Deception

Deception

ELEANOR LIGGENS

Blue Ink Media Solutions

Deception

Printed in the United States of America
ISBN 978-1-64133-819-6 (sc)
ISBN 978-1-64133-820-2 (e)

2024.06.03

Blue Ink Media Solutions
1111B S Governors Ave
STE 7582 Dover,
DE 19904

www.blueinkmediasolutions.com

TABLE OF CONTENTS

CHAPTER 1

Love Has No Boundaries

*I*t was a beautiful quiet evening of dinner and dancing by moonlight on Santa Monica beach in California. Johnathon Fitzpatrick drove up in his Mercedes AMG two door coupe to a luxury five story marvelously structured condominium building setting on five acres of property. The glass door entrance was lined with palm trees on both sides. The first three floors were squarely designed, with the last two floors shaped as complete circles, one on top of the other. Each room, six thousand square foot, was beautifully designed with a lake view and modern furniture. The main lobby had one receptionist desk and a huge Sputnik Sphere Chandelier that illuminated the entire room, hanging center ceiling.

It was mid-night when Johnathon brought his girlfriend, Erika, a gorgeous long blonde haired, brown eyed, and shapely figured female back to his second floor apartment for a night cap.

"Does your receptionist that buzzed us in the building work all evening, its midnight?" asked Erika.

"Oh no. Becky leaves fifteen minutes after midnight. If you don't have a front door key, you can't get in after she's gone for the day." Johnathon wanted to set the mood. He changed the subject. "I know you've worked hard all day waitressing, would you care for a drink my love?"

"Yes, please." Erika softly spoke.

"What's your poison my lady?" Johnathon turned on some soft music.

"Vodka, straight."

"Oooh, a woman after my own heart. I'll join you."

While Johnathon poured the drinks, Erika slipped away to the bedroom and dressed in something more comfortable. When she returned, she was dressed in a Victoria Secret embroidered baby doll sheer mesh bra, matching thong and see through mini shell top, all black. She relaxed, crossed one leg over the other and stretched her right arm out on the back of a lavish white leather sofa. She now awaited Johnathon with the drinks.

Johnathon came over with both glasses of Vodka. He stood close to her and handed her the drink. Erika was baffled at his lack of sexual assertiveness. She took a sip of vodka. "You know we've been seeing each other for a couple of weeks. You have bought lingerie clothing for me to keep here. Yet, we have not consummated our relationship. Am I not attractive to you?"

"Of course you are, my sweet. Of course you are. The clothing is a gift. You may take them home if you like."

Erika smile. "No, I think I like wearing them here. It shows just how beautiful I am, yes?"

"With a body like yours, how could any man resists?"

"Then come and sit beside me." Erika patted the sofa for Johnathon to position himself closely beside her.

Johnathon remained standing. "Erika if we act as if each night is a first date, it keeps the relationship fresh. It seems like we learn something new about each other every time we meet. That's why I didn't want to know everything about you the few times we met. Each encounter makes it seem like our very first date."

"Well we've met twice before. Sit beside me." She patted her hand on the sofa again. Johnathon sat down next to her. She stared into his eyes. "You're a masculine, tall, dark haired, blue eyed, hunk of a man." She started rubbing his hair on his head, from front to back. "I'm a hot cutie and I'm done with fresh, I'm ready for old."

"I just don't want you to think I am rushing you into anything. Erika I enjoy your company. I like our conversations and I want to get to know you for who you are, before anything else."

Erika gulped her Vodka until the glass was empty. Johnathon took a sip of his drink. With glasses on the coffee table, Erika adoringly glanced into his eyes and the loving gaze was returned. With the intense stare down, Erika reached for his right hand and placed it on her breast. "Is this fresh enough?" Johnathon followed her lead and they embraced each other with rapid kisses. She ripped the buttons from his shirt. Johnathon paused and slowed down her aggressive behavior. Erika watched him as he gently removed her shell from her arms. His arms soon wrapped around her back to unsnap her bra as warm and gentle kisses touched upon her neck. The bra fell to the floor. His tender lips caressed her breast as his hands moved gingerly to the lower part of her body. Erika's silk panties were removed. A loving smile engulfed her face. Johnathon gently lowered her back to the soft sofa pillows. Erika was passionately conquered by his gentle touches in all the right places. Their physical emotions heated up so quickly they never made it to the bedroom.

The next morning at Advanced Technology Systems Incorporated (ATSI), a stunning ten story, high tech, modernized office building, it towered high in the northern part of Los Angeles. The building from the outward appearance had staggered architecture. One floor extremely out and the other floor in, all the way to top. Totally tinted reflective heat resistant glass embellished the windows all around. The roof entailed a private helicopter pad for high-end specific clients and Johnathon Fitzpatrick's short distance client visits.

The first floor was open to the public with video's playing of all the latest technological devices the company had constructed. There were hand-crafted leather sofas and lounge chairs for all guests. A twenty-foot statue of a one-billion dollar bill set center of the first floor as a reminder of the company's goal. Not far from the main lobby was restaurant style dining, chef prepared meals or cafeteria style food ready to eat and a buffet for breakfast and lunch. To get to the second floor and above, were a set of three elevators, each one had a security guard armed with concealed weapons. They were required to check security badges. Each floor had hand and face recognition. To get on the tenth floor took a massive security check. It required face, hand, body and hair scan, plus a special security pass card. All offices on the tenth floor were glassed in with exclusive Bocote wooden office doors. Personalized name plates per staff member lined the hallways. Every floor shined with a black marble terrazzo with streaks of white coloring swiveled throughout the design. Stylish lights lined the hall ways. While all employees relished their fashionable modernized office furniture, every staff member felt valued.

Johnathon Fitzpatrick, the CEO of Advanced Technology Systems Incorporated (ATSI), sat in his huge modern designed office that had a six-foot vertically long, dark gray Espresso Wood, L-shaped, adjustable desk, in height. The conference table was adorned with eight black, cushy, leather chairs, a small drink bar and an executive style personal bathroom with shower and closet area also encompassed the room.

While at his desk making notes in a little black book, a faint knock was heard at the door.

"Come in." Calmly spoke Johnathon.

His Senior Vice President, Mark Atsu Townsend, a handsome man that stood six feet-one inch in height, light brown skin, small fro, thin sideburns, dark brown eyes, and go-tee, walked in. He was well dressed with black blazer, black slacks, white shirt, unbutton at the top and black patent leather shoes. "Good morning J." He observed Johnathon for a moment. "I see you scored again last night."

"And you say this because...?"

"You're writing in that black book again. Every time you have a night out, you make notes."

"Well Mr. Townsend, if you must know, I have to keep up with the ones that are just for pleasure and the ones that deliver in both categories."

"Both categories?" Mark was perplexed.

"Some stimulate my mind as well as my body."

"I see. Did last night meet both expectations?" asked Mark.

"No, I have seen her a few times. Last night was our first and last time in bed. I found her sexual ability a little lacking in some areas, plus her intellect for meaningful conversation about anything required additional education."

"One day J, your evil ways of treating women like under garments is going to catch up with you."

"What are you talking about, my friend? I wine and dine them. I treat them like queens when they are with me. As a matter of fact, they are overwhelmed by kindness and gifts until they beg me for physical affection. They almost attack me."

"Do you tell them before you wine and dine them J, that you're a married man?"

"No need. I don't let it go that far. But I do tell them I am not looking for a relationship."

"What about your wife, Johnathon?" Mark stated in a slightly harsh tone.

"My *wife*...?" He calmly spoke. "The only time you call me *Johnathon* is when you are annoyed with me. Are you annoyed or are you jealous my friend?"

"Your wife is a very nice person."

"My wife knows I work day and night to keep her happy. She lives in a five million dollar house. She has a private jet at her disposal. Our bank account is such that she can have anything she wants, when she wants it. What woman could ask for anything more?"

"How about a loving husband?"

"I fit her into my schedule to keep her oblivious to what I am doing. She is on my list to wine and dine once or twice a week too." With excitement in his voice, "But I am telling you Mark, some of the women I have met, are amazing. When someone said, "variety is the spice of life," I do believe that was an understatement."

"Well I guess showering them with lavish gifts and expensive meals before having sex with them would make any woman grabble at your feet." Mark didn't like the idea of toying with women just to get them into bed.

"Don't knock it until you've done it. Don't get self-righteous on me Mark. You're a single man. You have multiple women you date."

"Ahhh, yes. You said the magic word my friend, *single*. I don't see a girl more than three times if I'm not interested in her, not her body, her."

"That's where you're missing out Mark."

"Look... I didn't walk in here to get into your personal life or tell you how to respect women. I need to know if you've had a chance to look over the accounts on your desk. Out of eight accounts only one didn't close. Plus we have..."

"What do you mean, one didn't clos..." Johnathon was interrupted.

Suddenly, a buzz came over the intercom from Angela, his administrative person, five feet, six-inches tall, twenty-five years of age, with a shapely body. She was a petite, brunette, with long flowing hair that she maintained in a ponytail. She wore huge glasses.

Johnathon pushed the intercom button. "Yes... what is it Angela?"

"FedEx is here Mr. Fitzpatrick."

"Send him in."

Angela opened the door and waited. The FedEx man walked in and placed a small box upon Johnathon's desk. Mark waited patiently while Johnathon completed the transaction. Once the delivery man left, Angela closed the door. Johnathon sat at his desk and opened the box. Mark resumed the conversation.

"As I was about to say J, I need you to know we have some Japanese clients coming in next week for a presentation on what new technology we have on Cyber Security. Do you want to brief or do you want me to have one of our best analyst to do the briefing while you and I sit in?"

Johnathon had completely forgot about what they were discussing. To his delight, Fuente Don Arturo Gran Aniverxario Cigars were the best in taste and smell. He reached in the box and pulled one out. Johnathon held a cigar to his nose. "Hmmm, that aroma takes your breath away."

"Johnathon about the clients coming in next week?" Mark was trying to get back to business.

"Yes. How much are they offering if they want our systems and train their people?"

"If they like what they see and hear, eighty-nine million for two years to install and educate their staff."

Johnathon smiled. "I will do the briefing. That is… if you don't want to do it."

Mark laughed. "You know I clam up in front of an audience."

"Mark Atsu Townsend, you are the best damn technological engineer we have at Advanced Technology Systems Incorporated. All anyone has to say is, "This is what I want and how I want it." Then, somehow, some way, you make it happen. That's awesome. You're gifted my friend. I hit the jackpot when I hired you."

"Thanks J. I just need to get over my fear of speaking in front of people."

"It's easy. Just don't give a damn about what they think and only talk to what you know. Pretend their staff and you will see how words flow off your tongue."

"That's sounds simple enough." Mark was nonchalant in his response.

"It is. Anyway, set up the meeting for next Wednesday. I will do it."

"Consider it done."

Johnathon extended a cigar to Mark. "Have one?"

"No thanks man. You know I don't smoke. I didn't know you smoked either. I have never seen you lite up at the executive parties you host."

"It's a bad habit. I shouldn't have picked it up."

"Once a month you have them delivered here. Why don't you have those expensive cigars delivered at home?" questioned Mark.

"Catherine doesn't like the smell. The first box I ordered and smoked in the house, she hid the rest of them from me. Can you imagine how furious I was? A $7500 box of cigars and I can't smoke in my own house."

"Really… she knew you smoked before you married her?" probed Mark.

"Nooo. Truthfully, I acquired the practice after I married her. I told her I picked up the habit from one of my business client's at a corporate celebration, but I actually picked it up from one of my mistresses. So… I don't push her button about smoking in the house. To keep the piece, I have them delivered here and I hide them when I get home. She puts up with enough of my indiscretions, unknowingly. So when I want to relax, I get one from my favorite hiding place in a small safe behind a picture in the living room. I grab a glass of wine from the pool refrigerator and relax on the patio. As long as I smoke outside, I'm not stinking up the house with smoke. I don't want to risk her finding the box and discarding them again."

"So you just don't smoke around other people?" questioned Mark.

"Yeaah… no need in subjecting my bad habits onto to others. I only smoke when I am without guests at my home. I don't do it at the office. I don't want to offend any clients."

"Ok. Back to the files on your desk J. The clients we closed have a…"

"Speaking of clients." Johnathon interrupted. "That reminds me. A client of mine is sending a young woman here from the Global Banking meeting I attended in China last week. She will bring a thumb drive here tomorrow. Only you can accept it from her. I need you to drop the drive off at the end of the day to my house." Johnathon placed his black book and cigars into his desk drawer.

"And you can't retrieve this data yourself because…?" Mark was baffled as to why he wouldn't be at work.

"I am spending tomorrow with a very special woman."

"Verrry special? You mean the whole day? You know tomorrow is a workday?" Mark was confused. He has gone out afternoons for three or four hours, but never all day.

"Yes. She is very, very special. I have to be on time with her. Her schedule is short. She is in town for a day and I want to be with her every second she is here."

Mark shook his head. "When I get *this* thumb drive, why don't I just upload the data and send the information to your private server at home, like usual?"

"No!"

Mark was surprised by the outburst in tone. "Okay, Ok... J."

Johnathon observed his startled expression. He spoke calmly. "Look Mark, I don't want this information on a computer anywhere. Even though it's encrypted, the less possible places of retrieving the data, the better. I have got some business transactions going on that I don't want you to know about just yet. But I will fill you in soon."

Mark tilted his head and sighed. "But you're head of Advanced Technology Systems Inc. We are the best at what we do. What do you have to be afraid of with me uploading it?"

"Genius's like you my friend, hackers. Even though we are the best, we are one of the best. There is always someone better. You can never be too careful." Johnathon was slightly irritated. "Just... drop off the thumb drive."

"What about your staff meeting and other business affairs tomorrow?"

"You take care of them. When you speak, this company knows you speak for me. I have complete confidence in you."

Mark was shocked. "I'm always there with you. I may say a few words magnifying what you have spoken, but I have never made any decisions on the company's behalf."

"And you won't now. Answer questions. Take notes. Get back to me later. Clients don't bite and you know the staff. Just brief like we just talked about. I trust your judgement, Mark. If something serious comes up, put it on hold and we'll discuss later. Besides you've been with me since I started this company five years ago. You know what I know and you know where I stand on certain issues that matter. This is just for one day." Johnathon was getting irritated. "Now cover for me tomorrow and stop whining like some twelve year being left at home for the first time."

"So tomorrow I won't see you at all?" Mark was still a little unsure of himself.

Johnathon sarcastically tried to assure Mark. "Yesss… my son. I have confidence that I can leave you at work by yourself for one day. If you feel that you can't handle the responsibility, reschedule the staff meeting and the clients."

"No, no. You're right J. I got it. It's only two clients worth five million dollars each. I'll keep it brief and to the point."

"Fine, or you can get Brady to do the briefing if you feel unsure of yourself. But you greet and introduce Brady to the clients. Let me know how things go. Because tomorrow evening I assure you I will be tired of winning and dining. I won't feel like discussing anything tomorrow. I'm going to give Mikey a break tomorrow evening."

"Mikey?"

Johnathon looked down at his zipper. "Yeah, my other head."

Mark followed his gesture and had no expression. "Got it. What time are you going to be home?"

"Don't know. After being with this special lady all day, I have a couple of errands to run before heading home. Here…" Johnathon reached for a pen and paper on his desk. "I am giving you the combination to the gate. It unlocks the front door and silences the alarm when you punch in the code. Just set the brief on the coffee table or the kitchen counter. I'll get it. When you go back out the front door, the alarm resets and locks the house down."

"You don't want me to let you know I'm there? I mean… I don't want to get shot as an intruder."

"That won't happen. You see when the code is punched in, colorful lights all over the house flicker. That way, no matter where I am in the house or even by the pool for that matter, I know Catherine just got home. So if I hear a noise or see someone, I know it's her."

"You know its Catherine? No one else has the combination?" questioned Mark.

"No one. Not even my parents or hers' get a copy of the combination and I change the code twice a week."

"Not even the creator can by-pass the system?"

"Mark, I designed the system and installed it."

"Okay, what about Catherine?"

"I will let Catherine know you may be stopping by. So when she sees the lights flicker, she will know it's you or me." Johnathon was annoyed with the questions. "Just drop it off. Please."

"You're not worry that Catherine may pick it up and be curious as to its content?"

"Not in the least. She doesn't have a clue about my work. I have trained her to respect my work at home and at the office."

"Okay... No problem J."

Johnathon finished writing down the combination and sled it to Mark on his desk. "You memorize it and then destroy this piece of paper."

"Absolutely. Why don't you just text it to me J?"

"Phone hacking, my friend."

Mark shook his head. "Our revised technology on our phones are the very best in the..."

Johnathon spoke in a slightly harsh tone. "Didn't you just hear me?"

"How stupid of me. Right?" Mark stepped closer to his desk. "Let me have your pen so I won't forget what these numbers are for." Mark wrote on the top of the paper, 'Johnathon's home combination'.

Johnathon was reviewing the folders of closed accounts for the week on his desk, while Mark was writing. "Mark!"

Mark was distracted by J's tone. He saw the file in his hand. He placed the pen down and gave Johnathon his full attention. "What?"

As Johnathan flipped pages on the Atkin's Account, "Ten million. Who closed this account?"

"It's on the last page of the brief. I believe it was Brianna Delray."

Johnathon displayed extreme pleasure. "Awesome! We've only had her... how long? For ten months, right?"

"I believe so. She catches on quick. She was a good hire out of college." Stated Mark.

"Well, let's do lunch to celebrate. Then you can watch me in action and maybe take down a few tips on how to capture the attention of beautiful women."

"Sure J, just let me know when."

"Today, my friend, today."

"Ok, I will come back around eleven." Mark started to leave, but he remembered, "Oh J, there is one other issue if you haven't heard already from Angela and you haven't seen the file."

"Angela did text me earlier this morning, but I was too tired to read it. What was it?"

"It's the last folder on your desk. Javier lost the Anderson account." Mark uttered softly.

Johnathon spoke in a slightly angered tone. "Say that again."

Mark spoke a little louder. "Javier lost the Anderson account. It's there, in the folder on your desk."

Infuriated, Johnathon stood and slammed his fist on the desk. He pulled Javier's file and took a glance. "What! A seven million lost?"

"Yes. Seven million." Mark spoke calmly.

"Seven million!" Johnathon screamed. He immediately got on the intercom to Angela. "Get Hernandez in here!"

"Yes sir." Angela softly spoke.

"J, Javier is one of our best negotiators. He has a record of over fifty-five million in accounts over the past five years. Please take that into consideration."

"Have you talked to him?" Johnathon asked in an aggressive tone.

"Not yet."

At that moment came a knock at the door. "Come in." serenely spoke Johnathon.

Javier entered slowly into the room, only a couple of feet. "You wanted to see me Mr. Fitzpatrick?"

Johnathon stood behind his desk with his right hand on his hip. "Come closer."

Mark with a somber expression, stood to the far right side of Johnathon's desk.

Javier reached the front edge of Johnathon's desk. "Yes sir."

Johnathon threw the file on his desk toward Javier. "What happened with the Anderson case?"

Javier fidgeted with his hands. He was at a loss for words. He stuttered for a moment. "Well, I... I... ahh, I mean... I mean everything had gone well." Javier cleared his throat and began to speak with clarity as he remembered why Anderson cancelled the account. "As a matter of fact, we had shaken hands at the restaurant. He was going to come in and sign the papers today."

"Go on..." Johnathon's tone was calm.

"As I started to leave, I overheard him say to his partner, 'That half-breed greaser has a head on his shoulder. I guess he must have gotten his intelligence from his white half.' I went back to the table and punched him in the face."

"You're fired!" Screamed Johnathon.

"What!" screamed Javier. "Do you know how much money I have brought into this business?"

Johnathon still infuriated, leaned and slammed both palms to his desk. "I can't have you getting upset with clients because they called you a name. I have a reputation to uphold. You should have taken it as a compliment and signed the papers today."

Javier spoke in a soft begging tone. "But Mr. Fitzpatrick, those were my parents he was speaking of."

"I don't care if it was your children he was speaking of. Seven million dollars!" Johnathon glared straight into his eyes. "Get out!"

"Mr. Fitzpatrick I don't have anywhere else to go." Appealed Javier.

"Don't worry, I'll give you the rest of your yearly salary and I don't give a damn where you go. Now get out!"

Tears nearly came to Javier's eyes. He lowered his head and noticed the paper with Johnathon's home combination on it. He memorized the numbers. Javier glanced at Mark. Mark had no expression. Javier looked back toward Johnathon in desperation to keep his job, he begged. "Mr. Fitzpatrick please. It won't happen again."

"I'm making sure it won't. Now do I have to call security to have you removed?"

The expression on Javier's face went from sadness to resentment. "My work ethics, dedication, and the money I have brought this organization means nothing to you?" Javier stated with angry. "You throw me out like a stale piece of bread over one incident?"

"I will not repeat myself again! Mark call security."

Mark motioned toward the door.

Javier raised his hand to stop Mark from performing Johnathon's request. His eyes stayed focused on Johnathon. "No need Mr. Townsend, I'm leaving. You're going to regret this decision, Mr. Fitzpatrick." Javier stormed out of his office and slammed the door behind him.

Mark was solemn in tone. "J, he was a good man and a hard worker."

Johnathon ignored Mark's statement. He focused on Javier's reaction. "Can you believe he slammed my door? What nerve, after all this company has done for him."

"J… he did bring in a lot of money for us."

Johnathon was unsympathetic in his decision. "Mark, a seven million dollar account is worth swallowing your pride, especially when ten percent commission is yours. How long do you think we would keep our clients if word got out that we punch them in the face if they say the wrong thing to our representatives?"

Mark was silent and started to leave. Johnathon noticed the paper he had written his home combination on, was still at the corner of his desk. "Hey Mark, you're forgetting something." Johnathon picked up the paper and gave it to Mark.

"Oh yeah, thanks." Mark placed it in his blazer pocket.

"Hey, remember those numbers and destroy that paper."

"Got it." Mark walked toward the door.

Johnathon had a quick thought. "Mark before you go, I need you to do two more things."

Mark paused by the door. "And what might that be?"

"Tell Brianna to take over Javier's clients. Tell her to see if she can get the Anderson account back. If she does, there is a double bonus in it for her."

"And the other thing?"

"Let's do brunch at the Yacht Club. Now. After that little emotional episode, I feel like I need a drink."

"It's only nine-thirty J."

"So…?" Johnathon gave him a look that Mark understood completely.

"Give me an hour to put some things in motion." Mark slightly shook his head and walked out the door.

As Mark left Johnathon's office, he noticed Javier slinging books and papers across the room of his office. He smashed awards and stomped on company pictures. Mark wondered if he should go in and console Javier or just let him vent. He continued to his office.

Chapter 2

Business Conversation

At brunch, at the Yacht Club, Johnathon and Mark were seated at this elegantly designed edifice with an array of colorful real flowers that centered all the tables. There was chandelier lighting above, white table cloths, and plush gray seats that adorned the room. Waiters in black bowties and white shirts scurried the floor serving the exceedingly rich clientele. Brunch came with complimentary champagne or wine, if so desired.

Johnathon and Mark sat at their usual table, they were approached by one of their regular waiters. "Would you like your medium glass of Chateau Mouton Rothschild 2009 as usual Mr. Fitzpatrick?"

"No. Not today, give me a black Hennessey on the rocks with steak and eggs." Added Johnathon.

"And you Mr. Townsend, the Sazerac?" asked the waiter.

"Yes Rodney, with a splash of Rittenhouse Rye, please."

"Of course, sir. Something to eat as well Mr. Townsend?" asked Rodney.

"I'll take an eggs benedict." Stated Mark.

"Very good sir." Rodney left to fill the orders.

"I thought you strictly a wine man. Hennessey for brunch?" quizzed Mark.

"I am. I love my wine, but after this morning, I need something a little stronger."

"Speaking of this morning, don't you think you were a little hard on Javier? After all, over fifty million in five years of excellent effo..."

Johnathon interrupted firmly. "No. I sent a message with Javier to the rest of the staff. If you're thin-skinned, you don't belong on my team."

"Well I definitely think the message was delivered."

"Mark why do you think I treat my employees so well? They each have their own office space… Why?"

"Why J?" Mark nonchalantly responded.

"Because I want their thoughts of innovative ideas to remain with the company. I want them to feel like they are important to the organization and they are. Why do you think their commission on jobs they bring in is well within their favor? Because I want to keep their talent and knowledge within our corporation. What I cannot tolerate is thin-skinned employees who can't take an insult over closing a multi-million dollar business deal."

Mark was a little annoyed about losing a good employee. "No matter how much money they brought into the company?"

"Absolutely Mark. The client is always right, especially the multi-million dollar ones. You know reputation is everything. Business men talk. That's why I host executive parties at my house and have our clients bring guests. I don't' know Mr. Anderson's connections. His contacts could be influential. With that being said, if he let word get out that one of my representative's hurt or insulted him because of a comment he made… that one incident could cost our organization millions in referrals of other potential clients. That's why I am hoping Brianna can salvage that deal."

"Brianna is still green. Do you really think she can handle cleaning up a situation like that? You *really* think she can fix this?" asked Mark.

"With a double bonus on the line and her good looks, I believe she will exercise all of her abilities to get that client back for us."

"Well, I have already informed her of the double bonus you're offering. She took the case with a smile."

"Good."

The waiter returned with their drinks and placed them down on the table. "Your brunch is almost ready gentlemen." Rodney walked away.

Johnathon nodded and took a sip of his drink. "You know why I'm going to be the best tech security corporation on the west coast?"

"Enlighten me J."

"My objective is simple. You value everyone's opinion. No matter their statue." Johnathon leans a little closer to Mark so he can hear every word.

"Let me tell you a story. I happen to speak to a janitor in our building, just out of curiosity. I asked him what from our business stand point would he like to see invented. He told me since he worked late at night, a device that could detect the presence of someone within one-hundred yards of him would be great. Thus you invented the "Individual Remote Vibrator" that alerts anyone of the presence of another individual within one-hundred yards. That device has brought us over twenty-five million in sales revenue in one year. I have gotten 'thank you' letters from doctors, nurses, and executives that have appreciated the device. Why?… because they work late at night and walk through dim lit garages, cross streets with no lights, walked in shadowy open parking lots, and the device worked. They felt safer and I got the ideal from a janitor."

"A janitor?"

"Exactly Mark, a janitor. I value the ideals of every single person we have on staff. That's why I treat everyone equal. No idea is too small. So you get the staff on board with the mission of the organization and guess what I got?"

"I'm listening." Mark drank some of his Sazerac.

"Performance focused individuals working toward a common goal. Don't you see their bettering themselves as well as the organization? No better feeling than seeing something you visualized in your mind become a reality."

Mark was in thought. "So that's where you got that ideal of the Remote Vibrator?"

"Yes. That's why I want all my employees to feel like executives even though they aren't. I want them to present their ideas to me in the presence of their peers. If we create their idea into reality, they get their ten percent of the company's entire sales. What does this do for our business? It keeps the employees thinking and looking for fresh innovative concepts. No one gets complacent when you have competition. No one can take another person's idea if it's presented to everyone at the same time. We've had team collaboration on great projects. You know that."

"Yes, of course, I know and I applaud your fairness with the employees. But Javier was a good employee."

"I want to keep good people. So I pay them well and give them credit for a job well done. What I did to Javier was a warning to the others. If I treat you like executives, you have to treat our clients like royalty, no matter what kind of imprudent individual they are."

"I respect that. But…"

"No but's. They can't make any mistakes on the company's behalf. I won't tolerate it. Not by Javier or anyone. Reputation is everything."

Nonchalantly Mark agreed. "Okay J, if you say so." Mark took another sip of his drink.

"I say so." Johnathon changed the subject. "Anyway, I have a few clients lined up needing briefings on our latest technology. Some are willing to come here to LA, others want our staff to come there. I need you to line up our best techs. I will give you the countries when we get back to the office. Ensure they are updated on the culture of the country they visit and the personnel they are briefing. I don't need our people losing an account because they spit on the sidewalk or didn't take off their shoes because they didn't know about the culture."

The waiter returned with their brunch and served them. "Thanks Rodney." Stated Mark. The waiter departed. "Got it J. Now, next week, the agenda is…"

Johnathon put his hand up. "Hold that thought." At that moment two beautiful young ladies entered the club. "Turn slowly and observe the stride and elegance of these two gorgeous women that just entered this establishment."

Mark slowly turned his head to gaze at the women Johnathon referred to. They were beautifully dressed in designer summer wear with hats and sunglasses to match. "Hey man, if you love women like you do, why on *earth* did you ever get married?"

"Catherine is a beautiful woman too, but she isn't what I wanted for a wife."

"What?" Mark slightly laughed, while in shock by the comment.

"Yeah, yeah. She's has a great body, gorgeous legs… I know." Johnathon took a taste of his Hennessy. "I didn't want to get married to Catherine, but father insisted. He said a good looking woman on my arm at evening networking parties gives the other business professionals a sense of stability on my part. You know integrity and family… that kind of crap."

"Catherine is a sweet woman. She loves you very much. If I find a woman that loves me as much as Catherine loves you, making her my wife wouldn't be something I think twice about." Mark cut into his food.

"I did it to please my Dad. So to keep my passion going, I knew I had to find a woman that was naïve and would believe every word I said without questioning my motives. Catherine was it. Man you know me. I'm still into myself."

"That's for sure." Mark mumbled under his breath as he chewed his food.

"I care for Catherine, but just not how a husband should care for his wife."

Mark drummed up a slight grin and took a sip of his Sazerac. "If she only knew. Don't you know that it's better to dwell in the wilderness, than be with a contentious, angry woman?"

"She'll never find out. I cover my tracks very well." Johnathon cut a piece of steak and began to chew.

"So you don't love her." Mark put a small pinch of his eggs benedick on his fork and ate it. "Don't you know that love doesn't love anything? It takes a human body with emotions to show that love, to make you feel loved. Have you ever loved anyone J?"

"I know what love is. I came close a few years ago to loving someone once."

"Really?" Sarcastically stated Mark.

"Yeah. My Dad wanted me to finish college before I started my own business. While I was studying at Yale, I met this gorgeous, brunette, brown eyed sweetheart, named Penelope. She was so shy and very beautiful. She kept her head in the books. She would always sit on this one bench at school around noon every day, reading. It took me awhile to get her head out of the books and into me."

"Why didn't you just move on to the ones that would have given you the attention you wanted from just looking at you?"

"That would have been too easy my friend. I could get that anytime. But this girl… she was tough to get next to. I found the challenge invigorating. Mark I had tried everything, from a flight to Hawaii for the weekend, to dinner and a movie. I was about to give up until her roommate clued me in."

"Her roommate?" queried Mark.

Johnathon placed his fork and knife down and stared straight at Mark. "Yes. There was something about her that was different than all the other girls at Yale." There was a sincere, earnest tone of affection in Johnathon's voice. "I finally broke the ice with Penelope when I found out she liked poetry and red roses."

"Poetry, you?" Mark grinned.

"Yes, I hate poetry, but for her... I learned at least three poems just to get her to listen to me. Every time when we met, I quoted a poem and I brought her a dozen of beautiful red roses. Mark, the smile upon her face when she took the roses from my hand reminded me of a ray of sunshine beaming through a cloudy sky. It made me happy just to see her smile. She didn't want the rich material things I could have given her. She had a genuine warmth about her. A love for life and the beauty of the world. I enjoyed the walks we took along the beach. The evenings we spent together just enjoying each other's company. I loved our strolls in the park. The way she touched the flowers with such gentleness as not to disturb the petals. She'd watched butterflies glide through the air with elegance and admired their grace and beauty. Later, she would write a beautiful poem about what she saw that day. She read to me. I read to her." Jonathon broke out in a slight laughter... "The time we went swimming with the Dolphins and a Dolphin pulled my face gear off, I panicked so bad... afterwards we laughed so hard, we cried. A few months later from spending so much time together, she greeted me every time we met with a smile and kiss upon my lips. Her happiness was my happiness."

Johnathon spoke with a sound of glee, almost as if he could see her as he spoke. "With so much friendship, love and happiness between us, I finally got her to give in. She was excellent in bed. Who would have thought, beauty, brains and sexual stimulation were all in one package? But what really got to me was her innocent personality and her true affection for life. She was everything any man could have wanted. Then one day out of out of the blue, she told me she loved me."

Mark broke the trance. "Sooo... was that so insulting about her expressing her love for you? What happened to her?"

Then, suddenly Johnathon's tone changed. He picked his knife and fork back up and began to cut his steak. "I discarded her. I had to walk away from this one without saying goodbye. If I hadn't, she might have been Mrs. Fitzpatrick, for real."

Mark was benevolent in tone. "Would that have been so bad J?"

"For me, yes." Johnathon took a sip of his drink. "When she said I love you, deep down I wanted to say, 'I love you too'."

"Why didn't you?"

"I wasn't ready Mark. I knew I wasn't ready. I would have cheated on her and hated myself for doing it. If she found out my indiscretions, if we had been married, I don't know if I could have taken the hurt that I would have caused her. I was starting to love her just that much. I had begun thinking about how she felt. How she would prefer our relationship to be, instead of thinking about myself. I knew I had to get away."

"Sounds like she was a beautiful woman."

"She was Mark, inside and out." Johnathon had a blank stare, as if he could still see her face. "She really was." Emotions were flaring up for Johnathon. He needed to change the subject. He continued eating. "Enough about her. So what's your story? You're single. Don't you know variety is the spice of life?"

"Of course, but my father taught me better than to treat a woman like a pair of underclothing, something you change and get into every day."

"Don't put it like that."

"Well that's how my father put it. He taught me values and respect. Not just for women, but for mankind. I have to say for a step-father, he treated me as if I was his biological son. I never wanted for anything."

"You're adopted?" Johnathon was shocked.

"Yes, my mother died at child birth and my father left me on the door steps of a church when I was six months old according to the note that was left in my basket."

"Wow… huh?" Johnathon took another sip of Hennessy.

"A married couple at that church already had a little girl. They had complications at child birth with her and didn't want to risk having another child. They wanted a boy. So, they embraced me as one of their own."

"Well I must say, you did well for yourself for an adopted black child."

Mark's voice rose slightly. "Really… J!" He was aggravated by the statement. "I wouldn't have expected such racist criticism from your lips."

"I didn't mean anything. It's the truth though. It's just that most black families are so poor, that adding another mouth to feed is a rarity."

"And you know this because…?" questioned Mark.

"It's a statistical fact if you look at it."

Feeling insulted, "You know what J… this conversation is over." Mark took a sip of his Sazerac. He threw his napkin and a hundred dollar bill on the table and got up to leave.

"Hey man. Take your money back. You know this goes on my tab as a business brunch. Sit down, please. I'm sorry. I didn't know you were so thin-skinned too."

"Perhaps, but stereo-typing my race as poverty stricken isn't what I expected from a man of your professionalism." Mark was a little angry. "So I guess I'm fired liked Javier?"

"Don't be ridiculous. You didn't lose a seven million dollar account." Mark was irritated by Johnathon's remarks. He started to get up again. Johnathon smiled at him and took a sip of Hennessey. "No, no, sit down. You're right, I apologize. Let's get back to women. That's my favorite topic anyway."

"Naw man. Enough about women." Mark sat back down. "Let's get back to the agenda for next week."

"You're right." Johnathon took another bite of his steak. His cell phone rang. He pulled the phone from his jacket pocket. "Let me take this call."

Mark nodded and ate his eggs benedict. He watched Johnathon and overheard him say the word, 'sure'. He hung up that call and a second later he made a phone call and spoke the words, 'Prepare, Allison.' He hung up with just two words spoken.

Not really understanding the secrecy of the phone call, Mark was curious. "Another client?"

"No. I may be a little late coming back to the office after we finish eating and discussing next week's agenda."

Mark took a sip of his drink. He sighed. "How late? I have some clients coming in from New York. They are just interested in what technologies we have."

"I should be back around three or four. Is that good?"

"Fine. No problem J."

They consumed their drinks and their meals while concluding business. They went their separate ways after brunch was consumed.

CHAPTER 3

Catherine Meets September

This same day as Johnathon was having brunch at the Yacht Club, Catherine, Johnathon's wife was in Top's Fine Jewelry Store in downtown Los Angeles shopping. The store was filled with expensive diamond rings, Sapphire necklaces, watches and bracelets. Bright lights in the store illuminated the sparkle in each expensive gem. Catherine observed this dark skinned, five-eight inch tall, full-figured, African-American female that was casually dressed in black slacks and gray blouse. She was staring at a diamond tennis bracelet. Catherine walked close to the female to see what item she was observing in the jewelry case.

"That would look great on my arm while I am hitting tennis balls." Stated September to the sales representative.

"What's stopping you? If you're in a store like this, no price is too steep. The average cost of any item in here is fifty-thousand dollars. Just get it." stated Catherine.

September glanced up from the counter to see who made the comment. Maintaining her professional attitude, September responded to this stranger. "Indeed. I'm a retired Army Ranger. My retirement check allows me groceries, payment of my common bills and one vacation a year. You know what they say, a penny saved..."

Catherine interrupted, innocently commenting. "Is not very much... so why do you come in here if you can't afford to buy?"

September gawked at this woman. She observed her attire from head to toe. "Excuse me, Miss Thang. Who are you? Some kind of undercover cop. I don't know you? Why are you all up in my business?"

"I didn't mean anything. I overheard what you said to the clerk. So I'm really just curious as to why would you come into a store that you can't afford what they have on display."

"Like it's any of your business. I like to look and they have beautiful stuff that I want. I keep thinking to myself, one day... one day I will be able to walk in here and just say, 'I want that,' and walk out of the store without a second thought of the money I just spent to get it."

"I see." stated Catherine.

"No you don't see, judging by the way you're dressed. You probably can say 'wrap that up' or 'give me two of'em' or 'mail those to my house', without a second thought of what it cost." September was a little angered by the curiosity of this total outsider that had embarked on her personal space.

"Would that bother you if I could?" questioned Catherine.

"No, because I don't know you. Have a good day, *Miss Thang*." September turned and walked out the door.

Catherine followed her outside. "Hey wait." September paused on the sidewalk. "If you don't mind my asking, where are you headed?"

September was annoyed by her. She gawked at Catherine with her hands on her hips as if preparing for a fight. "Look, Miss Thang... What's your problem?"

"No problem. It's just that, I have nothing else to do and I would like to do something with someone. You appear to be alone, just shopping and I'm alone shopping too." Catherine spoke with purity and candor. Her expression was that of a little child wanting to go outside to play and needed mommy's permission.

September observed her demeanor and tone. Her aggressive attitude diminished. "I... ahh," She thought she really didn't have time for this woman. "I ahh... practice every day at this gun range." She glanced quickly at her watch. "I have an appointment. If I miss my time, I have to reschedule because they don't take walk-ins." September turned to walk away.

"You mind if I tag along?" asked Catherine. "I've never been to a gun range."

September faced Catherine eye to eye. "And you're not about to now. Didn't your mother ever teach you not to talk to strangers? I don't know you like that."

"Well I won't be a stranger if you get to know me. My name is Catherine Fitzpatrick." She stretched her hand out to shake. September observed her hand for a moment and didn't respond. Catherine pulled her hand back and gave September an innocent stare. "So please, I promise not to be a bother. I like to try and do things that I have never done before."

"Yeah. Like follow a complete stranger around?"

"Pleassse." Catherine's voice was very low-spirited.

September noticed her facial expression of curiosity and voice of sincerity. Her tough exterior weakened. "Well not in those high heels, Armani bag, and that tight fitting one piece navy blue dress. Definitely not with all that bling, bling jewelry all over your body to match that outfit. You would need a gun just to protect yourself as you walked in. Besides, you're not dressed for the occasion."

"Do I have time to change?"

September sighed and checked her watch once again, displeased at the fact that this woman wanted to go with her. "I guess. Why do you want to tag alone so bad? Clearly you're way out of my class."

"Like I said, never been to a gun range, something different. So follow me home. Let me change. I would love to join you."

"Let's go." September mumbled. "You barely know me."

They walked to their cars. "Thanks. I appreciate this so much. I'm so bored and all I do is shop. I want to do something distinctive, out of the ordinary, and gun practice is very unique from anything I have ever done before."

"Okayyy... ok, you've twisted my arm. Just stop talking." September stopped in her steps. "So how far are you from here?"

"Not far." Catherine was ecstatic, she smiled from ear to ear.

"Alright. I'll follow you. This is my Kia Forte." September pulled out the key and opened the car door.

"You can leave your car at my house and we'll just take mine. I'm driving this black Audi R8, right here." She was parked just in front of September.

September paused to admire the car, but doesn't let Catherine know she was awed by its beauty and design. "Fine. Let's go."

Minutes later, as they drove up to Catherine's home, she electronically opened the gates from her car. September parked in front of the house, got out of her car and noticed the curtains across the street move slightly. As September approached Catherine…"Say… do your neighbors watch you all the time?"

Catherine reached the doorsteps. September was right behind her. "That's an understatement. That's Mrs. Nosey body, Jenson. She's an old biddy with nothing else better to do. Her husband still works and doesn't give her the time of day. He still owns forty percent of shares in some football team and CEO of some company. He doesn't have to work, but he still does. I see him leave the house some mornings just like Johnathon."

"Well if she doesn't work and you don't work, why haven't the two of you rich ladies gotten together and painted the country. Between the two of you, you could probably fly to some new city or country every day, go shopping and sipping on Martini's and shit."

"Please don't curse around me. My father used to do it all the time. It just means your brain can't find the proper words to express your true feelings. At least that's what my mom told me."

"Wooo…." September slightly leaned back, aggravated by the comment. "Well excuse me Ms. Sensitivity. But *shit* is my true feelings. If you're going to be around me, you better get used to a curse word every now and then. You feel me? Or we can lose each other right now."

"Okay, ok." Catherine made the compromise quickly. She didn't want to lose her new found friend.

"So what's up with the rich lady across the street?"

"There is an age gap of thirty-five years between us. I don't think we have much in common."

"Then how do you know so much about her?" quipped September.

"Johnathon invited them over for dinner one evening. He wanted to know who he was and if he might be beneficial to his company. They talked. She and I talked. I was never so bored in my life. She likes to bake, sew, and play bingo at the Yacht Club on seniors' night. She actually brought a picture book of her twenty grandchildren over and wanted me to learn their names as she showed me their pictures."

"Why would you care about her grandchildren?"

"My point exactly. It was the only dinner we ever had." Catherine punched the key code in the front door, it automatically opened.

"You don't have a house key? What if you forget the combination?"

"I have a key to the gate and the house, just in case I forget the combination or gate remote, since we do switch cars a lot. I keep that in my purse."

Once inside, September observed the elegance and décor of this modern house as she relaxed on a chic, plush, gray leather sofa and waited for Catherine. September admired the huge living room with cathedral type ceiling, white marble floor, a wall décor of geometric abstract canvas paintings and a plush Persian rug beneath her feet. When Catherine returned in blue jeans and a white casual shirt, September was surprised.

"When we come back, you have to give me a tour of your beautiful home."

"Of course, let's go." Catherine was eager leave.

September was puzzled as to her attire. "I didn't think you owned anything so informal. I thought you might have a blouse and slacks, but jeans?"

"I'm really a down to earth country girl. I dress the way you saw me a few moments ago because my husband expects me to sustain a certain imagine when I am out in public."

"So won't he get upset if he sees you in jeans?"

"He doesn't have to know. We'll be back long before he gets home."

"Well in that case, heaven forbid he catches you. Let's hurry and take my car. I know where I am going." Stated September.

Catherine was excited. "Take me away."

They go back out the front door. Mrs. Jensen still had her binoculars peering out the window. Catherine looked across the street, waved and hopped in the car. September cranked the engine and it sputtered a little before the car cranked up to full gear. The sedan moved slowly.

"Are you sure we're going to make it in time in this thing?" Catherine was a little surprised by the gradual mobility of the car. "For a minute it felt like a minor earthquake. We can take one of my cars if you like?"

September was a little annoyed from the statement, but rightly deserved. "Sometimes it takes a minute to get moving, but it gets me from point A to point B. Sit back, relax and enjoy the ride."

Moments later, the car picked up speed. Mrs. Jenson continued her visual observance until the car was out of sight.

Once at the firing range, September went to her locker, came back with a leather bag, pulled out eight weapons and placed them at her firing station. She had a .45 Caliber Colt, Glock 32, Colt 1911 Classic, German Luger P08, SIG-SAUSER P228, and others.

Catherine was in amazement. "My goodness! Are you preparing for a war?"

"No. I just like to stay toned in firing my weapons in case I get called back on active duty."

"What….?" Catherine laughed. "How old are…?"

September gave her a look of anger before should could finish her sentence. "Look… I went in when I was twenty, made the rank of Lieutenant Colonel. I got wounded in Afghanistan and had to get out. So I retired at thirty-seven. Now… are we going to stand here all day and ask questions about my military career or do you want to learn how to shoot?"

"Please… you go first… ahh?" Catherine paused. "I just realized I never got your name."

September grabbed her Glock .45 and took a stance. "It's September."

"Sep… tem… ber?" Catherine had an estranged look upon her face.

September interrupted and gave that look of anger again. "Don't start nothin…"

Catherine was silent and just shook her head.

September reached for the mufflers hanging on the side of her firing stand. "Here. Put these ear muffs on." September changed her mind and picked up the Colt 1911 Classic and fired four rounds center mass of the target. Catherine watched closely.

"Wow!" exclaimed Catherine.

"Lady, I'm so good… I can pluck a fly's wing at 100 yards?" September stated with a smile. "You wanna try now?"

"Sure. That looks easy." Smiled Catherine.

September gave a slight grin and handed Catherine the gun. "It weighs a little over two pounds, but the recoil is manageable." She stood behind Catherine and assisted her in aiming the gun with her arms and trigger finger. "Now take a small stance spreading your legs apart to balance yourself."

Catherine stretched her legs almost her arm's length. "Like this?"

"What are you doing?" asked September.

"I'm stretching my legs."

"This isn't the wild, wild west. Just distance your legs far enough apart to have a good balance. Then aim the weapon at your target."

Catherine performed as instructed and aimed. "Like this?"

"Now relax, take a deep breath and slowly pull the trigger."

Catherine did as directed and hit the wall. They both laughed.

"Next time open your eyes." September was still laughing. "I didn't' think I needed to tell you that. But it is a prerequisite in hitting the intended target. We'll try each one of my weapons and see which one you like the best and we'll work with that one. For now, try again."

Catherine took aim and pulled the trigger. She hit the wall again. An hour later of much practice of body positioning, breathing, and pulling the trigger, September had worked up an appetite from being an instructor. After they left the gun range, Catherine told September to drive to one of her favorite dining area, Angelina's Italian restaurant.

"I hope you like Italian. They have excellent food here. It doesn't matter what you order, it's all delicious."

An hour later, they had arrived at a quaint little restaurant at the far end of town.

"As long as you're buying, then I will order whatever looks good to me on the menu."

"Then let's go in." Catherine led the way.

As they entered the restaurant, September noticed the ceiling. The ceiling hung fake shapes of garlic, like tiny light bulbs, pictures of Italian singers where on the wall, and tiny violins stood as center pieces upon the table. A waiter approached them.

"Mrs. Fitzpatrick, how wonderful to see you again. Your usual table?" asked the head waiter.

"Yes, please Leonardo."

"This way madam." Leonardo led them to Catherine's favorite table.

They were both seated as Leonardo left the menu on the table.

"Hey… Leonardo has seen you in blue jeans. Aren't you worried your husband will find out you look like a commoner today?"

"No, actually I come here quite often, alone. Normally I am dressed in my jeans and t-shirt when I come here. They know they are not to mention anything to my husband if we ever showed up here together again, which I doubt."

"Why is that?" questioned September.

"Johnathon thinks this restaurant is too low class for his taste. He thinks anything less than a hundred dollars a plate can't be good. We have been here only once and he hasn't been back since. But this is one of my favorite places because they do accept my attire. Plus, I love Italian food and spend much money here."

September gazed at the menu. "From looking at this menu, I wouldn't have cared if you walked in here naked as long as you could afford what's on it. Fifty-five dollars for a plate of spaghetti… really?"

"It does come with meat balls and the sauce is absolutely delicious."

"I wouldn't care if it came with a thirty-six thousand dollar bottle of Petrus 2012 wine. For a plate of spaghetti… that's too expensive."

"Well Johnathon thinks fifty-five dollars for a plate of spaghetti is too low class." Catherine placed the napkin on her lap. "If you don't mind my asking? Where did the name September come from?"

"My mother died giving birth to me on September ninth. My father thought it fitting to always remember her through me. So he always tells me he celebrates the love she brought into this world as he remembers the love he lost. He calls me his Sweet September."

"How beautiful and sad." Commented Catherine.

September was a little emotional from remembering. "Yes well…"

Catherine interrupted…"I want to thank you for letting me tag alone. The gun range was fun and actually exhilarating at the same time."

"You ain't seen nothin yet. Let me take you to my house. I had an obstacle course built in the backyard so I can keep my skills toned."

Catherine laughed. "You're kidding… right?"

September's expression was stern and unemotional. "I don't kid about my military training. I'm an ex-Army Ranger, Airborne qualified and always will be. Bring your skinny rich butt over and you'll see."

The waiter approached with water and warm bread for the table. "Would you ladies like something to drink before your meal?"

"I'll have the usual Leonardo. September?" stated Catherine.

"You wouldn't happen to have a bottle of Petrus 2012 wine laying around, would you?" asked September.

"No ma'am." Stated Leonardo.

"I thought so. Give me a Gin Negroni on the rocks." Stated September.

"Very good ladies." Leonardo left with the order.

"You don't mess around with your drink. Do you September?"

"Hard and strong with my liquor. That's how I do most everything, especially my men."

Catherine gave a slight grin. "I see."

"If you don't mind my asking, rich lady? What does your husband do if he thinks a hundred dollars a plate is the only way to get a good meal?"

"He owns his own tech business. He develops new technology for businesses and sells it to large corporations."

"So he's a Brainiac. I see why you spend so much time alone."

"What's that supposed to mean?" questioned Catherine.

"Brainiac's are thinkers. How he ended up marrying is a mystery, because they're usually always thinking about something technical and not about love and emotions. If they marry, it's usually not for love, but for convenience."

Their drinks arrived. Leonardo placed their beverages before them.

Catherine took a sip of her Sex on the Beach Cocktail. "I guess he took one look at me and love struck his heart."

"Ready to order ladies?" asked Leonardo.

September smiled and responded. "Give me the spaghetti and meat balls."

Catherine grinned.

CHAPTER 4

Catherine and September Bond

$\mathcal{J}$ohnathon left Mark after the Yacht Club Brunch for a few hours and went to his condominium. Here, he waited on the second floor condo suite for Allison. When she entered, Johnathon noticed this five-foot seven inches tall, long haired, brunette with a shapely figure walk in with a beam of delight on her face. Johnathon stood in the center of the living room. He held a red rose in his hand. A bottle of red wine sat center the coffee table in a bucket of ice.

"Allison, my sweet, when I got your call I was so excited. I rushed and got this rose for you." Johnathon handed her the flower.

"You remembered." Allison accepted and sniffed its fragrance with a smile.

"I will always remember things about you my sweet. However, I am so sorry I can't spend the rest of the day with you. This was such short notice. When you called I was at a business brunch. I didn't want to call back and cancel as I have not seen you since last month. So our time is short as I have a three o'clock meeting to attend." Spoke Johnathon.

"Johnathon, I realize your time is of the utmost importance. I am glad you decided to see me on short notice as I have thought of nothing but you since the time we last met. The lovely dinners in Hawaii and New York, our conversations and amazing sex we had. All, left me wanted to see you again. Being an international interpreter doesn't leave me much time in one place."

"I don't want to rush you today. We can just have a couple of drinks at a local restaurant or enjoy this bottle of wine and take pleasure in our own company for a few hours together."

Allison lovingly gazed into his eyes and moved closer to him. "I've been wanting your body since the last time we met. So let's dispense with the dialogue."

"I don't want you to feel as if I am hurrying you."

"I know, you've told me… you've got to leave. No more talk." Allison leaned closer to his lips and kissed them passionately.

"I don't want this to seem like a hit and run, because I've missed you too. However I don't want you to think all I want is…."

Allison interrupted before he could finish his sentence. "Shhh….my love." Allison removed his suit coat. Johnathon watched as she slowly unbuttoned his shirt. Following her lead he reached his arm to the side of her dress and unzipped it. Allison let her dress fall to the floor as she touched his chest with the gentleness of her hands. Her fingers slowly moved from his chest towards his zipper. As his pants fell to the floor and the shoes fly off their feet, Johnathon picked her naked body up and whisked her away to the bedroom, with the wine bottle in hand. No more words were spoken.

While Johnathon embarked on an afternoon of sexual pleasure with Allison. Catherine was still enjoying an afternoon lunch with her new found friend.

"You know rich lady, I think since you're having a hard time hitting the target. I am just going to get you use to firing a gun first."

"What do you mean?" Curiosity overwhelmed Catherine.

"There is a Paint Gun Club I go to just for fun. The building is huge. It's set up for novice, mediocre, and professional gun shooters. It's just off of Lincoln Ave. My brother owns it. We can go there until you get comfortable shooting a gun and then go back to the gun range to fire the real weapons again."

"I would prefer to stick with the real thing."

"We will go to the paint gun club and you'll see it's not half bad. We'll just do that a couple of times and I promise you we will get back to the real deal."

Catherine nonchalantly agreed by nodding her head. She glanced at her watch and realized the time had passed her by so quickly. She waved at Leonardo… "Check please."

September noticed Catherine's action. "In a hurry?"

"Look September, I have an evening executive party to prepare for tomorrow. I need to review my plans before I began implementing them."

"No problem. Let's get you home."

September drove in front of Catherine's home. Her car sputtered, then shut off. Catherine waved at her nosey neighbor as September walked toward the house.

Mrs. Jensen stared out of the window with her binoculars as usual. "Come quick Harold! Look baby. You missed seeing this woman early today."

"Because I was at work." Harold mumbled to himself. "You old biddy."

Gloria maintained her focus on the ladies across the street. "Catherine has a new person coming to the house with her. Some tall, lean, well-built black lady. You should come and check her out. She doesn't appear like Catherine's type of friend that she should be around. She looks like bad news."

Harold was undressing from his suit and tie. He mumbled, "You're bad news."

"What's that honey?" Gloria still had the binoculars on the house across the street.

Harold was tired and wanted to relax. "It's four o'clock in the afternoon. I just got home. Will you stop being so damn nosey. Why don't you go downstairs and help the maid cook something. Maybe that will give you something constructive to do with your time besides bugging me with nonsense. Better yet, why don't you go over there and ask her for her itinerary so you can stop wondering where she is and who she's with?"

"Are you kidding me, she wouldn't do that. Besides their lives are like a soap opera. They're the only real entertainment I have since you don't like to do anything with me anymore."

"I'm sixty-nine. What do you want me to do with you Gloria?"

Gloria placed the binoculars on the dresser and turned her full attention to Harold. "Quit working and let's travel and see the world. Lay with me a few times a month. I may be sixty-six, but I still like to roll in the hay every now and then. We're wealthy, healthy, and alive. Let's act like it. You've been working for the past fifty years and you haven't stopped. It's time to start enjoying the wealth we've accumulated."

Harold mumbled… "I enjoy it just fine in my house."

"Stop whispering. I can make arrangements for us to travel anywhere in the world right now. How about it, tootsie?"

Harold sighed. He headed for the closet to take off his suit coat, shoes and tie. He muttered again as if shocked by the statement. "With you? Huh, that will be the day."

"What's that dear?" Gloria turned her attention back to Catherine's house with binoculars raised.

"Hey honey, ahhh… too busy at work. Now is not a good time. I'm going downstairs, get in my recliner, enjoy a glass of Scotch on the rocks, turn on the TV and watch some real news." Harold put his house slippers on and left Gloria standing at the window with binoculars in her hand.

Gloria watched Harold make his way to the stairs. She soon turned her attention back to the Fitzpatrick's house. Gloria murmured. "Yeah, yeah, too busy, you old fart?"

Harold turned on the steps to watch Gloria for a few seconds gazing out the window, shook his head and continued down the stairs.

Once in the house, Catherine hung the house key on the key ring and immediately started upstairs to change her clothing.

Catherine spoke to September as she made her way to the bedroom. "Make yourself at home September. Drinks are in the refrigerator. Hopefully Johnathon will come home not long after I change and you'll get to meet him."

September started to admire the décor of the house once again. She went to the refrigerator and saw some Pepsi cans. She grabbed a can and placed it on the kitchen counter top. Catherine quickly outfitted in a casual white elegant flowered dress with a black Onyx necklace, earrings and shoes to match.

September continued to walk around the house. She admired the picturesque architecture and design of the home. As she made her way back to the kitchen and popped the can of a Pepsi, Catherine was on her way downstairs to the living room. She soon noticed the lights flickering. Catherine yelled to September. "Wow, just in time."

September stood in the middle of the kitchen observing the colorful lights flash on and off. "Just in time for what?" September rotated her head around watching the lights. "Did I win a prize for opening the Pepsi?"

"Nooo. Johnathon is home." Catherine met September in the kitchen.

"Then what the hell are the lights doing?" September was dazed by the different colors of orange, red, and blue flickering lights throughout the house.

Catherine smiled. "That's our silent alarm system to let one of us know the other is home."

"For a moment there, I thought it was New Year's Eve in June."

At that moment, Johnathon entered the living room. He saw Catherine and September in the kitchen.

"Oh hey Catherine. I tried to call you earlier today to let you know the executive party for tomorrow evening was cancelled. So I wasn't sure if I would catch you home by now."

He walked pass September and Catherine. They watched Johnathon grab another set of car keys off the hanger mounted on the kitchen wall. The key hook had ten different cars with the names of each automobile underneath.

Johnathon paused and noticed the two of them watching him. "Johnathon, this is September, September my husband."

Johnathon reached his hand to September. She stretched her hand out to greet him. Johnathon shook hands quickly and headed back toward the garage door.

Catherine was puzzled. "Babe, you just got here. It's just two-thirty in the afternoon. Don't you have a few minutes before you have to rush out? Where are you going? Why did you cancel the caterers for tomorrow's executive function?"

Johnathon stopped just before he reached the door and addressed Catherine. "Because a few of the regulars couldn't make it. They let me know at short notice. I had Angela to call our regular caterers to cancel after I couldn't reach you."

"Then what's the rush? Aren't you free for the afternoon? The three of us could get acquainted."

"Look Catherine, I really got to run. I wanted to get the Bentley to impress this older gentleman client instead of using the BMW. I still have meetings later today. I have one at three. If I don't hurry, I will be late. Mark and I are meeting later this evening with another potential client."

Catherine sighed. "Another late meeting?"

"I know Catherine. I hope you understand, its business. I am at the client's convenience, not mine. You know that."

"Well you better go. Tell Mark hello for me." Catherine sighed.

Johnathon exhaled hearing the insecurity in her voice. He paused to explain. "I know Catherine. Mark is the tech wizard. He tidy's up where I leave off and the meetings are wherever the client wants to meet. So this evening I told Mark we'd leave the office around seven. Then we'd head over to the Yacht Club to meet up with a potential fifty-five million dollar customer to go over some tech software he was interested in. Okay?"

"Then... You don't want to be late. I'll see you later, baby." Catherine spoke with a solemn voice.

"Much later Catherine. I may be really late. Don't wait up for me."

"Okay sweetheart." Johnathon turned toward the door. "Can I get a kiss baby?" asked Catherine.

Johnathon raced over to Catherine. Pecked her on the cheek. "Nice meeting you September." He yelled on his way out the door.

After witnessing the interaction of the two, September remarked. "Some relationship you two have."

Catherine took her phone from her purse and noticed no phone messages. She said nothing more as Johnathon was gone in the blink of an eye.

September noticed the car names under the key hooks. "Woow! A Bentley Continental, Mercedes AMG, BMW M8, Jaguar P450 Coupe, Rolls Royce Sweptail, Audi, Bugatti Chiron, Ferrari F60..."

Catherine interrupted. "You don't have to name them all. I know what we have. Come on. Let's have a drink out back by the pool. We can sit, talk and enjoy the evening air."

"Oooh, I like that ideal. Got any wine?"

September followed her through the sliding glass door to the pool area. Catherine grabbed a bottle of wine from the pool bar.

September admired the décor of the patio. "What a lovely setup you have here. The high multi-color brick fence line for nosey neighbors. The overhanging palm trees, the beautiful patio furniture, a gray granite pool, large enough to hold a party for... ahh... about two-hundred?"

Catherine smiled. "Yes, it's Elle décor, nine-hundred square feet and twenty feet in depth."

At that moment, September saw a pattern of lights hanging from areas of the pool wall. September flicked a switch near the house and beautifully designed circular lights came on dim. "These ambiance lights just make for a romantic setting. Ohhh, I could get use to this style of life real easy. You guys must really get down out here sometimes?"

"We use to. Johnathon let me pick the architect and he designed it just as I told him and wall-la. Home sweet home."

"It's beautiful. Did you decorate the house too?"

"Oh no. I'm not good at that type of stuff either. I had a designer as well. Told her what I wanted and she created it."

"Well I must say she did an excellent job. This patio furniture appears as if you could sleep on it. An island kitchen with refrigerator. I bet it's filled with lots of goodies to drink." September walked around the pool side and laid in one of the lounge chairs.

Catherine shouted, "Well since you like the lights so much let's leave them on. It will be dark soon. Alexa! Play classic music by Mozart." The sound of piano keys softly played with Bose speakers that echoed ever note.

September listened for a little bit. Then reclined in a patio chair. "I've got's to get me one of those Alexa things." As Catherine pulled the wine bottle from the mini refrigerator, her facial expression appeared melancholy. "Why the sad face? What's wrong?" Then, September noticed the label on the wine bottle. She stated with excitement in her voice as she sat up from her chair. "Talaria Vineyards, Cabernet Sauvignon! That's over a hundred dollars a bottle!"

Catherine perked up. "You know your wines."

"I'm always looking at things that I can't afford. I want some."

"With pleasure." Catherine blissfully grabbed a glass from the patio cabinet. She popped the cork, handed September a glass and poured the wine.

"Where is your glass rich lady?"

"Call me Catherine, please. I feel like a label when say rich lady."

"Ok Catherine. Where is your wine glass?"

"Not a wine drinker. That's why I have these." Catherine goes back to the refrigerator and pulled out a Seagram's Cherry Cooler and twisted off the top.

September slightly smiled. "Coolers, that explains the Pepsi in the refrigerator. You really are a down to earth girl."

"Excuse me?" Catherine was curious by what she meant.

"Rich people don't drink Pepsi's or coolers. They have that expensive stuff like sherry, vermouth and Champagne. Pepsi and coolers are for commoners."

"Well, meet your first rich… commoner." Catherine raised her bottle joyfully.

"I'll drink to that." September hovered the glass of wine underneath her nose and took a sip.

Catherine drank her cooler. "Hmmm, nice and cold. Drink up. There's plenty more where that came from." Catherine relaxed on the recliner right next to September.

"Ummm, that's good. So this is what expensive wine taste like."

"Does it meet with your approval?"

"As matter of fact, you can fill this baby up." September held her glass out. Catherine got up to get the bottle from the refrigerator and poured until September's glass was filled to the brim. "Just leave the bottle beside me. I'll take care of it."

Catherine placed the bottle down beside her and laid back in her patio chair. "You know September… I love my husband. Just listening to you brought back memories of how we used to come out here when we first got married and let our physical emotions run wild. But now, he is all about money, money, money and how he can get more of it."

"I take it you and your husband pass each other during the day. Or you see very little of him from the expression you had on your face a little while ago."

"You gathered correctly, if we see each other at all. It seems like I only have certain days of the week that are set aside for me and even that at times seems very limited, as you can see."

"I'm sorry. I can tell you love him."

"How so?" questioned Catherine.

"When a woman doesn't care about her man, she doesn't care where he goes or how long he stays. As a matter fact, she's happy to see him leave. But, when she is in love with her man, she doesn't want him to go anywhere unless she goes too. Your facial expression at the moment he walked out of that door said a lot."

"September I am so bored. I have everything and yet I have nothing. What good are things, if they aren't shared?"

"You are so right rich lady. I mean Catherine." September took another sip of wine. "Well I tell you what rich lady, I mean Catherine. When you need to share, I am going to help you. When you are not with your husband, you can be with me. I am on a mission to fulfill my bucket list and you can join me if you like. Between your boredom and your money, I can complete my bucket list in less than a year."

Catherine laughed. She seemed energized by the concept. "So you're only going out with me because I'm rich?"

September smiled and drank more wine. "You said it, I didn't. I told you about bringing strangers home."

Catherine laughed even harder. "With great pleasure, I would love to help you complete your bucket list."

"Consider it done, tomorrow we'll hit the paint gun game room, some racquetball, and go zip lining."

"Zip lining?" asked Catherine.

"Don't ask, just wait and see." September shook her head. "You rich ladies really don't get out much."

They continued their conversation and downed wine and coolers until the wee-hours of the morning.

CHAPTER 5

Rendezvous with the Ladies

That same evening, while Catherine and September relaxed by the pool, Johnathon held his briefing until six with his client. He called Mark to his office at around six-thirty to let him know he was leaving and wouldn't be working late. Johnathon headed to his condominium to meet Amoy.

When he arrived at the condo, he took his key out and opened the door slowly on the fourth floor. Suddenly he received a text on his phone. Johnathon read the text and placed the phone back in his coat jacket. Peering through the darkness of this candle lit room, he noticed a beautiful light brown skinned, shapely figured woman stretched out on the couch, sound asleep. She had on see-through white Victoria Secret lingerie. Johnathon tip-toed into the living room, sat beside her and kissed her softly upon her cheeks.

Amoy awoke. She spoke softly. "Hey honey bun. I thought you may had forgotten you asked me to be waiting for you."

"I'm glad you could make time for me on such short notice. I didn't mess up any of your business deals for this evening?"

"Not when I'm the boss. That's why I'm napping. It has been a rough day. I didn't mind taking a break after you called. I started sipping wine without you and it got the best of me." Amoy rubbed her eyes.

Johnathon leaned over and kissed her on the forehead. "Well I am glad you weren't too tired to see me."

"For you baby… I would move heaven and earth to get to you. You're the reason I have a growing successful restaurant business. It's moving faster than I expected. I can't thank you enough."

"You thank me enough when we are together."

Amoy kissed him passionately upon the lips. "I was dressed as your masseuse with only a thong on. I got chilly and decided to get into something a little more comfortable."

"You look beautiful just the way you are. Sorry I'm a late, my adoring Jamaican Queen. Things were a little hectic at the office. I needed to relax and all I could think of… was you." He took his suit coat off.

"No problem my love. I needed to relax too and I'm glad you called. You're here now. Let's help each other unwind." Amoy started to unbutton his shirt.

Johnathon stopped Amoy's hands. "Do you want to get dressed? It's only seven. We could catch a late evening dinner anywhere you like. My jet awaits your beckon call."

She continued with unbuttoning the buttons. "Get dressed?" She removed his shirt and gently showered his chest with kisses.

"You want dinner in New York, Las Vegas… Florida? Just say the word my sweet."

Amoy never looked at him, she continued her gentle kisses upon his chest. "I see food all day. Now all I need is dessert and I have it right here." She unzipped his pants. Johnathon soon relaxed in ecstasy of kisses and gentle touches of her hands and lips that were maneuvering around his entire body. No more words were spoken.

At the midnight hour, Johnathon left Amoy sleeping quietly in the bedroom with an empty bottle of wine laying on the carpet floor. He tiptoed out of the room and went down two flights of stairs and entered the room with Victoria. She was a blue-eyed, five foot-nine inches tall, beautiful brown haired woman with an hour glass figure. Her focus was on a Jimmy Fallon Show with a black Victoria Secret long sleeve sleepshirt on. He slowly walked over to the sofa. The room was dim with mood lighting and a bottle of red wine on the coffee table.

"Right on time my love. I wasn't sure you got my text since you didn't reply." Victoria popped the bottle of wine and poured two glasses.

Johnathon loosened his tie as he stood before her. "Hard day at work my sweet? Did you miss me?"

Victoria passed him a glass of wine and he sat down beside her. "Yes. Always. I finished my trial case. The jury found him guilty. When my flight got delayed from New York yesterday, until today. All I thought about was seeing you again. I hope I didn't drag you away from anything important."

"I was just with another client finishing late night business. Your timing was perfect."

Victoria took a sip of wine. She placed her glass back on the coffee table. She reached for Johnathon's glass before he drank and placed it on the table. Johnathon smiled. He stood, pulled her from the couch and removed the pajama shirt over her head. As it dropped to the floor, Victoria grabbed his suit jacket and pulled the coat off his shoulders. As she stood in front of him completely naked, Johnathon admired the curves and shapes of her petite body. She unzipped his pants and rubbed her hands all over his lower extremities. He groaned in ecstasy.

Victoria whispered in his ear. "Do you want to role play darling?"

"Yes, you can roll on and play with any part of me you want to."

Without further hesitation, she went down to her knees and continued to tantalize his lower area with her soft lips and moist tongue. He soon dropped to the floor and return the tantalizing oral motions between her thighs. They soon embraced in each other's arms, while kissing each other passionately on the lips. Physical emotions ramped up so quickly, they never made it to the bedroom.

CHAPTER 6

Johnathon Meets Nicolette

As the sunlight struck the window pane, Johnathon soon realized the hour. He dressed quickly and arrived at home. It's seven-thirty in the morning. He tiptoed into the bedroom hoping Catherine hadn't awaken. Once in the bedroom, Catherine was still sleeping in their specifically designed king size bed that could sleep four easily. While Catherine slept from her evening with September, Johnathon ruffled his side of the bed and jumped into the shower. When Johnathon came from the shower drying his hair with one towel and another towel wrapped around his waist, Catherine awoke. She saw him standing at the foot of the bed.

Catherine rubbed her eyes to clear her vision of him. "I'm sorry honey. I must have slept through your coming in last night. September and I sat up until one-thirty this morning just chatting girl talk and what we're going to do today."

"That's wonderful Catherine. I'm glad you have found a partner in crime to help keep you busy these days."

"Yeah. She's an ex-Army Ranger, retired."

Not really interested in her new found friend, he changed the subject. "On Catherine, please, in the midst of your activities today with this September person, would you ensure everything is in place for the executive party at the house this Friday? I do want everything to be perfect."

"Have I ever let you down my love?"

Johnathon leaned over on the bed and kissed her on the forehead. "That's my girl. I can always count on you. But I just wanted to remind you in the midst of having someone to hang out with, you might forget."

"I'm here for you darling… anyway I can help. Do you mind if I come by the office today and bring September with me? You really didn't get a chance to meet her yesterday."

"Not today Catherine. I will be in meetings all morning and with a client the rest of the day. Today is not a good day."

Catherine just shrugged her shoulders. "Oh honey, when you go downstairs to let Rosa in, tell her that I'm not hungry and not to fix me breakfast."

"Yes. I will do that." Johnathon slightly smiled, realizing Catherine had someone to keep her busy.

Catherine climbed from the bed to hit the shower. Johnathon dressed quickly as he monitored his watch the hold time he was getting dressed. He disappeared before Catherine was out of the shower. He let Rosa in and just told her to clean the house and don't worry about breakfast. He grabbed his Jaguar P450 keys and hurried out the door. He didn't want to be late.

This day, Nicolette arrived at his condominium. Johnathon had been waiting patiently in his master suite. A knock came gently on the door. "Come in." When she entered, he was standing in the center of the living room with a bottle of wine behind his back.

Johnathon couldn't take his eyes off of this slender brunette with bobbed hair. She was dressed with a diamond necklace and a tight black, hip-hugging dress, with a slit down the right side that exposed her thigh. She elegantly stood in the doorway. "Hello Mr. Johnathon Fitzpatrick, how are you?"

"Please come in." Johnathon glanced outside the door. He saw no one and closed it.

Nicolette glanced around the room. "What a beautiful home you have here, Mr. Fitzpatrick."

"Why so formal? I could understand when I was installing the security systems in your home in Italy and your husband was around, but why now?"

"I know… Mr. Fitzpatrick." Nicolette had a stern look and impersonal attitude.

Johnathon closed the distance between them and tried to kiss her on the cheek. She stepped away before he touched her. She continued a slow stroll into the living room.

"I didn't see any body guards outside. So how did you get away from your ninety year old husband?"

"Very carefully Mr. Fitzpatrick and the guards are there. Just not to where you can see them."

Johnathon moved closer to her. He still had the wine bottle behind his back. "You arranged this meeting with me to show you how love making should be done. Yes?" Nicolette just stared at him. "Don't let my good looks intimidate you. I assure you I am all man and up to the challenge. I would be a breath of fresh air from your old man."

"Don't flatter yourself Mr. Fitzpatrick. If I wanted an affair, there are plenty of eligible, more handsome bachelor's I could have picked from in Italy."

Johnathon slightly smiled at the smug comment. "When our eyes met at your home, I read them like a book. I know that glance very well."

"I'm sure you do Mr. Fitzpatrick. But what you saw and how you perceived my facial expression was totally... incorrect."

Johnathon walked closer to her again and pulled the bottle of wine from his back. "I took a chance that you may want something to drink while you are here. A bottle of 2008 Opus One Proprietary Red Wine."

"Yes, Napa Valley. How did you know?"

"While examining your home for security measures, I noticed several bottles in different rooms of your home. May I pour you a drink?"

"You may not. Put your wine away Mr. Fitzpatrick."

"Can we dispense with the formalities and you call me Johnathon?"

Nicolette was very serious and acute in tone. "No....we may not... Mr. Fitzpatrick."

Johnathon shrugged his shoulders. He moved nearer to her again. Nicolette stepped away toward a window view. She admired the city of LA for a moment before turning to face Johnathon. "The reason our eyes met, you reminded me of someone I knew long time ago, for a brief second, when I first saw you at my home... I thought..."

Johnathon interrupted. "I was someone you had known before."

"Yes, deeply." Nicolette spoke with sadness in her voice. She sat down on the sofa, placed her purse on the coffee table and pulled a designer cigarette case from her purse.

"Please don't smoke a cigarette. I can't stand the smell. I can offer you a cigar?" Johnathon placed the wine on the coffee table, reached in his jacket pocket and extended her the cigar.

"No thank you." Nicolette placed the case back in her purse.

Johnathon put the cigar back in his coat pocket. He sat closely beside her. Johnathon tried to place his arm around her shoulder. Nicolette stood and moved toward the window.

"What a beautiful view of the water and the city. I see Mr. Fitzpatrick that…"

He interjected. "Johnathon, please."

"I see Mr. Fitzpatrick that you clearly think I am here for your physical attributes. I assure you I am not. I wanted to see what kind of person you were… are. If knowing you was like…"

Johnathon intervened. "Knowing the one you lost? If you just let me, I will make you forget about any other man in your life."

Slightly aggravated by his intentions, "Clearly I was wrong about trying to get to know you." She gave him a glance of discontent. "I will be leaving now. So sorry to have wasted your time." Nicolette grabbed her purse from the table. Johnathon stood and slightly lunged to grab her purse from her hand. He placed it back on the coffee table.

"No, no, I'm sorry. Let me offer you something else to drink. I mean… let's just talk. Please. Normally I'm not so aggressive with women, but you told me you were on a short schedule for today, I thought…"

"Obviously your thought process with women is one-way. You thought wrong, Mr. Fitzpatrick."

"But for you to have traveled so far just to hold a conversation, it doesn't seem logical to me."

"Yes, I understand how you could have come to that conclusion. So instead of trying to get into my panties, why not try to get into my head?"

Johnathon had a solemn expression upon his face. "Of course, my apologizes. Let me get you that drink. May I call you Nicolette?"

Nicolette doesn't waiver from her position. "No, and I will take a Seltzer water if you have it?"

"Coming up." Johnathon went to the kitchen.

Nicolette sat back down on the couch. When Johnathon returned, he passed her the water in a glass and sat in a single sofa seat matching the couch across from her. "Tell me. How did you meet your father? I mean, your husband?"

Nicolette gave a slight smile to the sarcastic humor. "I love fashion Mr. Fitzpatrick. Not being the riches person in the world, a friend of a friend got me a ticket to a high fashion runway extravaganza. Giovanni was there. After the show was over, he had his driver to follow me and get my phone number. When his driver told me his name, I recognized it immediately."

"Giovanni Russo, the multi-billionaire."

"Yes." Nicolette took a sip of water.

"How could you refuse such an invitation? How many years does he have on you... forty?"

"Does it matter, Mr. Fitzpatrick?"

"And you're what? The same age as me? You don't look more than thirty."

"Can we get off the topic of my husband?"

"Of course. Tell me about this person I remind you of." Questioned Johnathon.

Feeling unable to talk about the relationship she once had, she stood and tried to depart. "Mr. Fitzpatrick I believe I have taken up enough of your time. I'm so sorry." She placed her water on the coffee table. "I must leave."

"No, no, please. I want to know. Obviously this person meant a great deal to you to come all the way from Italy just to have this conversation. Please... continue. I'm listening."

Nicolette bowed her head. She sat down and took another drank of water. She placed the glass back on the coffee table and began again.

"I met Rinieri, the man you remind me of, at Cascine Park in Florence. He was walking his dog and I was jogging. His dog broke away from him. The dog snipped at my leg and I fell. He was so apologetic. I told him not to worry about it. He helped me up. When he did, I looked into his eyes and he stared into mine."

"The same look you gave me at your home."

"Yes. I told him I was fine and started to jog away. He followed and insisted he pay me back with dinner. I accepted, just thinking... why not."

"At dinner, you two realized you had more in common than just a dog snipping at your heels." Added Johnathon.

"He loved fashion and so did I. The concept of owning our own fashion designer shop intrigued us both. We continued to see each other as friends. Over time we decided to go into to business together."

"Did your relationship ever become physical?" asked Johnathon.

"Not at first. Our idea was so strong in both our minds, after months of seeing each other, a business together was all we could focus on. We pooled our money together, but it wasn't enough to open a shop. I was a waitress at Essenziale restaurant. The money was good, but with expenses of living in an apartment alone, I saved very little. He worked at the airport, putting bags on planes."

"Not actually your high level executive positions."

Slightly angered by the comment, "Do not mock me Mr. Fitzpatrick! All of us weren't born with a silver spoon in our mouths."

"Are you suggesting I was?"

"Of course you were. I could tell by the way you carried yourself at my home in Italy and spoke with my husband about your company."

He didn't care for her analogy of his upbringing. Johnathon quickly change the conversation back to her story. "Please, go on Nicolette."

"Mrs. Russo, please."

"Yes, Mrs. Russo. Please continue."

"We thought with one less apartment, we could save more money. His apartment was bigger, so I moved in. He wanted me to stop work and focus on putting together our business plan, overhead, unique designs, and location."

"Why would he want you to stop work, you needed the money?"

"Without a prospectus or business plan, the banks wouldn't listen to us. I read books, took on-line classes, study other business models, and sought advice. We worked our fingers to the bone that first year. We knew our jobs, at the rate we were saving money, it would take us years to get where we needed to be. A loan seemed the fastest way to make our dream a reality."

"That's true." Johnathon was trying to be supportive, by being in agreement with her comment. "Go on."

"One night he came home from working two jobs. He was totally exhausted. I ran some bath water for him. He was so long in the bathroom, when I checked on him, he was sound asleep in the tub. I took the wash cloth and began to wash him while he slept. He looked so innocent, so peaceful, and when I leaned in just to kiss him on the cheek, he awoke."

"This time the stare was more intimate." Stated Johnathon.

"Yes." Nicolette was reminiscing, "Yes it was. We kissed one another as if we had been distance lovers, seeing each other for the very first time… even though we had been living together."

Johnathon had a smirk on his face. "That must have been special."

"You make lite of it Mr. Fitzpatrick, but it was… very special. I felt at that moment, I had found my mate in life. Our passion was to be more than what we were on the outside and our desire to climb to that next level of financial success was our goal together."

"But without physical contact? How long did this last?" asked Johnathon, curiously.

"Three years Mr. Fitzpatrick. Three beautiful years just getting to know each and working toward a common goal."

"Three years? That's a good man, if he was stealing it from another."

Nicolette gave him a stare of total discontent. "You don't see Mr. Fitzpatrick. Everything isn't about sex."

Johnathon was nonchalant. "You're right. I'm sorry. What was your plan?"

"To present an excellent business proposal to the banks, but without collateral, our requests were denied again, again and again."

"Yeah, I can see that."

"I wanted to quit after the tenth refusal. But Renieri looked at me with such loving eyes that day and said, 'Our vision will not be denied my beloved. We will never stop trying. We are not going to let the noise of the world destroy our dreams.' Nicolette spoke as if she could see Renieri speaking those words to her at that moment.

Breaking her trance, Johnathon intervened. "Yeah, Mark, my partner, always boosted my moral by saying his mother always told him from the Bible, 'where there is a will, there is a way'."

Soon realizing where she was, she focused back on Johnathon. "So, Mr. Fitzpatrick we never stopped trying. In fact, our efforts intensified."

"So why didn't you two just change your profession to where you could both progress and make more money?"

Incensed by the statement. Nicolette's tone was slightly aggressive. "You make that sound like a flick of the switch, Mr. Fitzpatrick. 'Just get a job that pays more.' That sounds like a statement from an arrogant rich man. When you have a passion Mr. Fitzpatrick, you don't just turn it off and move on like it never existed."

Aggressive with his tone, "Poverty knows no name Mrs. Russo, only no effort."

Slightly irritated by his comment…"That's where you are wrong with us. We weren't giving up on our passion just so we could go along with the status quo. If we had both gotten caught up in jobs where the money paid the bills and we were content, it would have been easy to say, let's stay where we are and be comfortable."

"What's wrong with that? You wouldn't have been hungry or deciding what bill to pay next."

"If you believe your passion is your God given talent, then pursuing your dream will eventually come true. We both believe that if we worked jobs we couldn't tolerate, once we reached our goal, it wouldn't have been hard to walk away from them. So Renieri started toiling days, nights and weekends. I went back to working days. One night on his way home, so tired from his labors, he fell asleep at the wheel, hit a tree and snapped his neck."

"Sorry to hear that." A hint of sadness was in Johnathon's voice.

"I just bet you are." Sarcastically spoken. "Excessive effort is was killed him. I guess you wouldn't know that when family can hand you millions to get started?"

"I'll have you know it wasn't millions, it was just a few hundred thousand. But I built my company up to what it is today."

"Clearly you don't get it." Nicolette grabbed her purse from the table. "Good day Mr. Fitzpatrick." She walked briskly towards the door.

Johnathon just sat there admiring her curvaceous body as she stepped away. Just as she reached for the handle and began to turn the knob, he scurried toward the door and closed it before Nicolette could leave.

Johnathon stood before her with his back and hand pressed against the door. "Look, I'm sorry. Please sit back down. I didn't mean to be insensitive." Johnathon stared into her beautiful browns eyes with much empathy. Nicolette was emotionless to his words. "I want to hear you out. Please sit. Can I get you another water?"

Nicolette gazed back at him. Not really sure whether to believe his actions. "No. No thank you."

"I understand why you had to see me. I am so sorry for your loss... sincerely." Compassion reigned a little more from Johnathon.

"You have listened to me Mr. Fitzpatrick, but I don't think you understand me. The hour is getting late. I must return to my hotel with shopping bags before I leave tonight or my husband will not believe I came to California to shop."

"It's only 4:30 in the afternoon, allow me to escort you to some of the most luxurious shops in LA. I assure you, you won't be disappointed. What time is your flight?"

"I plan to leave at eight tonight. What of your wife, if you are seen with me?"

"How did you know I was married?" asked Johnathon.

"I do my research Mr. Fitzpatrick."

"Well, my wife knows I have many clients. Some of them female and I might escort them to different areas of the city."

"Dining perhaps, but clothing stores?" questioned Nicolette.

"You let me worry about my wife. Let's depart so that you won't miss your flight. We don't want Giovanni to get concerned and come looking for you."

"I am the wife of a billionaire. I have my own private jet Mr. Fitzpatrick. I come and go as I please. I just told my husband I would be leaving at eight tonight."

"In that case, you can leave tomorrow morning. Let me take you shopping, dinner and show you the sights in LA. I assure you, I will not disappoint. Maybe I can pursued you to stop calling me Mr. Fitzpatrick."

Nicolette smirked. "I don't think so. Shopping will do. I will not miss my time to leave."

"Of course not." Johnathon reached for her hand to aid her from the sofa. She accepted and they left for the rest of the day.

Chapter 7

The Yacht Club

Back at Johnathon's office, Mark made preparations for the day and the rest of the week. Catherine decided to stop by Johnathon's office before meeting up with September. Mark was sitting in his executive office and noticed Catherine at the receptionist desk through his office window. Not wanting to discuss Johnathon's absence from the office, he went to his personal men's bathroom hoping she didn't see him at his desk. When he came out, Catherine stood in front of his desk waiting for him.

"Catherine…" Mark tried to act surprised. "To what do I owe the pleasure?"

"I was wanting to catch Johnathon by surprise. He told me he had a busy schedule today, but you got to eat sometime. I was hoping we could go to lunch if he wasn't too busy."

"Well, what did Angela tell you?"

"She said he was out with a client?"

"Then… there you go." Mark sat in his chair and started reviewing documents and shuffling papers on his desk.

"Well since I am here, why don't you join me Mark?"

Mark looked up at her. "Me?"

"Yes. You have a couple of hours you can spare. I asked Angela to check your schedule and she said you were clear for the next two hours before your meeting."

"J told me you were meeting up with a friend of yours you met the other day."

"I was, I mean I am. That's not until later this afternoon. She forgot she had a doctor's appointment at eleven. I will meet up with her around one-thirty or so."

"Well I know I have a couple of hours, but I like to make sure I am prepared for my meetings. So I always go over the agenda and my notes before I go into a conference."

"Mark are you that afraid of me or Johnathon? I don't bite. Besides, Johnathon considers you a friend, almost like a brother, versus a business partner. So I am asking nicely... please." Catherine smiled.

Mark smiled and reluctantly surrendered to her pleading. He stood from his desk. "Yes, of course, Catherine. I would love to dine with you. Anywhere special you would like to go?"

"The Yacht Club is fine. It's not too far from your office and you can get back here in fifteen minutes or so."

"Very well, after you." Mark stood and motioned his hand toward the door.

Catherine walked out. Mark was right behind her. He whispered to Angela on his way out. "If J calls, tell him I went to lunch with Catherine."

"Yes, Mr. Townsend." Responded Angela.

Mark raced to open the hall door for her. They both left.

At the Yacht Club, there was a hustle and bustle of waiters as the afternoon business lunch crowd had begun. However, Rodney dropped everything when he noticed Mark and Mrs. Fitzpatrick enter the club. He made his way to greet them both.

Rodney seated them immediately. "Mr. Townsend your usual?"

"Yes Rodney, and for you Catherine?" asked Mark.

"Let me have Sex on the Beach. A little heavy on the Vodka please."

"Very good." Rodney left.

"You're looking good, Catherine."

"Thanks Mark. So are you. How did your meeting go with your sixty-million dollar client last night?"

"Last night?" Mark's expression was that of confusion.

Catherine slightly puzzled to his expression, but soon dismissed the look on his face. "Yes, Johnathon told me he was meeting with you and a client worth fifty or sixty-million or so last night."

In Catherine's response, Mark knew Johnathon had used him as a patsy. "Ohhh, yes, yes. It went very well, but it's still not finalized yet. Just a few loose ends to tie up."

"Good. I hope you get it."

"Yes. I think J *stuck* the presentation pretty good. But, thank you for asking."

"Mark, now that I have you alone. I would love for you to do me a favor."

"Sure Catherine, if I can."

"You've known Johnathon and me for over five years now. He works too hard in my opinion to be the CEO of his own company. The late nights and some nights he doesn't come home until two or three in the morning."

"Yes, I understand. How can I help?"

"You're his right hand. There is nothing he does that doesn't involve you. Can't you fill in where he leaves off and let him come home at a reasonable hour in the evenings?"

Their drinks arrive. Rodney placed them down beside them. "May I take your orders now?"

"Catherine?" asked Mark.

"I'll just have the house salad."

Rodney wrote down the order. "And for you Sir?"

"Just bring me the Club Sandwich." Added Mark.

"Very good Sir." Rodney left to fill their orders.

Catherine took a sip of her drink. "Hmmm, that's good."

"I would have thought you partial to wine Catherine."

"No, I really don't like wine. However, Johnathon has so many wines in the cellar. He can name or pull out a dry or sweet wine, tell you what year it is and how long it fermented to get its flavor. I just like to keep it simple and tasty myself."

"But I have seen you at your home with a wine glass in your hand at the executive parties that you host."

"Only for show. Johnathon prefer I have wine in my hand. It looks more elegant than a glass with an umbrella or orange slice hanging from the glass rim or a cherry sitting on top. I would never pour myself a glass of wine."

"Okay, so the wine glass is just to please Johnathon when guests are around?"

"Yes, just between you and me, I wouldn't touch it on my own."

Surprised by the comment, Mark changed the topic. "So, you want me to take some of the pressure off of J, so he can be more of a husband to you."

"Please Mark, don't make it sound like he doesn't pay attention to me. He does. I just want more of his time. I want him home for dinner. I want him to take a day here and there so we can fly to Paris or Hawaii and just enjoy the day to ourselves. I want to make a candle light dinner with flowers at the table and a bubble bath for two afterwards. I want to do what single wealthy couples do. I want to keep the love alive between us." Catherine paused and bowed her head reminiscent of the way it was when they first got married. Then she looked back at Mark. "I love him so much. If you can do that for me I would be so grateful."

"You know Johnathon, Catherine. I can't make him. But what I can promise is, I will do my very best to take the work load off his shoulders and put it on mine."

"Can you try to pull him away from his client today? I will cancel my rendezvous with September."

Mark paused, recalling where Johnathon was spending his time. "Let's not pressure him Catherine, especially when clients are involved. Meet with your friend today. Give me a couple of weeks to work on Johnathon and you'll know whether or not I am getting through to him."

"Ohhh, yes. One more thing. You will be at this week's executive party as usual? I would so like for you to meet my friend, September."

"Of course Catherine. Have I ever missed one? They are just as important as the meetings we have here at the office."

Catherine smiled and lifted her glass. "A toast to brighter days ahead."

Mark mimicked her expression and raised his glass. "To brighter days."

When Mark returned to the office, a beautifully dressed Asian brunette arrived twenty minutes later. Angela escorted her into his office and remained there.

"Thank you Angela." Mark acknowledged his guest. "Would you care for something to drink?"

"No thank you." Stated the lady.

"Angela you may leave." As Angela left the room and closed the door… "Please sit down Miss…" stated Mark.

She interrupted… "No names. Thank you, no. I am only here to deliver this envelope only to you Mr. Townsend."

She handed Mark the package and walked out. As she left, Mark observed the medium size vanilla package with no writing on the envelop anywhere. Curiosity overwhelmed him. However, the temptation to open the package was soon squashed. He knew he could possibly lose his position in the company if he interfered with Johnathon's secretive endeavors. Mark soon placed the envelope in his desk drawer. He knew Johnathon wouldn't be home until later that evening, if at all. He would do as Johnathon instructed him earlier in the day.

CHAPTER 8

September Teaches Catherine How to Shoot

Catherine soon made it home after having lunch with Mark. September arrived shortly after. September glanced across the street and without fail, Mrs. Jensen was staring with her binoculars. September rang the doorbell. Catherine opened the door and she was dressed in a long white sun dress with casual designer slippers.

September entered and went straight to the kitchen and grabbed a Pepsi from the refrigerator. Catherine followed. "Sorry I took so long, its 3:30. I didn't realize my doctor would be so thorough doing a physical."

"No worries, as I told you, all my days are free. Want to go relax by the pool or take a dip since we missed our appointment time?"

September popped the top and took a swallow of Pepsi. "No. It's just three-thirty. Maybe since I am a regular customer at the gun range, they will try to squeeze us in. Let me call and see. Someone may have cancelled and I can still get a spot."

While September called, Catherine went upstairs to dress in more casual attire, jeans and blouse. When she returned to the living room, September was gulping down her Pepsi.

"Well?" asked Catherine.

"You're in luck. They did have a cancellation. We can have a four-fifteen spot if we get there in twenty minutes." September threw the can toward the trash container and missed.

Catherine was bewildered. She watched the can fly through the air and hit the floor. "You do see there is a lid on that?"

September smiled, goes over and placed the can in the trash. "Let's go before we lose that spot."

"I'll drive. I'm never sure if we are going to make it in your ja-loppy when I ride with you."

"That's fine with me. Can we take the Mercedes AMG?"

Catherine was delighted September didn't argue about the car. "Sure. Walk with me to the garage."

Once the garage door automatically slide open upon the body presence at the door, September was in awe. "Ohhh man! This garage looks like a dealership. Even the floor is tiled and waxed. My car is hot red too. Oh, can I drive?"

"It's got a lot of horse power September. You think you can handle it?" When they both got in, September admired the steering, black and red interior and the dash. "Johnathon will kill me if you put a scratch on this car."

"I know. I will kill me if I put a scratch on this car. A 630 HP GT 63 S, twin-turbo, 4.0-liter AMG V-8, with several modes, comfort, individual, sport, sport +, and race, high end 3-D surround sound, a..."

Catherine interrupted and was anxious to get going. She became annoyed with her observation of the car. "Can you just drive? I don't need a dissertation on the features of this car. I don't want to miss this spot."

"Chill. It isn't every day I get to sit behind the steering wheel of one of these magnificent machines. Let me just enjoy the feel and comfort. Besides, in this... I can be there in five minutes." Catherine's eyes buck slightly as she watched September. A joyful September was caressing the steering wheel, feeling the dash, and adjusting her body in the seat. She turned on the music and blasted the sound.

"Sometime today September." Catherine glanced at her watch. "Remember twenty-minutes? Well now it's fifteen."

"In five minutes. Buckle up and enjoy the ride." September started the car. She listened to the engine purr for a brief moment. Catherine hit the garage door button. September screeched the tires pulling out of the garage.

Mrs. Nosey body Jensen observed the burst of speed at which September drove out of the driveway.

They hit the gun range in ten minutes flat. Catherine was relieved no accident occurred.

Before September hit the locker for her weapons, "Let's do the Glock .45. I like that one." stated Catherine.

"Sure. I'll just get that one since that is your weapon of choice." September returned with the Glock and placed it on the shelf at their booth. "Remember what I told you about your breathing and stance."

Catherine picked up the firearm and again fired five rounds into the wall. September grabbed her from behind and held her wrist steady. "Did you not learn anything from the first time I showed you what to do? Keep your wrist steady and breathing controlled." September released her wrist and stepped to the side.

"Okay. Let me began again. I spread my feet apart like this, aim for my target. Hold my breath just before I fire."

"You listened. Alright, now do it."

Catherine aimed and hit the target. "Now do it again." Stated September. Catherine aimed and struck the target again. "Now do it again and again and again."

After one full hour September got hungry. "Our hour is up. Where are we going for a late lunch, early dinner?" September put her weapon away in her locker.

"I know this great place in the middle of nowhere. Let me surprise you? I'll drive."

"Lead the way." September followed and sat on the passenger seat.

Once at the Mom and Pop restaurant in downtown Los Angeles, September was bewildered as to Catherine's knowledge of such a quaint establishment.

"I know your husband would never approve of this place, the Country Diner. A rich lady like you? How do you find these inexpensive diners that taste so great?" quizzed September.

A waitress came over. "What can I get you ladies?"

"I'll have a Negroni if you have that?" asked September.

"No ma'am we don't."

"A glass of your most expensive wine." Spoke September.

"And for you?"

"I'll have a water, please." Answered Catherine.

"Very good. I'll be back with your drinks."

"In answer to your question September, most of the time I am by myself. I try to find places that aren't so ritzy because that's not me. My dad and mom love these places. Mostly because the service is excellent, the people are friendly and the food is good. But when necessary, I can play the part of the boogie rich lady."

"Johnathon doesn't know he has a down to earth wife, does he? How did you two meet?"

Catherine gave a small smile and reminisced. "My father was invited to one of those financial conferences. It was held by a wealthy billionaire showing common people how to invest. He wanted me to go with him to hear what this man had to say about increasing your wealth before retirement. Needless to say, I was dressed to impress."

"This is where you met Johnathon?"

"Yes. After the conference, there were snacks and drinks. People were mingling around. He came over. We talked, he asked me out after that night. You know, when we were dating he never asked about the foods I like to eat or the places I like to go. It was always about him. He took me to all the places he dined and activities he enjoyed, and we were always around his friends."

"So if you never got a word in edge wise, how did he end up marrying you?"

"Now that I am talking about it, it was a little strange. We dated for about three months. For those three months I was his queen, his everything, he called every day. We flew to Hawaii to watch the sun set and rise. We ate out at expensive restaurants and had private dinners for two at his house. We made love all day every day, some days. It was amazing. Though it never occurred to me that all that time we only did what he wanted to do. Except for the Italian restaurant."

"Sooo, how did you two end up getting married?"

"Just out of the blue one evening, having dinner at his home, he asked me. He called his maid from the kitchen saying we were ready for dessert. When the maid served me, a diamond ring was in the dessert dish."

"A little strange." Thought September. "A man of his wealth should have been more creative. I would have thought he would have wanted a huge crowd with his friends around to embrace the treasure he had found in you."

"That's not my Johnathon. He only expresses such affection when he is making love."

"You mean no hugs and kisses in public?" questioned September.

"Exactly. He believes such public affection isn't professional."

"What?" September grinned. "Professional? Oh, no, no, no. I know when I am out with my man, he'd better act like I am the only woman on the planet. Letting the public know that you love someone by holding hands or an occasional kiss on the lips, in my opinion, is what this world needs to see."

"Oh, but our wedding was unique and beautiful. We went back to Hawaii. We were in Oahu, Hawaii. Nalo Gardens. This place was filled with a variety of unique botanicals. The lush greenery set the stage for the ceremony, while the iconic Ko'olau Mountains made for a breathtaking backdrop. Just his family and mine, with a few of our very special friends of our domestic acquaintances were there. The first six months were a wedding bliss. We couldn't get enough of each other. "

"Let me guess… after that, he threw himself into his work and now… time with him has to be made by appointment only."

"I wouldn't say it's that bad, but close. I do get most Friday's when he is free. But sometimes I do feel like I'm not treated like a loving wife should be."

"Hell, I know you're not. I noticed when he left you the other day, he didn't say good bye *hon*, *babe*, or *sweetheart*. He called you by name and then you had to ask for a kiss. That's a true sign that there is trouble in paradise. Have you tried telling him how you feel?"

"Of course, but his heart is set on becoming a billionaire. So I'm afraid if I try to stand in the way of his dream, I will lose him."

"If you ask me, I believe you have already lost him. I think money is in the way. Money isn't everything. I know, I walk around looking at things I would love to have, but at the end of the day, I am thankful of the things I do have. Money may be a necessity and provide beautiful wants and desires, but it is not a substitute for life, love or happiness."

"I hear you September, but how do I make him realize that I am a part of his life? I asked his assistant today to try and free up some time for him, so Johnathon can spend more time with me."

Their drinks arrived. "What would you ladies like to eat?"

"Give me the T-bone steak and fries with string beans." Responded September.

"And you ma'am?" asked the waitress.

"The house salad. Thank you."

"Very good." The waitress left.

"Well, I just met him briefly and already I think he's a jerk. If you don't try to balance work and home, you're going to lose one of them." September was unsympathetic about Johnathon's behavior that day. "From what I see, he is willing to lose home. You have plenty of money. It's just the greed in him that's wants more and ignores you."

"Don't be judgmental September. Becoming a billionaire is not many people's dream. To become one takes a lot of hard work and effort. I applaud him for that. I want to be supportive, but I don't know how and I feel shut out."

"Why not try learning a little bit about the business, that way you can discuss it with him?"

"Yes, of course." Catherine sarcastically stated. "A lot of chips, analogues, worms, spiders, viruses, swarms and on and on… I have no clue."

"Yeap… who wants to learn about a bunch of critters." September laughed. "Well I was in the killing business, not the encrypted career. I see what you mean. I don't know Catherine. Just continue being the good wife. Maybe he will come around."

"I do try September, I do." Catherine stated with a solemn voice.

Their food arrived. The waitress placed their plates before them. "Anything else ladies?"

"Yes bring the dessert menu, please." Stated September.

"Are you that hungry September?" asked Catherine.

"No, I only ask for food at a restaurant when my stomach is full." September, sarcastically spoke.

"Will that be all ladies?" asked the waitress.

"Yes, please bring the dessert menu as well." Stated Catherine.

"Keep an eye for when I finish the first glass of wine, I will need another." Stated September.

"That will be all, thank you." They both watched the waitress leave. Catherine was concerned about September's ability to control the car if she drank too much. "I'm driving. The way you almost hit that pole and sober…"

September agreed. "That was just a little too much speed on that one road. But, you bet. I don't want a DUI in that baby of yours."

Catherine and September dove into her plates. "I better carry my high-end black card, if I am to keep you well feed."

September just smiled and nodded her head, while chewing on a piece of steak in the corner of her jaw.

CHAPTER 9

Mark Confronts Johnathon

When Johnathon left Nicolette after shopping and dinner, he returned to his condominium and met up with Ava and Krista at seven that evening. Heavily engaged in role play, wine, bodily foreplay and much sexual interaction all evening long, Johnathon lost all tract of time. He called Catherine to let her know that he was going straight to the office after spending the evening with Mark.

That day, Johnathon was at his desk writing in his black book and checking his calendar. Mark knocked. He entered Johnathon's office and saw him making notes.

Mark was a little annoyed. "Eleven o'clock. Are we keeping banker's hours now?"

Johnathon closed his black book and placed it in his desk. "What are you bickering about? You know I only come in this unpunctual when I have been with two friends late in the evening."

"I thought you said one very special lady?"

"Well she was on a time clock and had business to take care of as well. So I called up two other friends for the evening."

"Well it must have been an excellent two friends this time, because you're never this late. Did you get the package yesterday? When I arrived around seven, neither you nor Catherine where home."

"No. If you put it on the coffee table, I will get it when I go home tonight."

Mark was astonished. "You haven't been home yet? Yesterday must have been super awesome? Whoever they were, they must have five stars in your little black book?"

Feeling a little irritated behind the twenty questions... "None of your business my friend. What is your problem? You never ask me how my time went with my partners. Why the curiosity now?"

"Catherine paid you a visit... here, at the office yesterday."

"What! I told her not to come here unless I ask her to come. I told her I would be too busy to see her." Johnathon hoped Mark hadn't felt self-righteous on him. "What did you tell her yesterday?"

"That you were with a client."

"Okay... what was she doing here?"

"She wanted to catch you by surprise and have lunch with her loving husband. Some wives do that when they believe their spouses aren't having affairs."

"Don't go there Mark. It's not an affair if you have more than one partner. Besides, my personal business is none of your concern."

Mark felt it was time to be straight forward and aggressive. "Only when your wife ask me to take the heavy burden of business off your shoulders so you can spend more time with her. Then... it's my problem."

"She asked you to do that?" Johnathon was a little perplexed. "I thought she was having a grand old time with her new found friend."

Mark was still aggressive in tone. "Yes. Well maybe their conversations are about how nonexistent you are in Catherine's life."

Johnathon had a softer tone. "I'll take care of it Mark." He was still confused as to why Catherine came by when he told her not to. "I won't mention that you told me about her request. Now what's on the agenda today?"

"Ohhh... and one more thing."

"What's that?" asked Johnathon.

"The next time you want to use me as an excuse to get out of the house to go whoring around... you might want to let me know so I don't have a stupid look on my face when I'm questioned about it."

Johnathon spoke with sarcasm and a little anger. "Ok, for the record, I spent last night with you going over some business with a client. We drank a little too much and I fell asleep at your place. There's your heads up. Now you know if she ask. Let's get to the agenda, please!"

Mark just stared at Johnathon in disgust and shook his head. "Today we have a dry run of the briefing for Mr. Fu, CEO of Chen Bao Industries from Hangzhou, China. He'll be bringing all of his industrial plans and diagrams of the buildings he wants us to secure. He is worth twenty-seven billion dollars. He wants a top notch system to protect his main office on the twenty-third floor, plus five other buildings in the city."

"Ok, anything else?"

"He wants a security system to monitor all the floors and allow access to each floor to only the individuals that work in that area."

"We can do that. We can show him the security systems in place for just individuals, the facial recognition, voice recognition and the meticulous body scan. When does he arrive?"

"Tomorrow with his entourage."

"How much are we talking again?"

"A potential one-hundred-ten million for the main building. If he likes what he sees, we install security system in the other five building. All six buildings would be approximately three-hundred-ninety million over the next five years."

Johnathon raised an eyebrow. "How many will be in his team?"

"Ten."

"See to it that the briefing room is prepared with refreshments and my slides are ready to go."

"Already done J. All we need is a dry run today by you to see what slides you wish to use and in what order."

"Then let's move. I definitely don't want to lose this one. This one sell would equal the last two years alone. Oh yes. You know about the executive party this Friday night?"

"Of course, I haven't missed one yet. Catherine reminded me yesterday and Angela always makes sure the party dates are on my calendar. Plus, I have placed a reminder in my phone. I will be there."

"Good, because I want you to meet this new friend of Catherine's. Maybe you can get a sense of what she is all about."

Mark smiled. "She sounds intriguing if she keeps Catherine on the move."

"You'll see. Pick her brain for me. Find out what they have been talking about. Catherine doesn't usually disobey me when I tell her something isn't feasible. She should have never come to the office yesterday."

"I'll bet you're the number one topic they talk about when they're together." Mark gave a slight grin.

Johnathon stared at Mark, he wasn't smiling. They headed toward the conference room. After a dry run of the slides and they ensured all was in order for tomorrow's briefing, Johnathon headed back to his office.

As Johnathon entered his office, the intercom buzzed. "Mr. Fitzpatrick, line one." Stated Angela.

Johnathon picked up. "Fitzpatrick here."

"Mr. Fitzpatrick, Nicolette Russo. I wanted to thank you for lending your ear to me the other day. Our conversation gave me some relief from the past. Thank you for dinner and shopping as well. Your kindness will never be forgotten."

"It was my pleasure. If you need my ear again, I would love to let you have it."

Nicolette giggled over the phone. "Nooo... that won't be necessary. I believe I have come to terms with what I lost and I must move forward."

"I totally understand. If you are ever in L.A again, call me. Let me give you my cell."

"No thank you." There came a short pause over the phone. "I might use it. Thank you again. Goodbye, Mr. Fitzpatrick." Nicolette hung up the phone.

Johnathon was delighted to have heard from her. He got on the intercom. "Angela do I have anything scheduled on the calendar for Monday and Tuesday of next week?"

Angela checked quickly. "Not at the moment Mr. Fitzpatrick. Your calendar is free."

"Good. Put me down for a three day vacation starting this Monday. I will let Mark know personally and get me two tickets to Rome Italy for this Saturday as well. Thank you."

"For you and Mr. Townsend?" asked Angela.

"No, for my wife and I."

Angela was surprised by the request to include his wife. "Yes, sir." She immediately got on the phone to make the arrangements.

CHAPTER 10

Johnathon and Catherine in Rome

Johnathon and Catherine arrived in Rome, Italy that Saturday afternoon. They purchase the crown suite in the building with a view of the city. The room was twenty-six-hundred square feet of exquisitely designed living room furniture, master bedroom, dining area, and more.

Catherine stood at the hotel bedroom window with suitcases by the bed. "Oh honey, this view of the city is breath taking. I have to admit I am a little shocked for you to spontaneously want to take me on a vacation out of the blue. Is it because you landed that three-hundred-million dollar deal you were talking about?"

"No. I told Mark I haven't been spending enough time with you and I needed to change that."

Catherine thought at that moment her little chat with Mark may have worked. "Awesome, sweetheart. Did you plan an itinerary or do I need to gather a hotel pamphlet for attractions or tours they have for the city?"

"You go see what they have Catherine. Talk to the manager of the hotel for the best response. I need to make a phone call to a client I have here."

"Business!" Catherine was upset. "Really Johnathon. I thought we were here to enjoy one another. Not on some business undertaking."

Johnathon in a soft loving tone tried to explain his actions. "I'm not here on business. I've already done business with this man. It's just a follow up to see how he is satisfied with the work I've done." Johnathon walked over to Catherine and pecked her on the lips. "Now go and talk to the hotel manager and see what exciting things we can do while we are here in Rome."

"Why don't I just call?" Catherine sighed.

"In person conversations make for excellent results. Please talk to the manager, in-person Catherine."

Catherine left out the front door and slammed it. Johnathon immediately pulled out his cell phone in the bedroom suite and made the call.

"Mr. Russo, this is Johnathon Fitzpatrick. May we meet for lunch today if you aren't busy?"

"You're here, in Rome?" asked Giovanni. He sounded excited.

"I am here on vacation with my wife. I just wanted to see how my work on your home was holding up and if you were satisfied."

"Wonderful! Well since you are on vacation, you and your wife can join us on my yacht. Let's say tomorrow, for lunch and we can discuss your work then."

Johnathon was surprised by the invite. "Splendid, I look forward to it Mr. Russo. Where shall we meet you?"

"Meet me at my home tomorrow at noon. I will take it from there."

"Yes, sir. We will be there."

Catherine came back to the room and threw the excursion pamphlets on the coffee table. Johnathon heard the door and entered into the living room.

"Catherine, I am so glad you decided to join me on this short vacation." Johnathon smiled from ear to ear.

Catherine didn't share his enthusiasm. "I was surprised you asked. We haven't been on vacation together since our honeymoon last year. But now I feel as if this was just a business meeting and you wanted me along for show."

"This isn't business Catherine. We're going to enjoy ourselves while we're here, I promise." Johnathon kissed her on the forehead. "Now let's unpack and prepare for dinner."

Some tension was in Catherine's voice. She stepped into the bedroom, grabbed her suitcase and threw it on the bed. She loudly spoke to Johnathon still in the living room. "Why didn't you just tell me the truth instead of letting me think that this…" She looked around the bedroom. "This vacation was about us?"

Johnathon came into the bedroom. "It is about us. I guess I should have told you everything and I am sorry that I didn't. But this hard work is going to pay off. I was on the phone with Mr. Russo, my client. I called him just to see how my devices were performing for him. And to my surprise, he invited us to lunch on his yacht tomorrow. He's a billionaire!" Johnathon stated with enthusiasm. "Can you imagine the associates he must know? Just a couple of referrals from him could mean millions." Johnathon waited for a joyful response from Catherine. Her expression was that of sorrow. He reiterated in a soft tone. "Millions Catherine. It's just a small lunch on his yacht tomorrow for a few hours. Do you mind?"

Catherine sighed, thinking about being more supportive of him. A slight smile came across her lips…"Of course not, my love. Anything for you."

"Catherine you're the best. We are going to enjoy ourselves as well." Johnathon glanced back into the living room and saw the pamphlets on the table. "I tell you what? Let's go for a swim by the pool, then grab some dinner and dance the evening away. We'll look over those pamphlets at dinner. How does that sound?"

Catherine moved close to Johnathon and wrapped her arms around his neck. She kissed his lips softly. "We just got here my sweet. It's only three o'clock. Can we rest first, before we venture out?" She took one hand, unbuttoned his shirt and rubbed her hand across his chest. Johnathon watched her movement and decided not to participate.

Johnathon moved slowly away, closer to the bedroom door. "You rest. I am going down to the lobby and make arrangements for our dinner this evening."

With a heavy sigh… "That's what phones are for darling. Call, while I slip into something more comfortable." Catherine grabbed her suitcase from the floor, threw it on the bed and popped the locks. Johnathon noticed her behavior as she began to pull out her Victoria Secret lingerie.

Johnathon gingerly made his way to the living room and yelled standing at the front door with his hand on the knob. "Going to the lobby Catherine. I'll be right back. You go ahead and change. Just want to talk to the concierge face to face. The message of excellent service gets across better in person."

Catherine heard the door close. She let her lingerie fall back into the suitcase as she spoke softly to herself. "Very well darling. I will await your return." Catherine sat and fell back on the bed with her suitcase beside her in total disappointment and closed her eyes.

When Johnathon reached the lobby, in a short distance, he spotted a gorgeous brunette, beautifully dressed, legs crossed with one thigh showing as she sipped her drink at the bar alone. He thought he recognized her. As he walked over, she saw him out the corner of her eye. Then she fully turned to see him closely as he approached.

She reached her arms out. "Oh my gosh! Johnathon. What are you doing in Rome?"

When he reached her, he embraced her tightly as she was still seated. While peering over her shoulder, Johnathon noticed her room key on the counter. Then he faced her. "Amoy, might I ask you the same question?"

Amoy was excited to explain her situation. "Well if you must know, my restaurant business is taking off just as you said it would. Two Italian chefs saw my YouTube video of me cooking some of my dishes. They followed my recipes and tried them in their restaurants. They were so popular at their restaurants, they want to open one of my restaurant's here, in Italy. Isn't that the greatest! I am meeting them for dinner this evening to discuss a contract. I just came down to have a drink and unwind before our little conference at seven."

"Good for you." Johnathon spoke excitedly. He leaned and kissed her on the cheek.

"Yeah... I want to seem poised and professional rather than eager and willing to jump at the first price they offer."

"Well, have a figure or percentage already in mind to what you will settle for. Go bigger than what you will settle for. Most of the time, their final offer is more than what you would have asked for anyway. Be stern and straight faced. If they want it bad enough, they will meet or exceed your demands."

"Thanks Johnathon. I do have a figure already in mind."

"Good." Johnathon's roaming eyes gazed at her lovely body. He changed the subject. "Sooo....you are just passing the time at the bar until dinner?"

"Yes." Amoy took a sip of her drink. "How about you? What are you doing here?"

"My wife and I are here to meet with a client tomorrow. She is relaxing in our suite right now. We also, will be dinning in here later tonight."

"Well good for you." Amoy took another swallow of her drink and she looked back at Johnathon.

Johnathon observed her shapely figure and beautiful outfit once again. This time Amoy noticed his roaming eyes.

Johnathon spoke tenderly. "Amoy?"

"Yes, Johnathon." Amoy knew that tone of voice.

"Are you here alone?"

"I am. I'm only here for a couple of days to talk over this deal. I got here yesterday. I will be leaving tomorrow."

Johnathon was now staring into her eyes. "Let me help you pass the time. I will order a bottle of wine and send it to your room." Johnathon peeked at his watch. "Let's say... right now."

Without hesitation, Amoy sipped the last little bit of liquid from her drink. Grabbed her room key from the counter. Told the bartender... "Put my drinks on my room." She eased off her bar stool. She whispered in Johnathon's ear as she headed toward the elevator. "355."

Johnathon handed the bartender five-hundred dollars in cash and had a chilled bottle of 2017 Chateau Lafite Rothschild sent to room 355. He soon followed the perfume scent Amoy left behind.

The bartender yelled as Johnathon walked away. "Sir, you are short a thousand."

"Put the balance on Suite 907. Add another hundred for yourself." Johnathon never looked around and punched the elevator button.

Hours later, Johnathon was gone so long Catherine had fallen asleep on the bed by her suitcase. He came back to the room, Catherine was still sleeping. He awakened her by shaking her shoulders.

Catherine looked at her watch and gazed out the window. "Goodness! It's almost six my love and the sun is setting. I must have been more exhausted than I thought from our flight. Where have you been? It doesn't take three hours to make dinner reservations for two."

"I met this gentleman, in the lobby. You know me always thinking business. I approached him and we got to talking. I had a couple of drinks with him at the bar. I glanced at my watch, realized the hour and the next thing I knew, time had passed so quickly. I told him I had a dinner engagement with my beautiful wife. He gave me his number and perhaps in the future we can do business."

"Are you sure this vacation is for us? So far, I have not spent an hour with you since we've been here."

"Get dressed Catherine. We'll have dinner and I will take you dancing all night long."

With much gusto, Catherine grabbed her bag from the bed and raced to the bathroom to freshen up. Johnathon kept him promise to Catherine. At dinner, while Catherine went to the ladies room, Johnathon asked the waiter to have the bartender to double the vodka in her drinks.

Catherine returned to the table. "You want to leave now my love? Let's dance the night away."

"Not yet. I want to discuss the company business with you." Johnathon raised his hand to the waiter. "Bring another drink for my wife and I, please." The waiter in a distance acknowledged his request.

"I don't know if I should have another. After two you know how I get... very sleepy. I should just stick to the one drin..."

Johnathon intervened. "Nonsense Catherine we're on vaca. Let's enjoy ourselves."

"You're really going to talk shop with me?" Catherine was enthusiastic about learning more of what Johnathon did at work.

The waiter brought Catherine another drink and Johnathon as well. Catherine sipped away. Johnathon talked company business at her for an hour. As the third drank took effect, Catherine's speech became slurred. Johnathon ordered another one before she finished the one she had. He continued to talk as Catherine started her fifth drink. He let her swill so many Sex on the Beach cocktails that her head was spinning before they were to go dancing. As Johnathon observed Catherine, her face almost struck the table.

Johnathon knew she was in no condition to stand. "Ready to go dancing?"

Catherine could barely keep her balance in her seat. She responded. "Yes."

As she tried to stand, Johnathon had to race to catch her from hitting the floor. Catherine unable to function, was more than willing to go back to their hotel room after dinner. She was so groggy, she leaned on Johnathon until they got back to their suite. Passing out at the door, he picked her up, took her to the bedroom, undressed her, placed her in bed and allowed her to rest. He watched Catherine lay asleep for about thirty minutes until he felt sure the vodka had taken full affect. While she slept, Johnathon closed the bedroom door, went to the living room and called Amoy. To his delight, Amoy was resting in her bedroom awaiting tomorrow's travel. He wanted to see her again. She didn't refuse.

When Johnathon knocked on the door, he was barefooted in a pair of slacks and pajama top. Amoy was dressed in baby pink Victoria Secret lingerie. "Coming." When she opened the door, Johnathon stepped into the living room. Amoy closed the door, locked it and followed him.

Johnathon looked around. "Nice room."

Amoy smiled. "It's the same way it looked when you left five hours ago. It's not like your suite, but one day it will be." Amoy was puzzled as too his presence. "It's only nine-thirty my love, I thought you and your wife would be enjoying Italy's night life."

Johnathon stepped closer to Amoy. "When you are nearby, the only thing I want to enjoy is you." He grabbed her by the waist, pulled her tightly to his chest and kissed her passionately.

With little resistance, Amoy pulled back gently and stared lovely into his eyes. "After our earlier encounter of over three hours together, I would have thought you would have had enough of me."

"No my love. The time with you today, only left me wanting more." Johnathon kissed her again. This time she embraced him with open arms. Moments later, he started to remove all the clothing on her body as she in return did the same to him.

Once they both were naked, Johnathon grabbed her by the waist."Did you get an offer you couldn't refuse this evening?"

Amoy kissed his lips passionately. "Your advice was gold." She grabbed his hand. "Follow me my love. We left a few drops of wine in the bottle. We must finish it and not let it go to waste." Amoy led him to the bedroom. She pushed him on the bed, took the bottle of wine and let the remaining juices fall upon his chest and the rest of his body. She dimmed the lights and began gently with her lips and tongue to extract the liquid she had poured upon him. They both embarked upon another blissful moment in the bedroom.

Lunch with Russo

As the morning light hit the sky in Rome, Johnathon was excited about his lunch with Mr. Russo. He was dressed in casual attire. Catherine was dressing in the bathroom as he took in the view from the bedroom window.

"Catherine are you ready? I have a taxi arriving for us downstairs."

"Coming darling." Catherine stepped out of the bathroom, completely dressed in a beautiful summery flowered outfit with matching shoes and jewelry. "I must apologize for last night my sweet. I was so intent on listening about the business that I drank too much. You must forgive me for ruining our evening of dance."

"Think nothing of it Catherine. Come. The taxi will be arriving soon."

They both made their way down to the lobby. The concierge acknowledged that the taxi had arrived for them.

Once in the taxi, Johnathon and Catherine were driven to the town of Tuscan of Monte Argentario. Once they arrived at the villa, a servant greeted them at the door. He led them to the living room. Catherine was astounded by almost twenty acres of the villa filled with beautiful trees and flowers that covered the grounds. The beauty of the Desert Sunrise Brick surrounded the front door. When they entered the home, the back terrace had a dynamic panoramic view off the coast of Costa d'Argento. The living room was decorated with artistic paintings from every corner of the world. As Johnathon and Catherine admired the décor of the home with elegant modern furniture. Moments later, the Russo's came in the room.

Johnathon noticed them out of the corner of his eye. He called Catherine to join him as she stood near the terrace. "Mr. Russo, Mrs. Russo, how are you both? This is my wife Catherine."

Catherine stretched her hand out. Instead of shaking hands, Mr. Russo, six-feet tall, slender, gray beard and white hair with shades of black peppered threw out his head, dressed with black designer slacks and blue shirt. He kissed both cheeks of Catherine and Johnathon. Mrs. Russo stretched her hand to Catherine and Johnathon, each of them shook Nicolette's hand.

"This is a beautiful home Mr. Russo." Proclaimed Catherine.

"Yes, thank you. Call me Giovanni, please. I will be happy to give you a tour another day perhaps. But today I want to enjoy this beautiful weather on my yacht. Come, the helicopter awaits. This way. My Yacht is already at sea, but not far." Mr. Russo moved to the Heli-pad. They all followed.

When the helicopter was five minutes into flight, "This is a spectacular view of the town." Stated Catherine.

"If you are here for a little while, you must allow us to show you around our beautiful city. My yacht is not far." Mr. Russo looked out the window and pointed in a distance. "There, you can see it in a distance."

Catherine glanced in that direction. "My... that certainly is a beautiful boat Mr. Russo."

"Ship, Catherine." Johnathon glanced now and then at Nicolette. Nicolette kept her eyes on the scenic view of the water out the window.

"Thank you Mrs. Fitzpatrick."

"Catherine, please."

"Of course Catherine. Well Catherine, I will be happy to give you a tour once we land."

"That would be most delightful, Mr. Russo." Stated Catherine.

"Please. Let's all be informal. Call me Giovanni. We are here to enjoy ourselves. No more formalities, I insist."

Once the helicopter landed, they were immediately escorted to the dining area by the Captain of the ship. The dining room was a fifty-foot area with couches, love seats, dining table and bar. The buffet table was loaded with fruits and vegetable, shrimp, finger sandwiches, sorted cheeses, and so much more. The room was elegantly designed with a fully loaded bar with all types of wines and liquors. Johnathon and Catherine were seated on a sofa near the wall. Nicolette sat on another sofa across from them.

"Mr. Russo, brunch was prepared as order as you can see. We have dinner ready to be served at your request, sir." Stated the Chef of the boat.

"Thank you Enzo. Tell the Captain he may start the tour around the area as instructed." Stated Mr. Russo. "I will let you know when we are ready for dinner."

"Right away, sir." The Chef left and called the Captain from the scullery area.

"Please, if you didn't have breakfast, I know you are famished. Eat, enjoy." Stated Russo.

"Sir, what would you care to drink?" asked the bartender.

"Aldo, I will have my usual." Giovanni glanced at his guests. "Johnathon, Catherine if noon is too early for alcohol, I do have other non-alcoholic beverages. Aldo my guest will have…"

"A glass of your finest red wine for me and my wife." Stated Johnathon.

"Give my wife her usual as well, Aldo." Stated Mr. Russo.

As they waited on drinks, Catherine was fascinated by the beauty and size of the boat. She got up from the sofa and walked around the dining area. She admired the décor of the living space and the view out the window. Johnathon continued to throw glances here and there at Nicolette.

"This boat is very beautiful." Stated Catherine to all.

"Yes, two-hundred-twenty feet in length, swimming pool, elevator, gym, four bedrooms… come… let me show you around. Aldo hold Catherine's drink and mine until we return." Stated Mr. Russo.

Aldo nodded in recognition of Mr. Russo's request.

"Thank you so much, I would love too. Do you want to come Johnathon?" asked Catherine.

"No, I have been looking at a yacht for you. I already have a feel for what you want and will see on this ship. Go ahead and let me know what you like. We will look at a yacht together later this year."

Catherine smiled. "Well, Giovanni lead the way. I guess it's just you and me."

"I will be back momentarily my darling. You mine keeping Johnathon company until we return?" Stated Mr. Russo.

"Of course not, darling." Nicolette smiled.

Aldo handed Johnathon and Nicolette their drinks and returned to the bar. Once Giovanni and Catherine left, Johnathon immediately jumped at his opportunity. He got up from the sofa, glanced at Nicolette to join him at the dining room table, far away, so the bartender couldn't hear their conversation.

Johnathon reached for a piece of cheese and some grapes. He put them on a little dish. He turned to see where the bartender was. He was still behind the counter.

Johnathon moved closer to Nicolette near the buffet table. "You hung up on me so quickly on the phone, I didn't give you my number."

"If I recall, I told you I didn't want it." Nicolette tasted her wine and moved to the outside deck.

Johnathon followed her and took his wine, but left the little plate of food on the table. "We could be close acquaintances. You never know when you might need a friendly ear to listen."

Annoyed at his presence in being there, "Mr. Fitzpatrick... I..."

Johnathon interjected. "Back to being formal I see. Your husband insisted on first names."

Nicolette was slightly upset. "Why did you come here? What is it that you want from me? You have a wife, I have a husband. There is no place for this to go."

"I just want to be friends." He took a sip of his wine. "Just in case you need a warm body as a reminder of what you lost." Johnathon waited for a happy facial expression, but noticed only a stare of discontent.

"That's not amusing Mr. Fitzpatrick. I'm beginning to see that I made a mistake to have ever met with you."

"Nicolette, I assure you my intentions here are nothing but honorable. I called your husband to see how my work ranked in his eyes and he invited me to dine with him and his lovely wife. So here I am. Is that so bad?"

Nicolette drank more wine. "As long as there is nothing more, Mr. Fitzpatrick."

Nicolette moved back to the lower deck and took a seat. Johnathon remained on deck to take in the view. When Catherine and Giovanni returned, they noticed Johnathon on deck alone. Catherine took a seat on the sofa beside Nicolette.

Giovanni walked out on deck sipping a vodka to speak with Johnathon. "How do you like the ocean view, Johnathon?"

"It's breathtaking, Sir."

"Come Mr. Fitzpatrick, let us talk about your future with my business." They sat on a couple of dining chairs on that deck level.

Johnathon smiled. "You said Mr. Fitzpatrick. Does that mean you are fascinated with my work and more business is in my future?"

"Indeed young man. I love the sensors you placed around the grounds. They detect the slightest of movement and the weight of the object brings up a holographic imagine of the entity, size and build. My security team is very impressed. I have another building being built that I would like your expertise to handle."

"Absolutely Giovanni and if you have friends that are in need of my services as well, I would greatly appreciate your referrals."

"Of course, but first, I have a proposal for you Mr. Fitzpatrick and this is business. Your work is excellent, as a matter of fact, beyond excellent. It's brilliant. Its stuff people have never thought of before. Let me be blunt. I would like to own your company." Johnathon was shocked. His expression of surprise, exploded from his face. He drank more of his wine. "A comparable figure of which we both agree upon, of course."

Johnathon was still dazed by the offer. He was only looking for referrals, not even that, he just wanted to see Nicolette again. This offer was totally out of the blue.

Johnathon was tongue tied, angry, and emotionally disillusioned, but he maintained his composure. "Really?" He took another sip of wine. So he toyed with the ideal. "How much would this offer be?"

"Ooooh, let's say... half a billion dollars plus you remain CEO of the company with extraordinary benefits."

Johnathon paused. He felt insulted. "You think because my company is in its infancy I would let it go for such a ridiculous price?"

"You don't have to give me an answer now Mr. Fitzpatrick. Talk to your wife, business partner, whomever and get back to me."

Johnathon was clearly insulted by the offer. "Now since I'm Mr. Fitzpatrick, the business man. Well, I'm getting back to you right now. The answer is no. You don't have enough money to buy my labor, efforts, and ideals."

Giovanni smirked. "You don't know me Mr. Fitzpatrick, if I want something, I get it. No matter what the cost."

"You don't know me Mr. Russo. The answer is no." Johnathon was infuriated. His emotional expression was displayed directly into Russo's eyes.

Giovanni grinned and took a sip of his vodka. "This is your vacation with your lovely wife, Johnathon."

"Mr. Fitzpatrick to you."

"Let's not spend any more time talking business right now. Let's join the ladies and toast to our new business endeavors together."

"There will be none Mr. Russo, ever." Johnathon's appearance remained that of aghast and appalled.

"Come." Giovanni led the way to the ladies.

As the men came down to the lower deck... Catherine was trying to get more acquainted with Nicolette seated on the sofa.

"Mrs. Russo." Catherine caught herself and wasn't informal. "I'm sorry Nicolette. This boat is so beautiful and so is your home."

"Thank you... ahhh..."

Catherine interrupted, as Nicolette struggled to recall her name. "Catherine."

"Yes, Catherine, well thank you. It all belongs to my husband. He had it all before I met him. Now if you will excuse me." She rose from the sofa and headed toward the bar. "Aldo! I need a refill."

Catherine had a puzzled expression on her face as to the harshness of her tone. The men made their way below deck.

Mr. Russo saw his wife at the bar. "Oh honey while you are there, bring me a fresh vodka on the rocks. Aldo freshen every ones drink." Aldo moved from person to person and back to the bar. "Thank you Aldo." Giovanni lifted his glass. "We have a toast to make." Johnathon stared at Giovanni. "Johnathon is going to do the security on our new buildings and I have other friends that would be very interested in the work he does. We should be in business for quite a long time. A toast to our new friends." All followed Giovanni in raising their glasses, except for Johnathon. He didn't drink. He just glared at him.

Giovanni smiled and drank from his glass. Nicolette mustarded a smile and sipped her wine. Johnathon's face reamed of animosity. Catherine was grinning from ear to ear as she drank her wine. Soon she noticed that

Johnathon's appearance was that of despair. He didn't even drink. She wondered with such a grand business offer, how could he be so displeased.

"Let's eat!" stated Mr. Russo.

CHAPTER 12

Return Home

Johnathon awoke this Monday morning around seven in his California home. He noticed Catherine was not in bed beside him. When he reached for his phone, he noticed a text from an acquaintance. He soon made his way to the kitchen in his robe. Catherine was already downstairs seated at the kitchen table having breakfast in her pajamas.

Johnathon stood at the bottom of the steps. "Why are you up so early Catherine? You normally sleep until nine."

"Yes. Well, I asked Rosa to come over early today to fix breakfast. September and I are headed to the gun range. She has surprise events planned for this morning and later in the day. So don't wait up for me if by some chance you come home before one in the morning and I'm not here."

"Gun range? How did she know we were back?" quizzed Johnathon.

"I called her from Italy."

"How do you know I didn't have a plan to spend today with you, just the two of us?"

Catherine was feed up with the deceit. "Who are we kidding Johnathon? You had planned four days alone with me in Rome, instead, we barely spent two hours alone together the two days we were there. You didn't spend one day alone with me in any type of romantic setting. Why? I don't know. I guess business is calling your name no matter where we are." She took a drink of orange juice and got up from the kitchen table. She walked up to Johnathon with a blank stare on her face. "When you want the two of us to be together, I am quite sure I will know it." Catherine left him standing there.

Johnathon just gawked at her and sat down at the table. "Rosa just give me a juice and a piece of toast. I will be heading into to the office soon."

Before Catherine was almost up the stairs, she yelled back at Johnathon. "Let me know if you want to have the Executive Party this Friday or not."

Johnathon shouted back. "We'll have it!"

Catherine made a few steps back toward the kitchen at the bottom of the steps. She replied…"I'm inviting September just so you know. Just call or text me if you want to get together today for lunch." She spoke sarcastically.

"Even if you are with September today, you sure you could break away?"

"She's my friend, you're my husband." Catherine went upstairs to get dressed.

Johnathon just watched nonchalantly, not really caring about what she did.

September parked in front of the house. Mrs. Jensen pulled back the curtain to observe who was leaving first. Catherine came out and hopped in the car. September cranked the car. It rattled and shook a little bit. The engine eventually started. September jammed her foot on the gas. Catherine noticed the action and the car barely got up to ten miles an hour. Catherine waved at Mrs. Jensen as the car slowly pulled away from the house.

"I'm glad you got here early enough to where we can make it to the gun range in this thing. I would hate to miss our time."

September was slightly insulted. "Don't talk about Old Betsy like that. She doesn't like it. Just give her a minute. You know she'll pick up speed in a few seconds."

"Yeah, in three-hundred seconds it will get up to ten miles an hour. You know this ja-loppy is going to die on you one day. You need a new car."

"Old Betsy won't die. She's like the Eveready Battery. She gets old and keeps on running, maybe not fast, but running."

Catherine laughed and didn't pursue the issue. "What do you have in store for the day my friend?"

"We're hitting the gun range, racket ball court and going para sailing."

Catherine was excited. "Great! Well I don't know how to play racket ball. I have always wanted to go para sailing though."

"I made the boat trip for two this afternoon. That way we can change into our water outfits after the gun range and racket ball."

"I am so glad I met you September." Catherine beamed with joy. "I appreciate your company so very much. You make every day an adventure. My trip with Johnathon to Italy was a total fiasco."

"That doesn't surprise me." September kept her eyes on the road.

"We spent a beautiful afternoon on this yacht belonging to a billionaire."

"Oh a yacht? You have to take me on yours one day."

"We don't have one."

"Then how is Johnathon in the Yacht Club?"

"He shares his father's yacht, the 'Gold King' to be a member."

"You have to take me on it one day. I've never been on a yacht."

"Not me. His parents can't stand me. After they found out I didn't come from money, I was common trash in their eyes. I can't get on that yacht without Johnathon being with me."

"Well I know that's out then. I'm sorry Catherine. It makes life easier when in-laws consider you family."

"Yeah… well. Enough about the trip and in-laws." Catherine observed the scenery.

"Oh, I forgot to mention one more thing." Stated September.

"What's that?"

"You're buying me breakfast. I haven't eaten yet."

"It's eight o'clock and you haven't eaten? You don't fix breakfast for yourself anymore?" asked Catherine.

"Not since I meet you. You know some of the greatest Mom and Pop restaurants. Why do you think I wanted to pick you up so early? The gun range isn't until ten-thirty. I can't wait to see where you take me next."

Catherine grinned. "Drive to Old Fashion Grits, it's off sixty third and Lexington. They make a great breakfast and you can have whatever you like. I ate already."

"Great! You can watch me eat, because I hate shootin on an empty stomach. Just tell me where to turn."

Catherine was just thrilled to do anything but shopping. They drove off a little faster than what they began as September's car finally picked up speed. After breakfast, the gun range, racket ball and para sailing, Catherine had been thinking about how good she had gotten at firing September's weapons.

"September before you take me home, I want to stop at Sure Shot Gun Store."

"What for?"

"I've been using yours and I feel that I'm good enough now to have my own. I got a private locker today while you were putting your guns away."

"Well I have to admit, you have gotten really good. We'll have to start entering some local competition just to see how good we are."

"Sounds good to me. Let's hit that gun store." Insisted Catherine.

Without hesitation, September made her way to Sure Shot Gun Store. Once there...

"Hey Catherine this looks like you since you've gotten to be such an expert shot with my .45 Caliber. You know your husband may not take kindly to you buying weapons of mass destruction without his knowledge."

"He never pays any attention to what I do anyway. Why should he care?" Catherine walked over by September to checkout a gun that caught her eye. "Hmmm... Pink?"

"Why not? It matches your personality." Proclaimed September.

"But now I'm a skilled professional at firing weapons. I want something... bad-ass, like you would say."

"Did I hear a curse word?" Sarcastically questioned September.

"Don't even..."

September grinned. "I think I'm rubbing off on you a little bit. You know you can continue to use my weapons if you like?"

"No. I want my own. I purchased my own locker at the range and I want my own guns."

September glanced around the store cases once again and pointed. "Then how about that one... over there?"

"Where?" Catherine looked and saw where September pointed. They went over to admire a Sig Sauer 1911 Compact C3 .45 in the showcase.

September pointed to the one beside it. "Or... how about that one, the Beretta PX4 Storm?"

"Hmmm... no. I want something kind of sexy. Like that one with the colored handle."

"The Dan Wesson Valor Commander… do you know how expensive that is?" September gently slapped herself in the face with the palm of her hand. "What am I thinking? Let's get two."

Catherine smiled. "Sir, we'll take this one, the Glock G21, and the Titanium Gold Desert Eagle in .440 Cor-Bon in that case over there. If you have two of those, I will take two."

September was in awe of her weapon choice. "You know that Titanium Gold has a powerful recoil. It may knock your skinny butt back against the wall."

"I can handle it. Besides, on Friday's when Johnathon stands me up on our day together, I'll go to the range when I'm not with you and take out my frustrations."

September thought, Catherine's attitude had change. "What happened to that skinny, someday wanna be a mom person I met a few weeks ago?"

"She hasn't gone anywhere. She just got tough." Catherine directed her attention to the clerk. "Oh Sir, let me have that S&W 1911 E-Series as well. Can you make it special for me and put pearl handles where that black siding is with my initials on the bottom?"

"We can do anything you like Mrs. Fitzpatrick." Stated the clerk.

"Three guns in the house? You are begging for a domestic dispute."

"I won't take them home just yet. I'll keep them in my locker. When I start winning trophies, I'll bring them home."

The clerk interrupted. "You know ma'am with the purchase of four, you get a special case for them."

"Okay. Make these two with pearl handles and I'll take the Beretta PX4 Storm as well. Put my initials on all the weapons. Wrap them up with plenty of ammo and I will take the free case."

September gasped silently with her mouth open at Catherine. In a quiet tone underneath her breath… she stated. "What have I done?"

CHAPTER 13

Johnathon with Old Flames

As September and Catherine fulfilled their day with fun and gun purchases, Johnathon only stayed at work a couple of hours this morning. He needed to forget about the weekend with Giovanni. To Johnathon's delight he had received a text earlier in the morning. He left work around 10:00 a.m. to meet a client or so he explained to Mark. He immediately headed to his condominium. Johnathon met with Savvy on the second floor. She was a beautiful woman. A blonde, that stood five-foot, ten inches tall with a model's figure. She was already in a suite on the second floor indulging herself in a bottle of wine, awaiting his presence.

"Savvy my love. I was very pleased to have gotten your text at 4:00 a.m. this morning. I was beginning to wonder if I would ever see you again. You said two months on a modeling shoot, not four."

"You know how things go if the producer and photographer don't agree on the photo, it's a do-over." Savvy stretched her arms out. "I have missed you so Johnathon."

Johnathon walked over and gave her a huge hug and kissed her softly upon her lips. "I have missed you my sweet."

"Why don't you leave your wife and marry me. I can take care of the both of us."

Johnathon laughed. "You know that will never happen. When you're in town, if I got the time. We meet. That's it."

"I know your policy. Take the time given, or leave the key on the bed and don't look back."

"That's right my sweet. So are you leaving the room key or are you staying?" asked Johnathon.

"I will have to leave the key with Becky. I find myself calculating how to get back to you when I am away. I have never done that with any man before. I think I love you and I know how you feel about that."

"It's not happening Savvy. If you don't want to do this anymore..."

Savvy interrupted... "This will be my last time my sweet. So let's not waste it with conversation. I want to make love to you, now."

"I am all yours my love."

Savvy reached for his pant buckle and removed it quickly. Johnathon watched as her hands move methodically all over his clothing, removing each item with precision. She laid each item of apparel neatly hanging over the back of a chair.

"It's ok my love, you can just throw them anywhere." Stated Johnathon.

She ignored his comments. When done, Savvy reached for a warm glass of wine on the coffee table that she had poured herself earlier before he got there. While Johnathon stood in the center of the floor totally naked, she took the glass of wine and placed his lower extremity in it. As she dipped his external rod into the wine glass, she swirled the wine around it. She placed the wine glass back on the coffee table. Before a drop of wine could hit the carpet floor from his harden flesh, Savvy had already placed her lips around his swollen erectile tissue. She sucked gently. Johnathon moaned quietly.

As Savvy paused and stood before him..."What next my love. I am your slave."

Johnathon smiled... he reached for the bottle of wine from the coffee table. "Come with me my sweet, the bedroom is prepared as always for a sexual appetite you will never forget. You will scream for me to stop."

Savvy had a delighted facial expression. "No. I will scream for you to continue. I love your surprises."

"Since this will be our last time together, follow me and prepare to be blown away."

When they reached the bedroom, Johnathon gulped wine from the bottle and placed it on the night stand. Savvy laid in the bed as she observed his actions. He reached for a bottle of passion fruit body oil on the end table. He poured a small portion in his hand. He placed the bottle back on the end table. He gently caressed her breast and began to rub softly in a circular motion around her nipples until they harden. He slowly left her breasts and embraced her entire naked body, rubbing the lotion in all direction. Savvy moaned with delight. He rolled her body over and squirted lotion all over her back. Laying the bottle down, he took his left hand and rubbed the oil from her neck to her toes. He soon took his right hand and rubbed her enter thighs, one after the other until he entered the vaginal area, slowly moving in and out. He continued to massage the oil over every inch of her, slowly, repeatedly, with his other hand. As the gentle touches of his hands aroused her body explosively from head to toe, Savvy turned over and looked into his loving eyes. She reached for his neck and drew him near. She kissed him passionately upon the lips. Savvy soon pulled him down up her, sharing the oil from her body onto his. Johnathon removed his hand from her sensitive area and let his harden rod invade her warm, creamy interior. He pounded gently into her over and over again until screams of sexual pleasure erupted from both their lips.

Relaxed in bed from his sexual endeavor, Johnathon realized the hour. It was noon. Johnathon placed a call into Angela. Angela let Mark know Johnathon wouldn't be at work for the next two days and to tell his wife he had to fly out of state for an unexpected business meeting. Mark nor Catherine were none the wiser that the client was indeed a lover.

He and Savvy took his private jet to Hawaii. They enjoyed a beautiful dinner on the beach. He took her swimming, shopping and they indulged in more heated passionate sexual activity that evening and the next day in their room as the sun set and rose again. Knowing he needed to be at work the next day, they left for California early the next morning. Savvy was dropped off at her hotel around 8 a.m. She blew Johnathon a kiss and disappeared beyond the hotel doors.

As he left Savvy, Johnathon briefly stuck his head in at work. He touched basis with Mark and called his wife. Hours later, he left work and went to his condominium. There on the third floor he met Kayla, his regular on Monday's. Kayla was a gorgeous twenty-one year old brunette, studying cybersecurity in college.

"I missed you Johnathon."

"I missed you Kayla. I am glad you came by my office for a tour on what we do on cybersecurity as a college project."

Kayla spoke with a sexy voice. "It was the best idea I ever had. Come my love."

Kayla had made ready a bathtub with four candles, one on each corner of the tub. Johnathon followed leisurely. A bottle of Cheval Blanc 1947 Saint-Emillion on ice in a little bucket with two wine glasses already prepared by the tub. When Johnathon entered the bedroom she was already naked. He undressed quickly. With his clothes falling to the floor, she quickly moved to the bathroom. Johnathon trailed her as if hypnotized by the way her body moved. With the lights dimmed and the ambiance of the candles glowing, he saw her standing there. She entered the tub filled with bubbles and warm water holding two glasses of wine. Kayla stood in the middle of the bathtub as Johnathon sat on the back of the tub. She handed him a glass of wine. He sipped, she gulped hers in one swallow. They gazed into each other's eyes. She placed her glass on the floor and made her way to Johnathon. Before she reached his lips, she knelt down on her knees and dipped her head to his waist. She took one hand and gently pulled his harden extremity to her mouth and massaged it gently with both hands as her lips tenderly applied suction around it. Johnathon placed his glass on the corner of the tub and eased down into the tub. While his body was submerged underneath the water and bubbles, he relaxed his entire body as Kayla continued to manipulate her tongue to stimulate every inch of his physique. As gentle moans expel from his lips, Kayla maintained masterful maneuvers from his cheeks to his chest, occasionally dipping her head beneath the water.

Moments later, Johnathon reached for the soap. He pulled her up from his waist and returned the exquisite movement of rubbing the soap gently across her breast. When Johnathon rinsed the soap away, he wrapped his lips around her nipples until they rose and harden, one breast and then the other, seconds apart with his tongue circling each one as he sucked gently to keep them firm. Kayla now laid-back her body as his fingers found the lower part of her waist and he began to thrust his middle finger inside her warm flesh. As their bodies heated up the water, Johnathon climbed out of the tub. He reached for Kayla. He swept her up from the tub into his arms and carried her to the bedroom. Soaking wet, he threw her on the bed and climbed on top of her. Their bodies slid across each other like melted butter on a piece of toast. They wildly moved their hands and lips across each other's body. So sexually aroused was Kayla, that she reached for his harden rod that she missed so much and placed it inside her. With each forceful thrust of his body into hers, she kissed and wrapped her arms tightly around his back, pulling him toward her, as if to say harder, harder, harder until the scream of rapture finally expelled from her lips.

CHAPTER 14

The Executive Party

This Friday evening Catherine had out done herself with this Executive Party. The caterers had aligned a smorgasbord of delight. The dining room table was filled with lobsters, crabs, caviar, Iberico ham, string beans, Zuni stew, eggplant surprise, veggie pot pie, Polenta Dolcetta, mashed potatoes, top off with bottles of Silver Oak Cabernet Napa, a red wine. Food was flowing from the dining area to the pool area. Waiters hustled and rushed to keep wine glasses full and appetizers served. As the party got started, Catherine greeted all guests with a smile as they entered the living room. Everyone was dressed professionally with suits and elegant gowns. Johnathon was entertaining all the business men that had arrived around the pool area. Everyone was mingling with someone.

Catherine spotted Mark in the corner of the living room speaking to another guest. She elegantly walked over to where he was standing. Mark and Ted turned toward her.

Catherine greeted them. "I hope you two are enjoying your evening. Why in the corner of the living room when everyone is at the pool or the dining area?"

"A charming setting as always Catherine. I was just going over a little business with Mark."

"Thank you Ted. Enough business for now. Enjoy yourself. Eat. Drink."

Ted smiled. "I think I will. If you two will excuse me, I have to freshen my wine glass." He walked away.

"Yeah, talk again later Ted." yelled Mark.

"Glad to see you Mark."

"You as well Catherine. A glass of wine in hand. No fruity drink?"

Catherine looked at her glass. "Just the way he likes it."

"How was your trip to Italy?"

"I thought our plan had worked. Thinking Johnathon had taken your advice and this was an invite for a couple's vacation. Instead we ended up at a client's house for a day."

"Mr. Russo?" questioned Mark.

"Yes, how did you know?"

"He's the only client we have in Italy right now. Are you saying things didn't go well?"

"Not for being a lover's vacation. The day we got there he called this client of yours. We went to Mr. Russo's yacht for lunch. While there, Johnathon got offered another building to work on once construction was complete. I thought he would be ecstatic that he had another deal. By the time the evening came, Johnathon was so angry. He didn't want to spend another day in Italy. He left the yacht in such a huff."

Mark was extremely curious. "Did he say why?"

"No. We came back to the hotel, packed our bags and left the next morning. I had to talk him out of taking our private jet home that night."

"Wow. Sounds like something really went wrong. You've been back a few days now. He never mentioned any issues with Mr. Russo to me. Where is he now?"

"You know him. Talking business with someone I'm sure. I still need you to work on him. I want to be his wife... not his companion."

"These things take time Catherine. I just can't tell him to go home and I will handle things. He knows I am capable of doing his job if need be. However, he has to make sure his fingers are in every pie. Especially now with this issue you've mentioned." Mark paused in thought wondering what the issue could have been... "Just give me some more time. You'll know when he's starting to trust me more with the business and start spending more time with you."

"I'm sorry Mark. I don't mean to pressure you. I just love him so. Sometimes I feel like he just married me for my looks."

A blank expression came over his face and he bowed his head. Mark sipped his drink, looked at Catherine and mustarded a smile. "You know he loves you. Oh by the way, where is this friend of yours I've heard so much about? Johnathon tells me you two do a lot of physical activities together. Is this woman a fitness trainer?'

"Far from it." Catherine spoke with zeal and excitement. "Mark she is so much fun. Never a dull moment. She has Airborne Wings and she's an *ex-Army Ranger.*"

"Wow! Well I must meet her."

"She taught me how to shot a .45 Caliber pistol. I'm really good at it. Come look at the ones I have purchased. I have hidden them from Johnathon for now, but I will tell him about them soon."

Catherine took Mark to a specific section of the living room. She glanced around to see if anyone was observing her activity. It appeared all guests were elsewhere. Catherine opened the cabinet, pulled the weapon case out and placed it on top of the dresser. She pulled a tiny key from underneath the gun case, unlocked the box and pulled one .45 out. She handed it to Mark.

"Wow!" Mark gripped the weapon by the handle. He brandished it a little bit to get a slight feel for the gun. "This is a beautiful piece of hardware and the case too." He gave it back to Catherine. "Those are beautiful guns and you know how to use them?"

"Does a cat meow?" Catherine placed the gun back in the case, locked it, and placed them back in the cabinet.

"Oh really." Mark smiled. "You're that good."

"We are going to start entering competitions together."

"You and this woman?"

"Yes. September."

"Well where is this extraordinary lady?"

Catherine glanced at her watch. The hour was getting late. "September should have been here by now. I asked her to arrive at least ten minutes late."

Mark was a little confused. "Why late?"

"So everyone is already mingling and she could observe who to attack."

"Attack?" Mark was slightly stunned by the word.

Coyly Catherine explained. "You know what I mean. Not like that. She's a single woman looking for companionship."

"Ohhh, I see. Well on that note, where did you say your husband was?"

Catherine walked toward the dining area and glanced toward the pool area. "I don't see him. So he's probably in his study talking shop."

"Well if you will pardon me, I will try to find him." Mark left to find Johnathon.

Meanwhile, Johnathon had been in his study for half-hour already. He was entertaining an unknown guess that ask to speak with him in private. The gentleman stood five-feet, ten inches tall, muscular build, dark hair, clean shaved, back straight, in a black suit and tie. He held his glass of wine in one hand. Johnathon placed his wine glass on his desk and sat before him.

"Please sit, Mr. Tate." Tate sat down. "Who do you work for again?" asked Johnathon. "Which one of my guest gave you an invite to this private party?"

"I didn't say and I don't know. So I can't tell you."

Johnathon sipped his wine. "How is it possible that an uninvited guest is in my house, drinking my wine, enjoying my food, and you don't know the person that wants this high profile project done?"

"Maybe it was one of your guest. I don't know." Responded Tate.

"Which one?" questioned Johnathon.

"I don't know."

"What do you know, Mr. Tate?"

"I want the project we discussed done in six months."

"How do *you* play in this picture Mr. Tate?"

"You won't believe this, but I assure you its quite true. I have been down on my luck for the past year. I was eating out of garbage cans, sleeping in abandon buildings, and drinking booze from other homeless people that was willing to share. Then one day, I was sitting on a street corner in raggedy clothing and I had my hand stretched out, head bowed, hoping someone would give me a dollar or two to get a burger. This day, a beautiful black woman, casually dressed, walked up to me, placed a twenty dollar bill in my hand. I looked up and thanked her. With that much money I went to buy myself a full blown meal. I was just eating at this restaurant, alone. I was sitting such that I could see out the window on to the street. About ten minutes into my meal, this seventeen year old boy or so his age appeared, walked in and sat in the chair across from me. He placed on the table a small black briefcase. He didn't say a word and then he walked out. I stared him down as he stepped away to see where he came from. By the time he hit the door, I looked out the window and he was gone."

Johnathon entertained his story. "What was in the case?"

"To my total surprise, there was a note. It said, 'This two-hundred thousand dollars is for you to ask someone to do a task for me. You tell them what I want and when I want it. I stay in touch with the client until the project is done. Once I am informed by the client that the project is ready, I call a number and say the word 'complete.' The payout is wired to the provider, I deliver the product and the two-hundred thousand is mine to keep."

"Interesting and this someone is me to do the task? Then what?" Johnathon didn't believe a word he was saying.

"Then I wait until I am contacted again for another project."

"So who are you? Some type of lawyer, Army guy, mercenary or something?" quizzed Johnathon.

"Believe it or not Mr. Fitzpatrick, I'm nobody of importance. I'm just a messenger. I was also instructed to say nothing about myself."

"So you just take two-hundred thousand dollars from a total stranger, no questions asked."

Tate drank some more of his wine. "This is good stuff."

"I drink only the best. So who are you?"

"If you knew what I used to do for a living Mr. Fitzpatrick, you wouldn't ask me that question. As I was saying, I sat there for a few minutes and pondered who would do such a thing. I knew if I took the money and didn't follow the note, I would probably be dead in a matter of hours. Then I thought, if all I am is a messenger and I'm not doing anything illegal, then, what the hell. I'm just delivering a message."

"You're right. I don't believe a word you just said. However, how soon did you say you wanted this project done?" Stated Johnathon.

"Six months is his approximation for development."

"I would have to speak to someone with the knowledge to create the device you ask for to know if it could be done in that timeframe."

"A quarter of a billion will be placed in an off shore account in your name as soon as you say yes. The other quarter-million upon delivery of the product and its functional capability is confirmed. Can you guarantee Mr. Fitzpatrick that we will have what we need in the allotted time?"

"Like I said Mr. Tate, I can't guarantee anything. I have to speak to my expert technical consultants and let you know."

"The money will still be placed in an off-shore account for you within a week's time."

"If you have this capability of paying that much money at once, I don't want the money in my name."

"Of course Mr. Fitzpatrick. Does this mean you are accepting the offer?"

Johnathon leaned back in his chair. He paused for a few seconds in thought. He stood, took a pen and paper and wrote down an account number and a name. He handed it to Tate. "No guarantees Mr. Tate. However, place the money in that account under that name when you receive a 'yes' from me. It will not be me doing the work, but one or several of my associates."

"How long do we need to wait before we hear from you with an answer?" asked Tate.

"Give me a couple of months to work on these people and bring them on board. I need to be able to trust the people I pick to be silent about the project."

"I would think so, Mr. Fitzpatrick. However, my employer is eager to get this done as soon as possible. Two month is a long time to wait for an answer."

"Give me the time I asked to talk to some people that I can trust and I will let you know. That should give you plenty of time to take care of things on your end. Don't put the money in my account until you receive a 'yes' from me. Please."

"Will your partners be hard to negotiate with?" Tate asked. "We can persuade people, if need be."

"You let me take care of my end. How can I contact you to let you know if we are onboard?"

Tate stood. "You don't. I will convey your answer to my employer. Since you are my first client, I don't know how well your response will be received. I'm sure I will contact you very soon." Tate raised his wine glass. Johnathon did the same. "To saying 'yes', Mr. Fitzpatrick."

"Hopefully a yes, Mr. Tate." They both took a sip of their drinks. "You go out first and I will follow." They both put their glasses on his desk.

"Very well." Tate walked out the door.

Mark passed Tate coming down the foyer from Johnathon's study. He watched Tate go to the dining room. Mark proceeded down the hallway.

Johnathon smiled, still in his study. He softly spoke to himself. "Sell my company. Ha! Russo. I will be a billionaire soon." He waited a few more seconds to finish his wine. When he stepped out the door, Mark was standing there.

"Hey J… everything alright? Catherine was concerned."

"Walk with me to grab a drink." As soon as they reached the dining room, Johnathon's eyes were roaming the crowd for Tate and new faces.

Mark followed. "Catherine said you left Italy in a huff. Did something go down with Mr. Russo?"

Johnathon's focus turned to Mark. "Is there anything that woman doesn't tell you?" He grabbed a wine glass as a waiter passed by. He gulped all the wine in one single swallow as he observed his dining room guests looking for new prospects. Johnathon was in thought of the conversation he just had in his study. He spoke aloud not really speaking to Mark. "Perhaps this person that Tate spoke of might be in the mix of people in my house." He continued his roaming eyes around the room as Mark watched him.

"What?" probed Mark. Surprised to see Johnathon down a glass of wine in one gulp when he taught his executives and his wife professional etiquette. Mark thought, 'What was that conversation about?'

"Nothing. Keep socializing." Johnathon started to walk away. He placed his empty glass on a tray and grabbed another.

"Wait J." Johnathon paused and gave Mark his attention. "Catherine just loves you so much that anything that concerns your business, she thinks I can help make it better."

Johnathon started to observe his guests once again, not speaking directly to Mark. "Keep that thought. Perhaps you can Mark. Let's mingle right now and find out who our new guess are. Let's see if we can extract some new business deals for the future." Johnathon moved through the crowd while observing new faces. He tried to find Tate to see whom he might be consorting with, but it appeared he had already left the room and perhaps the party.

Mark watched Johnathon circulate among his guest as if he were searching for his long lost brother. He was perplexed to his peculiar behavior.

CHAPTER 15

September is Blind Sided

While Catherine was mingling among the guest, she wondered where September could be. September had an uninvited guest that appeared at her front door step. Just as September was prepared to walk out the door, her doorbell rang. She pondered, who could this be at this late hour of the evening.

September opened the door and to her surprise… "Antonio!" A tall, light brown skinned masculine man stood before her eyes. He had black slick hair, clean shaved, black slacks, and a black cotton shirt on with the top button unfastened.

He smiled with flowers in his hand. "Hello September." Antonio spoke in a slightly deep voice.

"What are you doing here? We were never to see each other again."

"I know my love." Antonio stretched the flowers to September. She took them and threw them on her front lawn. Antonio watched her actions. He turned and begged the question. "May I come in please?"

September stepped back and allowed him to enter into the living room. She closed the door.

Antonio noticed her attire. "You look stunningly gorgeous. The slit in that black dress just brings back memories of how I use to love rubbing on those lovely thighs of yours."

September spoke in a harsh tone. "What do you want?" But she still loved the way he displayed his open chest. "I have somewhere to be right now."

"I came by to tell you I'm sorry for all the pain I caused you ten years ago."

"So when did you get out of prison? The judge sentenced you to twenty years for treason."

Antonio stepped closer to her. "Good behavior got me out in ten."

"So why did you look me up? You want to steal some more military secrets from my laptop. Well news flash. I have since retired and I am enjoying life without you."

"Baby I just came by to let you know that you are the only one that got me out of prison alive. All I thought about was the beautiful memories of our lives together."

September moved closer to his face and aggressively spoke. "I am the one that put you behind bars, you sorry bastard. I loved you! And every time we met and you laid in my bed while I slept, only to ensure my slumber while you stole top secret information from my computer for another country. You know how hard that was for me to swallow. I took an oath to this country to defend it. I was not just in the Army, but part of an elite team to protect and defend our country." She yelled. "I am an Airborne Ranger! I am dedicated to serving my country with my heart and soul. You stabbed me in the back and for what? A few dollars."

"Those few dollars were going to secure our future." September sighed and stepped away from him. "Baby I came here to say I'm sorry. I still love you. If I could turn back the hands of time, I would."

September grew angry just thinking about what could have been. "Save the untruth for your next trial. Knowing you, if money means that much to you to betray your country, it won't be long before you're back behind bars."

"Do you really mean you're not happy to see me?" Antonio moved closer to her and softly touched her right cheek with his hand.

Momentarily, she remembered her love for him. September peered at his open chest and gazed into his eyes, lovingly. She quickly realized she was letting her guard down. Her poker face immediately reappeared and she slapped his hand away. "You need to leave Antonio. What was is in the past, can't be relived. I don't need any of your foolish behavior back in my life. I got somewhere to be right now." She searched the room for her car keys.

Antonio spoke sympathetically. "September you were the first person I came to see when I got out."

September got in his face and pointed her forefinger toward the door. "Get out!"

He reached in his pocket and withdrew a picture of the two of them snorkeling in the Bahamas. Before he could show it to her, she pulled a hunting knife strapped to her thigh and shoved her forearm into his neck. She penned him against the wall with the knife to his throat.

He was putty in her hands with both his arms dangly down his side. Antonio spoke softly as if her actions were 'ok' with him. "Still the same old September. Always on the defensive. I didn't come here to hurt you. I came to love you… if you let me."

He slowly raised one hand that held the picture of the two of them together in the Bahamas. September saw the smiles on their faces, the sun shining in a distance, the beautiful blue water and sandy beach in the background. She slightly tilted her head to the side staring at the picture in his hand. She was in awe that he had held on to it all these years.

September still had the knife to his throat. "Why? Why are you showing me this?"

"I've been in a lonely hotel room for the past two weeks gazing at this picture. Wondering… if you would take me back. Finally I got up enough nerve to come over in person, hoping you hadn't found someone else. I wanted to see if you still loved me as much as I love you."

September tried to remain uncompromising. She stared into his eyes and push her forearm into his neck a little harder. "Well you got it wrong." She raised the knife a little closer to his neck as well. "I don't."

"Well I do… still love you." Antonio pushed the picture slightly closer to her eyes. She glanced at the picture and then once more into his eyes. Her once buried emotions rose again after peering at the picture. She realized the love and desire she once had for this man was resurfacing. She pulled the knife from his neck and released her forearm from penning him against the wall. He stood before her, holding the picture in his hand. September was motionless looking at it.

September glanced toward this lover she once knew, almost teary eyed. She softly spoke. "I've got some where to be. You need to leave." September brushed past him and opened the door with the knife still in her hand. Antonio walked toward the door and gradually closed it. She stared at him. He placed the picture back in his pocket.

Antonio slowly reached for her left hand and held it gently in his. "I don't see a ring on this finger." She jerked her hand away. "I don't see any other car parked outside with someone waiting to take you somewhere." She bowed her head. He lifted her head with one hand. "I don't see hatred in these beautiful brown eyes." Tears were forming as he spoke. "I believe you were waiting to see if I was coming home to you once again." They gazed into each other's eyes adoringly.

"Tony... I..." September quietly spoke.

Antonio interrupted her. He placed her hand to his cheek. "If you want me to leave September, you don't have to pull a knife or a gun. Just tell me to leave." She stroked the side of his face gently. "It's just that easy. Say leave, and I will walk out of your life, right now... forever." Tears began to flow heavily. He reached with both hands and used his thumbs to wipe her tears away.

September melted into his eyes lovingly. "I do still love you. But we can't, we just...."

Before she finished the sentence, Antonio leaned forward and touched her lips gently and quickly pulled back. He waited for resistance by her words or her knife to his gut. He gazed into her eyes and found only love. He leaned forward to kiss her again and was met with passion upon his lips. Her hand went from his cheek to loving arms around his neck as the knife fell from her hand to the floor.

As September's evening was heating up physically, Catherine was concerned about her. So terribly concerned that September didn't make the Executive Party that she tried to call after everyone had left late that evening. Unable to reach her that night, Catherine called her the next morning around eight o'clock.

September reached for her cell phone on the end table by the bed. "Hello." She whispered as she climbed out from under the covers and made her way into the living room.

"What happened to you last night? I was worried after you didn't show. I was hoping to get you acquainted with some of my friends and Johnathon."

She uttered softly, "I ran into an old flame. It was totally unexpected." September peeked her head around the corner to see if Antonio was still sleeping. "He looks like a baby when he sleeps."

"Ohm, I know that tone. Well I guess you and I won't be seeing each other anymore."

"No, on the contrary. Nothing has changed. He caught me at a weak moment. It ends today. I will come over later today."

"You mean we are still on for today?" asked Catherine.

"Of course. I know. I missed an appearance with you last night, but that didn't change my plans for today. I will explain it all when I see you."

September got off the phone and scrawled back in bed. Antonio felt her movement. She leaned over behind him, kissed him on the cheek and wrapped her arms around his chest. He gently held her arm close to his body and continued to rest.

Later that day, September drove over to pick Catherine up at her house in her sputtering car. Catherine came out and waved at Mrs. Jensen. Catherine got in. Five minutes later the car picked up speed.

"Why don't you let me drive?" asked Catherine.

"Because I know where I'm going and I don't like people telling me to take a left, then no, I meant right… then I am slamming on the brakes until you make up your mind which way."

"You want to drive one of my cars?"

"Yes, but I don't want to get you in trouble with hubby." Minutes later, they were on a long road that seemed to be out in the middle of nowhere.

"Where are we headed today?" asked Catherine.

"It's a surprise." September kept her eyes on the road.

"Speaking of surprises, the old flame you spent last night with…"

"Yes, we worked together a long time ago. There is good reason you don't fall in love with the people you work with. We dated for two years while we were in the Army together. I got wounded in the Afghan War. So I was waiting for my release papers from the Army. Once I got them, a year later, I finally got the paper work to be a member of the Central Intelligence Agency, CIA. Tony was still in the Army. After I got out of the Army, we lived together for two years while I was working with the CIA. We dated so seriously, we fell in love or at least I did."

"So what broke up the relationship?"

"He live with me for months at a time. I had things at his house, he had clothing at my house. While he slept in my home, he hacked into my laptop and stole top secret information related to the government. So I put him in jail for being a traitor to his country."

"Why did he do that?" Catherine was stunned.

"He had cut a deal to be paid a quarter of a million dollars on every top secret he could deliver to this foreign country."

"I'm sorry September."

"Not nearly as sorry as I was. I truly loved him Catherine. But after I found out what he was doing, I didn't hesitate to put his ass away."

"You're really hard on the ones you love."

"No, the ones you love sometimes hurt you the most. He didn't get anything he didn't deserve. I would do it again if the situation was the same."

"No second chance?"

"Not with me." September had a flashback of last night's sexual encounter. "Maybe. I don't know. When that man is around me, I forget what planet I'm on. I don't know."

"Well, I guess it's time to change that subject."

"Yes, I would say so." September was solemn in response.

Catherine peered out the window and saw nothing but grass and trees. "Where are you taking me anyway?"

"Look ahead. We're here." September pulled up to this huge hanger. They both got out of the car.

Catherine read the sign on the building. She was shocked. "Sky Diving School. Are you crazy?"

"No, I just wanted to show you something different."

"Sky diving?" questioned Catherine.

"Don't knock it until you've tried it."

"I have never wrapped my head around jumping out of a perfectly good airplane."

"You'll see it for the excitement that it is. The adrenaline rush. The YAHOOO of living life to the fullest." September beamed.

"If you don't mind my asking, you learned how to jump…"

"82nd Airborne baby!" September stated proudly. "One of the best training experiences in the Army I ever had."

Catherine took another look at the hanger. "Can't do it, September. I will have to pass."

September walked up to Catherine, placed her hands on both of Catherine's shoulders and stared her in the eyes. "After all we have done together, do you trust me?"

Catherine bowed her head and sighed. She looked up at September. "Let's go! Let do it!"

"That's my girl." September smiled.

Soon they were both suited with parachutes for the ride of Catherine's life.

Catherine paused with one last question. "Hey, you going to let me meet the man that has September's heart?"

"I put him in jail for treason ten years ago. He got out a couple of months ago, showed up at my door last night. I gave him some relief from being in prison for ten years and told him to stay out of my life. End of story. Sex is good. I just don't think I can forgive him. Now let's go jump out of a perfectly good airplane." September scurried toward the aircraft.

Catherine watched September as she stepped away. Then, dashed to catch up with her.

CHAPTER 16

Nicolette visits Johnathon

This Monday morning Johnathon was behind his desk as usual making phone calls and flipping papers on his desk. He was strictly focused on a strategy for approaching Mark about Tate and his own new business endeavor for becoming a billionaire. Suddenly his concentration was interrupted.

Angela soon buzzed the intercom. "Mr. Fitzpatrick you have a visitor."

"Did I have someone scheduled at this hour?"

"No sir. She says her name is Nicolette Russo."

Johnathon's emotions tightened up. He quickly responded. "Send her in Angela." Angela walked Nicolette into Johnathon's office. "That will be all." Johnathon quickly stated.

Angela closed the door immediately. Realizing since he didn't offer her a drink or any type of refreshment, she concluded that this conversation wasn't about business.

Johnathon came from around his desk to face her. He glared directly into her eyes. "Well….to what do I owe this pleasure? Did he send you to beg me to sell my company… again?"

Nicolette was dressed in a low cut pastel blouse with Armani shoes, bag and gloves to match. She bowed her head, pulled her black leather gloves off her hands and held them in her palm, while her purse hung from her left wrist. She knew she owed him an explanation. Her eyes soon met with his. "No Mr. Fitzpatrick, I came to apologize." Her personal expression was that of emotional disappointment in her own behavior about the events that took place.

Johnathon was still mesmerized by her beauty. However, he maintained his anger. "Who are you apologizing for? You?... or for him? You lied to me when you came to my condo. Giving me that sob story about you and that so call boyfriend. Did he even exist?"

Nicolette had a solemn voice. "No, Mr. Fitzpatrick. No I didn't lie. It was all true."

"And the phone call the other day, about using my number, he asked you to call me that day, right?"

"Yes." Nicolette softly spoke.

"So you and he were in on a conspiracy to get me to sell my company. So was he hoping you would soften me up or seduce me to the point where I would just give my company away?" Johnathon stared at her. Nicolette stared back, not answering. Then he screamed... "Answer me!"

Nicolette blinked her eyes and slightly flinched as if startled by the outburst. Calmly she spoke..."I came to apologize for all of it. Good day Mr. Fitzpatrick." Nicolette was almost tearful, but enough was said. She turned and sauntered out of his office.

Johnathon watched her leave, still infatuated with her beauty. The moment Nicolette disappeared from his sight, Johnathon received a phone call.

"Line one, Mr. Fitzpatrick."

"Thanks Angela." Johnathon pushed the button to receive the call. He placed it on speaker. "Fitzpatrick here."

"This is Tate."

Johnathon was shocked. "How did you get my office number?"

Tate ignored the question. "My boss is willing to give you thirty days. I will check in with you once a week just so you don't forget. The money will be in your account by the end of the week."

Johnathon spoke aggressively. "I told you don't put it there unless you get a 'yes' from me."

"Mr. Fitzpatrick, it better be a yes. Have a good day." Tate hung up.

"Wait... Tate..." The phone went dead.

Now Johnathon knew he had to approach Mark soon, but when would be the right time.

CHAPTER 17

Johnathon's Proposition

A week later... Johnathon was driving into work. He noticed a stretch limo outside of Marie De La Roche Fashions. He realized it was Nicolette's limo. She was shopping for purses and shoes. He entered the store. She was dressed in a tight-fitting dark blue skirt with a light-blue wide collar blouse, black heels and a blue purse on her arm. A wide brimmed black hat set off her stunning well-fitted outfit.

Johnathon stepped in behind her. "Mrs. Russo."

Nicolette glanced toward the voice calling her name and then continued looking at purses. "Mr. Fitzpatrick. I thought our paths were done being crossed."

"I felt as if I didn't give you a chance to explain yourself that day you were in my office. Do you care to have lunch with me at Phillippe's Restaurant? I will meet you there at noon today."

Nicolette didn't look at him. She replied. "I will meet you there at noon."

At noon, Nicolette was on time as Johnathon was already seated at a table, waiting. The restaurant only served the elite of the elite. It had an elegant design of chandelier lighting, gray cushioned chairs, white table cloths and crystal vases shaped as doves for center pieces. The butlers with bowties were scattered serving exotic meals and pouring expensive wine. When Nicolette walked in, she noticed Johnathon right away. Johnathon rose from his seat as she elegantly strolled to meet him. He pulled her chair out and she graciously accepted.

"I wasn't sure you would come Mrs. Russo."

"I did feel as if I owed you an explanation as well as an apology Mr. Fitzpatrick."

The waiter arrived at the table. "What would you like to drink Miss?"

"Just Seltzer water, please."

"Nothing stronger than that?" asked Johnathon.

"It's noon Mr. Fitzpatrick."

"And for your sir, would you like a refresher?" asked the waiter.

"No. No thank you." Johnathon spoke without observing the waiter.

"I will be back with your drink ma' dam." The waiter left.

"I will be quick and to the point Mr. Fitzpatrick."

"Please do. I have a three o'clock appointment and I need not be late."

"It was true. My husband asked me to soften you a bit so he could make an offer to you for your company. I refused, he insisted. So I did it."

"Why didn't you tell me the truth when you met with me at my condo?"

"Because everything you said was true. The stare I gave you at my home was because you reminded me of someone I loved. I couldn't tell you the truth because when I looked at you I saw Renieri. When I think of Renieri, I think of honesty and truthfulness. So instead of performing my husband's wishes, I decided to get to know you for myself. I wanted to know if you had the same morals and integrity that he had."

Johnathon hadn't heard a word she said. "What about the phone call at my office?"

"I lied to my husband when I returned home. The phone call was again, my husband's ideal to try once more. I told him you weren't interested in any proposal for your company. That selling your life's work wasn't an option. Then suddenly, out of nowhere, you appeared on our doorstep as if you had changed your mind."

"Well Mrs. Russo I thank you for that. You were right. I have no intention of selling my hard work. Also I feel as if I owe you an apology as well. I am sorry your first perception of me was tainted with a gigolo type behavior. That is not who I am. But I appeared on your doorstep to see *you* again. After the story you told me that day, I thought about the words you spoke. I wanted to know more about *you* as an individual."

"After you left the yacht that day, my husband was furious with me. When he talked to you about the proposal, you had such a surprised expression on your face that he knew that I hadn't mention it at all. Now he has bodyguards on me 24/7."

"I noticed them by your limo. Why?"

"If I didn't talk to you about the proposal when I met you, what did I spend time doing with you for an hour and then we went shopping and dining."

"Your chauffeur told him?"

"Of course. He thought I was intimate with you when we were alone in your condo that day. It took me a couple of days to convince him that nothing happened. Even though he says he believes me… I am stuck with body guards."

Johnathon twirled his drink in his hand, bowed his head and then looked into her eyes. "I only wanted to see you once more. That was the only reason I came to Italy. I didn't mean to cause a marital dispute."

"You have a strange way of showing it. What did you expect my husband to do? Leave the premises while you make a move on me. Then what about your wife Mr. Fitzpatrick?"

Johnathon chuckled a little. "I didn't come to Italy to get into bed with you. I just wanted to see you again, that's all. I… I don't know what I expected. I just… I just needed to see you again."

The waiter returned with the water. "Would you like to order?"

"Mrs. Russo?' asked Johnathon.

"The Chef's salad will be fine."

The waiter looked at Johnathon.

"Make that two."

"Very good Sir, Ma'am. I will get that right out to you." The waiter left.

"Why are you here in L.A? I didn't know you were here, so it wasn't to harass me again. Why did you come?"

"No, Mr. Fitzpatrick, it wasn't to see you. I shop for American style clothing from time to time. Some I like very much. As I told you before, I'm into fashion. I also oversee a homeless children shelter, a domestic violent rehab center for battered women and a couple of other charities here in L.A. When I leave you, that's where I'm heading."

"No way…" Johnathon chuckled. "A pretty rich girl running a homeless shelter for homeless kids and battered women?"

"You see Mr. Fitzpatrick, this is where you don't see... *me*. The story I told you was true about me wanting to have my own business. My husband won't let me because he wants me at his beckon call."

"But you're running these shelters?"

"No, I'm overseeing the shelters. I love children, I want to help battered women and others that are less fortunate than I. I promised myself after I became a thriving fashion designer, that I would give back what I didn't have coming up as a child. So... since my business didn't work out, I persuaded him to allow me to run several shelters with my name behind them. He thought it a great ideal because it looks good for his businesses."

"Which is?"

"Real Estate, food markets, liquor companies, etc... I come to LA to check things out from time to time. I take photos with the kids, snap shots with some of the women, while surveying the building, ensuring quality care of the individuals staying there, that type of thing."

"So you really don't care for these kids or women. They are just a front for his businesses, a tax write-off?"

"On the contrary, I love these kids and helping others. I want to run these charities. I have my name behind them, but he won't let me. To be truthful, I want my own fashion company, but he won't let me, I want to come and go as I please without chauffeurs and body guards, but he won't let me."

"Just leave him and start your own business."

"You still don't get it. I guess a rich Ivy League man like you with daddy passing down millions to his son... wouldn't get it. You've never had to choose between having to eat or pay the electric bill, or paying the rent versus paying the car note to get to work so you can pay the rent."

"Pleassse... spare me the poverty lecture Mrs. Russo. You've already given it to me, remember?"

"Yes I have and you still don't get it. You see Mr. Fitzpatrick, with what money do I leave him with? He would let me go without a dime in my purse and I would be right back where I was before I met him. Penniless."

Johnathon sighed. He stared at his drink. He thought for a few seconds. He leaned forward with both elbows on the table. He crossed his fingers. Then he confronted Nicolette straight in the eyes. "What if... what if I loaned you the money." Nicolette paused for thought. "I mean... think about it. I could kick things off for you. You tell me what you want and how you want it and I can make that happen. You keep your business running when you are not with him. You control it with a laptop or iPad from your home in Italy. Of course you'll need someone to manage things here, but you have the final say over the entire business."

Nicolette sat with her back straight against the chair, totally silent. Her eyes moved down on the table as if the concept of her own business could be a possibility. She looked back at Johnathon. Johnathon watched her facial expression as if her cheeks raised to simulate a slight smile at the possibility.

Their salads arrived from the waiter. He placed their food before them. "Will there be anything else?"

"No thank you." Johnathon's still focused on Nicolette.

The slight smile soon disappeared. "Why would you want to do that for me, the liar?"

"Because I do see... *you*. I believe what you have told me about your desire to have your own business..."

Nicolette sighed and thought for a moment. "I will have to think on this Mr. Fitzpatrick."

"While you're thinking Mrs. Russo, there is only one person that can change your circumstances..."

"It's you... Mr. Fitzpatrick?"

Johnathon spoke with passion and concern. "No, not me. Take a good look in the mirror. See that person for who she really wants to be. Do you want to be a person controlled or a person free to make her own choices and decisions about her own life?"

Nicolette glanced at Johnathon as if he just made perfectly good sense about her situation. "I hear you. You want me to make this leap of independence with you?"

"I want you to make that choice for yourself. I'm just offering the opportunity. Only you can open the door to your freedom."

Nicolette was silent. She gazed into his eyes. Johnathon could see how deep in thought she was. "I... I..."

Johnathon interrupted. He leaned back in his chair. "Well Mrs. Russo, here's what I'm going to do. I am a busy man. If you change your mind, I will be at my condo tomorrow evening at nine-thirty. If you want to move forward, meet me there and we can discuss further. If not, I will take that as a no and I will trouble you no further on the ideal of controlling your own business. In the meantime," Johnathon glanced at his food. "I think I will enjoy this salad."

Johnathon took his knife and fork, stared at Nicolette while cutting his lettuce and tomato. She glared at him as he chewed and sipped his wine. He returned the look. Nicolette rose from the table. Her thoughts were racing and she walked out.

When Johnathon got back to the office for his three o'clock appointment, Mark met him at the door.

"Hey J, some guy named Tate was here looking for you. I normally know all of our clientele and I offered my services, but he said he only wanted to speak to you. I told him you had a 3 p.m. appointment and he wouldn't be able to see you today."

"Where is he now?" asked Johnathon.

"He looked at his watch, then left. Is this someone I need to be concerned about J or you got this?"

"I got it Mark. Is everything ready for the brief or do you want to do it?"

"Actually I had gotten prepared to do it. I thought about what you said in building my confidence. I should face my fears instead of shying away from them." Lately... you have been spending more time dealing with what's in that black book of yours, than about this company you are trying to grow. Don't let your other head start doing the thinking for you."

Johnathon ignored the comment. "I'm glad to see your confidence is building Mark. I think I will let you handle the presentation. I need to get some things in motion for another client. Go ahead and take care of it, please."

"Sure, no problem." Mark left for the conference room surprised at Johnathon's actions. He didn't even ask to see his presentation before he gave it.

Johnathon went to his office. He sat in his chair glaring into space. Moments later, he grabbed the phone and got things in motion for Nicolette. He called in favors, got his own staff to draft a business plan, had research done for locations and checked his business financial status.

Mark was headed home, when he noticed Johnathon through his office window still seated in his chair around 6 p.m. He knocked on the door. Johnathon waved him in as he hung up the phone.

"How did the briefing go Mark?"

Mark was so excited. "J, you would have been proud of me. Let's say you and I go to the Yacht Club… right now and celebrate my first twenty-five million dollar deal?"

Johnathon leaped from his seat. He hugged Mark. "I knew you had it in you." Then he sat back down and reengaged in the paperwork he had in front of him.

Mark watched Johnathon as he read papers. "You know I'm used to creating and making things work, not briefing them. But, I have to say, it was invigorating to me to talk about what I invented and then sell it. So, let's go have that drink."

"I would love to Mark," Johnathon doesn't look at him. "But I got a call from an old friend. She needs some assistance and I will be meeting with her on some proposals."

Mark was still enthusiastic. "Understood. How about tomorrow?"

"Uhhh… tomorrow is not good either. I will let you know when." Johnathon maintained his visual on the papers in front of him.

"Hell J! You can't spare a couple of hours right now. The time will be long gone to celebrate. The adrenaline is pumping now." Johnathon didn't budge. Mark was visibly upset. "Just forget it. I will leave you to whatever."

Mark closed the door. He was clearly irritate over Johnathon's response to his accomplishment of performing his first single brief and landing the deal. Johnathon continued his quest of gathering information for Nicolette's potential business.

CHAPTER 18

Girl Trouble for Johnathon

Johnathon left the office after working long and hard on Nicolette's business plan to unwind at his condominium. This evening around eleven, after beautiful moments in bed with Cynthia, Johnathon decided to cut the evening short. This very beautiful blonde, with a curved body, lay naked in bed resting against the pillows. She lit a cigarette while Johnathon, nude, started to get dress. He sat on the side of the bed putting his socks on. As smoke entered the air, he turned on the air filter at the end table to cleanse the room of second-hand smoke. Cynthia ignored his action and continued to puff away. He reached for his shirt off the floor and continued to get dressed.

Cynthia questioned him while she leaned on the pillows in bed. "Hey baby, why do we only get together on Tuesday's at seven and Thursday's at three? I would like to see you more often than two days a week."

"I don't want to see you more than two days a week." Johnathon continued to get dressed.

Stunned by the comment, "What's that supposed to mean?"

"That I don't want to see you more than two days a week. It's not complicated. I told you I don't want to get emotionally involved with anyone and that means you, Cynthia."

She put the cigarette out in the ashtray by the end table. She reached for him while he was buttoning his shirt on the edge of the bed, and pulled him back into her lap. He gazed up at her.

"I was hoping to change your mind after seeing you enough times, but you're not really giving me a chance. You're out of the room by three or four in the morning, like you have to wake up with someone else besides me." She looked at the clock on the end table. "It's eleven-thirty. Where are you going baby? It's too early for you to leave me."

He sat up from her lap and stood beside the bed with just his shirt and briefs on. "Look, we had a nice evening dinner out, took in some moonlight, and had great sex. Tuesday and Thursday for a few hours, that's all you get. Take the days and time I give you or leave them? Right now I need to be somewhere else. I have to go."

"I want to see you more often than a few hours twice a week. Are the other days taken by another woman or shall I say, other women? Is my time up for this evening? I thought I had until midnight or three in the morning?"

"As a matter a fact, if you must know, yes. Yes on both counts."

Cynthia paused in thought and grew angry. "So what number am I?"

"Really sweetheart. You're ruining this moment. We just had a beautiful time together. Can't we leave it at that?"

"This condo isn't your home, is it?"

"No… Cynthia it's not."

"Are you married too?"

"Yes, if you must know. Yes… I am." Johnathon grew annoyed with the multiple questions as he sat on the side of the bed putting his shoes on.

"Ohhhh….how stupid can I be?" Cynthia angrily announced. She leaped up on her knees in bed. Johnathon stood and moved away from her. "I should have known for months we've been together only on Tuesday's and Thursday's at a certain time. Now it's all coming together. I guess it didn't matter at first, what… with private jet trips, the dining in the most expensive restaurants, the laying on the beach in exotic places, all only on Tuesday's and Thursday's."

"You're telling me you didn't have a good time?" quipped Johnathon.

"I'm telling you, you asshole, that I had a great time!" Cynthia angrily spoke. "I want to see more of you. I love you. I want to be with you, not just on Tuesday's and Thursday's. I was hoping to be more than just another pretty face."

"That's not happening, ever. I like you, but that's all you are, just another pretty face to me. We have fun together and that's it." Johnathon's temper rose. He spoke in an aggressive tone. "If this has gotten to be too much for you, we can end this right here and now. I don't need complications like love creeping into my lifestyle. So tell me now. Does it end tonight?"

"Do you love your wife?" asked Cynthia, emotionally disturbed.

"That's none of your business?" Irritated by the comment, Johnathon forcefully zipped his pants up and straightened his tie. In that moment, frustration took over. "You know what? I'm going to make the decision for you."

"Wait Johnathon… " She reached for him and wrapped her arms around his neck, still naked, she tried to kiss him. He pulled back from the bed and placed his suit coat on.

"It's over. Take my number out of your cell. Delete it. Act like you never knew me." Johnathon adjusted his coat around his shoulders. "When you go out the door, be sure you have everything. If you leave something, I'm burning it. The door locks behind you. Leave the key on the bed or give it to Becky on your way out."

"Johnathon, my love… I…"

Johnathon interrupted…"Do it! Or I'll just change the lock."

Cynthia was baffled as to his affairs. "How do you keep it all straight?"

Annoyed with her questions and wanting to insult her, he explained. "It's quite simple really. The fourth and fifth floor are permanent residence, females I see when I want. The third floor is for regulars like you on a scheduled weekly basis. Becky handles everything. She arranges the room. Moves the clothing in and out per female. The second floor is for quickies. Women I only intend to see once or occasionally. The first floor is just for me to relax and unwind from a long day from everyone. You should consider yourself lucky I even made you a regular."

Cynthia, outraged over the information she had just learned, stood from the bed with tears in her eyes. Infuriated from not knowing the total truth, she lashed out at him. "I want you to know I am not some kind of back woods sleazy whore you can just sleep with at your beckon call." Suddenly she reached for the lamp on the end table and threw it at him. He stepped aside, watched as the lamp flew against the wall and cracked into pieces.

Johnathon turned to look at her and softly spoke. "Ooooo... such anger. I'm not going to make you pay for that. It just goes to show me that you never know anyone until the dark side comes out and exposes itself. I would have never taken you for the physically violent type." He straightened his tie. "Never set foot near this building again. Enjoy the rest of your life... without me."

Cynthia reiterated her circumstance. "I am not some cheap hussy you can just pick up on the street and throw me to the curb when you are done, like a piece of trash."

Johnathon stated in an aggressive voice. "Really, I beg the differ. You have been here on your designated slot, right on time, just like my other women."

Cynthia yelled..."You don't know who you are messing with. I have friends in high places."

Johnathon had put his suit jacket on and was completely dressed, "I have friends in higher places. I promise you that right now you may be a Senior Executive for one of the largest marketing firms in L.A., but not only will you not work there and lose you cushy one million dollar job, but you won't be able to find work anywhere in this country. So let's see whose friends are in higher places."

"You'll regret the day you ever saw me."

"I already have. Leave the key and don't look back. Whore!" Johnathon slammed the door behind him.

Cynthia fell to the bed in tears. She pounded the mattress with her fist and water trickled from her eyes rapidly, she vowed to herself... "You will pay for my hurt and pain Johnathon Fitzpatrick!"

As he left a teary eyed Cynthia, he went down to the second floor. Johnathon waited for half an hour in the living room of another suite. At 11:30 p.m., suddenly he heard the key turn in the door. He stood from the sofa.

"Rachel, sweetheart, look what I got for you."

A beautiful long-haired brunette with an hour-glass figure stood in the doorway, airline bags in hand. "I know my calls are unexpected. I hope I didn't take you away from anything important."

"Rachel nothing is more important than seeing you my love. I would have moved heaven and earth to spend time with you this evening."

"Oh Johnathon, it's such a joy knowing I get to see your handsome face after such a long day of serving grumpy passengers."

He stood dead center in the living room with a smile on his face. Johnathon pulled Inglenook Cabernet Sauvignon Napa Valley 1941, a $24,675 wine bottle from behind his back. He reached for the remote on the coffee table and the lights dimmed and classic music began to play. He poured two glasses of wine and offered her one.

Rachel placed her bags on the floor and took a sip of wine. "Ummm…. just what the doctor ordered." She moved closer to him, placed her wine on the coffee table, and then kissed him passionately upon his lips.

As Johnathon placed his glass down, she reached into one of her bags… "Look what I brought you my love."

"More cigars. You know I'm hooked on those. I started ordering these instead of waiting for you to bring them to me." Johnathon took two of them and placed them in his pocket. "Let's go enjoy a glass of wine and a cigar in the Jacuzzi. The water is warm and full of bubbles, just the way you like it. While you relax and puff away, I will massage every inch of your body." He grabbed the wine bottle off the dining room table. Rachel grabbed the glasses.

Rachel smiled. "Lead the way my love, I am putty in your hands."

Johnathon took her by the waist. They both strolled, kissing one another on their way to the bedroom.

CHAPTER 19

Business Meeting with Johnathon

On this morning, Johnathon dressed in a three piece suit and tie after Catherine left with September. He headed for work. When Johnathon reached his office, he checked on the points of contacts he had made the previous day. He had paper work of architectural drawings sent to him and he had phone numbers of points of contacts for fashion designers and seamstresses. He knew if Nicolette met him at nine-thirty this evening he wanted to show her he was serious and a man of his word.

Mark hadn't seen Johnathon all day because he had been in staff meetings, on conference video calls with overseas clients, and putting out company fires. Mark was going to call Johnathon over an emergency situation that had just occurred that night. Walking back to his office from a staff meeting, Mark peeked toward Johnathon's office and noticed him sitting at his desk.

Mark knocked on the door.

"Come in." Johnathon was reviewing the company's financials.

"There you are J, I'm glad to see you." Mark stood by the door. "We have an issue."

"What might that be?"

"Kenneth was in a car accident last night. He has broken ribs and a concussion."

"Will he live?" Johnathon never looked up from the papers he had before him.

"Yes, but that is not the problem. The problem is that he was to be on a plane this afternoon to Brazil pitching our security system to a potential eleven million dollar Brazilian client tomorrow afternoon."

"So get someone else to do it."

"J I have reviewed the schedule of all twenty of our employees with the skill set to deliver this particular type briefing and they are all booked for today and can't leave by three."

"So you do it Mark."

"I can't. I'm scheduled to meet with an African client at four today to discuss a thirty million dollar potential deal. No one is left but you my friend to catch a flight in time to brief Kenneth's client tomorrow in Brazil."

Johnathon had his head buried in papers and never gave Mark the attention he was expecting. "How much is this potential client worth that Kenneth has?"

Mark tilted his head slightly to the side, puzzled, as he had just told Johnathon the value of the client. Realizing Johnathon was in another zone, Mark repeated himself. "Eleven million."

"Call the client. Explain what happened and see if we can postpone for a month."

"J… I didn't see anything on your schedule for tomorrow or today. You can handle it." Mark's tone was a little frantic with a sense of urgency. "We're talking eleven million."

Johnathon's tone was harsh. "No… I can't do it." Johnathon put the paperwork aside for a moment. He acknowledged Mark's presence. "Are you trying to tell me what to do? I can't leave the country today and that's that. I have a client I am meeting today and it will be worth a whole lot more than eleven million. So either postpone the briefing or cancel all together."

Mark was shocked. Normally Johnathon would have moved heaven and earth not to miss any client over five million dollars. Mark spoke softly. "I'll see what I can do J."

"Great. Now disappear, I have much to do."

"Do you want me to tell you how I will handle it? And do you want to know what's on our schedule for this week with clients and how much money is at stake?" asked Mark.

Johnathon's voice was softer. "I do not."

"Do you want to let me know whom you are working with in case you need my assistance?"

"I do not." Johnathon's head was buried in the paperwork before him. "I will keep you informed on a need to know basis. That will be all. Please take care of Kenneth's client if you can. Shut the door on your way out."

"On it J."

Mark stared at Johnathon baffled at his actions when he was always involved in all of the cases. He was either doing the brief, preparing the brief or listening to the brief of someone. Something was different, Mark just couldn't put his fingers on it. He watched Johnathon for a few seconds and saw how he was rummaging through papers and making notes. Mark closed the door trying to make sense of what just happened.

That evening Johnathon awaited Nicolette in his personal condominium suite. He checked his watch for the time, nine-forty. He came out to the main lobby where Becky was seated. He watched through the glass doors for headlights and saw none. He turned and headed back toward his suite. Seconds later, he heard the main doorbell ring. He looked and saw Nicolette.

Johnathon called to Becky. "Hurry. Buzz her in." He raced to the door to open it for her. "I was about to give up on you."

"For being ten minutes late?"

Johnathon glanced at his watch. "Eleven."

"I'm not the one driving." Annoyed with the question, Nicolette spoke bitterly. "Did you bring me here to discuss my punctuality or my fashion business?"

As Johnathon talked to Nicolette in the lobby, Amoy walked in. Nicolette noticed she had a key to the glass doors and didn't need to be buzzed in.

Amoy spoke, "Hi Johnathon." She continued to the elevators and pushed a button.

"Hi Amoy." Johnathon replied.

"She lives her?" questioned Nicolette. "Am I interrupting something?"

"Yes, she lives on the fifth floor."

Just at that very moment, Melanie walked in without being buzzed in. "Hi Johnathon."

"Melanie." Johnathon responded.

She went to the elevators and pushed the button to the fourth floor. Nicolette noticed she had a key as well to the front doors.

"Are you sure I am not interrupting anything?" asked Nicolette.

"Of course not. Let's go."

"Which floor is yours?" enquired Nicolette. She hesitated to move.

"You remember. I'm right here on the bottom floor as usual. This way." Johnathon placed the palm of his hand in the middle of her back to edge her in the right direction.

As they walked to his suite, "Are those women friends of yours?"

Johnathon opened the door to his dwelling. Nicolette stood in the doorway still asking questionings. She awaited his response. "I wouldn't say friends, more like acquaintances."

"Really? Do most of your female acquaintances have keys to your residential building? You and your wife don't live here. Do you?"

Johnathon was slightly angered by the questions. "It's my condominium that I utilize from time to time." Nicolette stared at him without saying a word. Johnathon glanced back at her and responded. "No. My wife and I don't live here."

"So what are these woman to you?"

"If you must know. I, from time to time pay them a visit late in the evenings."

Johnathon edged her further into the living room. Nicolette entered slowly, still asking questions.

"There are five floors. Are they all full of female acquaintances?" Johnathon ignored the question and said nothing. Nicolette immediately went on the defensive. "If you think I am going to become a part of this haram that you've got going on, you can just forget it! I don't see you like that Mr. Fitzpatrick and if this is some kind of scam to lure me here to get in bed with you... well... let just say..."

Johnathon interrupted calmly. "Absolutely not. I'm a man of my word. I meant what I said at lunch yesterday. I believe you can start and maintain your own business. "This..." Johnathon pointed with his hand upward to the ceiling, referring to the floors above him. "These women that you've just witnessed are my past time. They mean nothing to me."

Nicolette gawked at him in amazement and disgust. "So you just use them for your play toys?"

Johnathon's tone was softer and that of innocence. He walked closer to her face and gazed into her eyes lovingly. "I don't take advantage of anyone, especially women Mrs. Russo. These women have a choice. I am very upfront with the ladies I caress in my arms. I tell them I don't want a relation..." Johnathon paused, a little annoyed at her curiosity. He walked away from her. In a split moment, he turned to face her. "Hold it, just a minute. I didn't ask you to come here and pass judgement on me. I want to show you what I have accomplished so far in getting your business off the ground. That is... if you are done with the twenty questions and we can get down to why you came here in the first place."

Nicolette soon realized Johnathon meant business. "Ok, let's get started." Her voice was stern.

"Come into the study. I have everything laid out there." Once they reached the study, Nicolette noticed the table filled with papers. "Can I get you a seltzer water before we commence?"

"Yes." Nicolette pulled her light jacket off and placed her purse on the table where the papers were.

"I will be right back." Johnathon talked on his way to the kitchen... "As you can see there, I have identified some locations. I have surveyed most of the buildings. I've review financials in new construction or renovating a building. More stuff like that is all right there on the table. You can look at them and I'll be right back with the water." Nicolette observed all the effort he had put together in just a matter of a day.

When he came back to the study, Nicolette had already reviewed two floor plans for her shop. Johnathon handed her the water.

"What do you think Mrs. Russo?"

"This one is five-thousand square foot and this one is nine-thousand. Why such a huge difference?"

"That's why you are here. I didn't know how big or small you wanted to start. Whether you wanted to be able to sew and showcase fashion in the same store or you wanted two different locations. There is so much I don't know. So I just accommodated for everything."

Nicolette just looked at him and was thrilled with his efforts. "Well, let's see." She was in thought of his question. "If we can, I would prefer two different buildings, one to showcase the fashion designs and the other to make the designs. Is that possible?"

Johnathon grabbed his note pad and sat on his beautiful white leather sofa. Nicolette took her water from the table and followed him. She sat right next to him.

"Of course." Johnathon mumbled 'two locations' to himself as he wrote it down. "Nicolette, you need a manager. I can call you Nicolette?"

"No. Let's keep it professional Mr. Fitzpatrick."

"You are my business partner now. Right?"

"Potential. Mr. Fitzpatrick."

"Very well. Do you have a manager in mind? One that can thoroughly run the company without having to call you to make decisions for every little thing."

"Yes. I want you to call Elisa Martinez. I went to her shop one time and told her how I admired her work. When I mentioned I was a designer as well, we became friends. We talked design and fashion. She said if I ever opened up my own shop she would be interested in putting my designs together for me. She is currently working for Marcus Royal. She will not work for pennies. We have to steal her away. She knows the fashion industry inside and out. Make her an offer she can't refuse. Her talent to create what is put on paper is magnificent. She knows who to bring under her."

"Got it. Give me her number." Nicolette took the pen from his hand and wrote on his pad. "What about the building space? How much for sewing and how much for the store?"

Nicolette gave him the pen back and watched Johnathon take notes. She interrupted… "You have got me so excited about this. It sounds as if you plan on sparing no expense."

"That's right. We have to start big and I can do that for you. I know people. I have money…"

Nicolette interrupted… "What if things don't work out? I will owe you and what do you want in return for all of this effort you're putting forth to help me succeed?"

Johnathon looked at her. He took his pencil and tapped her on the nose. He smiled. "You have to think positive Mrs. Russo. If this is still your dream, then you will do everything in your power to ensure it succeeds. After listening to you, I believe that. And what do I want from you? Just a thank you. Nothing more."

Nicolette formed a slight grin. "If this is a business deal Mr. Fitzpatrick, you shall get a percentage of the profits."

Johnathon knew not to argue. "As you wish Mrs. Russo. We can discuss numbers later. Right now let's try to make this work." He continued to write on his note pad.

Nicolette watched him while he made annotations and wondered if she was doing the right thing. Nicolette felt a feeling of excitement, exhilaration, possibility, and then sadness and fear set in, what if Giovanni found out. Then at that moment, she watched Johnathon. He moved from the sofa to the drawings on the table. As he pondered over his work for her, she saw his eagerness to get things accomplished. Nicolette soon dismissed those thoughts of sadness and fear and assisted Johnathon further in generating ideas for her business.

CHAPTER 20

Tate Visits Johnathon

The next working day, Johnathon was blissful from his evening before working with Nicolette. The smile he had walking into his office soon dissipated as he approached his office door.

Angela stopped him before he entered. "Mr. Fitzpatrick a gentleman insisted on waiting for your arrival. I offered him a seat in your office."

Johnathon could see Tate through his glass office window. "Thank you Angela. It's fine. Just poke your head in with me to see if he would like a drink."

"Yes, Sir."

Johnathon opened the door and Angela was right behind him. Tate was seated in a chair across from his desk. Johnathon was not surprised to see him.

"Mr. Tate." Johnathon went and sat behind his desk. "Would you care for coffee or a Danish before we talk?"

"Yes, I will take a coffee, black."

"Angela…" spoke Johnathon.

Angela replied. "Right away, Mr. Fitzpatrick." She closed the door behind her.

Johnathon was slightly aggravated. "Tate what are you doing here? Just because I gave you access to the fifth floor doesn't mean I want to see you unannounced. Don't do it again unless I call you here."

"I said I would check with you every week."

"You said your boss gave me thirty days for an answer. It's only been two weeks. You were here last week. Did you ever hear of a device called a phone?"

Tate ignored the comment. "And I said I will remind you every week until I get an answer."

"Need you show up at my office? You have my work phone number. You could have called."

"Phone calls don't leave impressions. You blow me off and wait until I call again. Since I am here, I want you to see my facial expression."

Johnathon leaned back in his chair and awaited this emotional threatening stare that was supposed to petrify him. Instead Johnathon heard the calmness in his voice.

"Mr. Fitzpatrick, I haven't been a man of violence for quite some time and I'm not about to start now. You have been paid a quarter of a million dollars in said account. This is week three. Why wait until the last minute to give me a decision?"

"Because I have other pressing issues within my own organization that needs my attention." Johnathon was a little frustrated. "I'm not jumping through hoops for something as illegal as what you are asking me to do. I told you I had to find trustworthy people." Johnathon paused. "As a matter of fact, you shouldn't have put the money there until I had responded to you."

"You're not hearing me Mr. Fitzpatrick. It would please my boss if you made a decision now. The money is a sign of good faith."

"You can go back and tell your boss I will give him his money back. I am this close," Johnathon portrayed his forefinger and thumb to show a tiny distance between the two fingers. "from reaching five-hundred million dollars on my own. I don't need his money."

"Mr. Fitzpatrick…" A knock came at the door.

Johnathon glanced toward the door. "Come in Angela."

"Two coffees Mr. Fitzpatrick." Angela placed a coffee before Johnathon as he turned his attention to Tate.

Tate returned the gaze to Johnathon as Angela handed him a saucer with his coffee. Johnathon and Tate stared each other down. Tate took the coffee from Angela without recognizing her.

"That will be all Angela." Voiced Johnathon.

Angela noticed the intense stare down of both men and immediately closed the door. Tate took a sip of coffee, his eyes never left Johnathon. He stood up and placed the cup upon Johnathon's desk. He straightened his suite coat and adjusted his tie. He leaned on his desk with both palms, never looking away. "One week Mr. Fitzpatrick. It better be a 'yes'. I will see you soon."

Tate was uneasy over Johnathon's indecision. However, he felt if he could get Johnathon to move faster, it could be a few extra dollars for him getting the client to move ahead of an agreed schedule. This was uncharted territory for Tate, since he was unsure of how the boss would react without an answer soon. He walked toward the door and glanced back at Johnathon. Their eyes met with a firm stare down and Johnathon's eyes followed him as he left.

Johnathon, not knowing who he was actually dealing with, felt confident that he wouldn't be pressured to produce the item in question. Besides, Tate hadn't threatened bodily harm or did he?

CHAPTER 21

Catherine Goes To New York

Another morning sunrise hit Johnathon in the face. He and Nicolette had spent the entire evening getting the details of her company plotted out. Nicolette left for Italy that morning. Johnathon called from the condo to his office to let Mark know he would be in late and that he spent the night with him. Johnathon called Catherine to let her know he spent the night with Mark at his home.

Catherine's cell phone rung while she was eating breakfast. "Hello, sweetheart. Another late night with Mark?"

"Yes Catherine. I'll be home by nine tonight, promise. So Friday will be all yours."

Catherine felt in her heart that he would not keep his word. She was feed up with waiting her turn over his job. At that moment, Catherine made a spontaneous decision while on the phone. "Don't bother Johnathon, I've made plans to take my jet to New York this afternoon."

"But what about Friday Catherine. Since the executive party is postponed, Friday should be our day."

"The jet is already fueled and ready to go. September and I are spending the weekend in New York. I will see you late Sunday evening."

"I'm sorry I didn't make it home last night. I will make time when you come back. Monday will be all yours. Anything you want, just you and I."

"Johnathon don't lie. Work has always come before me."

"I'm not lying Catherine. I will cancel everything and the day will be yours."

"We'll see. Gotta go, love you."

"Be safe in New York. Bye."

Johnathon immediately got on the phone and called Nicolette.

Catherine called September. "You got plans for today?"

"Just the usual. I thought you were prepping for Johnathon tonight and tomo..."

Catherine interrupted..."Great! So cancel them. I have made plans for us for the weekend starting today. How would you like to fly without jumping out of the plane?"

"What do you mean?"

"Come to New York with me and go shopping? In my private jet."

September screamed. "Yes, yes!" When she calmed down... "You're buying, of course?"

"Of course. Don't pack anything but a toothbrush. We'll get everything else there. I will be over in fifty minutes to pick you up in the limo."

Catherine waited for a response. September had already hung up the phone to grab her toothbrush.

Forty minutes later, Catherine arrived in her limo. September hopped in the car and immediately looked around. "Boy, this is nice. "You made my day my friend. I love spontaneity. But I thought today was a prep for the glorious day tomorrow with hubby?"

Catherine was very solemn in tone. "It was supposed to be."

September scrutinized Catherine's expression. "Are you ok?"

"No I am not. I have everything I could possible need or want in this world, except my loving husband."

September gave her an ear full. "Can't you see you're his show girl? He doesn't love you. He's that man that wants his cake and eat it too."

"Johnathon has his moments. I know him constantly working all the time doesn't always make for a healthy relationship."

"Come on Catherine. Do you really believe that? Right now, knowing that you're gone, he's probably jumping for joy."

"Why does your thoughts always have to be so distrustful of men?"

"Because I've known a few in my time and I've seen the kind that you have right now. You're so full of him and catering to him, you can't see the forest for trees."

"I trust him. What is a marriage without trust?"

"I just hate to see you get hurt by a man that doesn't give a shit about you. I just wish you would stand your ground and be a strong woman." September's tone was a little aggressive. "Tell him how you feel."

Catherine spoke softly. "I am a strong woman when I need to be. How do you think we are on this trip?"

"This trip... this is nothing. He's only too happy to see you leave for an extended period of time. That's why when you're home he's never there, with you gone that makes it all the better. He doesn't need to make up some excuse for not coming home."

Catherine was a little irritated by all the comments. "I trust him. I'm a strong woman. I don't care what you say."

"Oh really. I'll bet you haven't told him about the guns, have you?"

Catherine hesitated. "Well... ahh... I'm getting around to it."

"What if he tells you that's not becoming of a lady? Are you going to take the guns back?"

"No, of course not."

"Do you have the guts to tell him that?" quizzed September.

"Of course I do." Catherine spoke with confidence. "That's just one of the many things I enjoy doing with you. Since I've gotten so good at it, I started studying about shooting guns. I mean like... distances, wind velocity, the weight of the gun, the grip, my breathing and how all that plays a factor in how accurate you are at hitting your target. You don't do that and just give it up because someone else tells you too, especially if this sport is your passion."

"Bravo!" September cheered and clapped her hands. "Good for you. Now when Johnathon tells you to get rid of them, I will be more than happy to take them off your hands."

Catherine just smiled. They reached the airport, Catherine took September down a special corridor only for private plane owners. Once on the jet, September admired the spacious aisle, the luxury plush beige leather seats and dark oak wood tables on each side. Minutes later, they were in the air.

With the seatbelt sign off, September moved about the air craft. "This jet is beautiful Catherine." September looked out the window and then sat down at a table. Catherine joined her. The flight attendant entered with their drinks.

"A Negroni." September was delighted it was already prepared. She took her drink. "Wow. Thank you for the special treatment."

"September, I just want to thank you. I haven't had so much fun these past few months since after the week I got married. This evening will be my treat."

"Thank you Catherine. When you called, you knew I would jump. I have never flown in a private jet, shopped in New York, stayed at an expensive hotel and changed into an evening dress to watch a Broadway play, all in one day. This will be my very first time."

"It's my pleasure. It's the least I could do since you let me into your life." Catherine smiled.

"I haven't done so many rich, extravagant things since…" September paused in thought.

"Since when?" asked Catherine.

"Since never. Since never, ever. Cheers!" September gulped her drink. She yelled. "Waitress!'

"Call her Jenna. She prefers her name." Catherine sipped her cooler.

"Why don't you have Sex on a Beach? We are just having a good time."

"Because I, after two of them, I become light-headed and non-functional."

Jenna came out with refreshments and more drinks. "Ma'am here you are."

"Thank you Jenna." She grabbed her drink from the tray. Jenna also placed food on the table. "Finger sandwiches?" September spoke as if disappointed in the edibles before her.

"I don't want to dine on the plane." Catherine raised her drink. "I have a nice dinner planned once we arrive. We paint the town, do some shopping and I have tickets for an Opera at Teatro alla Scala."

"Tea what?"

"Just forget it. We're going. You'll love it. It's something different and I didn't see it on you bucket list. So you can add the Opera to it."

"I'll drink to that." September lifted her glass.

Catherine raised her glass as well. They both toasted. They flew away looking forward to a beautiful, splendid sun shinny weekend of buying clothing, purses and enjoying the theatre.

Chapter 22

Strictly Business with Nicolette

Meanwhile, Johnathon had called Nicolette to let her know that he would be free for the weekend. She in turn had one of her girlfriends to call her, requesting her presence back to L.A. Giovanni was none the wiser and didn't object. Nicolette arrived late that Friday evening. She met Johnathon at his condo. He had Seltzer water and wine chilled upon the coffee table when she arrived. Nicolette was dressed in tight black slacks with a white loosely fitted blouse, jewelry and purse to match. Johnathon admired her body movement as she entered his suite.

Nicolette stood in the middle of the living room floor, she turned to see Johnathon still standing at the door.

"How did you manager to have the weekend free after spending Thursday evening with me?" asked Nicolette.

Johnathon was solemn and intent on getting down to business. He moved toward her. "My personal affairs Mrs. Russo are not open for discussion. Here is the plan for this evening. In about a half-hour Elisa and my architect, Peter will arrive. I have been working with them over the past week on a building structure and design. They will be working with you to ensure this is what you want. Peter and Elisa will get a feel for your desires of how you want the building structured and the rooms designed. He will put it all together. When I know what you want and how you want it, I will set the wheels in motion for construction. How does that sound?"

Nicolette realized Johnathon was all business and responded in turn. "Excellent, Mr. Fitzpatrick."

"Please help yourself to the water or wine. It's there on the coffee table." Johnathon grabbed the bottle of wine from the chilled bucket. He poured himself a glass and sat on the sofa.

Nicolette grabbed a water. Set her purse on the coffee table, reached for a cigarette from her purse. She started to lite it up.

Johnathon noticed her action. "Please don't smoke that cigarette. It leaves a terrible smell in the furniture."

Nicolette immediately put it away and sat on the opposite end of the couch from Johnathon.

"If I might ask you Mrs. Russo, how were you able to get away from your grandfather for the weekend?" questioned Johnathon.

"Please do not insult my husband's age or him. He has treated me well over the years. I take his kindness with the utter most respect. In answer to your question. My personal affairs are none of your concern."

"Very well." Johnathon drank some wine. "Back to business. I am willing to spend ten-million on your business, more if I have too. That being either new construction or rehab."

"Mr. Fitzpatrick, I have no desire to put a strain on your finances. If this endeavor hurts you financially in any way, we can end this right now."

"I assure Mrs. Russo, if I wasn't able to perform such a task, I would not risk my business to create yours. I was just letting you know because you mentioned a percentage of the business or money will be paid back with interest."

Nicolette sipped her water. "I do not wish you to own nothing that I possess. Therefore, what percentage of interest do you want to place on any amount that is spent on the business?"

"Let's say five-percent."

"Done." It wouldn't have mattered to Nicolette what number he would have thrown at her. "Paid in full after five years of profit or sooner."

"Very well Mrs. Russo. I will have my attorney draft the papers that way. We can sign those after we get the construction under way."

"Agreed."

There suddenly came a knock. "I will get that." Johnathon went to open the door. Upon entering, Elisa raced to hug Nicolette. Peter shook Johnathon's hand. "Well everyone… let's have at it. I have the plans laid out in my study."

They all followed Johnathon.

CHAPTER 23

The Gun Ranges

*J*ohnathon returned home about 4:30 a.m. that Monday morning and snuck into the bedroom with Catherine as she was sound asleep. He eased under the sheets and fell asleep. Catherine was so exhausted from her flight from New York the day before, that she didn't here Johnathon when he climbed into bed. However, she knew today was to be her day. As the daylight shined through the curtains, Catherine arose and saw her husband in bed. She went to make breakfast. After breakfast was ready, she woke Johnathon from his slumber with a gentle kiss to his forehead.

Johnathon opened his eyes. "What time is it Catherine?"

"It's eight o'clock, my love. You promised me that after I came back from New York you would spend time with me. Don't you remember? You promise me today, all day. We will do whatever I wanted. I let the cook go for today. I have readied breakfast for two. Now I await your company at the breakfast table, my sweet."

"Let me shower and freshen up and I'll be right there."

At the breakfast table...

"Honey, I'm just letting you know September will be at the executive party this Friday."

"September... yes. The black lady, right? You've been seeing? What an unusual name, but okay." Johnathon vaguely remembered their encounter. "I thought you did invite her to the last party we had."

"I did, but she couldn't make it. So I'm just making sure it's still ok."

"If it makes you happy, of course."

"I'll ask her. Thanks dear."

"Good. I'll be down in a few for breakfast and the day is yours Catherine."

Catherine was headed back to the kitchen when she remembered, "Oh… Johnathon, dress in something very casual. You might get dirty."

"We might get dirty?" Johnathon was puzzled. "Are we wallowing in mud today?"

Catherine disregarded the comment and made her way downstairs. Twenty minutes later Johnathon joined her. Johnathon was dressed in a light blue shirt and dark slacks with black patent leather shoes. Catherine was dressed in jeans and blouse with sneakers on.

Johnathon began to eat his eggs and toast. "The way you're dressed, I hope no one we know sees us. What do you have planned for today anyway?"

Catherine was exuberant. "It's a surprise."

After breakfast Johnathon and Catherine drove off in the BMW. Mrs. Jensen watched Catherine and Johnathon drive away together. Thirty minutes later, they reached their destination. Johnathon noticed this huge building. He observed a huge sign that said Jamal's Paint Gun Club, 'Fire for Fun'.

Johnathon spoke in a slightly harsh tone. "What side of town are we on? What are we doing here Catherine?"

"We are going against Team Red and we'll be Team Blue. I have already arranged it." Catherine was excited. "You're going to love it baby."

Johnathon was a little agitated. "You've arranged it? Arranged what?"

"You'll see sweetheart." Catherine went to the trunk of the car and opened it. Johnathon saw the case.

"What's in there?" asked Johnathon.

"Our weapons for the game."

"Weapons! You brought paint guns? That's what you put in the trunk. I thought it was a couple of sandwiches and some wine for a day at the beach or something."

Catherine lowered the trunk down with the case in hand. "Come on honey. It's fun. You'll enjoy it. I did, when September first brought me here."

"September… that figures." Johnathon mumbled to himself.

"What's that dear?"

Johnathon was a little annoyed about the situation. "Nothing Catherine. It's your day. Lead the way."

Once they entered, Catherine had Johnathon put on a vest and goggles. "If I get my shirt and slacks tainted with paint, guess who's buying me new clothing?"

"With pleasure my love. Now let's go have some fun."

Catherine led the way. After an hour of dodging paint shots and getting hit several times with the vest on, Johnathon was a little displeased about the entire event. However, he put on a face for Catherine as they headed back to the car.

"That was interesting. You only got hit once. You're pretty good."

"September and I do this twice a week." Catherine put the guns back in the trunk. She headed for the driver side. "But you ain't seen nothing yet."

Johnathon opened the door and sat in the passenger seat observing this new person that seemed to be his wife. "Ain't..." he repeated quietly. He was realizing September was having a huge influence on Catherine's mannerism and language. Catherine cranked the engine. "Where are we headed now?"

Catherine grinned. "It's another surprise."

Forty-five minutes later they were at the gun range.

"What is this?" asked Johnathon. "We just left a gun range."

"Come on in. Let me show you what I can do."

As Johnathon got out the car, he noticed Catherine headed straight to the trunk again. He read the title on the edifice. Another vast sign said, 'Big Jakes Gun Club'. She pulled out another case and carried it toward the building. Johnathon followed.

As they approached the building..."What's in this case? Let me guess? Guns."

Johnathon trailed her. Catherine signed in at the desk and took her booth. "Put these ear plugs in honey."

He took the ear plugs. She opened the case and to his amazement, two .45 Caliber weapons already loaded and ready to shoot. Johnathon was fully shocked and totally speechless. "Catherine you mean these are real weapons? I thought you were coming here to shoot BB Guns or something?"

"Watch this baby."

Johnathon put the ear plugs in his ears. He observed his coy, beautiful, meek wife that he thought he had in the palm of his hands place two bullets center mass into a silhouette. He watched her again fire five shots center mass into another silhouette.

Totally astonished. Johnathon took the plugs from his ears and yelled. "My goodness, Catherine! This is what September has been teaching you?"

"This is just for sport honey… pastime. You want to try?" Catherine stated with glee. Catherine placed the .45 on the deck. "September and I have signed up for competition in and around the local areas. You see how good I am."

"I see how good you are!" Johnathon was angry. He grabbed her tightly by the arm to make her face him. With an evil stare to her face, he acknowledged his disappointment of her actions. "I don't want my wife to be known as some gun toting, gun slinging cowgirl that has nothing better to do with her time than to fire bullets into a silhouette. Why don't you get into some charity or something and bake cookies for the homeless. You'd be good at that." Johnathon jerked her arm slightly to ensure she was receiving his message. "It's one thing to have a little fun with the paint guns, but gun competition? Are you crazy?"

Catherine eased her arm out of Johnathon's grip. "Well darling, I'm sorry. I found something I love to do and I'm sticking with it. I'm pulling my trophies and guns out of the cabinet at home and putting them on display for all to see."

"You've already been doing this without telling me!" Johnathon was visibly irate. "You have lost your mind. I don't want you to see this September person anymore."

Catherine's tone was aggressive. "You mean like I don't see you, but maybe once a week."

Johnathon just gazed at her briefly. "I'm leaving. Give me the keys." She handed him the keys from her pocket. Johnathon headed back to the car. He got in the driver's seat and awaited Catherine.

Moments later when she arrived at the car, she threw the case in the back seat and he spun off in a frenzy. Johnathon glared at her. "You know loaded guns can't be in the backseat."

"Well you're driving." Johnathon immediately pulled over to the side of the road and popped the trunk. Catherine grabbed the gun case from the backseat, got out of the car and tucked the case underneath a blanket in the trunk. She got back in the passenger seat and Johnathon burned rubber driving away.

Johnathon was bemused at her behavior. "What's gotten in to you Catherine? Your attitude has even gotten more belligerent. Your language, using the word, *ain't*. Wives of multi-millionaires do not use words like *ain't* or enter gun competitions."

Catherine spoke aggressively. "What do they do Johnathon? Sit at home, plan executive parties, bake cookies for charities and wait to be fucked and told what to do next in order to satisfy their husbands? Do you want a wife or a maid?"

"Wow! What an attitude. You're cursing at me and what that's supposed to mean?"

"You work all the time. You act like I don't even exist now that we're married. You give me a slot like I'm one of your clients that you have to appease once a week. You call that a marriage?"

Johnathan was completely caught off guard by Catherine's arrogance. "I see where this is going. This September woman is filling your head with suspicions about nothing. You need to leave her out of your life from this day forward. Do you understand me?"

Catherine raised her tone. "I will *not* stop seeing her. I will continue with the gun competitions and she will be at the executive party this coming Friday."

Johnathon's voice was intense with anger. "What if I say no?"

"Then you better get used to seeing a lot more of me. Because I will be at your office every day waiting for a moment to spend time with you, from the time you wake up, until the time you are ready to come home."

There was a long pause of silence by Johnathon. Then Catherine heard a heavy sigh. Johnathon's tone softened. "Fine! But I expect you to carry yourself with dignity and elegance as much as possible at these competitions."

"Have I ever done anything less?"

"I don't know since you've been hanging out with this woman and doing competitions behind my back."

Johnathon drove in the driveway and the garage door opened. Johnathon doesn't even look at Catherine as he got out of the car. "I don't even know you anymore." He slammed the car door and walked in the house.

"You haven't tried to know me!" Catherine followed him.

Immediately, Catherine entered the house and placed her .45's on the fireplace mantel. She pulled her other weapons out of hiding from the living room cabinet. She had her weapons placed in a specifically constructed solid oak wood trimmed gun case. The case was designed with mounted glass on top so any one can admire the two .45 Caliber's magnificent design without opening the box. A key was necessary to unlock the case to gain access to the weapons. Johnathon didn't say a word about her placement of her guns in the living room, along with a few trophies for all to see.

CHAPTER 24

Executive Party II

This Friday, when September arrived at the Executive Party, she observed all the men guests were in suits and ties. All the ladies were elegantly outfitted. September was donned in an elegant white party dress with one sleeve off and a slit down both sides of the dress displaying both thighs. She was not going to be out-done in style by any other woman there.

Catherine greeted her. "My, don't you clean up well."

"Hey, what can I say? I never know who I might meet. Who knows, I could find me a sugar daddy and be able to afford some of that stuff I'm always looking at with you."

"Not likely here. Most of the men are married and the single ones are still playing the game."

September was observing the men of the party. "I'm game for playing the game. Now do you want to step aside so I can find some of these single hones that may be looking for a sugar mommy?"

Catherine smiled and moved aside following behind her. September stepped further into the living room.

Catherine had displayed her trophies of marksmanship in the living room. Two .45 caliber guns with pearl handles were right next to her trophies in a locked glass case and the other two weapons were locked underneath the cabinet. September stopped in her tracks gazing at her trophies and guns that were displayed against the wall above the fireplace mantel. Catherine strolled up beside her.

"My... this is bold to display your trophies and guns. Johnathon let you do this?"

"No, I let me do this. This is my house too. He is barely here anyway."

"The guest haven't asked you about the trophies and the guns?"

"Of course they have and they've asked Johnathon too. He plays it off like a past time for me, but he doesn't like it. He's made that very clear."

"Well good for you Catherine. I am proud of you for standing up for yourself." September turned to face Catherine. "Now how are you hiding the bumps and bruises he put on you once he found out you did this behind his back?"

Catherine grinned. "No bumps, no bruises."

"Good." September glanced around the room only to see a couple of male guests she wouldn't mind engaging with.

"September let me get you a glass of wine."

September still gazed at one individual in particular. "No I see your butlers have that all under control. I will just grab one off those trays they are carrying around. You go mingle with the stuff shirts and other tight dresses. I will drink and observe. Thank you."

"Well make yourself at home."

"Ohhhh, don't worry, I intend to." September elegantly stepped away.

Catherine moved to socialize with the rest of the guest. While Johnathon entertained a guest in his home office, discussing business details.

After September's conversation with a particular gentleman, she stood near a wall attentive to the clientele in the room. Mark noticed her being observant of the guests. He went over to her.

September glanced at Mark from head to toe coming in her direction. She placed a smile on her face.

"Why is such a beautiful woman standing alone?" questioned Mark, with a wine glass in his hand.

"My, my... thank you very much. You're not half bad looking yourself. What do you do to make these executive parties of the Fitzpatrick's?"

"I am Vice President of the company." Mark stated proudly.

"My, my, again. I'm impressed. That must mean you are pretty smart at something."

Mark played coy, "Oh I can hold my own. What is your name? If I may ask?"

"It's September."

"Ohhh… so you're September."

September was flirtatious in body motions. She touched his hand and pulled it back. "You've heard my name." She took a sip of wine. "Good things I hope?"

"Actually, I just heard it a few days ago when Catherine stopped by the office. She mention she was meeting you later to go shoot guns or something like that the other day."

"Yes well, I have been teaching her how to shoot at Big Jake's Gun Club that I belong to. Now she is a member as well."

"Oh really, a member?" Mark sounded surprised.

"Yes, she has gotten quite good at it. Didn't you notice her guns and trophies in the living room?"

"Yes, she showed them to me."

"Well, she actually enjoys the competition between her and me. So much so, we got tired of beating up on each other that we thought we rather beat up on other competitors. We do tournaments in and outside the area. Catherine and I have smoked them all."

Mark raised an eyebrow. "I guess that's a good past time for two beautiful women?"

"When you are a single woman that walks alone, it's a good skill to have."

"Well remind me not to get on your bad side, Ms. September." Mark wasn't quite sure if he should continue the conversation. "If you will excuse me, I must make my rounds with the other guess. Perhaps in the future we could get together for drinks?"

September admired his masculine body structure. "Well let me give you my number."

"Just tell it to me Ms. September. I will remember."

"It's 213-777-8955."

"Got it. Well I must continue to mingle with the other guest Miss September for…."

September interrupted… "Miss Jones."

"Ms. Jones, until we meet again." Mark raised his wine glass and bowed his head. September stretched her right hand out for a kiss. He stared into her eyes briefly, he smiled. Then he swiftly kissed the top of her hand. He started to leave her.

"Wait. I didn't catch your name."

"It's Mark. Mark Atsu Townsend."

September gave a slight grin. "What kind of name is Atsu?"

"It's African."

"African? How does African fit in with Mark?"

"Perhaps over dinner sometime we can discuss, as it is a long story." Mark smiled and stepped away.

"Perhaps, Atsu." September mumbled. She watched him leave admiring his masculine body motion. She resumed her observation of the other guests.

Catherine saw Mark walk away from September and approached him. "What do you think of her Mark?"

"Miss Jones?" He glanced back in her direction. "She is something else Catherine." Mark took a sip of his drink. "Where is your old man? I don't mean to talk shop today, but that is what these executive parties are all about."

"Really Mark, now?"

"I will be brief Catherine, I promise."

"If he is not on the dining room floor or by the pool entertaining, you can rest assure he is in his study talking shop."

Mark nodded and smiled in jest. "Well I will go drag him out for you."

When Mark went down the hall to the study, he heard high tempered voices. He made hast to the door to try and hear what was being discussed. The closer he got, the volume of tone increased. When Mark reached the door, he listened with one ear.

"Look Tate… I'm not telling you again. The answer is no!"

"My boss can make your life miserable, or he can enhance your wealth beyond your imagination. Why not take the latter Mr. Fitzpatrick. You have until this Monday or you will see what my boss is capable of. Good day."

Mark overheard the last few words. He raced back to the dining room of the main party. He intermingled with the guests while glancing at this guy call Tate come down the hallway. Tate grabbed a glass of wine, gulped it down and left.

Johnathon emerged from his office and saw Mark speaking with some high profile individuals that have already invested in his company.

Johnathon interrupted Mark's conversation with some clients. "Excuse us Blake… Marcus." Johnathon pulled Mark by the arm to the side. He whispered. "Mark have you met her yet?"

"Met who?" Mark was surprised by the question. He thought Johnathon would have wanted to discuss what took place in his study.

"You know, September?"

"Well, yes. I just met with her a little while ago. She's something special."

"Really? Where is she?" questioned Johnathon.

Mark turned and gestured with his head in the area he left September. Johnathon took off in her direction like a bull headed for a red cape. September was mingling with a gentlemen guest.

"Excuse me Connor." Johnathon interrupted quickly. September drank some of her wine while Connor relocated. "So September."

September was unemotional as she stared into Johnathon's eyes. "I'm surprised you remember me. Our first meeting was a passing glance." She took another sip of wine.

Johnathon spoke in a whisper. "I'm not impressed with what you've been teaching my wife about guns and taking her to competitions."

"Well she seems to have a knack for it. So if I were you, I would just let her be herself instead of trying to shape her into what you want her to be."

Emotionally charged from her words, Johnathon's eyebrows rose and his lips tighten. Anger clearly engulfed his face. "Look!… You… low life, antagonizing bitc…"

September interrupted…"Ott, ott, ahh. Don't be angry. This is a party. You don't want your guests seeing veins pop and your face turning red. Making a scene at your own party would be *very* unprofessional. Wouldn't you say? Your red face wouldn't go well with that black tie you have on." September gave a slight sneer and took another sip of wine.

"She has made it clear that she's not going to stop seeing you, but I want you to know…" Johnathon leaned toward her ear and whispered. "I don't like it one damn bit." Then he stood six inches from her face.

September leaned forward into his ear. "You know… that's just too damn bad." She moved back from his ear, looked him straight in the eyes and spoke softly. "I've seen men like you that try to manipulate women because they don't want to lose their little show piece. I've dated one. I'm telling you to let your wife be her own person and respect her for who she is."

Johnathon outraged, moved so close to her face he could breathe her same breath. September didn't budge. "Don't give me advice. You're messing with the wrong man. I can make your life miserable."

September smiled. "I can make your life more miserable. I know your wife very well. Now if you don't want to see her on the front page of the New York Times or CNN with a picture of her skydiving off the Empire State Building, I suggest you go play with your stuffed suits and put a smile on your face. People will start to think things if you spend too much time with me. Now mosey along and entertain your guests, tough guy."

September quickly left Johnathon glaring at the wall. She swiftly found Connor and resumed her conversation. When Johnathon turned to face his guests, Mark observed emotional anxiety upon his face. It was obvious the confrontation between the two of them was not a pleasant one.

CHAPTER 25

Johnathon Approaches Mark about Tate

The next morning at the office on Monday, Johnathon sat behind his desk. He was deep into work for his own business as well as Nicolette's. He confirmed his own business deals for the week and ensured Elisa had everything she needed for designing clothes. He managed the construction of both buildings as planned for Nicolette. After all was in order he knew he had to approach honest Mark with a proposal that Tate had given him, plus his own endeavor for becoming a billionaire. He knew he couldn't just tell him straight out or should he?

Soon there came a knock at Johnathon's door. "Come in."

Mark opened the door and stuck his head in. While his left hand was leaning on the door handle, "Hey J, just checking to see if I need to go over this week's schedule with you and if you needed anything before I head to my office."

Johnathon was solemn in his response. "We need to talk Mark. Let's have dinner tonight at the Yacht Club. Meet me there at seven."

Baffled as to the tone of his voice and the matter that needed to be discussed out of office, Mark agreed. "Okaaay. Sure J." He paused in thought. "What's up? I mean its nine-thirty now. I can just sit down. I don't have a presentation until one and..."

Johnathon interrupted, stern in tone. "I don't want to talk here. Seven, at the Yacht Club."

Mark nodded and existed his office.

At the Yacht Club for dinner….

"The usual drinks gentlemen?" asked Rodney.

"No. Give me a Hennessey on the rocks, instead of a wine." stated Johnathon.

"Yes please Rodney, my usual." Spoke Mark.

Johnathon watched Rodney leave. "I'm going to be blunt and I need you to have an open mind."

"A Hennessey instead of wine. Must be really serious. I'm listening." Mark figured it had to be a problem stressing J out.

"Mark you remember the disk you brought me a few weeks ago?"

"Yes."

"Well, what was on the disk wasn't notes from a business meeting."

Mark leaned back in his chair, mystified by Jonathon's secrecy. "What's going on J?"

"I have been traveling to Colombia. I have met with some high level drug dealers that want us to help them smuggle their drugs into the U.S. without being detected."

Mark leaned forward. Callous in tone. "And just how are we supposed to do that?"

"They want to be able to detect any electrical equipment from coast guard ships, helicopters, radars or individuals within a twenty mile radius using a miniature stealth submarine." They also want to be able to carry a ton of dope in this sub. That deal is me.

"Again, and just how are we supposed to do that J?"

"Every ship has a radar system on board. Every helicopter has electrical systems that control their instruments. So, I told them I had the best of the best working for me and that you could figure it out. On that disk was the schematics of every ship and air device the coast guard has.

"Why did you do that Johnathon?" Cynically speaking…"You have all you need. You're successful financially. Our net worth as of last year was over three-hundred million dollars. Why do you want to run the risk of going to jail and losing all that you've worked for?" Mark's voice rose slightly. "We… are… in our infancy, J!" Mark pounded his fist on the table slightly.

"We get paid a half-billion dollars from the Cartel now. Half up front and half when the project is finished. We could be a billion dollar company within a year, instead of five or ten years. But that's not all, remember the guy Tate that came by my office?"

"Yeah."

"He wants us to develop an Electromagnet Pulse (EMP) weapon that can render any electronic device useless. The distance is three miles away. Further than that would be a plus. If their boats are infringed upon carrying their drugs, they can use it to render their would be captives powerless.

"If the Colombian Cartel is you, then where did Tate come from?"

"I don't know. He just showed up at the Executive Party one day and offered me a half-billion dollars for an EMP weapon."

"And you're going to take money from a man you don't even know?"

"I know. I have a quarter-billion dollars in an off shore account in an anonymous name right now, they insisted."

"Who are *they*? They promise to break a leg if you didn't cooperate?"

"Not yet, but I thought about it." Johnathon had an eagerness in his voice. "One time deal. A half-billion from the cartel and Tate... we're billionaires."

Mark shook his head. But what is the rush J in being a billionaire? We are gradually making our way to that point without doing anything illegal. The secret project I have going on right now for our company can net us billions, legally, and your business stays legitimate. Let's keep the business clean. What are you thinking?"

Johnathon was slightly angered. "What? What? You're working on something to save the U.S. from cyber-attacks? Teleportation? Hover Cars? What Mark? You won't tell me what it is or how long it would take you to finish whatever it is you're working on. This is now. You can do this within months or a year. I'm thinking I don't want to take another five years to raise three-hundred million dollars.

"What are you talking about months or a year? You have no idea what it takes to create a single weapon that fires EMP or developing a stealth sub carrying a ton of drugs under water undetected." Mark just stared at him. "And you know what? Neither do I. I haven't the slightest ideal."

"I know when you put your brain to work, you can do anything."

"You're crazy J. It would have to be a cloaking device that renders a mini-sub undetectable under water. In other words, a silent sub or what it takes to create a device that could detect moving targets at five-thousand yards in the water or air and render them powerless. It's next to impossible. When active sonar transducers emit an acoustic signal or pulse of sound into the water somehow we would have to render the transducer incapable of detecting the sound waves of the sub. If not, the sub should be able to detect the ship's engine noise or vibration that's in the area without it being seen or heard twenty miles away. Isn't that what you said?"

"Yes. Something like that."

"The EMP, I would have to duplicate what the military has already researched in order to get an idea of where to even start. Without that blueprint it could take months of research to develop it."

"They are willing to wait. Whatever it takes to get the job done. I want more money now." Johnathon paused. "Listen to this Mark, I was thinking instead of building some type of cloaking device for their sub and motion detectors, plus the EMP weapon, we could kill two birds with one stone.'"

"How? How... Johnathon did you get yourself in such a huge mess? Two illegal deals."

"I have an idea that could only take you months. We have motion detectors just not at the range they are asking for. You could tweak those. As for the cartel, they know it won't be easy, so you have all the time you need. The wait will be worth the reward."

Mark was unsettled. "They each want something different."

"Maybe I can sell the Cartel on just the EMP weapon? It would accomplish the same mission."

"You can try." Mark leaned back in his chair again. "I don't think it would work because they want to carry tons of drugs as well. There strategies are different."

"If no ships or air craft can come close to them, they can carry tons of drugs on their boats."

Mark thought. "Maybe. How much are the cartel paying again?"

'Half-a-billion."

"And Tate?"

"Half-a-billion."

"If I do this, it could land us both in jail."

"Not if we play our cards right."

"You can't spend a billion dollars if you're locked up for the rest of your life." Mark saw the waiter coming and spoke no more.

Their drinks arrived. "Would you gentlemen like to order?" Asked Rodney.

"No thank you Rodney." Spoke Mark. Johnathon and Mark watched the waiter leave. "J if you crawl into bed with the cartel, one time is never enough. Once you give them what they want, they come back for more. You've spent these last five years calling the shots for your own business. You're willing to give all that up for a billion dollars? And you don't even know who this Tate guy is or works for. This just sounds ludicrous Johnathon."

"I'll tell you what Mark. I can make it a one-time deal for both projects one-billion each. With a price tag like that, nobody will want to come back asking for anything else."

Mark shook his head, realizing Johnathon hadn't heard a word he had said. "It's never a one-time deal J. If you give your soul to the devil, you will never get it back." Johnathon shook his head. "Johnathon it never ends well. The devil always wins."

"I will ensure we win. One-time Mark, just one-time. We will never do work for either of them again, I promise."

Mark took a sip of his drink and rested back in his seat. "One-billion each. What makes you think they will pay such a steep price?"

"Let's say one-billion dollars, take it or leave it. That maybe enough to deter them from pursuing the projects. Then we won't have to worry about it." Johnathon smiled.

"You think they won't flinch on asking for that much money? They could just say the project or your life." Mark sipped on his drink.

"If they kill me, they won't get it. If that's my price and they want it bad enough, they'll meet it." Johnathon spoke as if he was willing to sacrifice anyone or anything to make this happen.

Mark was in thought. He questioned Johnathon's logic. However, one billion dollars was a lot of money. "If I do this… it has to be just this once. I will not have my life controlled by gangsters."

"Yes. Sure. Of course." Johnathon smiled.

"When you put that many positive words together, it sounds like you're lying."

"I will make it clear that we are done. Let's toast to Two-billion." Johnathon raised his glass. Mark was hesitant. "Trust me Mark, they will know nothing about you. It's just this one time and we will be billionaires."

"I don't need the money J. My two million a year is good. But I am only doing one project at a time and I can get whomever I need to assist me?"

"Yes. Let's do this one thing and I will never ask you to take such a risk again. One-billion will be yours. No one will ever know you're the man behind the scenes."

Mark paused. "I love you man, but I think you're making a mistake by biting off nothing you can chew. I just have a bad gut feeling about everything."

"Just this once Mark. I'll make it work."

With a heavy sigh…"Alright. Just for you J." Mark lifted his glass and they both drank to this future endeavor. "To do this and come up with the technical device needed to detect against the FBI and coast guard, you said their devices are all on the disk? Plus the schematics for the sub that they want."

"Yes. That's what's on the disk I have. I told them what you might need. They retrieved the data. I have broken the encryption and put it in plain language for you to understand. As for Tate, I don't have anything. Maybe they already have what you need for the design and mechanics of the weapon."

"Ok, I will need those if they have something."

Johnathon was delighted. "I will ask Tate. Thanks Mark. I know once you commit, you are a man of your word."

"I don't want my name ever revealed to either of them." Mark gave him a stern expression.

"And it won't be Mark. These deals are strictly on me. I'll try to sell them on one device. But if I can't, while you are working on the cartel devices, can't you manage another team for the EMP weapon?"

"Now you're trying to tell me how to do it. I'm a perfectionist. I don't want to concentrate on more than one project at a time, especially of this magnitude. You know what J? Forget I said yes. Let me think about it for a couple of days? I think the money has left my head spinning. I'm not thinking straight about all the effort that it's going take to even get one done, not to mention two. These are massive projects, I just don't know." Mark downed another swallow of his drink.

"Absolutely, I thought you might have some reservations. I know you are a man of morals and integrity. I respect that about you. That's why if you decide not to do it, I will understand. I am not going to twist your arm on this one. I don't want your conscious bothering you. But I have to let you know if you don't do it, I'll have to find someone else."

"You're putting a guilt trip on me." Mark drank some more.

Johnathon could see the discontent in Mark's face. "Thank you Mark. You know you're the only one I can trust."

"I'm not going to jail."

"Of course not. I will take care of everything. Mark you know I love you like a brother. Help me out on this one." Johnathon gave an expression of assurance that everything would work out by giving Mark a slight smile. He hoped he would give in.

Mark sipped his drink and stared at Johnathon. "Hmmm."

CHAPTER 26

Swim Suit Executive Party III

At this particular Executive Party, Mark was socializing with guests in the living room. He noticed Catherine standing alone by the pool with other guests mingling in the area. Catherine was dressed in a one piece, tight fitting black bathing suit with white trim all around. One trap was over her shoulder and the other shoulder was bare. Mark had on loose fitting black trunks, Versace sandals, with his masculine six-pack abs exposed.

Mark approached with a glass of wine in his hand. "What a lovely idea with the swimsuits Catherine. It's a beautiful day for it."

"It wasn't my idea, it was Johnathon's." Catherine stated with wine in hand.

"J's ideal?"

"Yes."

"Well, I like it. It gives everyone a chance to see how we look underneath the tight dresses and three piece suits."

"To bad that when we pull off our clothing, we can't see what's in our hearts."

"Would you really want to know that much about anyone you meet Catherine?"

Catherine's roving eyes observed her guests. "I think so Mark. At least you could identify the snakes from the kittens."

Mark changed the subject. "You and Johnathon must enjoy this pool area you have here. I don't know if I ever told you, but it is quite breathe taking. I love this portion of your home the most. The décor, so intimate and relaxing."

"The only time we come out here since our wedding, is to entertain. However, Johnathon does love his moments out here alone. He takes a glass of wine, an expensive cigar and relaxes in the pool just looking up at the stars at night."

"You're not a part of that ritual?"

"I think he takes the cigars out because he knows I hate the smoke. He knows I won't join him if he lights up. So that alone prevents any intimacy that could possibly take place between us out here."

Mark drank some of his wine. "I'm sorry. Where is the old man anyway?"

"You know if he is not out here by the pool or jabbering business in the living room, he is conducting business in his study."

"Of course. I haven't seen your friend September, is she coming? Or did Johnathon stop that all together?"

Catherine responded with a slightly aggressive tone. "I live here too Mark. Johnathon doesn't always have the last word." She gave him an angry glance. "She should be here soon." Catherine walked away.

Mark watched her leave, totally stunned, as Catherine had never spoken to him like that before. He thought perhaps September was making a difference in her mannerism.

Meanwhile, in the study Johnathon was conducting business.

"Mr. Fitzpatrick one billion dollars is very steep. I am here to offer you the other quarter-billion before the project is complete as a show of good faith."

"One. One billion. Take it or leave it Mr. Tate. I really don't need your business."

"Let me make a phone call."

Johnathon watched Tate stepped to the opposite side of his study.

Minutes later. "Alright Mr. Fitzpatrick. You will have one billion placed in your account when the project is complete."

"Good. I appreciate you waiting a little longer to get a 'yes' from me. It wasn't easy getting people on board."

"No problem. We want what you can deliver. Have your people began working?" asked Tate.

"They will start after I have received half payment in my account. By the way, do you have any information or data on EMP?"

"I don't know."

"Otherwise, my team will have to start from scratch. I mean research, collect materials, experiment and heaven knows what else. This could take some time if you have nothing."

"Consider it done. I will be in touch with you next week."

"Great Tate. To becoming business partners." Johnathon lifted his glass.

Tate followed Johnathon's lead and gulped his wine down. Tate placed his glass on Johnathon desk. "Good Day." Tate turned the knob on the door, paused and faced Johnathon. "Oh by the way, was the swimsuit party just to make sure I wasn't packing any steel to threaten you with?"

Johnathon spoke sarcastically. "On the contrary, I just wanted to see what you looked like in swim trunks."

Tate laughed and walked out.

CHAPTER 27

Catherine and September on another Adventure

*O*n this day Catherine took September horseback riding at her country club. While trotting along a scenic route on Country Club grounds, Catherine expressed her concern over Johnathon being more distant than he has before.

"September, I'm a little more apprehensive about my relationship with Johnathon."

"Noooo?....Less attentive to you than when I first met him?" Sarcastically spoke September.

"Yes. Now he barely comes home at all. He's says he's with Mark, but I'm afraid to ask Mark for fear of him mentioning it Johnathon."

"It would be like you checking up on him. Then just ask him Catherine. Come out and say what's on your mind. Are you fucking somebody else?"

"I can't do that. I don't want to give him a reason to leave me acting like the jealous wife. What if he really is working diligently for our future?"

"Yeah don't say anything. That's what he loves about you. You're the church girl, the happy-go-lucky girl, the nothing bothers you girl, and the I'm sorry honey-type girl, even if you are right and he's wrong."

"What if he comes out and tells me the truth? That he is having an affair. What am I to do?"

"Leave him. You heard of alimony?"

"I can't do that."

"Don't you get it Catherine? You're not the one he wants as a wife, in bed, or on his arm. Only when he needs you to be there for him. For instance, hosting executive parties or going to dinner at a clients' house. I look at him and see him wanting the wild one, the ring my bell one, wanting someone that will make his body explode with ecstasy without taking the drug... he wants..."

"Stop! Just stop. September." Catherine interjected. "That's not true. My husband loves me."

"On what planet Catherine?"

"I think I am over reacting to his efforts in trying to become a billionaire. I just need to be completely trust worthy and when he reaches that goal, life will be *us,* together, all the time."

"Ooooh, don't be so naive. You're just trying to make excuses for him. You want to tell yourself he's working for you, so the abandonment you feel when he is not with you won't hurt so badly."

"I'm not trying to cover any hurt. I just love him so much."

"I don't doubt your love for him. I doubt his love for you."

"He loves me September." Catherine insisted.

"In your fantasy world or this one where he sees you by appointment only?"

Catherine spoke earnestly. "He still loves me. I know it. Our anniversaries are so romantic, he accommodates me like he did on our wedding day."

"One day out of 365 days for the last five years. Yeah... that's true love." Spoke September. "If he loves you so much, then where is the family? Why aren't you two swimming in children? It's not like you can't afford to have seven or eight."

"I wanted children, but he didn't. But he agreed to let me have one to keep me occupied."

"To keep you occupied? My word, it sounds like he's allowing you to have a hobby versus a family. So what happened?"

"I was two months pregnant. Johnathon was working late as usual one night. I started spotting. I didn't think much of it at first, but as the evening grew late, the spotting increased. Suddenly there was so much blood, I knew I was having a miscarriage. My stomach hurt so badly, I could barely walk. I dragged myself from the bathroom to the bedroom. I tried to reach my cell phone off the end table. To no avail, I passed out before my hand got to the phone. Fortunately, Johnathon did come home late that night. He found me by the bed and called 911."

"Ohhhh, I'm so sorry Catherine."

"We tried once more and the same thing happened. The second time I almost died, because I had lost so much blood before Johnathon came home."

"You passed out again and almost bleed to death. Why was he not being more attentive to you, if he knew you might be prong to having a miscarriage?"

Catherine was on the defensive. "He is working hard to make sure that if we have children, they will never want for anything."

"Are you ever going to try again?"

"I would love to, but I'm afraid. It's so heart breaking. So I take precautions now to prevent any more pregnancies."

"I am so sorry, Catherine."

They got off their horses when they came upon a beautiful lake. "Can we just sit here a moment?" Catherine dismounted and took a seat on the grass by the water. Catherine started to gaze out over the small lake on the grounds. September got off her horse and sat beside her. "Say… what happen to you? Did that old fling prevent you from coming to the executive swim party I had the other day?"

"I'm sorry I missed the pool party. But Antonio did come back that night. He rang my bell in more ways than just the front doorbell."

Catherine observed the open land and smiled. "Good, perhaps you can give him a second chance."

"Maybe. May I ask you a question Catherine, if you don't mind?"

"Of course. I consider you a dear friend. Ask me anything September."

"Do you suspect Johnathon of foul play?"

Catherine deliberated for a moment. "Sometimes that thought crosses my mind. I know his late hours are constant. I know he is doing it for the both of us and I am hoping that one day he will want to try and have a child again."

"Do you really believe this man wants children… with you?"

"Once he reaches that monetary goal he is so passionate about getting, I know our lives will be different. The time he is putting in now will be the time we will be spending together in the near future. Hopefully with a family. I have to have faith and trust that there is no other woman and the work he is putting in, is for us."

"Catherine as your friend, I don't see it that way. Can't you see or you don't want to see? He's using you. The late nights, all the trips away from home without taking you along. They can't all be just business?"

"Yes, yes they can." Catherine grew angry. "You just don't understand. What's a marriage without trust?"

"You've said that before. Okay, I'm not going to fight you on this, but just do one thing."

"What's that?"

"Be yourself. If you wanna wear blue jeans to a restaurant, wear them. If you want to fly to Paris with tennis shoes on, wear them. Whatever you used to do before you met him, do it. Marriage is supposed to be what he loved so much about you when he met you. Not trying to make you into someone he wants you to be."

"I hear you September."

"All I'm saying is… don't alter the lifestyle you love. Stop living under his umbrella."

"September if I please him, he will always love me."

"How far has thinking like that gotten you?"

Catherine became irate again. Her tone was slightly harsh. "You don't get it! I *love* him. I trust him. That's everything right there September, love and trust." Catherine glanced at her. September didn't say a word. "Let's ride back. I don't want to hear anymore from you. I got this."

September didn't push back. She started to observe the beauty of the land, while holding her horse's reins. Catherine got on her horse. She watched September just sit there. A few seconds later Catherine trotted back to the Club House. September wasn't far behind.

CHAPTER 28

The Beginning of a Love Affair

Johnathon and Nicolette met for months off and on. They worked together professionally, buying the buildings, positioning equipment, and hiring employees. Elisa and Nicolette established a network with other fashion designers. Elisa oversaw design and production when Nicolette couldn't be there.

As everything started to come together, Nicolette was so excited. The opening of her designer store called Reneiri Fashions was just a week away. She met Johnathon at his condo at ten in the evening to discuss the grand opening.

Johnathon's silent alarm went off to let him know someone had entered his suite. When he reached the living room, Nicolette stood there, beautifully dressed as always. He gazed lovingly into her eyes, he leaned toward her face, she turned her lips away and he kissed her on the cheek. Nicolette placed her small hand held black purse upon the coffee table and sat on the sofa.

"I have invited all the fashion designers, press, and fashion store owners I am associated with to be at your opening Mrs. Russo. Since I cannot be there, be sure to mingle with all of them. Some of them can do great things in aiding the further development of your company. Talk to Amari Hadiza, a female African designer, her country is deep into exotic colorful fashion. Just say you know me."

Nicolette had a saddened expression upon her face. "I am sorry you can't be there to introduce me yourself."

"It's best. Now, I have a chilled bottle of your favorite wine in my refrigerator. Allow me, unless you prefer a Seltzer water?"

"Please do Mr. Fitzpatrick. I will take a glass of wine."

Nicolette relaxed on the sofa and awaited his return. Johnathon set two glasses before her on the table. "Say 'when' Mrs. Russo." He began to pour.

"When."

Johnathon handed her glass to her and poured himself one, then sat beside her. "To your success. I have no doubt your designs will take off."

They both took a sip of their wine and placed their glasses on the coffee table.

"I believe we have reached a point since we are now partners that you can call me Nicolette."

"I have always been at the point where you can call me Johnathon."

Nicolette smiled. "Mr. Fitzpatrick…"

Johnathon gave her an estranged look as if 'Johnathon' was what he was hoping to hear.

"I mean Johnathon." Nicolette stated in a solemn voice. "I have to admit, I never thought this day would ever come true for me. You have been very meticulous in your efforts to make this happen on my behalf."

"Well, I do get ten percent until you pay me back, with interest. So we both benefit."

"I also want to thank you for being a perfect gentleman and an excellent business man. I just don't know how to thank you enough."

"You can thank me by not failing. Your success is our success and that is how I see it." Johnathon rose from the sofa. "I have a meeting to attend to with my VP at the Yacht Club. I must leave now. I believe you have everything you need for the opening. If not, I'm just a phone call away. So if you will excuse me, I need to gather some papers. I will walk you out." Johnathon stepped away.

"Johnathon wait." Nicolette stood from the sofa. She moved closer to him, stared into his eyes and kissed him on the cheek. "Thank you… for everything."

Johnathon was mesmerized by the look in her eyes. He had a desire to sweep her off her feet, but he remained professional. "The pleasure is all mine, Nicolette. Meet me back here after the opening is over. Let me know how it went."

Nicolette continued an adoring glare upon his face. Johnathon had seen this look before. "A VP at the Yacht Club at this hour of night, what day is it?"

"Excuse me?" Johnathon was puzzled.

Nicolette was being coy and malicious. "What day is it? Is it Ms. Thursday's turn at ten tonight?"

Johnathon laughed. "Oh you think you know me now." Johnathon slowly leaned forward and gently kissed her quickly upon her lips. He leaned back waiting to see her reaction. A glowing passion beamed from her face. Nicolette's arms flew around his neck so quickly even he was surprised. She pulled his lips back to hers. Johnathon embraced the moment and began to unzip her dress. Following his lead, Nicolette unzipped his pants. Both their clothing fell to the floor. He admired her beautiful well structure body as she unbuttoned his shirt. When the shirt fell from his shoulders, his physique delighted her expectations. He wrapped his arms around her naked waist and slowly eased her to the sofa, kissing her breast and lips franticly.

Nicolette, breathing slowly in heated lust, asked… "Aren't you going to miss your appointment?"

So involved was his desire to ravish her body, Johnathon responded. "What appointment?"

He continued his quest of pursuing every inch of her body with his lips and hands. Soon the emotional craving to truly connect as one, overwhelmed them both. The intrusion of Johnathon's lower body extremity into Nicolette was a welcomed ecstasy that they both embraced with extreme pleasure.

<h1>CHAPTER 29</h1>

Mark and Johnathon on the Stealth Sub

As weeks passed, Johnathon met with Mark once again to discuss the status of his research and progress. Johnathon entered the research lab in the basement of his building. Mark was toiling away on schematics and producing tech items to ensure the success of the sub.

"Mark where are we with getting this done? I've got Tate and my Colombian contact scrawling up my butt every month on this."

Mark pulled out a new design from the one Johnathon had given him to work from on the stealth sub. He spread the new design of the sub across a hug marble table, square in shape.

"I couldn't work from the one your Colombian friend gave you. The sub won't be able to deploy more than one-hundred feet rather than five-hundred with over a ton or more of drugs on it. It won't have to deploy that deep if we can get these two devices incorporated on the sub." Mark pointed to sections of the sub that needed to be altered. The wiring was all wrong and this connector to the mainframe of the panel was too large. So I had to redesign the connector." Mark showed Johnathon the old schematics of the sub compared to his new design. "Look at the wiring here." Mark pointed to the old design. "Now if we can connect our Quantum chip… here," Mark pointed to the mainframe of the submarine dash console on his design. "and the technical panel here, the instrument dash board I designed will be able to keep the sub silent and undetected from any ship's radar system. Plus the sub won't have to dive so deep with tons of drugs in order to be undetected." My team and I built the prototype with my design. We just need to test how the sub maneuvers with the weight and not be detected by radar." Johnathon observed Mark's new schematics.

"Well, if this works, how can they turn it down?" Thought Johnathon.

"We believe we have developed the devices to do what they want."

"Fabulous. After you test and it works, show me and I will present it. What about the EMP weapon for Tate?"

"There is only one problem."

"And that is?

"With Tate's EMP design none of the technical gears and apparatuses I created will fit in a gun type form. Instead of a gun. It has to be a mechanism, like a remote controller. I already have my prototype built. I have it over here. In the vault. It hasn't been tested yet. "You will need to show Tate my design and these specifications. See if he approves."

"If it works, I don't think he'll care if it's the shape of a banana."

"Let's do it my way, or it could take another year trying to figure out how to incorporate his design to get what he wants." Added Mark.

"It's already been one year for you to put all this together. That's why he gave you the schematics to the Electronic Magnetic Pulse (EMP) type weapon. To help you expedite the time. I don't know if Tate's employer wants to wait any longer." Johnathon paced the floor. "Whatever you have that works, I'm sure he will go along with it."

"Look." Mark goes to another table and unveils a huge device. Johnathon followed. "You see our design for the EMP system. It may be a little bulky, but I assure it will work. We will be ready to test by the end of the week. Just let your friends know I had to make the devices my way."

Johnathon stopped pacing and stood before Mark. "Ok... ok. Put the schematics on a disk and I will get it to Tate and my Colombian friend and we'll go from there."

"There is no compromise on this. Shove it down their throats if you have to, but this is it. With my design it will do everything they want done. Tell them, you don't tell an artist how to paint."

Johnathon smiled. "I will deliver the message. How long before testing is complete?"

"Give us another three to four weeks to finish testing to ensure no glitches. If all goes well, they will have their devices in a month. So I will keep you posted."

"Great. I don't want the blueprints until testing is complete. I will just tell them a little more time and they will have what they need."

Mark nodded. Johnathon walked out. He was jubilant about being a billionaire in almost a month.

CHAPTER 30

The Love Affair

On this day, after work, Johnathon visited Nicolette in her store in Los Angeles. In this building she had her office and a huge twenty-thousand square foot room built for the creation of her designer fashions. Johnathon walked past Elisa on her way out of the building. She smiled and nodded her head. Johnathon passed sewing tables, cases of thread and racks of beautiful expensive colorful fabric to reach Nicolette. Johnathon tip-toed to Nicolette's elegant office. It was designed with a beautiful black leather sofa, a medium sized Serpentine Mahogany desk, modern lights overhead, huge eight chair conference table and a black leather guest seat that sat in front of her desk. She was shuffling papers and checking her laptop.

Johnathon stood in her doorway, he observed her deep in thought. Nicolette was so focused, she didn't notice an intruder in her doorway.

"All work and no play makes for a dull evening."

To Nicolette's surprise… she looked up from her laptop. "What are you doing here?"

Johnathon moved forward and sat in her black leather guest chair. "You don't answer phone calls and you don't let me know when you're in town. To be truthful, I've been pretty busy myself, with work of course."

"Of course."

"Now that everything is pretty much under control, I wanted to see you again."

"After all these months, I thought you had gone back to things as usual." Spoke Nicolette casually.

"I had."

"Isn't Elisa keeping you informed of the business profits and event scheduling?"

"Yes and things are going nicely. But why aren't you informing me? You're my partner?"

"You said it yourself. Things were back to normal."

"If you're implying my lady associates, yes. But I told you they are my pastime, not my passion."

"Yes, well, why did Elisa tell you this time when I was here, when I have asked her not too? What did you promise her?"

"I told her all I wanted to do was take my business partner out to dinner."

"Liar. I've avoided you all these months for a reason."

"And that is…?"

"I was honoring your tradition and trying not to interfere with your routine of beautiful women at your beckon call or repetitive schedules."

Johnathon smiled. "The two times we had sex at my condo, I would have thought you couldn't stay away from me."

"The first time was to thank you for starting my business. The second time was a mistake. I only came by that evening to let you know how the grand opening went. Since it did happen, I felt I didn't owe you anything but money."

"Now, that I have caressed you tightly and know those sweet moments of surrender, I kinda like making love to you." Johnathon moved from his chair and got closer to Nicolette. He turned her swivel chair to him. He bent down so he could stare into her eyes.

Nicolette sat firm with her back straight and arms resting on her seat. She gulped slightly, trying not to expose her desire for him. "Are you searching for something Mr. Fitzpatrick?"

"We're back to Mr. Fitzpatrick, are we?"

Trying to resist her desire for him, she remained firm in her spoken words. "We're business partners, right? We must keep it that way."

"Well business partner, when I look into your eyes, I get lost in your beauty and all I want to do is find myself in you."

Nicolette slightly smiled, but remained unyielding. "Cute, but I do my very best not to concede to temptation."

"Like you did after the grand opening?"

"I shouldn't have come by after the opening celebration that night. But... I..." Nicolette bowed her head for a moment and then looked back at Johnathon earnestly. Her tone was soft and solemn. "I felt a certain way."

"Like you do now." Johnathon shifted his lips closer to her's.

Nicolette eased her chair back a little. "Don't flatter yourself, Mr. Fitzpatrick. It was just that... I felt that whole evening with the designers, investors and other guests, the drinking and socializing, that you should have been celebrating it with me. My dream had finally come true." Tears formed in her eyes. "Without you, none of that would have been possible. That's why I came back that night and I shouldn't have. I'm sorry."

Johnathon leaned closer and kissed her lips gently. She didn't resist. "Hmmm." He licked his lips. "I love the sweet taste of your lips. It's almost like dessert." Nicolette just smiled. He stood straight up. "Come." He stretched out his hand. "After a hard day, I know you can use a good dinner... business partner, and that's all it will be."

Nicolette took his hand and rose from the chair. She grabbed her purse. Johnathon led the way out. She turned out the lights to her office and locked the building door.

Once in Johnathon's car, he drove straight to his condo.

Nicolette recognized the direction he was going. It was not to a restaurant. "I thought you were taking me to dinner?"

"Once I found out you were here, I had a chef to make dinner for the two of us."

Several minutes later, they both entered his condo. Johnathon yelled when he walked in. "Chef Alfred, we're here."

"Very good sir. The table is ready on the terrace sir, just as you specified. Would you prefer drinks before dinner sir?" Chef Alfred stood there and waited for a response.

Nicolette had sat on the sofa. Johnathon came behind her and massaged her neck. "Relax." He continued to rub her neck and shoulders. Nicolette relaxed under the motion of his hands. "Ohhh, you feel tight." He leaned and whispered in her ear. "I have chilled Seltzer water or your favorite bottle of wine. Which do you prefer?"

"I will take that wine. It has been a long day."

Johnathon spoke. "Chef Alfred, bring the bottle of wine and two glasses please." Johnathon made his way around the sofa and sat beside Nicolette.

Nicolette whispered in Johnathon ear. "Can you release the chef? Whatever he has cooked, just have him place it on the terrace and leave. I just need to unwind without being professional."

"Your wish is my command." Johnathon got up from the sofa and relayed that message to the chef.

Chef Alfred did as instructed and soon left the condo suite. Johnathon joined Nicolette back on the sofa. He poured the wine for two.

"Why didn't you just take me to a restaurant and let me go home?"

Johnathon handed her the glass of wine. "I don't know. I feel now that your business is beginning to take off, I need to get to know Nicolette again. It was so much fun working with you to get it started, I kind of miss that."

Nicolette took a sip of wine. "I haven't changed. I'm doing exactly what you would expect me to do and that's run the business so it will succeed. I can't do that if every time I come to L.A. I'm trying to meet with you in between your affairs, when it's not necessary."

Johnathon took his glass of wine and Nicolette's from the coffee table. "Come. Let's eat." Nicolette followed him to the terrace. He put the glasses on the table and pulled a chair out for Nicolette to sit. She complied and he sat across from her.

"Why all of this Mr. Fitzpatrick?"

Johnathon was still captivated with her beauty. "Since our last encounter, I've missed you."

"Mr. Fitzpatrick there is no need for the condo, the wine or the ambiance of this evening. We are two married people who have individuals who love us. There is no reason to go down this path of deception. You should take me home."

Johnathon hit a button from a remote that sat on the table. The outside lights dimmed, romantic music began to play. "Let's have dinner first."

Nicolette wasn't impressed. "Home Mr. Fitzpatrick."

"That's funny. You speak of deception. It's too late for that. Isn't it? It appears you have done an excellent job of hiding your business from Giovanni."

"That's different."

Johnathon walked over to her and reached for Nicolette's hand. She placed her hand in his. He pulled her from her chair. Johnathon slowly placed his arms around her waist and pulled her body close to his. So close, their lips almost touched, but didn't. Then he took both hands and placed them in his. They danced slowly from side to side. "I don't want anything, but this moment with you." He stared into her eyes lovingly.

Nicolette's emotional desire was ramping up. She wanted to resist. "I can't do this."

"If you really feel that way, answer me three questions. If either one of your answers are no, I will drive you back to your hotel, after we eat." Johnathon smiled. "Scouts honor."

Nicolette beamed slightly. She stopped dancing and gazed into his eyes with both her hands in the center of his chest. "What are your three questions?"

"Did you want me the first time we made love?" softly spoke Johnathon.

Nicolette's smile disappeared. Her eyes were intimately focused on his. In an enticing voice she proclaimed. "Yes."

"Did you want me the second time we made love after your grand opening?"

Faintly, Nicolette replied. "Yes."

Johnathon held her tighter and came less than an inch from kissing her lips. "Do you want me now?"

Nicolette swallowed gently, she hesitated slightly and pronounced adoringly. "Yes."

She didn't resist when Johnathon kissed her affectionately. She immediately removed her hands from his chest and wrapped them around his neck. He removed her beige jacket from her arms, and then her blouse. He unzipped her black pants from the side of her waist as she removed his shirt. Now that Johnathon had her completely naked, he picked her up and whisked her away to the master bedroom. He walked into a completely candle lit bedroom with red rose pedals all over the floor.

When Nicolette saw the rose pedals, her expression of amazement gleamed from her face. "Is this for me?"

"I had hoped so."

"What if I hadn't come?'

"They would've still been for you." He kissed her lips again and continued to carry her to the master bathroom. There were more red rose pedals upon the bathroom floor with a stemmed red rose on the side of the tub. There was a lit candle at each corner of the bathtub. Nicolette was in awe. Once he reached the tub, he gently lowered her into perfumed scented warm liquid, filled with bubbles. Red rose pedals laid on top of the suds. As she relaxed from the warmth of the water, Johnathon removed his pants and shoes. He joined her. Once in the tub on the opposite side, he handed her the stemmed red rose. "This is for you." Nicolette inhaled the fragrance of the rose and smiled at Johnathon. He took her left foot and placed it on his chest and began messaging it with his warm soft hands. He kissed each toe and performed the same motions with the other foot. Nicolette dropped the rose to the floor and leaned back in the tub. Her eyes were closed as she enjoyed the relaxing movement of Johnathon messaging her feet. He soon got on his knees. With both hands on her thighs, he massaged both legs at once, stroking them gently up and down. Nicolette never opened her eyes. He took his right hand and slowly rubbed up her inner thigh until he reached a very sensitive area. Nicolette gave a small gasp. He was gliding his middle finger in and out slowly of her lower body. Nicolette groaned with pleasure of every movement of his actions. Suds covered Nicolette from the neck down, Johnathon then gently blew the soap suds away from Nicolette's breasts. Once they were exposed, he kissed each breast briefly. Then he took a rose pedal from the suds. Johnathon slowly stroked the rose pedal around and around each nipple until it had harden. He kissed each breast softly after each motion. Nicolette moaned a little louder as he still maintained his slow thrust of intrusion underwater and manipulated the rose pedals upon her breast. So tantalized by the movements of Johnathon's hands and lips, Nicolette grabbed him by the neck and kissed him as if he were a long lost lover. Johnathon responded to her emotional outburst by returning the passionate kiss and replaced his hand in the water with his harden extremity. His thrust upon her inner body intensified over and over again. Water and suds exploded to the bathroom floor like a tidal wave. No words were spoken, only screams of passion echoed off the bathroom walls.

CHAPTER 31

A Gift To September

The next morning when Johnathon started to leave for work, he saw September drive up. He also looked across the street and noticed Ms. Jenson with her binoculars as usual watching Catherine and September drive away. He got into his car and went to the office. That day September took Catherine to Fort Moore Army Base to the obstacle course. They ran it twice. They had lunch on base and then hit the racquet ball courts and later to the gun range.

As the afternoon wined down, Catherine took September for a body make over. They got their nails done, body massage, and hair done. When September drove back to her house late that afternoon, there was a brand new Mercedes Benz AMG Roadster 3D SQUIR in front of her house.

September was shocked. "What is that car doing in front of my house? If that's Tony, he is going to get an ear full."

They got out of the car. September admired the vehicle. "Boy this is a beauty. He doesn't have that kind of money just getting out of jail." She glanced at Catherine and continued to admire the car. "Do you think...?" Catherine just watched her move around it. "But he is not climbing back into my life by buying me stuff." She took another look at the car. "However, it is an excellent start." September scanned the area, she waited for Tony to pop out from somewhere. Minutes past. September stared at Catherine. "So where is he?"

"It's not Tony." Smiled Catherine.

September eyeballed the car once again. "If it's not Tony then..." September saw Catherine had this huge grin on her face. "It's from you? Why would you do something like this for me? It's beautiful Catherine." Once more, she walked around the car admiring its style, elegance, and interior. "It's mine?" September stated with excitement. "It's mine!"

"It's yours, my friend." Catherine reached in her purse, pulled out the keys and handed them to her.

September took the keys and immediately raced to the driver side. When September got in, she popped the door lock and Catherine got in. She placed her foot on the brakes, hit the start button and the engine purred. "You're giving this to me?" With a puzzled expression on her face... "What's the catch?"

"No catch. I got tired of you driving me around in that ja-loppy of yours. I desire better for someone that treats me with graciousness and respect. But that's not all. Get out of the car."

"Do I have to? I just got in. It purrs like a kitten that just finished a bowl of milk."

"Our day isn't done. You can drive until your heart's content later. Now go grab a few things for an overnight stay. Just a tooth brush will do."

"What are you talking about, another overnight stay?" September was confused.

"We are taking a trip in my private jet to the sunny beaches of Hawaii to enjoy massages, hula dancing and drinks. We'll be picked up shortly." Before Catherine could finish 'shortly' September was already at her front door. Catherine followed. They spent about ten minutes in the house. When they walked out, the chauffeur opened the door for both of them.

"What's the limo for? I thought it was only for special occasions."

"This is."

"Ooooaa, I like the sound of that."

"Does Johnathon know you are gone for the weekend?"

"He barely knows I exist these days. I just told him I would be out of town for the weekend, I didn't tell him where."

September smiled. "Well let's fly!"

.

CHAPTER 32

Love Affair in Hawaii

As time passed, Johnathon and Nicolette had been meeting as often as they could with her visits to Los Angeles. Since Catherine was gone for the weekend, Johnathon made plans. At the condo this Friday morning, Nicolette had just arrived and made herself comfortable in the living room. Johnathon entertained her thirst with a Seltzer water.

"Nicolette, your trips back to the states have to be more frequent my love. You know I can appear in Italy at your beckon call?"

"You know I can't change my routine from when I come for my charities. I have already made excuses to come here a little more often than normal. Now my visits are short at the charities and I barely go into the office because I am spending time with you. Elisa is pretty much running the business now. I have to remain discreet to my husband as to not arouse suspicion."

"I know. I just miss making love to you."

"Oh Johnathon and I you as well. But, right now he is none the wiser of my relationship with you or my business. I must keep it that way if I am to inherit his billions once he breathes his last breathe upon this earth. Besides…" Nicolette crossed her leg, showing a lot of thigh. She drew a small compact gold case with the initials N. R. on top from her purse. She pulled a cigarette from the case to smoke. "What of your wife Johnathon?"

"I thought you were giving cigarettes up. Why don't you try one of my cigars? They smell much better."

Johnathon turned on an air filter system on the end table.

"I'm sorry darling. I forgot how much you hate the smell of cigarettes. I have got a lot on my mind lately. I'm sorry. Turn that off. Come and help me relax."

Nicolette placed the cigarette back in her case and into her purse. She stood from the sofa and started to unzip her skin tight dress from the back. Before she could finish, Johnathon raced around her and completed unzipping her clothing. When the dress fell to the floor, he gently touched her neck with his hands and removed her diamond necklace. It dropped to the floor. He softly, with his fingertips, felt his way from her neck to her buttock as he admired the naked flesh before his eyes. He slowly turned her to face him. He took a step back to admire the curvature of her breast and shapely figure. "I can't get enough of you." Nicolette didn't say a word, but had a coy expression upon her face. She slowly moved toward him and wrapped her arms around him. Seconds later, she ran her fingers through his hair while kissing him passionately. The kiss never ended while Johnathon was trying desperately to remove his shirt. Nicolette pulled back and helped him. He slightly pushed her to the couch. He sat beside her. She ripped the buttons from his shirt. Frantically kissing his body, she maneuvered her tongue across his masculine chest and caressed his nipples with her lips. Soon the passion between them heated up, Johnathon paused. His pants soon fell to the floor. He slowly got up from the couch. Adoringly, he pulled her up from the settee. They stood flesh to flesh as he cuddled her breast gently in his hands. As the couch was no longer sufficient for their movements, he swept her off her feet. Once in the master bedroom, he gently rested her on the comforter, and scrawled on top of a waiting hot body of flesh. No more words were spoken.

Mark was in a frantic mode at the office. Mark was working the stealth sub in a specific basement room in the building and keeping the company running while Johnathon was preoccupied. Suddenly he got a call from Angela. He raced back to his office. Five clients had decided to converge upon the office at once. He called Johnathon's cell phone to inform him that he only has three techs in the office that could deliver briefings on their devices capability for which each client was looking for. Johnathon didn't pick up.

Mark called Angela on the intercom. "What is Johnathon's schedule for today?"

Angela replied. "His schedule is vacant for today."

"What! I put a briefing on his schedule for a twenty-five million dollar clie..." Mark paused. "You know what... never mind. Then did he tell you where he would be?"

"No sir. He did not."

"Thanks Angela. Keep me posted if he calls in. This is the sixth time in the last three month he has disappeared without a word to me where he was going. What time is Mr. Ferguson to arrive today?"

"I have him for a brief at 5:00 p.m. sir."

"Okay I will take him. Angela have the other two clients when they arrive to watch the videos of our new technology devices until I can get to them. Have Baker to set up the conference room now for Mr. Foster."

"Yes, Mr. Townsend."

Mark never heard from Johnathon on this Friday.

As Johnathon rolled out of bed this Friday afternoon, he admired Nicolette as her head rested upon the pillow.

"What are you staring at my love?" asked Nicolette.

"You my sweet. I am just admiring your beauty."

"You say that to all your women?"

"But I mean it when I say it to you."

Nicolette turned her body in the opposite direction from which Johnathon was standing.

Johnathon raced to the bed. He faced her. "Get up. It's almost four."

"So."

"I have a full weekend planned for us this Saturday and Sunday. My jet awaits. We are flying to Hawaii this evening to lay on the beach until the sun sets. On Saturday after breakfast, we'll go island hopping, whale watching, snorkeling with the dolphins....whatever you want to do. When we get hungry we'll attend a Luau and a candle light dinner just for two. When we are exhausted from our activities we can rest our bodies on each other enjoying a balcony view. We'll admire the ocean view from our bedroom and awake in each other's arms and watch the sunrise."

"Oh Johnathon, that sounds fabulous. But what of your wife this weekend?"

"She surprised me and said she was flying away to Italy or somewhere shooting guns with her new best friend."

Nicolette was in thought. "Italy? Johnathon what if Giovanni sees your wife without you in Italy. You don't think he would stop and ask her where you…"

Johnathon interrupted. "Don't give it a second thought. I'm not really sure what she said or where she went. Let's not spend our time on what ifs. Are you ready for the weekend I have planned with you?"

Nicolette smiled. "When do we leave?"

"When you get dress."

Johnathon pulled Nicolette from the bed and pressed her naked body against his. As their lips met tenderly, he picked her up and carried her to the master bathroom. They climbed into the shower together. As the warm water trickled down their bodies, Nicolette lathered her hands with soap and washed Johnathon from neck to toe. So emotionally charged by the movement of her hands around his lower body, they embraced in each other's arms once more. Johnathon raised her up and rested her back against the shower wall. At that moment, with one smooth single stroke, he penetrated her lower body. While warm water massaged their naked skin, she wrapped her arms around him. Soon the masterfully manipulation of his lips around her breasts and continued thrust of him into her lower body brought screams of pleasure from both their lips.

Hours later they flew to Hawaii for the weekend. They spent the weekend laying on the beach and the evenings participating in luaus. They laid under palm trees, drinking wine, and making love until the midnight hour in their hotel room. Just before the sunlight struck the Monday morning sky this day, they strolled to the beach hand in hand to watch the sun rise over the ocean as they embraced each other.

Meanwhile, September and Catherine relaxed in sun chairs on the same beach. September saw the couple. The male appeared to have Johnathon's same features. To confirm her suspicions, she alerted Catherine to take a look. Catherine lowered her sun shades and stared in that direction, but doesn't believe it could be her man. She dismissed the possibility and continued to rest in her chair.

Catherine glanced across the ocean. "I love to watch the sunrise over the ocean, September. I wanted you to see this because it's a once in a lifetime moment. One you will never forget, as I will never forget on my honeymoon with Johnathon."

September continued to gaze in the direction of the couple trying to get a better look at the male. After listening to Catherine, she soon took in the magnificent view and enjoyed the moment.

CHAPTER 33

Tension from Mark

When Johnathon came to the office that Monday afternoon, Mark was visibly angry. His eyebrows were quenched together, lips were tight and he didn't even knock before he entered. Johnathon was sitting behind his desk on his cell phone.

"Where have you been?" furiously questioned Mark.

"Let me call you back my love." Johnathon hung up the phone. He spoke calmly. "Since when do you not knock before you enter and since when have my weekends become a concern of yours?"

"Since you have been neglecting my phone calls with issues that require your input. I put a twenty-five million dollar brief on your calendar for this past Friday and you don't even have the decency to let me know you aren't going to do it."

Johnathon was still in a blissful moment from his weekend with Nicolette. "Oh yes, my apologizes. I told Angela to clear my calendar and I would inform you later to handle the brief. I guess it slipped my mind. But you handled it, right?"

"Right."

"Great. Now what's up?"

"I'm concerned about you. Arriving at work in the afternoon… What's up with that?"

"None of your business. How are the projects coming along?"

"I'm worried about you." Mark paused. He maintained his expression of rage. "J when you are here, you aren't here. What has gotten into you?"

With a smile on his face, Johnathon got up from behind his desk and casually walked toward Mark. "Nothing my friend. Oooh, did I tell you Tate is willing to use your redesigned schematics for the sub."

"Great. I assumed as much when you didn't get back to me right away. I was doing it my way anyway. It's the only way it will work." Mark stared at Johnathon. Johnathon seemed to be in a stupor of happiness. Mark's tone was still aggressive. "Don't try and change the subject. You know you have a business to run. Plus I had to pause work on the projects to take care of office business."

Johnathon placed his arm around Mark's shoulder. "That's why I have a second in command. When I am not here, you take care of things."

Mark moved away from him still furious over his behavior. But he spoke with a calmer voice. "Look Johnathon, we had glitches on both devices when we tested them. It's going to take some time to find out how to fix them."

Johnathon wasn't the least bit upset or worried. "Okay. I didn't tell them your timeframe. So they aren't expecting anything soon. I told them you were getting close to finishing."

"I guess it's a good thing you did. Because trying to finish the projects and run the office is putting me behind in getting those projects out of my hair." Johnathon just smiled at Mark. "Look J, if you're spending more time with Catherine, I get it. That's fine. You want me to run the business… got it. Just stop leaving me in the dark about you, when I am expecting you to do certain things. Plus don't be angry if I make a decision to do something and it's not what you would have done. I don't want to hear aggravation or disgust coming from your jaws after I tried to get in touch with you to discuss an issue."

Johnathon sat back in his seat, still smiling. "Look Mark…"

Mark remained calm, he interrupted. "No you look Johnathon. In another three months or so that sub and EMP device will be ready from the changes. We will need to tests them again. You need to be there, because I am not showing my face to a bunch of gangsters. And your business needs you too. You haven't held a staff meeting in the last couple of months, I have."

"Mark…"

Mark interjected again. "I get it. You got something else going on that I probably won't know about until the last minute. But I'm telling you right now, whatever it is, I am not doing anything else illegal."

Johnathon was still in a lighthearted mood. "I know. Look buddy, just keep running things. I'm fine. I will be in and out of the office. Don't call me, just take care of it. I won't be angry and I got you with Tate and my friend. Take your time and do it right. I will do the presentations when you're done. They will not know you exist."

"Just be sure they don't."

"Oh yeah, don't call Catherine either. She's on some gun competition tour with September or something. She doesn't know where I am or what I'm doing."

"Has she ever." Mark mumbled.

"What?"

"Yeah J, no problem. Just remember I'm not doing anything else illegal."

Johnathon just nodded his head. "Mark, once we're done with this, we're done."

Mark stared him down and walked out of his office. Johnathon picked up his cell phone to finish his conversation with Nicolette.

CHAPTER 34

Passionate Love

A month later, Johnathon took his private jet to Italy. He had Nicolette's daily routine monitored by a private investigator. He knew her every move. He followed her to a private boutique where she had an hour set aside every Thursday just for her personal shopping. When she arrived, she found a beautiful dress she wanted to try on. When she entered the dressing room, to her surprise…

"My God! Johnathon." Nicolette whispered. "What are you doing here?"

He took the dress from her hand and placed it upon the rack. He grabbed her by the waist, pulled her close, kissed her cheeks, neck and lips quickly and passionately. "Haven't you missed me? It's been four days since we last saw each other. Are you trying to end our relationships?"

Nicolette smiled and rubbed his cheek. "No, of course not, my sweet."

"You were supposed to come to L.A. a couple of days ago. Elisa called you. She said you were coming. I waited for hours at my condo and not so much as a phone call."

Nicolette pulled away. "Yes. I have missed you, but you know I'm not do back in L.A. until next week. "An impromptu moment for Giovanni occurred. He wanted me to go away with him to one of his business meetings and I couldn't make up an excuse that was important enough for me to keep my trip to L.A."

"All I could think about for the past few days was our magical moments in Hawaii and our evenings together these past weeks."

"Johnathon you know we have to be discreet. Our relationship depends on our deception of routines being normal." Nicolette moved closer and tugged his coat. "I only said yes, because at first he was going alone, and at the last minute he change his mind and wanted me to go with him. If my schedule to the U.S. is increased without good reason, he will want to know wh…."

Before she could finish her sentence, Johnathon jerked her by the waist toward him and affectionately ravished her lips. Without any resistance, she returned the emotional outburst. Seconds later, she pulled back slightly. "You know I have security guards outside the boutique waiting for me."

"Of course. That's why I'm in here and they're out there." Johnathon rubbed her breast and raised her dress to touch her thighs.

Nicolette smiled slightly to his response. She began kissing his face all over. "What about the owner?"

"She has been paid handsomely for her silence." Johnathon was unzipping her dress.

Nicolette softly spoke. "Johnathon we can't do this. Not here. Not now."

He halted his actions and gazed into her eyes. "Then when? Can you figure out a way to get out tonight and meet me? You tell me where and I'll be there."

Nicolette lowered her head and sighed. "Johnathon… I…"

"Shhhhh…" Johnathon raised her head with his forefinger. He kissed her luscious lips again. He maintained his passion as he had completely unzipped the dress she was wearing. When her clothing slide from her body, he caressed her breast delicately in the palms of his hands. Nicolette was panting softly as she unbuckled his pants and Johnathon removed all his upper clothing. As they stood flesh to flesh, the fever of the moment intensified. Johnathon picked Nicolette up in his arms, placed her back against the wall and slowly began to grind her lower body. Small groans of ecstasy eased from the dressing room door.

Moments later, he slowly lowered her to the floor. Their sexual position changed, Johnathon laid sideways beside her, with her back to his front… he continued to pound her lower body rapidly, until finally a moment of ecstasy burst from both their lips. She soon rested her head upon his arm, facing him as he laid next to her hot naked flesh. "I see you missed me too." Johnathon echoed. Nicolette reached for his lower extremity and performed hand motions to arouse it again as her lips reached for his. They engaged in another passionate eruption of affection. An hour later, she started to put her clothes back on and he does the same.

"I must leave now. Please zip my dress." Nicolette turned her back to Johnathon.

Johnathon smooched her neck as he zipped her garment. "You know this will be one of those moments when we look back at our relationship and laugh."

"Really? Is that where your head is right now. I'm hoping the owner doesn't talk." Nicolette opened the dressing room door.

"I am staying at the Hilton downtown. I have suite #2 on the top floor. Get word to me if you can make it. I will wait all month if I have to."

Nicolette put her shoes on. "I will come to see you tomorrow. Be patient. It maybe late afternoon before I can get there."

"My time is your time my love. I will be there as long as it takes to see you."

Nicolette kissed him on the cheek and walked out of the fitting room with the dress she took in. She grabbed five more dresses off the rack, a few purses and some shoes. She purchased them all to appear as if she had been shopping the entire hour. She walked out of the store. Her body guards and chauffeur drove her away.

The owner signaled all clear and Johnathon emerged from the dressing room. He stepped to the window and watched her car disappear around the curve. He walked out into the street and signaled for his limo. He had the owner paid a bonus of an extra fifty-thousand American dollars to remain silent of the affair.

Later that evening, Nicolette arrived at the Hilton with one of her girlfriend's and purchased Suite #3. Nicolette and Francesca arrived with shopping bags and suitcase. Her girlfriend was aware of the charade. Nicolette immediately went to the adjacent door and knocked gently. Johnathon opened the door with no shirt on. He noticed Nicolette dressed very casually as she stood in the middle of his living room with her back to him. He closed the door slowly as he winked at Francesca. Nicolette heard the door lock.

Johnathon displayed his masculine chest and six pack ab physique, with just pajama pants on and bare footed. Johnathon slowly moved toward her and wrapped his arm around her. "How did you break away from your husband? I didn't expected you until tomorrow."

"I told him an old friend came into town and she wanted to know if I could have a girl's weekend out since she was only in town for a couple of days."

"Obviously he agreed." Johnathon now had his arms around her waist and kissed her shoulders and neck. "I was hoping you would be able to get the suite next to mine."

Nicolette turned to face him. "Most thirty-thousand dollar a night suites aren't taken unless there is an event or an occasion this time of year. But you do know there are guards across the hall waiting for my beckon call."

"But there are none outside my door." He kissed her softly upon the cheek.

She moved away to another corner of the room. "Johnathon... I..."

Johnathon interrupted. "I see he is pretty protective of you."

"If you were a billionaire, you don't want anything to happen to the things you love."

"Or possess."

A slightly harsh tone, Nicolette spoke. "He doesn't possess me. He's just controlling." Her tone became softer. "He loves me so very much."

"Same thing. Enough about him." Johnathon leaned to kiss her.

Nicolette embraced his affection. He bent over to grab her skin tight dress from the seam and raised it over her head. Johnathon gently placed both hands on her hips and removed her undergarment. He grabbed her entire body up off the floor and whisked her away to the bedroom. As he laid her softly upon the bed, he positioned himself gently on top of her and whispered in her ear. "I'm breaking my own cardinal rule."

"What might that be?"

"I'm chasing you." He kissed her affectionately from head to toe. She laid there in rapture, engulfing every single movement of his hands across her breast and body. His tongue moved slowly up and down her thighs until they caressed the most sensitive area of her body. Soft moans echoed from her lips.

"Oh Johnathon... you feel..."

"Shhhh… don't scream my sweet. Your body guards may come over. Enjoy the moment my love."

At that instant, he removed his pants, climbed on top of her and gently began to ease into her lower body. Slowly pounding her with each tender stroke, silent screams of emotional pleasure echoed from Nicolette.

Minutes later, they rested for a moment, laying there, he held her in his arms. Her head resting upon his chest as he stroked her hair. "Do I have you for the weekend?"

"Yes. I had to devise a plan. When I just want to get away without him knowing where I am or who I'm with or I just need a little piece from the body guards and security, Francesca works with me to do that."

"And what might that plan be?"

"I have another friend that arrived here before me. She could pass for my twin sister."

"Do they know who I am?" asked Johnathon.

"Of course not. I don't tell them where I'm going or who I am with."

"Those two ladies are in your suite right now? I only saw one." Johnathon smiled. "You think we could do a three on one?"

"That's not funny." Nicolette was serious.

"I'm just teasing baby. Go on."

"Tomorrow a maid will come to the door of my suite delivering breakfast. She will come in pretending to serve us. I will change clothes with the maid. I will walk out as the maid. My friend that resembles me will dress in my clothing and paint the town with Francesco tomorrow. The two of them will go to restaurants, shopping, and evening plays. I will remain unseen until they leave the hotel. Then I will come back up here to go out with you. I will alert them when we are coming back to our suite. They will arrive in my suite for the evening, before we come back. My guards will think my friend and I have settled in the room for the day. You and I will arrive an hour or two later. The guards should not suspect anything."

"That's pretty clever."

"I don't do it often. Only when I am tired of being watched."

Johnathon kissed her once again. "It's still very clever."

"Johnathon…" She scrawled out the bed and stood before him naked.

He gave her his full attention. "Utt oh. What did I do wrong? Aren't you ready for round two?" Catherine walked to the shear curtains of the bedroom. She had her back to him. She pulled the curtain back slightly and gazed out the window. "What is it my love? Tell me so I can make it right."

She slowly turned and climbed back into bed with a bowed head. "I think I am falling in love with you." He took his forefinger and raised her head. She stared lovingly into his eyes. "I find myself when I am with my husband on outings and making love to him, thinking of you."

He smiled. "Really?"

Nicolette placed her head back on his chest. "I am distracted and in a daze sometimes around my husband. When he ask me what's on my mind, I lie and tell him something else. But the truth is, I'm thinking of you."

Johnathon rubbed her arms and brushed her hair with his hand. "My sweet. I must confess. I feel the same way about you. I find myself counting the days until our next meeting. That's why I came unexpectedly to Italy. When you didn't come to the condo last week, and the beautiful weekend we had and the lovely evenings we've spent together… the urge to see you again caused me to defy all logical reasoning. I just wanted to hold you in my arms, no matter how risky for both our sakes."

"I don't want to give up my billions Johnathon."

"I don't want you to either. But you have your business now Nicolette. You don't need him."

"How long would it take for my business to have billions as Giovanni does now? You see I already have it at my whim."

"I understand wanting money and wanting it now. Would it make a difference if I were a billionaire?"

"I love you so much, at this moment, I don't know if it would matter." Nicolette appeared solemn. "Oh Johnathon… I need you to take this chain of love off my heart and let me be free."

He pulled her body close to his and with loving arms held her tightly. "I'm going to tell you a story. Years ago… in college, I was starting to fall for a girl I had met. She was beautiful and intelligent just like you. I left her because I was young and wasn't sure of what loving someone really meant. At that time I don't think I really cared. But since I've met you, you have made me realize how special loving someone can be. What good are all the material things in the world, if you don't have someone special to share them with? When I am with you, I am most happy and everything that I have, I want to share with you. I promised myself… that if I ever found that kind of love again in someone, I would never let her go. I believe I have found that love again, with you."

Nicolette gazed into his eyes. "Do you really think you have found that kind of love... with me?"

Johnathon paused. He gazed lovingly into her eyes. "Without a doubt my love. I know heaven is missing an angel, because I am holding her in my arms right now." He leaned down and kissed her passionately. They fully embraced and once again their physical emotions flared. No more words were spoken.

The next day, Johnathon had chartered a yacht for the rest of the weekend. That afternoon, it was just the two of them, the captain and a small crew of servants. They both were lounging on the sofa at the rear end of the yacht in bathing suits.

"Where are we headed Johnathon?"

"Nowhere my sweet." The waiter brought two glasses of wine on deck and served them. "Thank you." The waiter left. Johnathon stood and extended his hand, pointing at the spectacular scene of the ocean. "We are just going to enjoy the picturesque view. Go skinny dipping off the coast and enjoy our day together. I have arranged dinner and a movie on this yacht for the most beautiful girl in world. I didn't want to risk your relationship with your husband by being seen somewhere where he may have prying eyes."

Nicolette tasted her wine. "He really is a good man. He doesn't care where I go, only that I am protected when I go."

Johnathon placed his glass on the table and sat close to Nicolette. He spoke quietly in her ear. "What if something were to happen to him and he wasn't around anymore. Would this upset you?"

Nicolette was shocked by the comment. "What are you talking about?"

"What if he suddenly had an accident?"

Her tone grew harsh. Nicolette jumped from the sofa with wine glass in hand. She stared at him. "Johnathon you aren't serious. I may not love him like I love you, but I do care for him."

Johnathon was a little intense in tone of voice. "He's like a father to you. He's twice your age. This way you inherit his billions."

"That may be true, but he's my husband. I will not be a part of any kind of murderous scheme to kill him and I don't want you to do something to make that happen."

"Who said anything about murder? I was just speaking theoretically."

"Good. Besides, I have been thinking."

Johnathon grabbed her hand and pulled her to sit back down on the sofa. He leaned her body against his chest as he wrapped his arms across her shoulder. "What about my sweet?"

Nicolette gazed out to the ocean while she laid in his arms. "Everything... everything is so perfect when we are together. When it's just you and I, I think... what a life we could have together. Then, reality takes center stage."

"What do you mean, my love?"

"I believe you only want me because you can't have me Johnathon. How do we even know that what we feel is really love?"

"I'm here with you, when I should be working."

Nicolette sat up from his embrace. She gazed into his eyes. "Do you love me? How do you know?"

Johnathon grabbed her hand and held it tight. "Of course, I love you." He paused in thought. "What's wrong? Tell me. So I can make it right."

"We're what's wrong. You have a condominium of beautiful women in and out of your life at your beckon whim. How can you not feel something for some of them?" Nicolette pulled her hand away and walked to the edge of the ship with her back toward him.

Johnathon stood and walked up behind her and placed his hands upon her shoulders. "Where is this going my love?"

Nicolette turned to face him. "I love you so much Johnathon, that on evenings when I am alone in bed, I fill my pillow with quiet tears of sorrow on the nights I think of you in the arms of another woman, even your wife."

"But my sweet, these women mean nothing to me, including my wife. I married only for convenience. I have never loved her."

"But this is why I think you may only feel this way about me. You don't see me every week like you do some of the women you have at your condo. If I were on a weekly schedule like the rest of your women, I could be just another number in your playbook of maidens."

"Oh my sweet, you could never be just another number." Johnathon put his hands around her neck and drew her lips close to his.

She pulled away and walk to the other side of the yacht. Nicolette paused in deep thought. "I think we need to end this, now."

Johnathon shocked by the comment. "What!" He walked in hast to her.

Nicolette faced him and spoke sincerely. "Maybe I love you because of the successful business you help me establish. That evening you seemed like my knight in shining armor. You helped me to do something I couldn't have accomplished on my own. That was the only time I meant for that to happen. As we met more and more I found our meetings intriguing and exciting."

Johnathon's voice was empathic and sincere. "I did too Nicolette. I love you. If you asked me to stop the rain from falling or pull the moon from the sky, with all my determination, I would try to make this happen in order to make you happy. That's how much I love you. Let me be your shadow. That way, where you go I go and you will never lose me or I you."

"Do you? Do you really love me that much Johnathon? Well, I'm not sure I really *love* you. Maybe my love for you is because you helped me start a business, or your appearance is so much like Renieri's, or maybe because when we make love it's *so* different." Nicolette smiled. "It's in the bathtub with bubbles and wine, in the bed with you stroking my breast with red rose pedals, the shower with warm pulsating water hitting our bodies, or making love on the dining room table or on the floor... or do I really, really just love you for who you are... which is the scary part." Nicolette paused and waited for Johnathon to say something. He does not. "Take me back Johnathon. I will alert the girls to cut their shopping spree early and meet us back at the hotel."

"I don't want to lose you. I love you. If I can't have you, I don't want anyone else. I have never said those words to any other woman in my life, even my wife."

"I only think that we love each other because we can't see each other as often as we like. I have to admit... the making love, along with the suspense of trickery, deceit, lies and not getting caught by our spouses is what kept us going. But since *love* has creeped into our equation, it's no longer the excitement for me, but emotional hurt and pain that I feel when I am not with you. My heart is burden with grief. I feel guilty about my vow to Giovanni. I feel guilty about my love for you." Nicolette tarried and her eyes glanced away from Johnathon. He came closer. She stared back at him. "It's confusing for me right now Johnathon. I need to think. I believe distance and time will give us a chance to rationalize our emotions and think logically. Right now this affair can only lead to disaster for the both of us."

Johnathon was speechless, but he agreed. "Alright my love. I can understand how you feel. If distance is what you want, we will end the relationship after today. To prove that I love you, all I want is for you to be happy. I will call upon you no more, but today is mine. If this is to be our last moments together, I don't want to waste another second talking." As Johnathon stood in front of her. He gazed into her eyes, tenderly. She returned the passionate expression. No more words were spoken. Seconds later, he kissed her feverously and she didn't repel his action. He picked her up and carried her down to the bedroom suite of the yacht. Their weekend was filled with love and friendship as they felt they had to part ways from one another.

CHAPTER 35

Affair with Olivia

Johnathon thought on the flight back about what Nicolette had spoken about their relationship. Maybe he did want her because their relationship was exciting with the lies and deceitfulness. Perhaps not getting caught by their spouses or that he couldn't be with her on a regular schedule is what made him want her more. When Johnathon got back to the states this day, he poured himself into work and the women at his condo. He decided to dive into developing his company further and working with Mark to finish the projects. However, he needed to test his theory of love. Johnathon kept a three o'clock appointment this day at his condo.

Olivia met Johnathon on the second floor. She knocked.

"Olivia… right on time." Spoke Johnathon.

She jumped into his arms before he could even offer her a drink or evening dinner out on the town. She immediately ripped his clothes off and took him to the floor. Before Johnathon could say stop, she had already raised a bulge in his pants. Without hesitation, Johnathon eased her thirst for sex.

Moments later, Olivia came from the bathroom totally naked. "Ready for round two, my sweet. This time let's take it slow. I ran some warm water with bubbles."

Johnathon was pulling his pants up. "No. This was our last time. I don't want to see you anymore."

"What?" Olivia was totally in shock. "My job as an archeologist takes me away for months at a time. I had just gotten back in town yesterday. I was about to call you when I got your call."

"I just wanted to be sure you were going to be here. I know you are out of town a lot."

"I'm here baby. Let's have some more fun."

Johnathon was solemn in tone. "It's not that I don't see you often enough. I just don't want to see you anymore."

"You know Johnathon, I think I'm falling for you. I haven't seen you in a few months and all I could think about is the times we've spent together and how beautiful they were. I feel I have heaven here on earth when I am with you. You've captured my heart with a rope and put a knot around it. No other man makes me feel the way you do when we are together."

"Unfortunately sweetheart, I don't carry rope. You did that to yourself. We only see each other when you're in town. So you can untie the knot and put the rope back in storage for the right man, because I'm not him. And I meant what I said about not wanting to see you again, no exceptions."

In a soft tone Olivia repeated her feelings. "I think I love you Johnathon. The times I'm here you have always made me feel as if I was the only one. Like just now. It was beautiful."

"It's my nature. I treat all my ladies that way Olivia. I told you I don't want love or a relationship. Why is that so hard for ladies understand?"

"Ladies?" Olivia, shocked to hear she wasn't the only one.

"Yes, other women. You didn't think with you're being gone for months at a time that I would sit around waiting for you… did you?"

Olivia pondered for a minute. "I thought or felt we had a connection but…"

Johnathon interjected. "That's exactly what I mean. *You* thought. Did you consult me with your thoughts?"

"The way you treat me when I'm with you, I didn't think I needed to. You had always shown me so much kindness and passion in our relationship."

"My life is complex. I enjoy the company of a beautiful woman and sexy ones. You fill that need when you are in town."

"Oh my God! You don't care for me at all?"

"On the contrary my love, if I didn't, you wouldn't be here."

Olivia became incensed by his comment. "I'm just another number in some little play book of yours. How do you keep it all straight? Is it with 'stars' or 'check marks' you put beside our names? Why did you even look my way if you have others?"

"Variety is the spice of life. Never the same flavor two days in a row. Different women intrigue me. But after this sexual moment, I no longer feel the desire to be with you again."

"Oh my God. I'm part of haram. I don't know what else to say." Olivia sat down on the couch deep in thought.

"I want you to take all your belongings and go. I have found someone I believe I want to be with. If this upsets you... great. Don't look back. I'm going to have Becky to take your name off the list."

Visibly angry at this point of the conversation. "List? Wow! What a fool I've been." Olivia stood from the couch. "Do you think you can treat me like a piece of tissue?! Just use me and then throw me away when you're done?"

"Yes. We are done Olivia. You knew the deal before we started seeing each other. If you didn't want to know it before, I hope you know it now. Love was never in the equation." Johnathon paused in thought. "You know what, just leave now. Becky will be informed to never buzz you in again. I will have her mail whatever you personally want from here."

He turned to walk out. "You Bastard! My heart is not to be played with like some string on a fiddle. You will regret this moment."

"I already have." Johnathon slammed the door. He mumbled to himself. "Another one that curses. Gees."

Olivia cried out... hoping he heard her through the door. "This will not end here!" She softly spoke to herself as she stared at the door. "I promise you that." She stated as Johnathon could no longer hear her words.

Johnathon felt nothing during this encounter. His thoughts were with Nicolette. He continued to test his other women and compare them to Nicolette.

CHAPTER 36

Johnathon Tells Mark about Nicolette

While Johnathon had been serenading Nicolette and his other women, Mark had been running the business, giving briefing, holding staff meetings, putting out company crisis's and working on the illegal projects. At work this day...

Johnathon knocked on Mark's office door. "Come in."

"Mark..."

To Mark's surprise. "Do I know you?" he questioned sarcastically.

"Look Mark. I know I have been pretty non-existent for the past few weeks, but I'm back now. Can you brief me for this week's schedule?" Johnathon closed the door and silently whispers. "How are our special projects going?"

"Are you sure you want to know what's going on? Maybe I should brief your other head. It's the one that's been busy."

"That's not funny. I've got some things going on I need to talk to you about. I need you to listen."

"Not now. This week is very busy. In twenty minutes, Brianna is giving a brief to a fifty million dollar client on our cyber system that intercepts viruses, reverses the action and detects the origin."

"The Virus Detector. Great."

"You can sit in or go to your office and get caught up on the schedule for the week and I will brief you later."

"Deal. I will go to my office. Perhaps we can hit the Yacht Club after the workday. I need to bend you ear."

Mark gave him a facial expression of discontent. He got up from his desk with papers in hand and headed to the conference room. Johnathon watched Mark as he left. He went behind him and headed to his office.

Hours later, Mark went to Johnathon's office and briefed him on how well the company had been performing. He had the extra projects on hold keeping the company afloat. Johnathon was gratified with the office performance.

"Thank you for the brief Mark. I'm sorry for not being around to help run the company."

"I haven't been working on the projects for that very reason."

"I know. I've been telling them we're running into issues every time you test, but you're getting close. They are accepting that for now."

"Well your company is doing great J. We have exceeded the organizational goals for this quarter."

"I knew our company could be better than our expectations dictated per quarter if our people just put their heads down and try to exceed it."

"Well they did this quarter. That's why I planned to have an office party this month. You will be there. Yes?"

"Yes of course. Let's have a drink. I'll drive." Johnathon was solemn in tone.

Without hesitation, Mark followed Johnathon to his car. Once at the Yacht Club, they had their usual drinks.

Mark was curious of Johnathon's activities. "What's up buddy, what's going on with you these days? You've been letting me handle all the meetings and presentations of clients without any interference or oversight. Don't get me wrong, I am finally glad you're putting more confidence in me to handle things, but this isn't like you. Plus I need to brief you on the presentation of the illegal prototypes. I need to let you know where we stand on those and give you a full brief. You got time for me or are you spending more time with Catherine?"

Johnathon was stern and stone faced, almost in a daze. He took a sip of his drink. "What I tell you now my friend must remain between you and I until I can figure things out. Right now I just need to talk it out with someone."

"Well I am here for you J. I'm listening."

"It's not Catherine I'm spending time with. You know the woman I told you about that is very, very special to me when she comes into town?"

"Yes."

"Well, I strongly believe I have developed a perpetual love for her. I believe I want to be with her forever."

"Ohhhh… man." Mark sat up in his seat, shocked by his words.

"Yes I know, right? Me?"

"What about Catherine?"

"I think a divorce is in order. You have said yourself I don't respect and treat her as a loving wife should be treated."

"I know, but… "

"I don't love her Mark and never have. I told you that."

"Yes… I know, but I thought, maybe, just maybe, you would try to work things out. Spend more time with her. Learn to love her as a wife should be loved."

"That was never going to happen. I found more enjoyment with the other women I was seeing than with Catherine. But now, love has entered into my life."

"Love? You my friend?" Mark grinned.

Johnathon started to mumble without really addressing Mark eye to eye. "I am trying to find out if their values and morals has changed since we first meet. I'm trying to see if perhaps Nicolette was right in that respect."

"Nicolette?"

Johnathon continued to ramble on. "Maybe because I didn't see her as much is why I wanted her more or if her virtues are what impressed me."

"Hey buddy, what are you talking about? Give it to me straight Johnathon. Why are you rambling?"

Johnathon finally gave Mark direct eye to eye contact. "Months have passed and I have grown weary of my playmates. I realize that none of them compare to Nicolette. Their thoughts, mannerism, perfume smell, laughter, nor sex felt the same or any better than Nicolette. In fact, the sex was less intriguing than it used to be. After weeks of trying to get over her, I wonder if she is thinking of me. I thought Nicolette would have tried to call or reach out to me by now."

Mark was perplexed. "Who is this Nicolette you keep talking about?" He paused in thought. "Nicolette? That name sounds familiar."

"It should. We did some work with her and her husband in Italy a year back."

Mark jaws dropped, totally stunned. "Nicolette Russo? Are you crazy?"

Johnathon spoke softly as if he wanted her name to flow off his lips. "Nicolette Russo, the love of my life."

Mark spoke with agitation in his voice. "Russo? The wife of billionaire, Giovanni Russo?"

"That's the one."

Mark's tone was a little harsh. "Oh my God. He's our client Johnathon. How do you think that's going to go down?"

"That's just it. I don't know. She loves me. I can feel it when I am with her and I love her."

"Wait a minute. When did you get so love struck? Variety is the spice of life remember?"

"I know Mark. You remember Penelope, the girl I told you about in college?"

"Yes."

"Well Nicolette reminds me so much of her. When I first met her, I thought she was a gold digger for marrying such an older man. Then she tried to assists her husband in buying my company out from under me."

Mark was astounded. "What! When was this?"

"It's a long story, but as our meetings grew casual, the physical pleasure grew. We started seeing each other when we could. She would fly in on business. I helped her start her own business."

"So this is why your work efforts have suffered. The moody attitude. It's all making sense now. What business?" Questioned Mark. "I didn't think the old man would let her work. He was so controlling when we were there."

"She told me she takes one-hundred million dollars a year and gives it to charity."

"She can afford to do that J. One-hundred million to her is like us spending a hundred dollars on a few drinks."

"I know. But she not only donates money, she is involved in charity projects, battered women, vagrant children, building wells and schools in Africa, taking dilapidated buildings here in L.A. and turning them into homeless shelters, donating to failing hospitals in poor communities that help people without health insurance, that sort of thing. I have watched her in action in some of these places. She has a heart of gold like Penelope did. The money she has as a billionaire's wife isn't just for her, it's for humanitarian efforts. She cares for others more than her shopping sprees or exotic vacations. I can't let another one slip away."

"Wow! What about her business? What is that? Does Giovanni know?"

"Reneiri Fashions and no he doesn't know."

Mark was surprised. "Reneiri Fashions? That's hers?"

"Yes."

Mark just stared at Johnathon in thought. "It seems you have meet your match once again my friend. I take it you don't want to let this one out of your life from the way you sound?"

Johnathon stared at the table. "I don't Mark." He gave Mark his full attention. "I have spent the last couple of months trying to make sure that Nicolette is what I want and I found the other women in my life don't even compare to her. I don't want to touch them anymore. All I can see is Nicolette when l am with them and assessing them to her. Once I came close to not even performing in the bedroom. You know that's not me."

"Nooo... Not Johnathon Fitzpatrick." Mark sarcastically smiled. Johnathon gave him a look of, *not funny*. "I know you can just get rid of the other women. But, how does Catherine fit into this picture?"

"Two-hundred and fifty million for her name on the dotted line of divorce papers should be enough."

Mark sighed... "We are barely a four-hundred million dollar company and you would give your wife over half. You really must be in love."

"I am." Sincerity rang in Johnathon's voice.

"I'm glad you finally found love, even if it is in the wrong place. Just to hear you praise someone else besides yourself though, is shocking."

Johnathon smiled. "I'm not that bad?"

"Oh yeah man... you are or you were."

"After knowing Nicolette this past year, I have found a new reality for the love of life. I believe I want to be around this one for the rest of mine."

"You know if somehow you end up with Nicolette, you don't even come close to Giovanni's billions. These charities she is sponsoring will suffer after a few years. If you spend a hundred million in a year, you lose almost a quarter of your profits. We need every single person we have on staff just to maintain a consistent profit on average of over eighty mil a year per person. Will she be willing to settle for less? Have you two even discussed such things?"

"No, how close are you on finishing the projects? With one billion under my belt and the company thriving the way it is, I can maintain her life style and mine."

"Giovanni is an eighty-five billion dollar man. You'll have one and a half. Besides I thought you might lay low for a while once you received all of that cash. Feds maybe lurking."

"I don't care. I will use it for her if I need too."

"Oh man. You really are love sick. She doesn't know anything about the deals, does she?"

"No of course not. She never will. One time shot, remember. You've got to finish soon or guns will be in our faces."

"Noooo, a gun in your face. Do you think I can just pull these devices out of the air? They take time J, especially working on them by myself with just a couple of individuals. You know that. Not to mention running the company, *by... my... self*, while trying to work on them. The team I have, think they are working on an office project. I just call them in when I need their technical expertise. Two different devices that require different components, prototypes, and demonstrations. These efforts are at least a month out on fixing the glitches. I needed to go and test all the components to see where the hick-ups were, but unable to do it."

"Why? You were almost there?"

Mark raised his voice. "I was there until running the company became the priority."

"Right now, Tate and Antonio know this. I was just hoping you could be superman and work the company as well as the projects." Johnathon paused. "I'm sorry. Right now I just need an ear. Just hearing myself speak aloud helps me to think."

"I hear you, but I am not advising you at all on anything. I'm just listening."

"I know Mark and I appreciate your ear. Now, what I need to do is discuss it with her."

"Nicolette or Catherine?" questioned Mark.

"Nicolette. I need to know if she will have me."

"I totally agree Johnathon. Do you really believe you love this woman that much?"

"Mark you just don't know. I lay in the bed with Catherine, I think of Nicolette. I lay in the pool with a glass of wine and a cigar, I want her beside me. Then I gaze up at the stars and I wish she was loving me. I think of her so much, I pause in my footsteps because I can't breathe just to catch my breath, wishing so desperately that she was in my arms."

"Yeah, J. You've got the love bug. I wish I could tell you what to do, but this is a true mess."

Johnathon mustered a slight grin. They both took a sip of their drinks as each of them contemplated what their next move would be to resolve their issues.

CHAPTER 37

Johnathon Eradicates his Women

When he got back to the office the next morning, Johnathon called Becky. He had her to tell all his playmates on the second and third floor that the condominium was closed now and forever more. He would tell Amoy and Melanie personally. He called his personal attorney to make arrangements for a divorce settlement with Catherine in the coming days. Later this month he would put the condo up for sale.

Now, Johnathon needed to tell Catherine he was planning to leave her. But instead of telling her, he thought his actions would speak louder than his words. He didn't pick up the phone when she called, he wouldn't come home for days. This time he would do something so devastating that any wife would want to divorce her husband.

But before he did the unthinkable to his wife, he needed to break the agreement he made with Nicolette not to make contact with her ever again. He needed to know after two months of silence, did this woman still love him as much as he loved her. He would call her and ask if they could meet once more. He thought he would be met with opposition.

Johnathon took his cell phone from his pocket and dialed her number. As the phone rang, his heart pounded with fear. A soft voice answered. "Hello my love."

Johnathon exhaled hearing the words she spoke. "My darling, I know I agreed to never seeing you again, but my heart is tattooed with love for you. My days seem worthless, my nights seem lonely even though I am not alone. I understand how you feel, because all I want now is you Nicolette."

"Oh Johnathon… I…"

"Don't say no my love. I will come to you."

"No, Johnathon I will come to you, tomorrow. Much has changed since we last met. I have missed you too. I will be out early tomorrow morning to the U.S. I will give you the details as they evolve. Wait for my call my sweet. You will hear from me soon. Bye my love."

With great delight, Johnathon perked up like a school boy who just got a date with the most gorgeous female of the cheerleader squad. He immediately got on the phone and called Mark into his office.

Mark knocked and entered Johnathon's office. "What's up buddy?"

"Tomorrow I need you to cover for me, all day."

"Is she coming?" quizzed Mark.

Johnathon stood from his desk and paced the floor. "Yes, she will be here tomorrow morning. I will tell you what you need to know in case Catherine appears unexpectedly at the office tomorrow. She is due back from her competitions tonight."

"You got it my friend. Not that I am happy about what you are doing, I just believe Catherine is a good woman and she deserves better."

"My sentiments exactly. I am headed home to see what state Catherine is in. I will make my excuses to her for tomorrow. So I will inform you later. I will try to be a cordial husband this evening so she won't feel slighted tomorrow."

"Don't act out of character or you will arose suspicion. Just be yourself. If you don't love or care for her, don't act like you do now. Stay out all night and come home late."

"You're right. I will stay here until late trying to figure this thing out."

Mark paused, observing Johnathon's emotional distress over Nicolette and Catherine. However, work must continue. "Look… J, I know you're preoccupied. I planned the office party at the Yacht Club for two weeks from now at happy hour, since this Thursday is your anniversary. I just need you to show up and give your congratulations to the group and especially Brianna Delray, Grayson Hartman and others that did exceptionally well this quarter."

"What did they do?" asked Johnathon.

"Not only did Brianna get the Anderson case back, but she brought in five more of Mr. Anderson's client's, each worth twenty-one million or more.

Her persistence and drive to stick with him to get him back these last few months could net us a hundred and thirty million dollars in the next three years. That's already on top of the fifty million she has already received from Mr. Anderson this year. Grayson grabbed thirty-five million from a couple of clients in New York."

Johnathon didn't seemed thrilled. He spoke solemnly. "Awesome, I will be there. I told you we have good people. Just got to keep them motivated."

Mark nodded, surprised at his reaction to almost one hundred and ninety-million dollars in team effort. Months ago he would have leaped for joy. Mark left the room. Johnathon sat for a few more hours until night fell upon the city of LA and headed home.

That Tuesday evening, two days before Johnathon's anniversary, he was deep in thought of how to tell Catherine how he felt about Nicolette. Was the truth the right way to go or should he act in such a manner that she would scream for a divorce. He would test the waters with Catherine about September. Perhaps creation of a disturbance in the relationship right now would cause Catherine to despise him. Johnathon that evening at home, decided to test the waters.

"Are you still inviting that woman to the executive party this Friday?"

"It's September and yes. Yes I am."

"I see she has been a big influence on you with those .45 calibers in the living room. You got a lot more trophies."

"You noticed. Now do you care?"

Johnathon couldn't bring himself to speak ill of her hobby since he was about to devastate her with a divorce. "Those are beautiful guns Catherine."

"Yes." Joyfully Catherine spoke, a little surprised by the comment. "I have become quite the shot. You should come with us to the competition in San Francisco next Tuesday and check me out."

"I already know you're good, my love. The trophies speak for themselves. I'm proud of you."

Stunned by his comment, Catherine had geared up for a fight about September or the trophies. "You're not angry about all the trophies?"

"No, why should I be?"

Still in shock, Catherine continued with the gun conversation. "Great! September and I are going to start entering in more contest around the state to test our skills against some of the best here and around the...."

"Great!" Johnathon interrupted.

Catherine was dumbfounded by his behavior. She continued with the conversation. "As September would say, I can pluck the wings off a fly at hundred yards."

"I would say that's pretty darn good. Maybe one day when I get sometime I will take in a contest. She's converted my wife into a high powered weapons expert."

"I wouldn't say all that." Catherine smiled. "But I do enjoy shooting for fun and now for competition and... I'm good at it."

"How often do you two go to the paint gun club? I did find that a little enjoyable."

"Tuesday's and Thursday's at noon if you want to join us sometime."

"I will think about it. Maybe I will work some things around my schedule to join you." Added Johnathon.

Still stunned by the conversation, Catherine didn't know how to react. She gazed at her wrist watch. "Johnathon, its midnight on a Tuesday and you're home. You're holding a conversation with me. Something you haven't done in years. Is there something on your mind you want to talk about?"

"There is my love, but not right now. There could be some huge deals going down at work. I'm going to call off the executive party for this Friday."

"Why?" Catherine was perplexed as to his strange behavior.

"I just need to be prepared for these deals. I'm going to bed now. I will be working heavily with Mark these next couple of days. So I will be either very late coming home or not at all tomorrow." He kissed Catherine gently upon the lips and walked upstairs.

"What's going on?" Catherine mumbled to herself. She yelled to him, "Oh Johnathon, tomorrow morning I am taking the jet to New York and I will be back late tomorrow evening. Perhaps we can make it our day, all day Thursday."

"Ok." Johnathon continued to climb the stairs to the bedroom. He thought to himself, what fortune, Catherine will be out of town all day Wednesday. He had a slight smile on his face knowing that his anniversary was on Thursday.

As Catherine watched Johnathon ascend the stairs, she was bewildered to his gestures of affection and attentiveness to her trophies and gun skills. She felt in her heart and mind good things were about to take place in their relationship. Perhaps Mark had finally gotten to him to spend more time with her and their anniversary was this Thursday.

The ladies flew away Wednesday morning with breakfast drinks and food served before them onboard her jet. Catherine was excited about the conversation she had with Johnathon.

"September I finished a wonderful conversation with my loving husband yesterday."

"What? You finally had a meaningful conversation after six years?" September smiled in just.

"Yeah. He complimented me on my trophies and gun skills. He even called me his love and kissed me on the lips before he went to bed."

"Oh my gosh!" September stated as if worried.

"What? He's going to try and make a go of our marriage. He pretended like he didn't know it was our anniversary was tomorrow. I played alone. I knew that's why he cancelled the executed party, because from Thursday to Sunday, those days are ours. He did that before, but the sweet words about my weapons and trophies did catch me off guard.".".

"Or not. It could mean he's ready to cut you lose. Where are we headed anyway?"

"Our anniversary is coming up this Thursday or tomorrow and I ordered this special wine called Petrus 2016 red wine in Pomerol, France. I know he doesn't have it, because he tried to get it for the last executive party we had."

"Does he know?"

"Of course not. I'm trying to surprise him too. I told him I was going to New York."

"So we're going to France?"

"Yes. This way he can get his surprise set up for me tomorrow. It's usually something different of grand proportion that I am always so pleased after the weekend is over. I think that is why he was so sweet to me." Catherine was beaming with joy. "Tomorrow is going to be so exciting. I can hardly wait to see what my four day wedding anniversary celebration will be like this time."

"Oh he's going to set it up alright." Doubted September.

"Stop being so cynical. He has always treated me like a queen on our anniversary. That is one day he has never disappointed me. He tried to have me fooled thinking the executive party was going to be Friday when our anniversary has been from Thursday to Sunday. But when he said he was cancelling it, I knew he hadn't forgotten."

"Ahhh... huh. So you think his sweet behavior is because he is planning this fabulous wedding anniversary? Well I believe this one will be very different from all the others." September stated with a bit of sarcasm.

"He'll be so excited once his sees a whole case!" Catherine spoke with much enthusiasm.

September sighed. "Okay, if you say so."

"Chill out. He loves me. Relax and enjoy the flight."

September smirked, leaned back in her cushy leather seat and yelled... "Jenna! Another coffee and orange juice please."

Catherine just smiled at her. September returned the grin with a gut feeling that Catherine was in for a huge disappointment.

On this Wednesday, Johnathon was prepared for his day with Nicolette. He had her favorite wine iced in a small bucket on the coffee table, red roses in a vase beside it, a vanilla folder, and a small box wrapped with a pink bow ready for her to unwrap. He awaited her presence at the condominium and stood glaring out the glass doors. Once she arrived beautifully dressed in a one piece tight fitting Rails dress... Johnathon let her in.

"Where's Becky?" asked Nicolette.

Johnathon kissed her on her cheek and then escorted her to his suite. She placed her handbag on the coffee table noticing all the items that were already staged there.

He walked over to her and let his emotional affection explode upon her lips. She responded in turn and then pulled away. Johnathon looked a little surprised by her action.

Inquisitive, Nicolette had to ask again. "Where's Becky, your receptionist?"

"Becky only works from ten to six now. She is making sure the rooms are cleared after the women come and remove their things."

Nicolette was stunned. "What?"

"The building is ours my love. No more occupants on any floor. As a matter of fact, the building will be up for auction by the end of the month."

Nicolette was surprised at his words. "Why, Johnathon?"

"You… my love. I thought about what you said on the yacht that day. About me not being able to have you. So… when I came back, I tried to resume my old habits and forget you." Johnathon paused. "Move on as if our relationship never happened."

Nicolette turned her back to Johnathon. "And?"

"I found that the females that I once enjoyed so lustfully was not what I wanted anymore. I broke the relationships off with all of them. I found myself thinking of only you, even as I laid in bed with them and with my wife."

Nicolette was saddened. She bowed her head. "I know Johnathon. That's why I wanted to talk to you in person. I can't go on this way. As much as I love you and want to be with you, it will never work." Johnathon walked toward her and turned her around by her shoulders. Tears began to form in hers eyes.

"I have never felt about a woman like I feel about you, right now, this very moment. When I was alone one night, I wrote a hundred pages of how to tell you how much I love you. I sat there and stared at what I had written. Then I burned them all, because I realized my actions would speak louder than my words."

"What do you mean?"

"I knew in order for you to realize how deep my love is for you, I had to get rid of the other women, the condo, and here…" He reached for a vanilla folder off the coffee table and handed it to her.

Nicolette opened the folder and pulled papers out. She glanced at the first page and shock struck her face. "Divorce papers."

"Yes." Johnathon quickly reached for the small black box wrapped with the pink bow and handed it to her.

Once she unwrapped the box and opened it, her jaw dropped in complete astonishment. "A diamond ring. Oh Johnathon…"

"Yes, my love. Will you marry me and be the love of my life?"

Nicolette walked around the room gazing at the ring. Tears began to trickle down her cheeks. She gave back the ring and moved to the terrace. Johnathon placed the ring on the coffee table and followed her. He placed his arms around her waist and kissed her gently upon her neck. He turned her to face him and with loving eyes and tears flowing down her cheeks, Johnathon kissed her lips. She didn't resist. As the kisses continued upon their lips, cheeks and neck, Johnathon unzipped her dress from behind as she unbuttoned his shirt. Both were completely naked. Passionate, physical emotions took control as he swept her into his arms and carried her to the bedroom. As he gazed into her eyes, he placed her upon the bed, placing his body next to hers'. One hand softly glided up her thigh until his middle finger landed inside her. Nicolette's body was already flowing with juices. Johnathon quickly eased inside her and stroke her steamy hot flesh with his harden rod, until the ultimate moment of sensation struck them both. Moans of sexual pleasure echoed off the walls.

In the bedroom, moments later, Nicolette rested upon Johnathon's chest. She was in deep thought. While Johnathon relished in the fact that Nicolette loved him and now all he needed was for her to say *yes* to be his wife. He kissed her on the head and rubbed her arms for a continued show of affection. Nicolette knew she must tell him why she came.

"Johnathon." Nicolette rose from his chest and looked him in the eyes.

Johnathon stared back with a smile. "What, my love?"

"I can't accept your offer of marriage."

Johnathon sat up from the pillows in bed. His tone of voice was a little harsh. "What are you saying?"

"It wouldn't have been right to tell you over the phone. I had to see you, to feel you, to make love to you one last time. I am saying this can't go on."

Johnathon reached to hold her hand. She allowed the gentleness of his touch. "I know. I get it. That's why I position myself so we can be together. That's why I am leaving my wife. I want *forever,* with you. I finally realize what it means to love someone more than anything else."

"Johnathon…." She paused, bowed her head and then looked back into his eyes. "I know how you feel. Since we've been apart, I thought about leaving my husband. My business is thriving, you love me and I love you, but…"

Johnathon pulled his hand away from hers and interrupted. A little angered…"*But* what? There is nothing else. We started the business so you could have your freedom. So you didn't have to be tied to someone you don't love or care about. So you don't have bow to his beckon call and now you're saying, *but. But* what, Nicolette?"

Nicolette slowly got out of bed and went to gather her clothing in the living room. Her tone was that of frustration. "I knew I shouldn't have come."

Johnathon followed her into the living room butt naked. "You came because you love me. Don't throw us away."

Nicolette reached for her dress and started to put it on. "While I was thinking about you, I also thought about all the good things Giovanni has done for me."

Johnathon spoke in an irritated tone. "It doesn't matter what he's done. You don't love him. Would you rather be faithful and unhappy, than be happy and in love?"

Nicolette paused in thought of his words and zipped her dress as far as she could. Again tears formed in hers eyes and she stared at Johnathon. Softly she spoke. "I don't know. But what I do know is I made a promise to another man."

Johnathon grabbed her by the shoulders. He pulled her lips close to his and with much yearning and passion, kissed her as if it was the last time. Nicolette placed her arms around his neck and returned the lustful desire. Completely naked in her arms, he raised her dress, rested her on the sofa and pounded her inner body once more. Moments later, Johnathon walked to the center of the living room almost in tears. "I love you."

Nicolette observed his facial expression. "Give me some more time. I do love you. I am… I'm just so confused right now." She remained on the sofa to put her shoes on and noticed the ring on the coffee table. Tears streamed down her cheeks again. "I have to go. Just give me some more time, please." She grabbed her purse from the coffee table and rushed out the door.

Johnathon watched as she left. When the door closed, he picked up the ring, poured himself some wine and stared at this sparkling diamond. He thought to himself… his plan for Nicolette had not changed. He just needed to give her a little more time. With that time, he would continue to free himself of all bondage that would prevent them from being together. Now that his ladies were gone, it was Catherine's turn. He needed to be free of her. Making Catherine hate him was his new plot. If he botched their anniversary day which was fast approaching, he felt Catherine would despise him enough to want a divorce. His usual routine was to shower her with gifts, love and affection on that day. Then wine and dine her with friends in a different state of epic beauty and dynamic entertainment. It was not to be on this anniversary.

CHAPTER 38

Missed Anniversary

*C*atherine returned from France with a beautiful wrapped case of wine. September helped her place it in the cellar. This Wednesday evening Catherine went to bed thinking Johnathon was going to surprise her as usual on her wedding anniversary. Especially in their last conversation, he called her his love. The celebration was just hours away. Catherine went to sleep that evening in anticipation of her glorious anniversary day.

On this Thursday morning, its 8 a.m., Catherine woke and Jonathon was nowhere to be found in the house. She immediately got dressed and called September. September arrived in front of Catherine's home. Near tears, Catherine stood in the doorway. Mrs. Jensen was suspicious of how September obtained such an expensive car.

September sprinted to the door. Catherine stood there in tears. "What's wrong? You sounded distraught over the phone. Why the tears? "

"Johnathon didn't come home last night." Catherine walked further in the house and paced the living room floor. September followed.

"Has he ever done this before on your anniversary? Is this the first time?"

"Yes. He has never broken or missed our anniversary since we've been married."

September was very calm. "Well, did you call him?"

"Yes, but the phone rings and goes to voice mail. He promised to delegate the work and come home to spend time with me every anniversary. Why would he do this on our special day?"

"Something could be wrong or maybe he worked later and fell asleep at the office?"

Catherine was still pacing. Tears streamed down her cheeks. "Noooo... September. He has always kept his promises to me for our anniversary."

"Stop pacing the floor. Calm yourself. Call him now."

When his cell phone rang as the sunlight struck the window pane, Johnathon reached for his phone and soon realized that Catherine had tried to reach him three times. Rolling out of bed at his condominium suite, he admired his beautiful Nicolette laying there naked. Her exquisitely curved body positioned picturesque with the face of an angel made him smile. He soon dressed to leave for work. He kissed Nicolette on the cheek and she awoke. Nicolette smiled at Johnathon, still sleepy.

"My love I am so happy you came back yesterday after our last conversation."

"As I laid in my hotel room, I realized you were like a drug in my veins. I just needed to see you. I know now I can't leave you. Oh Johnathon, what are we to do?"

Johnathon realm with joy. "I must go to work now. Would you do me an honor my love?"

"Anything my sweet." Nicolette spoke with a tender voice.

"Wear my ring when we are together." Johnathon took the box from the end table, took the ring out, pulled her wedding ring off and place his engagement ring on her finger.

Nicolette beamed with joy as he placed the ring upon her finger. Johnathon leaned toward her lips and kissed her lovingly. "I have a surprise for you when I return this evening. Wait for me. Don't change your mind."

"You know I have to leave tomorrow."

"I know. Today is Thursday my love. Find a way to stay until at least Sunday. I just want you to wear it for a few days until you have to leave."

"I'll make up some excuse. I will be here when you return." Nicolette closed her eyes to slumber once more.

Johnathon kissed her on the forehead, dressed and left her resting in bed.

Meanwhile, Catherine hung up and dialed again. Johnathon's phone rang and went straight to voice mail.

"Call Mark. Perhaps he might know where he is?" stated September.

Catherine called Mark. Mark was already at work and saw the call was from Catherine. He decided that whatever Johnathon had done, he wasn't getting involved. Mark let the call go to voice mail. He continued his daily schedule.

September was thinking if this man loved work so much, if he isn't dead, where else would he be. "Let's go check his office."

Catherine ran to the kitchen, grabbed her purse and keys. She and September left hastily for Johnathon's office. Mrs. Jensen was excited when she noticed Catherine's and September's acceleration in leaving the garage. Gloria knew something had to be wrong.

Once they reached the office building, Catherine and September found Johnathon at his desk. Catherine raced pass Angela and stormed into his office as he stood up in a motion to leave. September stayed outside next to Angela's desk. Catherine slammed the door behind her.

"You didn't come home last night." She spoke in anger.

Johnathon declared in an unemotional, intense tone. "That's very observant of you. But if you must know, I was with a client. If you will excuse me, I have a brief to give in twenty minutes. I must get with Mark to ensure everything is in order."

"Do you know what today is?" Catherine spoke in a soft but aggressive tone.

"It's Thursday. Now excuse me." Johnathon grabbed some papers off his desk.

"Our anniversary is today. You have never forgotten." Catherine's eyes teared up.

Johnathon spoke softly, dispassionate by her watery eyes. "I haven't forgotten this time either. I thought you may want to spend it with September. So I scheduled a very important meeting for today instead of spending it with you." Johnathon looked through the glass window of his office. "I see you brought her with you. Now you two can spend the rest of the day together without any interference from me. This client I have to brief is worth one-hundred million and anything he wants, he will get, including all of my time today. So you go mosey off with your best friend and shoot some guns. I will continue to ensure my company thrives. Now, get out my office Catherine. I have work to do."

Catherine was baffled, shocked, and frustrated all in one expression. Johnathon picked up some more papers on his desk and headed to the door.

Catherine earnestly spoke. "Baby... Johnathon wait." Johnathon paused at the door with his back to her. "You know I love you. I have been waiting for you to say something, do anything to show me that our love is strong and you want our marriage to work. But I have been drowning in nothing but disappointment from you for the last few years of our marriage. Every day it keeps getting worse. If you don't see me as your wife, how do you see me?"

Johnathon turned and faced Catherine. "What makes you think I ever loved you?" Catherine held her hand up to display the ring on her finger. "A mere symbol of my deception. I have never loved you."

Johnathon continued out the door leaving it open. He stared at September angrily and continued to Mark's office. September peered at Catherine standing in the doorway weeping uncontrollably. Catherine walked out of the office with her head hanging down. September put her arm around her shoulder. "Don't cry Catherine, he's not worth your tears."

Angela watched sadly as both Catherine and September walked out of the building together.

CHAPTER 39

Johnathon at the Night Club

September got Catherine in her car. Tears were flowing heavily from Catherine's eyes. It was obvious that she was feeling dejected. When they arrived at September's home, once inside, Catherine went to the kitchen to fix herself a Scotch straight, on the rocks. September grabbed the bottle, placed it back in the cabinet and gave Catherine a lecture.

September spoke firmly. "You know you don't drink hard liquor."

"Right now I just need to drown my sorrow."

"Not with me you're not. If one man doesn't want you, there are plenty of fish in the sea. The way you get over one man is to go fishing for another."

"Did you forget I'm married?"

"I didn't say you had to marry him."

"Oh September leave me be. One sip of Scotch and I'll be out for the rest of the day."

"You are not going to spend your anniversary drinking yourself to death because he is refusing to spend time with you."

Catherine spoke sincerely. "I love him September, even though he treats me like crap sometimes, I..."

September interrupted. "All the time."

"I still love him. Without him, what do I have? Nothing. I don't have a full college degree in anything. I don't have money in the bank in my own name. Everything I have is bought with his money. I'm losing him September. I can feel it."

"Catherine don't you get it by now. You never had him."

Catherine hung her head down over the kitchen counter. September stepped over to her. Tears trickled down Catherine's face. September kissed her on the cheek. "You have a friend in me." Catherine smiled slightly. "Now before you called, I had a full day scheduled for myself. Since you are available, we my friend, are going to complete my activity list for today and tonight will be a totally amazing evening."

Catherine perked up a little. "Oh yeah, like what?"

"Well since this is your anniversary, I've got something special for you. We are going to celebrate today like it was your birthday, with a bang. Now let's get busy. Go change into your jeans."

Catherine spoke nonchalantly. "September I really don't feel…."

September interrupted. "Go get changed woman."

"My clothes still in the guest room?"

"Why wouldn't they be?"

"Of course. I guest Antonio hasn't moved in yet."

September ignored the comment. "We got para sailing and jet skiing for the rest of the afternoon, but first you have to feed me. I missed breakfast racing to see about you today."

Catherine sighed. "Let me go get changed."

"I will be right here." September went to the refrigerator and grabbed a Pepsi.

Twenty minutes later, they are off to the races.

So much fun they had all day, Catherine forgot it was her anniversary. They walked to September's car from playing the last activity of the day, racket ball at the gym.

"Today was great!" exclaimed Catherine.

"Well wait until you see tonight."

"Tonight?" Catherine stated with a tired voice.

"Yes, there is this real expensive night club we're going to."

"Night Club?" Catherine really isn't in the mood. "I really don't feel up to it."

"I didn't say you had to pick up a man. We're just going to have some fun." September smiled. "I'm not taking no for an answer. Now let's go get cleaned up and party the night away."

September drove Catherine home. Mrs. Jensen watched as September drove Catherine into the driveway. Catherine got out of the car and leaned down and begged the question. "You think my hubby will be home, its 7 p.m.?"

"I think he made it perfectly clear about how he felt about today." September kept the engine running. "Now go get dressed like you're worth a million bucks. I will pick you up around ten-thirty. Now that I have the right car for the valet, let's have some fun." September burned rubber with her new car headed home to get dressed.

Mrs. Jensen noticed their every move.

While Catherine got dressed she noticed her wedding pictures on her vanity table. She stared at them for a few minutes. She sat on the bed holding one picture in her hand and burst into tears.

When September arrived back at ten-thirty that evening, Catherine was dressed in a sleek black Amani short sleeve evening gown with purse, shoes, and jewelry to match. September was also dressed in black.

Mrs. Jensen still spied from across the street. As Catherine climbed in the car, September waved and blew Mrs. Jensen a kiss. "Leave her alone, September. She thinks she's being inconspicuous when it's dark. You don't want to ruin her day by letting her know she is painfully obvious."

"Say my friend, I was thinking, can we use the limo for tonight instead? Let's drive up like celebrities."

Catherine thought for a second. "Sure. The chauffeur is at my beckon call, but why?"

"If you saw the cars that drive up to this place, you wouldn't ask that question. I know mines is nice and fits the protocol, but…"

Catherine interrupted… "Just for you." She peeked at her watch. "I will see you at… let's say eleven-thirty. That's time for the driver to get here and us to get to you."

"Okay. Sounds good." September drove her car back home.

Catherine arrived on time in front of September's house. When she came out, September was dressed in a light blue evening gown with white gloves and a diamond necklace, watch, and purse to match. The chauffeur got out of the car to open the door.

"You changed clothes from…"

September intervened. "After I saw you in black. I wanted to be in something different."

"I'm glad to see you putting to use the clothing we bought in New York."

"Of course my friend. I have been trying to get my hands on and wear this type of clothing all my life. Now I have some place to wear it thanks to you. So thank you." The driver pulled off.

As September adjusted her seat in the limo, not to wrinkle her gown, Catherine was curious. "Where are we going again? Tell the driver."

"It's called 'All the Way' driver. I called to see if we need reservations. They said walk-ins are welcome. Oh yeah, they raised the cover charge to $25,000 per person."

Catherine was slightly astonished at the price... "Twenty-five thousand dollars! For a night club? What was it before the increase?"

"Ten-thousand."

"September at a $25,000 cover charge, how do you know about this place?" quizzed Catherine.

"You know how I like things I can't afford. I Googled it long before I met you. At that time, it was ten-thousand. Inflation?" Catherine shook her head. "What are you complaining about, your husband is not here. Let's enjoy ourselves. There are four levels to this place. There is Jazz, classical, POP, and rhythm and blues music per floor. Each deck beautifully designed with the décor to meet the style music being played. We'll get a private booth, a bottle of champagne or wine of choice, with appetizers. There are two levels of booths on one floor. One booth is directly on the dance floor for the drinkers and dancers and the other sits high above the dance floor for those that just want to drink, chat and watch others dance. Just wait and see. If you don't like it we can leave. Just to be nosey, I frequent it a couple of times a month to see what kind of cars and people drive up there."

"Were you impressed?"

"Very much so. Wealthy executives and an occasional celebrity." September spoke with a smile. "We arrive in style just like them and you can flash your black card."

"You mean I'm paying for all of this?"

"You didn't think I was?"

Catherine just grinned. "It's my day. Let's go have some fun."

"Yes, yes, let's parrr... ty." September motioned in her seat some dance moves and smiled.

"If I don't like it, we can leave?"

"You would walk out on a $25,000.00 cover charge that is non-refundable? If I paid $5.00 dollars to get in some place, you best believe I'm shutting it down. I'm going to be asking the clean-up crew to take the glasses off my table."

Catherine laughed. When they drove up, valet gentlemen dressed in black suit and tie race to the car. One opened the door and another escorted the ladies from the car to the entrance. A valet sat in the limo and showed the driver where to park. Once at the door, a concierge greeted them. He was dressed in a tuxedo.

"Ladies, how are you this evening? Your first time at All the Way?" questioned the concierge.

"Yes." replied September.

Catherine reached for her card. He took her card and tapped it on the machine. He asked... "Have you ladies been here before?"

Catherine was quick to speak. "No this is our first time."

September was admiring the elegance and style of the lobby as she peeked past the bodyguards. She observed guests at a bar, dining tables, and a group lounge areas.

"You are in for a treat, ladies. We have four floors. I am sure you will find something to your liking. To enter a floor your must have a key card. What style of music do you prefer?" Asked the host.

"What if we wanted to visit all four floors?" asked September.

"That would cost each of you another ten-thousand dollars." Spoke the concierge.

"Done." Stated September.

Catherine stared at September. The host stared at Catherine. She handed her card back. The host tapped her card again.

"Here you are ma 'dam." The host gave her card back. "Please stand in this spot right here. Your master key is on its way."

The host let them enter... They stood in the lobby while he attended to other guests.

Catherine was observing the beautiful architecture of this magnificent edifice. She was also a little nervous about being at a club. September noticed Catherine's emotionally discomfort. "What's the problem?"

"I don't know how to dance. So… Jazz would…"

At that moment a handsome masculine, blonde hair, blue eyed man dressed in a black suit walked up to them. "Mrs. Fitzpatrick?"

Catherine smiled and spoke flirtatiously. "Yes, that's me."

The young man graciously handed her a master key card to each floor. "The elevators are around the bar area there," He points. "to your left. Each button is designated to a particular dance floor. Swipe the card across the white light at the elevator. The music is labeled by floor. Enjoy your time Mrs. Fitzpatrick." He looked at September. "Ma'am". He stepped away.

"I heard that soft sexy voice. That's what I am talking about." proclaimed September. "Now there's a man you might want to get to know?"

"Oh come on September. He looks nineteen."

"I didn't say you have to marry him. We are here for a good time. Let's live a little. Hell, I'll dance with a sixteen year old if he is here." Catherine shook her head and smiled. "Well, we don't have to dance."

The host came back and saw them still standing there. "Have you gotten your key ladies?"

"Yes." Spoke Catherine.

"Good. Just to let you know, the first bottle of wine or champagne is on the house after that every drink is charged. You also have you own personal waiter at each booth. Once you sit down at a booth, you are tagged with that booth and the waiter. No one else can take your seats or orders. This way if you decide to change booth's just to get another free bottle of wine or champagne it won't happen."

"With a cover charge of $25,000.00 that would be uncharacteristic of your customers. Would it not?" asked September.

"You would be surprised at those who just want to come in to check the place out and all they have is that one fee just to get in here. That's why we raised the price. Mixed drinks are five hundred dollars, two-hundred for a beer, one-thousand or more depending on the type drink you have. A bottle of any kind of wine, champagne is two-thousand dollars or more. Enjoy ladies."

September and Catherine strolled through the lobby observing the clientele. They pushed the Jazz button for the top floor. "Let's start out slow." Stated Catherine.

"Well, if we get bored with the jazz room, let's be adventurous and move about to check out the entire club. Who knows what floor we may find most intriguing and want to stay there?" September facial expression beamed with happiness.

"No problem."

They take the elevator to the fourth floor. September was astounded by the ambiance of the lighting in the room and the amount of people that were there just for Jazz. "There is a lot of rich folk in LA that love jazz. I guess you don't know how many until you start hanging out where they hang out."

September found a table. They sipped a few drinks, Catherine had Champagne and September drank wine. They sat for an hour at the top level chatting.

"This is nice, but I want to have some fun. Let's go straight down to the POP floor and dance a little. Who knows who we might meet? Some cute rich single dudes." Stated September.

"Lead the way." Catherine followed.

When September put the key in the door for POP music and it sled open, she immediately scanned the area for an open booth.

"I'm going to the ladies room. Do you care to join me?" asked Catherine.

"No. I'm going to see if I can find an empty booth so we can skim the entire floor without missing a face. I never know what kind of eye-candy will catch my eye."

"Eye-candy?" asked Catherine.

"Yes. Gorgeous hunks, cutie pies with pretty faces, or both. I will be right here when you get back."

Catherine disappeared. The music was bombing to the ear. September bobbed to the beat as she scanned for an empty booth. It appeared as if there were over a 150 people on the dance floor. September eventually spotted a booth. This seemed like the popular spot as there were only three booths available out of ninety plus on the top level. September saw one she preferred and walked toward it. While she was standing by the booth, she observed the dance floor once again. When Catherine returned, September's eyes suddenly bucked as she gazed at the group of people enjoying the music on the lower level.

Catherine watched September's expression of awe. "Is this our booth you're standing beside?" September was still staring at the dance floor with her mouth wide open. With the music booming, Catherine leaned closer to September's ear. "What are you gawking at? Have you found your eye-candy?"

September hasn't taken her eyes off the dance floor. "Not only did I find a booth, but look what else I found?"

Catherine squinted in the dimness of the light. She walked over to railing, "That looks…" Catherine leaned and squinted a little harder. "A little bit like Johnathon."

"A little bit… that is Johnathon. No wonder he works late and can't find time for you on your anniversary. He's too busy working."

"September I am sure there is a perfectly good explanation for why he is here with that woman. Johnathon loves me." Catherine continued to stare at them dancing. She mumbled silently to herself. "He has to love me."

"On what planet? Give up the denial. Wake up and smell the roses Catherine. That's why you are upstairs with me and he's down there dancing with another woman… because he loves you so much."

"That's not fair." September pointed to Johnathon on the dance floor. "That's! What's not fair on your anniversary! I wouldn't be surprised if that was really him I spotted on the beach in Hawaii that time. It appears to be the same woman too."

Catherine gazed back over the balcony. Johnathon was swinging, laughing, and dancing to the music with great delight. September leaned over the balcony to get a better look at the woman.

"Wait! Step back September, I don't want him to see us. I know that woman." They both stepped back from the balcony so they couldn't be seen from the dance floor.

"He's working September. That woman is one of my husband's clients. Sometimes they entertain their clientele by dining out."

September peeked at the dance floor once again. "Does that look like they are dining out? It looks more like they are partying out. Have you heard from him today since you spoke to him at his office this morning, just to wish you Happy Anniversary?"

"Nooo, but I haven't called him either."

"Let's go ask him if she's a client."

"Look September it's okay. Let it be. She's married too." Catherine turned her attention from September and observed the joyful faces and body movement of both Johnathon and Nicolette.

"No Catherine, if this is work he will take her home and go home. It's 1 a.m. in the morning. If this is pleasure, he will take her home and go inside. Let's follow him when he leaves."

"No September, I trust my husband."

September still exasperated over the fact that Johnathon was on the dance floor. "Don't you want to know if he is cheating on you? You owe it to yourself to see if you have been his second hand maiden."

Catherine thought for a second. "Very well. But I'm sure this is work. He and Mark take their clients out to clubs and restaurants to discuss business sometimes. I know her husband."

"Well, let's just see which one she is… a wife or a mistress."

They remained inconspicuous and continue to watch Johnathon and Nicolette the rest of the night. Catherine and September observed them for the next couple of hours as they danced and drank enjoying each other's company. When it appeared they were getting ready to leave Catherine yelled. "I'll have the valet get the limo."

"No. Have the limo driver go home. Call us an Uber, quickly. I will keep an eye on them until you get back."

Catherine left immediately and did as instructed. Minutes later, Nicolette and Johnathon waited for his car to arrive outside the club, Catherine and September stood inside the lobby gazing out the windows.

"How long did that Uber say before he would be here?"

"He should be pulling up any second across the street." Stated Catherine.

Johnathon's car arrived. He seated Nicolette in the passenger side and soon got in on the driver's side. They slowly pulled away.

"Where is that Uber guy!" quietly yelled September.

"There he is!" Catherine yelled.

They both scampered across the street. September was still eyeing the Jaguar as it slowly made its way down the road. They both hopped in the Uber.

The Uber person was taken by surprise as they were both dressed elegantly with expensive jewelry, but yet they called an Uber.

"Where to ladies?" asked the Uber driver.

"You see that Jaguar just up ahead?" asked September.

The Uber driver glanced in the direction. "Yes."

"We need you to follow it." Spoke Catherine.

The Uber driver appeared puzzled. He hesitated to pull off.

"Now!" yelled September.

"Yes ma'am." The Uber driver, sped off in a hurry. He tried to catch up to the Jaguar.

"Keep your distance. Two car links." Quipped September.

Minutes later, Johnathon pulled up to the condominium where he maintained his private suite. He opened the door for Nicolette. As the Uber driver slowly drove pass the building, Catherine and September peered out the back seat window. "What kind of building is that?" asked Catherine.

"Stop." September spoke to the driver. "Go back pass the building." The Uber driver does a U-turn and continued to drive slowly. "It's either an apartment building or a condominium, take your pick. They soon noticed Johnathon usher Nicolette with his hand around her waist. He kissed her cheek as they made their way through the front door.

"Do you kiss your clients after you take them home?" questioned September.

"He's just being nice since he knows her. He'll be out in a minute." Replied Catherine.

The driver almost passed the building when… "Stop the car!" Yelled September. The driver pulled over across from the building. "Did we tell you to leave?"

The Uber driver soon got the hint. "Hey ladies this is not what I do."

September and Catherine ignored his comment. "I don't think he's dropping her off." Commented September. They both continued to watch the building. Three minutes passed.

The Uber driver was getting impatient. "Ladies I have other fares if this is not your destination. We need to leave."

September got upset. "What other fares do you have at 4 a.m. in the morning?"

Puzzled to his situation, "Sleep… if you must know. So I can drive again today. Now if you ladies need to be dropped off somewhere, I will be glad to take you, otherwise I'm leaving you here."

"We'll make it worth your while just to shut up and do as we ask." September turned to Catherine. "He's right. If Johnathon was coming out, he would have been out by now. We will come back tomorrow and check this place out."

Catherine was in a daze. She spoke softly with tears rolling down her cheeks. "On my anniversary. You're right."

September observed Catherine's depressed demeanor. "Driver take us too 3547 Nation View Terrace. You're staying with me tonight my friend."

As the Uber driver pulled in front of September's home. She reached in Catherine's purse, grabbed two-hundred dollars cash and tipped the Uber driver.

CHAPTER 40

Johnathon Calls Tate and Mark

On this gorgeous sunny Saturday Johnathon saw Nicolette off at the airport. He was now laying in his pool enjoying a cigar, while Tate sat across from him in a lounge chair. Catherine hadn't returned home since she saw Johnathon on Thursday night at the club.

"I invited you here because I need something done for me." Stated Johnathon.

"I was hoping you had finished the project and ready to give me the word 'complete.'"

"Soon."

"Do you have the schematics? My boss would like to take a look at them."

"Why?"

"You can understand his impatience. It's been almost a year."

"Right now I need something from your boss."

"What might that be? You will get no more money until the project is complete."

"No money. I need him to make someone have an accident. It must look like an accident."

"How do you even know my boss is in that kind of business? You've never even met the person."

"Don't ask questions. Remember you're just the messenger. Deliver the message." Insisted Johnathon.

"I transferred a half-billion dollars to your account in Switzerland and now you want to hire *my* boss?" quizzed Tate.

"How much?" questioned Johnathon.

Tate stood and walked closer to Johnathon. "How would I know? This must mean a great deal to you?"

Johnathon screamed. "How much!?"

"I tell you what. Let me get back to you on that. I will deliver the message. It's not like he must have a sign on his wall stating a shot in the shoulder $10,000, a shot in the head, a million."

"You do that Tate. Get back to me as soon as you can. I want it done soon."

"I will be in touch Mr. Fitzpatrick. You better be sure this is what you want."

"You let me worry about that. Just deliver the message."

Tate started to walk out. Then he paused at the sliding glass doors to the living room. He turned to address Johnathon laying face up in the pool with shades on and cigar in his mouth. "How much are you paying?"

Without hesitation Johnathon spoke. "Whatever he ask."

"I will do it myself Mr. Fitzpatrick. Two-million cash dollars." Replied Tate.

Johnathon flipped over in the pool. He put his cigar out in the ashtray next to him. Dripping wet he came from the water and gave Tate a surprised stare. "You can make it look like an accident?"

"Yes, but you will owe me one."

"Owe you? What's the two-million dollars for if I am going to owe you after I pay you?"

"That business I was in, I gave it up. I was good at making people disappear or causing freak accidents. I will do this one thing for you." Tate paused in thought. "If something goes wrong and I need to disappear, I will depend on you to make that happen. So when I call you… you better be like a fuckin fire engine heading to a fire. Understood?'

"Deal." Johnathon smiled with delight not having to wait for an answer.

"Who is it? Name only. Leave the rest to me."

"It's… Russo."

"The billionaire, Giovanni Russo?" asked Tate.

"Yes."

"Five-million. He will be difficult to get to. Why him?" probed Tate.

"That's my business."

"When do you want it done?"

"Soon. I will let you know."

"I will devise a plan on how to get it done. When you are ready with a date, I will execute. Since this is between you and me, let me give you my number." Tate reached in his pocket for a pen.

"Don't write it down. Send it to my phone and don't use your real name."

"How will you know it's me?" asked Tate.

"Get a burner phone and send your text as Otto to me."

"I'll get one now." Tate thought if he gets five million, perhaps he could leave the life of being messenger, make one last kill and just disappear.

"Good. Now leave me. I will give you an update on the project next week."

"Hurry Mr. Fitzpatrick. Time is ticking. It's been twelve months alre... ."

Johnathon intervened. "Well we're not exactly making pencil sharpers are we? Now leave."

As Tate walked out the front door, he received a text communication. The message was 'Get the schematics and confirm possession. We will eliminate Fitzpatrick'.

Tate was shocked. Now he had a dilemma. Once he got the schematics, if Fitzpatrick was killed before he got the five million... how could he turn his life around.

Johnathon continued his leisure in the pool now that Tate was gone. He suddenly felt the urge to call Mark. He dialed on his cell phone.

Mark was relaxing in his million dollar home. His body in a recliner, feet cocked up, watching sports on TV. His cell phone rang by the table.

"Hello."

"Mark, I am leaving Catherine for Nicolette. I know I am in love with her." Mark was silent. "What?... No lecture on morality and marriage?"

"I'm not your father J. You've already heard my spill. What do you want me to say? Thou shalt not commit adultery. You should honor your wife as God honors the church."

Johnathon sighed. "Something like that."

"Or do you want to hear, 'go for it.' Follow your heart or your ego, whichever is dominant?' Mark paused and waited for a comment, none came. "It doesn't matter what I say, because the final decision rest with Johnathon Fitzpatrick."

"Look Mark. You know me."

"Right, I know you. That's why I can't tell you what to do or how I feel about the situation, because it's not about me. It's about you and what makes you happy. If it's not Catherine, then do you J. But whatever you do, just be honest about it so she won't feel guilty for the marriage not working out. Catherine deserves that."

Johnathon was in thought and didn't say a word.

CHAPTER 41

Is Johnathon Cheating?

This Monday morning Catherine was still over at September's house discussing what they observed with Johnathon last week. September was fixing breakfast for the two of them. Catherine sat at the breakfast nook as September cracked eggs, fried bacon, toasted toast, and poured orange juice.

"Has Johnathon called you?"

"No."

"Are you going home today? You think Johnathon maybe upset about you spending the weekend with me?"

"No. Not after what he said to me on our anniversary day. We haven't talked. But I'll go home this evening."

"With your cheating husband, when you go home tonight play this song." She pulled out a record by The Jones Girls.

"What's that?"

"Listen." September played it on her turntable.

"Who has a turntable?"

"I do. Now listen." September played the '45' record. 'You're gonna to make me love somebody else. If you keep on treatin me the way you do'. September sung and danced along.

Catherine listened for a minute and then interrupted. "September I'm not going to love somebody else unless he wants a divorce. Our vows were to love in sickness and in health. Until death do us part, not divorce."

"That's right and now he's making you sick. So we need to cause his death."

"I don't think that's funny."

"Well, it wasn't meant to be. If you try to push your affection on him and shower him with love when he doesn't love you, he's going to run like a hungry Cheetah chasing a Gazelle."

"Look… September if Johnathon doesn't love me anymore, I'm not going to try and force him to love me. I just wouldn't do that. I need love voluntarily. My father once told me if a man doesn't want you, let him go. If he doesn't come back, it wasn't meant to be."

"Smart Dad. But that still doesn't take away from the fact that your husband is a low down dirty snake-in-the-grass."

"Now September, I'm sure there is a perfectly good explanation for what we saw. Mrs. Russo is a married client."

"Yeah, an adulteress client and on your anniversary."

"How can I know for sure if she is having an affair with Johnathon? I just don't want to make an assumption from sitting there for five minutes. He could have just made sure she was safe in her apartment."

"Well let's just test that theory." Thought September.

"How's that?" probed Catherine.

"Here's a plan. We follow him and see where goes for this entire week."

"You devised a plan already?"

"That's what Rangers do. They assess the situation and create a plan to solve it."

"But what do we follow him in?"

"Rental cars, Ubers, taxi's, whatever. Tomorrow we will go and check out to see if the building has rooms for rent."

Catherine was almost in tears. "Ok, September. Let's see where this leads. I pray you're wrong."

That week Catherine and September followed Johnathon's every move. They rented cars and used Uber drivers not to be spotted with their own vehicles.

This day September went up to condominium. The front designer glass doors were locked. She knocked. Becky saw her and buzzed the door open. She only let September come as far as the lobby desk.

"May I help you Miss? Are you lost in this neighborhood?" questioned Becky.

"Yes. I mean no. I was just driving around and looking for a place as I am new to the area. I noticed this building had a beautiful view of the city and a waterfront behind it. I just knew it had to be some apartments or condominiums. I was wondering if I could purchase one."

"I am sorry but that is not possible as this property is privately owned by one individual."

"Who is that so I may inquire about living arrangements?" spoke September.

"Sorry again, but the residents here are only recommended to stay here by the owner. The owner gives the keys to the residents. That's why no rooms here are for sale."

"You mean the owner finds the tenant, instead of the other way around?"

"That is correct. If you were one he had singled out to reside here, you would have a key to those glass doors and a key to one of the condos. However, I believe the owner will be auctioning off the building soon. Either way you can't reside here. Now if you will excuse me, I have paperwork that needs to be finished by the end of the day." Spoke Becky.

"Of course, thank you for your time." September left. Becky hit the automatic doors to lock behind her. Catherine was hiding in the back seat of the rental car.

When September sat in the driver seat, Catherine engaged her with a question. "What did you find out?"

"Johnathon owns the building. He personally hand picks the women that live there."

"What? Women?" asked Catherine.

"Yes, he gives them the key to the front door and to the rooms."

"What! Is the building full? How many rooms does it hold?"

"Hey… hold on." September calmly spoke. "I didn't interrogate the woman. She may have gotten suspicious and alerted Johnathon of my actions. We will follow him for a couple more days and see what happens. You just remember to be yourself when the two of you eventually see each other at home."

"That's easy, since I rarely see him anyway. Now I know why the late nights." Thought Catherine.

The next day, Catherine and September followed him again in a different rental car. Its 2:30 in the afternoon and they see Johnathon go straight to the condominium. He parked his car in the building garage. They drove past, and waited for him to leave.

As they sat in the rental car, two hours past. "Catherine, if this is where he spends his afternoons or evenings, we can be sitting here for hours and we didn't bring food."

"Is that all you can think about is food right now when my marriage is on the line."

"He's your man, not mind!" September, a little agitated from her stomach grumbling. "When I get hungry, I need to eat."

At that moment, Johnathon came out of the garage with a passenger in the car. "Hey! Look!" Screamed Catherine.

September saw the car with the two of them as well. "Ok, let's go. I hope he is headed to a restaurant."

Catherine cranked the engine and began a slow drive behind Johnathon. They followed him to his private jet location and noticed the two of them get out. Minutes later they saw Johnathon's private jet leave the area. Catherine broke down in tears.

"What are the tears for? She could be a client. It's not the same woman." Spoke September.

"A client that is already at your personally owned condominium and then leave two hours later in your private jet? Give me a break." Sarcastically stated by Catherine.

"Now you're beginning to see what I have been trying to tell you all along. So now can we go get something to eat? I don't think this rental car can fly. Besides, it's almost five o'clock and I'm starved."

As tears rolled down Catherine's eyes, she headed for the nearest restaurant to fill September's craving for food. Moments later they were seated at a restaurant, Catherine eyes were red. The waiter came to the table.

"Something to drink ladies?" asked the waiter.

"Yes, I will have a Negroni and she will have a Pineapple Pina Colada." Answered September.

Catherine's head was bowed. The waiter left.

"Catherine, you had to have a feeling with the late nights and sometimes not coming home at all, that Johnathon was having an affair. We saw him at the nightclub and from yesterday. Why are you letting this get you down? Now you have a more vivid picture of why you aren't his number one woman, even though you're his wife."

Catherine looked up at her. "Really September. That hurts. Nicolette is married. We don't know who that lady was we just saw him with. Why? I don't understand. Why?"

"Reality does hurt. Lust! Love! Who cares? Now what are you going to do about it?"

Catherine was in deep thought. The waiter returned with their drinks. "Are you ladies ready to order?"

"Yes. I will have the Chicken Marsala with extra gravy and mushrooms. Does that come with anything?" asked September.

"Corn, broccoli, mashed potatoes and garlic bread." Stated the waiter.

"Perfect. Hurry and bring that." September took a sip of her drink.

"For you ma 'dam?" asked the server.

"Nothing. Thank you." Said Catherine.

"She'll have the same." The waiter left. September placed her napkin in her lap. "You can't think clearly on an empty stomach."

Catherine had a thought. "September our jets have to have a log sheet for clearance to our destinations. We can go back there late tonight and find out where they went and when they plan to come back. Plus the names of the individuals are logged as well."

"Sounds good. Let's eat first." September took a sip of her drink. "You know how to get in?"

"I got it covered. I'm friendly with the flight manager." Catherine felt she had to know where he was taking this woman and others he had been with.

Once dinner was done, they returned to the private jet area. Catherine reviewed the logs of the past month. "Look September. Look at the last six months."

"Oh my God. Look at all the different women." September was amazed.

"Today was Amoy. The week before Amoy, it was Melanie. Then Nicolette and the week after that it was Nicolette again and on and on and on."

"All different women. Some of them more than once. Trips to Hawaii, Paris, New York, the Virgin Islands and others. Do you want to believe they are all clients?" questioned September.

Catherine walked out of the flight manager's office in tears.

CHAPTER 42

Plot to Murder

After September had seen enough of the actions of Johnathon's infidelity, she was hatching Johnathon's demise. She was sketching and scratching on a piece of paper in her kitchen. Catherine came from the living room and sat on a stool at the counter.

"Hey, I thought we were just chilling tonight and watching some movies with popcorn. Your sofa is real comfy."

"How can you talk like that? After all, we've seen your husband's manifest. Flying all those women to Hawaii, New York and other places. You know he entertained in a five story condominium. He's a liar, a deceiver, and just a plain old asshole."

Catherine peered at the paper September was writing on. She saw what appeared to be a design of her living room and pool area. "What kind of diabolical plot have you hatched up?"

"I have guns, knives, hand grenades, poison… how do you want him to die?"

"Are you crazy? I don't want him to die. I've thought about it. If I lose him, I have nothing. I am willing to accept my role as the other woman rather than his wife."

September slightly angered because of Catherine's approval of Johnathon's actions. "I wish you could hear yourself right now. You sound ridiculous. I love you like my blood! But you don't get it?"

"What do you mean?" Catherine was perplexed.

"We've been following him for a couple of weeks. The only woman he's been with lately, since we've been tailing him, is Mrs. Russo."

"Okay, what are you saying?"

"He's not seeing women anymore. He's seeing her. Which means he loves her and divorce is in your future."

"No. He married me. She's married." Catherine began to tear up.

"I am not going to stand by and watch this... this... thing run over you like you don't exist."

"If I kill him. I go to jail. I can't enjoy life behind bars September and I won't. Like you said, alimony if he wants a divorce. I can live with that."

"I can't. I will do it for you."

"No, September. You are the reason I can accept what is happening to me right now. I don't want you going to jail either. I need you to help me get through this."

September paused in thought. "What?"

"With you, we can continue our friendship and he can have his affair... affairs or even a divorce. I don't need him to enjoy my life when I have you."

September ignored her words. "I can make it look like an accident."

September hadn't heard a word she said. Catherine spoke in anger, "How? Look at all that stuff you have listed on the plan you drafted up. You going to blow him up, stabbing to death, poison him... how September?"

"I have been thinking about this for a week now. I have it all put together. You said for the past week he has been coming home around midnight every night laying in the pool. Perhaps Nicolette is back in Italy now."

"So? Where is this going?" Catherine was baffled. "No September. I know you are doing this for me, but no."

September reached for a folder on the counter top where she was drafting her plan. She pulled pictures from the folder and gave them to Catherine. There was Johnathon coming out a restaurant with his arm around the waist of Nicolette, he was shopping at different stores with her. There were snapshots of him bordering his private jet with her, gentle kisses of him and Nicolette in his car, and worst of all sex on the beach in Hawaii, where they had their honeymoon. Catherine burst into tears uncontrollably. September raced around the counter and placed her arms around her shoulders until the flow of tears finally turned into sniffles.

September slid one more picture in front of her. "And look at this picture. It was a picture of the condominium location, a huge sign in front, stating "For Sale at Auction". He selling the building. He's giving up the women."

Catherine sniffed. "You're right."

"He is giving up the condo. I think he's finally found the love of his life."

Catherine was perplexed. More tears flowed down her cheeks. "Where did you get all those pictures? We didn't take those pictures or follow him to Hawaii."

"I know. I could tell us following him was getting to you. After we stopped, I hired a private investigator to continue. Cost me a little bit of my savings, but I figured… what the hell. This past week he has only been with Nicolette."

Catherine sighed and regained her composure. "You think he's given up the condo to only be with Nicolette?"

"Precisely."

Catherine stared at the photos. Incensed by the passionate display of affection that should be hers, "What's your plan? Johnathon is at a company party this evening."

"Then he should be there until at least midnight. I am going to poison all the wine bottles in the pool frig tonight. We will come back to my house after I do it. We will wait until about ten or eleven before I take you back home. He should drink soon wine tonight or for sure tomorrow. When I drop you off from our day of activities later tonight or tomorrow evening he should be passed out, half-dead or dead somewhere in the house, hopefully in the pool."

"What do you want me to do?"

"If he is in the pool, make sure you turn him face down in the water to make it look like an accidental drowning. Make sure an untainted wine bottle is by the pool. Then get rid of the other bottles in the frig."

"What if he is not in the pool?"

"Then drag him there and make sure his face is in the water." September stated as if it was common sense.

"How can you be so sure he will drink the wine?"

"You said yourself lately he has been coming home between midnight and three in the morning just lying in the pool with his cigar, not talking to you. Probably contemplating how he's going to get rid of you."

"Not nice September, not nice." Peering at the photos, Catherine conceded. "Okay, let' go."

September smiled and gathered all her military tactical equipment and utility belt as if ready for battle.

CHAPTER 43

Company Office Party

This evening is the 7 p.m. Advanced Technology Systems Incorporated (ATSI) Office Party at the Yacht Club. The entire club was rented out for the event. At the office party Mark and Johnathon both had drinks in their hand at the bar and discussed how the evening would go.

"Mark I am truly delighted you put this on. The numbers for this quarter is remarkable. I'm glad you are taking care of business with the office and staff. I know I have been a little out of touch."

"A little… I would say a lot. They've noticed you haven't been around as usual. This is just to let them know you are still alive and on top of how the company is progressing. I put this on in your name. I told the people you want to thank them for their hard work and exceptional efforts for this quarter. That is why I put the party on a Thursday so an extra bonus would be Friday off. Did you read the memo on the people who were outstanding in sales?"

Johnathon sighed. "Yesss. I will make my speech and then leave. I need to call Nicolette about some things we need to do. She is back in Italy right now. I just feel as if I need her in my life to make it complete."

"So when do you intend to let Catherine know?"

"She already hates me for missing our anniversary. We haven't been talking when I do see her at home. So telling her I never loved her will only make her want the divorce even more. I intend to serve her with the divorce papers tomorrow evening."

"You're sure about that J? What if Catherine doesn't want a divorce?"

"I really don't care what she wants. This is what's going to happen. I just need to know from Nicolette that she will be mine. After I call her tonight and the answer is 'yes' there will be no stopping my plans."

"Your call J. I just hope things work out the way you want them to. Well… let's get your speech over and you can do what you need to do."

Johnathon gulped the remaining juices in his drink. Mark went to the podium to introduce Johnathon.

"Ladies and gentlemen!" Mark yelled amongst the chatter and laughter of the staff. "Let me have your attention please. Our great leader has a few remarks to say about this quarter's earnings and acknowledge those who out performed our expectations. Mr. Johnathon Fitzpatrick!"

Everyone in the room clapped as Johnathon made it to the podium. "Thank you. Thank you everyone." Johnathon waved one hand to silence the audience. The claps stop. "It is I, who should be clapping for you. Six-five million more this quarter than our goal, is exceptional effort. An organization can only survive with good people to work it. Not only are you good people, but outstanding workers. That's why your Christmas bonuses will have an extra one-hundred thousand dollars in it this year for all of you. And for the three outstanding people that brought in an extra six-five million dollars by themselves… Ms. Brianne Delray, Nicolas Franks, and Grayson Hartman, an extra one-hundred and eighty thousand in their bonus checks. Again, I want to thank you all. Food and drinks are on the house. The bar and dance floor are open until the last one of you leave. So enjoy yourself until your hearts content. Tomorrow is a day off for everyone. I will see you all on Monday."

The entire staff clapped. Johnathon stepped off the podium and walked over to Mark at the bar.

"Hey I need the schematics and the prototype. Are they ready?" asked Johnathon.

"I can drop them off tomorrow morning at your place. Say around eleven. You remember how to demonstrate the weapon, right?"

"Yeah." Johnathon sighed.

"I have made arrangements for the prototype sub to be shipped to the address of your liking. I just need the address."

"Great. I will contact everyone tomorrow to let them know everything is ready. Well done Mark." Johnathon started to leave and then he thought,

"Hey Mark, if you feel like stopping by tonight before Catherine gets home, I would love to bend your ear just to listen to me or talk business. Here's the combination." Johnathon wrote on a napkin and handed it to Mark. He took the paper and looked at it. Mark paused in thought, balled it up and gave it back to Johnathon.

"Maybe tomorrow when I bring over the weapon. If you want to talk then, we can grab some brunch. I'm going to hang with the staff tonight. One of us needs to party with them just to show some love. Talk to you on tomorrow if you want to, or if you're still moody, I can bring things over on Monday for sure."

Johnathon smiled, patted Mark on the shoulder. "Tomorrow is fine." He headed out the door.

Mark grabbed his drink from the bar and began to mingle with the staff.

CHAPTER 44

Attempted Murder

Johnathon laid relaxed in the pool after leaving the party after he had confirmed Nicolette's feelings for him were true. Catherine and September were standing in the kitchen having drinks. Now that the plan was set, they put on Army green camouflage outfits and blacken every inch of their hands not to show any skin. They put on black masks that covered their entire face, only their eyes were visible. They used a rental car to drive to Catherine's home. They pulled up in the back of the house. Catherine was suddenly having second thoughts and doesn't want to get out of the car.

"Maybe we should think about this some more?" quipped Catherine.

"What's to think about? We have watched him night after night have an affair with this woman and other women apparently for years. Personally I don't see how you can stomach such behavior from the man you say you love."

"What about going to jail for the rest of our lives, especially you September? Every day I have been with you, it's been something audacious and exciting. Can you truly spend the rest of your life behind bars without going crazy?"

"I know, but I couldn't spend the rest of my life with a cheating son-of-bitch who wines and dines other women, while my best friend has her heart broken. When it's you who should be loved by him every single day of your life, because you're a good person Catherine. You deserve better."

Tears formed in Catherine's eyes. She realized September was right. "I do still love him though."

September was aggressive in tone. "Are we doing this or not?"

"I…" After a long pause, and tears were wiped away, Catherine reached over and handed September a piece of paper.

"What's this?" asked September.

"The gate code to disable the entire alarm system. Once disabled, the doors are automatically unlocked and the entire system is down. It's like a reset code, where the alarm system checks itself for flaws. It will get you through the gate and into the house. The lights won't even flicker. It has to be put back on in thirty minutes or security will call and if no answer, a police car is dispatched."

September looked at the paper. "Why wouldn't security alert the police once the system is disabled?"

"Because the code you put in tells security the system is rebooting for a system's check."

"Aren't you coming in?"

"I can't watch you poison the wine bottles. I don't think I can bare cruelty to an individual I made an oath to, to love forever."

"Spare me the sentimental bull-scrap. If I had found my husband with other women in some condo he bought for them or jet flights to Hawaii… let's just say, he would have become another Jimmy Hoffa very soon." September was aggressive in tone. "Now come on! He's not home until midnight or one or two in the morning."

"Don't make me do this!"

"What are you saying? You want to let this go?"

"Yes. Maybe we can go to counseling?"

"What?! September was flabbergasted.

"My love is stronger than my hatred right now September. We don't have the right to take anyone's life."

"That's just what I mean about a 'good girl', always wanting to do the right thing. Then I will do it by myself for my own conscious." September snatched the paper from Catherine's hand, memorized the code, balled the paper up and threw the paper back at her. September opened the car door and started to leave for the house.

"September wait."

A few feet from the car, she paused and turned toward her. "What Catherine?" September quietly stated in disgust.

"Nothing."

A few minutes later, September was behind the house. Under the cover of darkness about 10 p.m., September quietly maneuvered her way to one of the entrances to the house. She punched in the code. Once she entered the kitchen, she heard two rapid shots of gun fire. She pulled her .45 Caliber from her utility belt, loaded the chamber and raced toward the noise. Silently, she moved from the kitchen to the living room looking for Johnathan. Suddenly, another gun shot rang out. By the dimness of the pool lights, September saw a glimpse of a totally black clothed figure race from the patio area.

Mrs. Jenson had binoculars trained on the house as usual. She heard the shots as well.

"Harold! Come over here. Did you hear something that sounded like firecrackers? There is something strange going on over there."

Harold was laying in the bed, asleep. He was groggy. "Look Gloria, will you stop watching that house? I'm trying to sleep." Harold turned to put his back toward his wife, and tried to continue his rest.

Gloria noticed his reaction to her words. Realizing Harold wasn't going to be any help, she resumed her observation of the house. Her visibility was limited with the darkness of the evening. She couldn't get a glimpse of where the shots came from. She put the binoculars down and got dressed to get a closer look of the house.

September moved quickly to try and get a closer look at the culprit leaving the patio. By the time she got to the glass doors the perpetrator had vanished. There in the pool laid Johnathon's lifeless body, floating face up. She holstered her .45 and pulled a flashlight from her utility belt. She stepped closer to observe the body. Three bullets had gone through his forehead. Recognizing the gravity of the situation, September quickly made an exit from whence she came. She rushed back to the car to alert Catherine. Catherine was standing outside the car.

Anxiety was in Catherine voice. "I heard the shots. He was home? Why did you shoot him? You should have just left if he was in the house."

"Stop talking. I didn't shoot." September was hastily opening the door. "Someone else shot him. Get in the car." September sat in the driver seat, staring through the passenger side window, wondering why Catherine wasn't in the car.

Catherine got in. September started the engine. "Stop! Tell me what happened in there."

Out of breathe, September began…"You said he wasn't going to be home."

"Well… he was. So tell me what happened."

September sighed. "As soon as I got in the kitchen, I looked around and didn't see anyone. I was slowly making my way to the living room when I heard the shots."

Catherine became hysterical. "What do you mean? I heard you fire your gun."

"Noooo… not my gun. If I were going to use my gun, I would have put my silencer on it so there wouldn't have been any sound. As I raced toward the patio door, he fired or someone fired another shoot to his head. By the time I made it onto the patio, I caught a glimpse of a figure running away. I stopped, looked at the pool, and there Johnathon was laying belly-up with gunshot wounds to his forehead."

"Are you saying someone else killed him?"

"Dah… Yes. That's exactly what I am saying." September started to shift the car into drive. "Now we need to get the hell out of here."

"STOP!" September put the car back in park and looked at Catherine in disgust. "You didn't call 911!"

"Are you fucking crazy? Sorry… that sentence needed a curse word. Look at me and how I'm dressed. I have two field knives, two hand guns, a small bottle of poison and strangling wire around this utility belt! Just what would I tell the cops when they showed up? It's Halloween in December and I'm playing a CIA operative instead of Santa. I think they would suspect I did it."

"He maybe still alive." Catherine hoped it really didn't happen.

September spoke softly. "Noooo, I don't think so. He looked pretty dead to me. He's floating like a wine cork in a bowl of water, face up."

"How would you know for sure? Did you take his pulse?"

"When you have seen as many bullet wounds as I have in my military career, you recognize a fresh kill when you see one."

Catherine was insistent. "We have to get help. He was just shot minutes ago. There may be some chance he is still alive." Catherine fiddled with the door knob and started to get out of the car.

September reached over and closed the door shut. "No! He had three direct bullet shots to the head. We stick to the plan!"

"No. We have to call 9-1-1 now!"

"Now I am beginning to understand why he married you. The brain has left the building. Look!" September paused and took a deep breathe. "Let's calm down. You're being irrational Catherine. Look at how you're dressed." Catherine paused and observed her attire. "Let's stick to the plan. We go back to my house and change clothes. You come back home and pretend to be shocked. The cops are going to blame you anyway."

"Me?"

"Yeah, you. Don't you watch Forensic Files and NCIA?"

"NCIS." Catherine corrected her.

"Whatever. They always suspect the spouse first. Now let's get back to my house and get you changed so you can get back here. Your neighbor across the street will help you verify the time you arrived once you drive in front of the house. Above all else... don't forget to act surprised and distraught when the police arrive."

September started to put the car in drive again.

"No! Turn the car off. You go and I will call 9-1-1 when I get in the house. There may be a chance that he's not dead."

"Now I know you're crazy? That nosey neighbor of yours probably already called the police. I'm sure she saw you leave this morning with your car and she hasn't seen you come back. So if you act like you are just coming home two hours from now... get the picture? She can't say it was you."

"Drive me around the front of the house. I'll just tell the police you drove me home, because I had too much alcohol at your house after playing with our paint guns."

"Catherine do you know what you are doing? You're still in military dress. We're sitting here in a rental car."

Catherine was deep in thought. "Rental car. That's right." She thought. "I got an ideal."

"What...?" angrily shouted September.

"No. If you drive in front of the house, drop me off, she'll see only me. She won't know it was you if you don't get out of the car. I can say you were an Uber. We stick to the plan, just a little sooner that's all. We were playing a war game in your back yard with paint guns, just like we've done on numerous occasions."

"Who's going to believe we were playing paintball at this hour of the night?"

"We'll think of something. Hurry! Pull one of the paint guns out of the trunk and shoot me with it." Stated Catherine.

"I can't! You idiot. This is a rental car. The paint guns are in my car at home."

"Ok, ok, that's right. Let me think." September stared at Catherine with disgust. "I got it. When you get home, shoot yourself with the paint gun. Make it look like I was the victor and you couldn't get a shot on me. That would explain why I don't have paint on me when the police come to the house."

"Really… that's the best you can do. I trained *you*, remember. We go to gun competitions. *We* have trophies. It sounds stupid anyway. That won't work." September glanced at her watch. "Ohhh shoot!"

"What?"

September glanced at her watch again. "I forgot to reset the security system. You've got fourteen minutes before the police are alerted about your alarm."

Catherine checked her watch. "Okkkk….you're right." She thought for another second. "Come back in the house with me. I'll fix the alarm. You go the garage and get the paint guns I bought for Johnathon. We'll shoot ourselves. Then you drive me in front of the house so Mrs. Jensen can see me."

"That's the dumbest thing I have ever heard."

"You got a better ideal? I have got to get to that alarm."

"I guess it's all we got." September paused. "You know what else? I think Johnathon knew whoever killed him."

"Why do you say that?"

"He was in the pool. He was relaxing. He would have seen the lights flicker for…"

Catherine interrupted. "But he could have thought it was me coming in the house."

"Yeah... you're right. But someone knew the combination or Johnathon let them in." September glanced again at her watch. "Yeah. Let's hurry. We are down to nine minutes. Your nosey neighbor probably called the cops already."

They both raced back inside the house. "Go in the garage and get the guns from the cabinet marked, 'GAMES' in big bold letters."

"So what are you going to do?" asked September.

"I am going to check on Johnathon."

"You don't want to look Catherine."

Catherine ignored her warning and headed to the pool area. September shook her head and raced toward the garage. A wine bottle and two glasses, one by Johnathon and the other near the edge of the pool by a patio chair is what Catherine observed. Then she noticed her husband lying face up with scattered bullets holes to his temple as bloody water surrounded his head. His arms and body stretched out as if he had been crucified. She placed her hand over her mouth and began to weep. September arrived at the pool area only to see Catherine standing there in tears.

"What are you doing? She sprinted up to Catherine, grabbed both shoulders and shook her. "Get yourself together. I told you not to look. This is no time for sympathy." September pulled the paint guns from her utility belt. "Here. Take a gun. Is the alarm taken care of?"

Catherine took a gun from September. Bucked her eyes... "Oh..."

Catherine and September raced toward the alarm system in the kitchen with seconds ticking down. They both looked at each other... Catherine punched a six digit code and the alarm was reactivated.

"Whoow..." they both said simultaneously staring at each other.

"Now let's get this done. Ok you shoot first." Stated Catherine.

"Here? In the kitchen? There will be paint spatter all over the place."

"You're right. Then where?" questioned Catherine.

September paused for thought. "In your master bathroom, at least after you call the police you can clean the bathroom before they get here. Let's go."

September followed Catherine to her master bedroom. September saw a thirty by thirty white plush carpeted room with a lavish sofa, huge King size bed with modern furniture, and a sixty-five inch television…"All these months you have never invited me to your bedroom. "Wooow… its nice."

"Will you come on?" Catherine was a little impatient.

Once there, they shot each other five or six times in the bathroom shower. Paint spattered all over the shower floor and glass.

"Let's go." Stated Catherine. They wiped there boots on a towel Catherine had placed beneath the shower doors. They both hurried to the car and got in.

Once in the car… "You still want me to drive you in front of the house?" questioned September.

"Yes, my neighbor needs to see that I am just getting home."

"So what are you going to tell that nosey bitty if she comes over?"

"We started early afternoon with the paint guns and sat around and had a few more drinks. Now you're driving me home because I drank more than you. Now take me around the front so we can get this over with."

"Catherine, we can still stick to the plan. No one will be the wiser."

"Not anymore. Not with all that paint spatter in the bathroom. Now hurry so I can get in there and call 9-1-1 and clean that mess up before it dries."

September stared at her. Catherine's expression depicted sadness, but her demeanor was strong.

Suddenly…" Oh shoot!

"What now?" quizzed September.

"The alarm system was disabled for more than twenty minutes. All I did was reactivate the alarm. There is a security code that needs to be sent in to the grounds authorities to let them know the owners were the ones that disabled the system and not criminals. Otherwise, grounds security can could come over and check on the house or alert the police."

"How long do you have before security calls to find out if you just forgot to punch that code in?"

"Twelve minutes."

"Then you better hurry."

Catherine looked at her watch. "I've got seven minutes."

"Go!' yelled September.

Catherine dashed back to the house. She reached the outside alarm and worked frantically to enter the code. As she was entering the security code, her nosey neighbor stood on a stool casing the grounds with a flashlight and binoculars. She spotted Catherine at the side entrance tinkering with the alarm system. Catherine saw the light upon the alarm system. It shined from a distance. She immediately finished her task. Catherine turned toward the brightness of the beam, only to see a figure holding the object in question. Catherine sprinted toward her. Mrs. Jensen was unable to clearly identify her in military dress, face paint, and black mask. When Catherine came closer, Mrs. Jensen was so frightened, she fell off the stool and dropped her binoculars and flashlight. She immediately ran back home as fast as her legs would carry her. Catherine noticed that she was no longer there and rushed back to the car.

Almost out breathe… Catherine got in the car. "My neighbor saw me."

Desperation set in with September. "What! Now what? I can't drive you in front now with the uniform on. She'll know or suspect it was you."

Catherine thought. "She is surely going to call the police. It would take too long to go back to your house and get changed. I need to get in the house with plain clothes on, right now. If the police comb the house…"

September interrupted. "The paint gun story is out the window. What do you want to do?"

"Take me to the nearest clothing store."

"Why don't you go back in the house, get changed and come back to the car."

"September she already saw me. Besides she may have already called the police. If she has, I wouldn't have enough time to clean the shower, change clothes and get rid of the evidence."

"She doesn't know it was you with all this stuff on."

"I know. Let me think September."

"You can't be sure that's she is calling the police right now."

"I don't want to take that chance now. Let me think."

"Well the only store open at this hour that I know of, is Wal-Mart. I don't think you are going to find five-hundred dollar blouses and sixteen-hundred dollar skirts in there."

"What choice do I have? She has already seen me in this uniform. Let's go. I am sure she's calling the police. I have to get in there and get that paint spatter off the shower walls and floor."

While September stepped on the gas and headed toward the nearest Wal-Mart. Gloria scurried toward her house. She ran in screaming. Harold pulled the covers over his head to ignore the sound.

"Harold! Harold!" She ran down the hallway to the bedroom. "Wake up! Wake up!" She tugged on the covers of the bed. Harold held them tightly.

"Can't you stop watching that house for a second? Do you know what time it is? Some of us have to work tomorrow. Now let me go back to sleep old woman!"

"I saw someone trying to break-in to the Fitzpatrick's house."

Harold pulled the covers from his head. "Sure you did. You know there system is the best there is, we have one."

"Listen, you have to get up and help me. I think I heard gun shots earlier and when I went over there, I saw someone fully dressed in a military uniform. They could be on their way over here since they saw me."

"I doubt that. You can't run any faster than a turtle. They would have surely caught and killed you before you got back here. Now let me go back to sleep."

Disgusted with his behavior over a serious matter, Gloria left him in bed and debated whether to call the police. She took another pair of binoculars from her dresser drawer, resumed her surveillance and pondered calling the police.

CHAPTER 45

Police Suspicions

Meanwhile, Catherine and September made hast to get to Wal-Mart. They discussed a new strategy to eliminate Catherine from being a suspect in Johnathon's murder. They soon pulled up to the doors of Wal-Mart.

"Once I go in to buy the clothes, you call me a ride." Catherine got out of the car. The passenger window was rolled down.

"A cab, Uber, Lyft, which do you prefer?" smiled September.

"I don't give a fu…! You're making jokes and Johnathon is dead."

"Ahhh… you almost cursed at me. I guess Johnathon was right. I'm wearing off on you. At a loss for words are we?"

"Now's no time for jokes September. This shouldn't have ever happened."

"I'm not sorry he's dead."

Catherine was sad and angry. "Well this isn't the time for jokes. This situation is not funny. Get me whatever. I just need that ride when I come out." .

"Now? You want me to call?"

"No, tomorrow. Yes! Now!" Catherine was annoyed by the cynical sarcasm.

"You don't have to yell."

"Just do it." Catherine felt flustered.

"Ok, consider it done. What's the plan again?"

"We can claim we both had too much to drink and I called a cab, Uber or whatever to get home."

"Got it." September was in agreement.

"You go home and stay home. I will call and tell you what happened with the police later so we can get our story straight."

"Oh before you walk in there, take off the mask." September threw her a towel from the back seat. "Wipe off the paint around your eyes. It might make you look a little suspicious about buying something versus stealing something."

Catherine looked at her dress, hopped back in the car, and removed the mask, the paint from her face and the vest on her body. She looked in the car mirror. She glanced at September. "How do I look?"

"Lay your hair down a little bit. Pulling off that vest over your head ruffled it."

Catherine smoothed her hair down with her hands and grabbed a credit card from her purse. She got out of the car. September started the engine with cell phone in hand. Catherine gave September a thumbs up. September returned the motion. Catherine watched her drive away. She immediately dashed into Wal-Mart. Catherine found some jeans and a casual top. She caught the Uber back to her house. When she got out of the Uber, she had a Wal-Mart bag in her hand. Gloria noticed the car and ran across the street to explain to Catherine what she saw.

Mrs. Jensen, nearly out of breath, screamed. "Mrs. Fitzpatrick!" Catherine turned to recognize her presence. "There was a strange person roaming around your house."

Mrs. Jensen noticed the bag in Catherine's hand, but was too excited to ask why she had a Wal-Mart bag.

"I'm sure it was nothing Gloria, go back home. You yourself know our home is alarm proof. No one can get in without the combination."

"Well I'm sorry, but the police are on their way. I just called them when I saw you get out of the car. The person I saw was dressed in military clothing and appeared to be trying to break into your home."

Catherine cringed and tighten her grab on the bag with the military clothes in there, knowing now that she got a good look at someone. "Thank you Gloria, I will go in and make sure everything is ok. You stay here and be sure to let the police know it's this house. I appreciate your help."

"You don't want me to get Harold to go in with you?"

"No. You may stay here for the police or go back home Gloria. I got it. If something is wrong, I will be sure and yell."

Gloria slowly walked toward home. After Catherine entered the house, she immediately returned to the pool. She was spellbound at Johnathon lying there lifeless. She knew at that very moment, there was nothing to try and save. Time was of the essence with the police on the way. Her plan had to be flawless in order to free herself of suspicion. She immediately went upstairs. She hid her military clothing and boots. Washing down the bathroom shower was next. She called 911 sounding hysterical. Now she needed a front. Someone to help corroborate her story. Catherine raced across the street and rang franticly Gloria's doorbell.

Gloria hurried to the door. "Catherine what's wrong?" .

Harold came from the bedroom in his robe. "Yes what is it my dear?"

"Come quickly. He's in the pool and I can't get him out by myself."

Harold and Gloria both looked at each other in disbelief and followed Catherine home. Once at the pool area, they both stared in awe of Johnathon's body floating motionless above the water. Harold pulled his robe off and leaped into the pool in his pajamas. He dragged Johnathon's body to the edge of the pool. Catherine and Gloria grabbed Johnathon's arms to pull, while Harold pushed to get his body out of the water. Catherine immediately started CPR under the dimness of the ambiance lights.

Harold looked at his wife. "How long ago did you call 911, hone."

"They should be here soon." Gloria answered.

"I called them too." Stated Catherine as she continued CPR.

Harold soon noticed the bullet wounds when Catherine came up for air from Johnathon's lips. "He's been shot in the head Catherine. I don't think CPR is going to help."

The police and paramedics arrived minutes later. They pounded on the door. Catherine raced to answer it, while Harold and his wife stood in awe over Johnathon's body.

"Where is the person in distress?" asked one of the paramedics.

Catherine pointed to the backyard pool. Gloria was standing in the patio doorway waving her arms for them to come her way. Catherine waited for the police.

When the police arrived, they immediately taped off the area of the house. While Catherine brought the Detective to the pool, Harold and

Gloria were telling their story to another police officer. Detective Farland interrupted the other officer. "I got this. Go assists the forensic team in gathering prints and taking pictures." The officer walked away. Detective Farland, late forties, five feet, nine inches tall, dark hair, black pants, white shirt, and light black leather jacket leaned over and examine the body briefly noticing the three bullet shots to the head. He pulled out his note pad and pen. He addressed all three of them standing by the pool.

"My name is name Detective Joseph Farland. You are?"

"This is my wife Gloria." Stated Harold.

"I called." Responded Gloria.

"I am Harold Jenson, next door neighbor."

"I'm Catherine. That's my husband laying there."

Gloria interrupted. "I called because I saw someone in a military uniform trying to break into her house."

"Military uniform? Are you certain?" asked Detective Farland.

"What time was this?"

"About ten-forty-five or so" Detective Farland wrote in his note pad. "I shined my flashlight directly on them. When they turned towards me, I couldn't get a clear look at their face because it was covered with a black covering of some kind. Only the eyes were visible."

"You couldn't make out the color of the skin with just the eyes showing?" questioned Detective Farland.

"No... the eyes had dark coloring or paint around them." Stated Gloria.

During this conversation Catherine had her eyes focused on Johnathon. Her arms folded praying Mrs. Jensen couldn't say anything to identify her.

"Are you sure it was a military outfit Mrs. Jensen?"

"Oh yes Detective, like the military wear. The ahhh, ahhh..."

Detective Farland interrupted, "The camouflage outfits."

"Yes." Gloria stated.

"Could you tell if it was a man or woman?"

"No. As soon as they noticed me, I took off running."

Harold interrupted... "Probably more like a slow trot."

Gloria stared at her husband. Detective Farland was writing all of this down on his notepad.

Detective Farland, "Where were you Mrs . . . ."

Catherine intervened. "Fitzpatrick. I was at a friends' home. I just got back a little while ago and found my husband in the pool."

"And you called 9.1.1.?" asked Detective Farland.

"Yes." Answered Catherine.

"Why did you remove the body from the pool?" inquired Detective Farland.

"We thought, or I thought if I could give CPR to him, I might be able to save his life." Stated Catherine.

"With three bullets in his head? You shouldn't have moved him Ms. Fitzpatrick."

Catherine realized she was speaking calmly in responding to the questions. She needed to appear more emotional over his death. She tried to appear infuriated over the comment. Catherine's tone was more aggressive. "You really didn't expect me to leave my husband lying there like that, did you? I had to try and see if there was some possibility of life still in him."

"You got your neighbors to help you?" asked Detective Farland.

"I couldn't do it alone. After I called 911, I ran over to their house."

"You should have left things as they were."

"Well pardon me detective, if you come home and see your loved one in distress, what else was I supposed to do?"

"Dead." Stated Gloria.

Everyone looked at Gloria. She gave a smug expression.

Catherine's attention went back to the Detective. "The first thing comes to mind isn't to wait for the police, but to try and help them."

Detective Farland raised his voice slightly. "With three bullet holes to the head. It should have painfully obvious your husband was dead Mrs. Fitzpatrick."

"Really Detective?" asked Harold.

Detective Farland lowered his tone. "Ok. I'm sorry Mrs. Fitzpatrick. So you weren't home. Where were you?"

"I was playing paintball with a friend of mine at her place." Tears began to flow from Catherine eyes.

"Tonight, until midnight?" questioned Detective Farland.

"Yes." Catherine began to stutter as she spoke. "She ahhh… dropped me off because she thought I… ahhh had a little too much to drink. When I came in the house I found my husband like you see him now."

Mrs. Jensen coughed. She thought to herself. That didn't look like September and it definitely wasn't her car. Mrs. Jensen kept quiet.

"So you just got home. "What time did she drop you off?"

"I think around eleven-thirty or midnight." More tears began to flow heavier from Catherine.

"And who would that friend be?" Detective Farland continued taking notes.

"September... September Jones."

"And where might we find Ms. Jones?"

"She lives at 3547 Nation View Terrace in Ingle town."

"Do you have a phone number?"

"Her number is 213-777-8955."

"Where did your husband work Mrs. Fitzpatrick?"

"He owns that Advanced Technology System company. That building in the heart of...."

Detective Farland interrupted. "You mean that ten story modern designed building belongs to your husband?"

"Yes." Catherine slightly bent over with a continued flow of tears streaming down her cheeks.

"Do you know of anyone who might want your husband died?" Detective Farland ignored her anguish.

Catherine's used her hands to wipe her tears away. "I never knew his business clients, but we entertained a few of his closest associates. We had executive parties on every other Friday."

Harold interrupted... "Detective can't you see she is in no condition to continue this questioning tonight. Please give her some time to get over this emotional shock. I am sure she will be more stable to answer questions at a later date."

Detective Farland sighed. "Yes, of course. Forgive me. I will pay a visit to his office tomorrow. However, if you could write down the names of his associates for me, that would be great. We can talk tomorrow. Let's say ten. In my office. We need to talk while events are still fresh in your mind. Ten would be great if you could?"

Catherine muddled under her breath. "I never meant for this to happen."

"What did you say?" asked Detective Farland.

"I said 'how could this happen." Responded Catherine, emotionally distraught.

Gloria wrapped her arms around Catherine. Detective Farland was puzzled to her actions and expression of verbiage. 'Why would she think something like this could possibly happen, unless she had something to do with his death?' So he thought.

"What time did you arrive home again Mrs. Fitzpatrick?"

Harold interrupted again. Aggressively this time. "Detective!"

"Yes, yes of course. I will have my men to wrap up here as quickly as possible and we will talk tomorrow Mrs. Fitzpatrick."

Catherine just nodded her head. "May I go to my bedroom?"

"No. When I said as quickly as possible, I meant four or five days." Stated Detective Farland.

Gloria still had her hands wrapped around Catherine's shoulders. "Would you like to stay with us Catherine dear?"

"That would be a good idea. This whole house is a crime scene. We need to inspect all the rooms."

"Thank you Gloria. Let me gather some bedroom things and pack a few clothes." Stated Catherine.

"Good Mrs. Fitzpatrick. It's best." Stated Detective Farland.

Harold, Gloria and Detective Farland watched as Catherine ascended the stairs. When Catherine was out of sight, Detective Farland approached Mrs. Jensen.

"When did you see Mrs. Fitzpatrick arrive Mrs. Jensen?" Detective Farland still had his note pad out ready to write.

"It was around ten forty-five or so." Answered Gloria.

"When did you see the intruder?"

"It was around ten or ten-thirty. Something like that."

"And you called 9-1-1 at eleven-thirty. Why so late if you saw someone at ten-thirty?"

"It was someone else's house and it was no way for me to get in a call to the Fitzpatrick's. I don't have their number. Besides the intruder was on the outside and I thought perhaps I scared them away. I thought about it after I got back to my house. About an hour later, Catherine rolled up. I thought it's better to be safe, than sorry. So about eleven-thirty or forty-five or there about, I called 9-1-1. I told her what I am telling you right now."

"I see. Did you hear any gun shots?"

"Yes."

"About what time was that?"

"Sometime after nine. I don't remember actually since so much has happened since that time."

"Why didn't you call 9-1-1- then?"

"Again Detective, it's not my house. I don't know what they could have been doing. I didn't know it was gun fire until Mrs. Fitzpatrick alerted us her husband was in the pool, lifeless."

"Thank you. You two may leave, but I will be calling on you to answer more questions as they develop."

Harold grabbed his wife around the arms. "We'll be around Detective. We aren't going anywhere." They went to wait for Catherine by the stairs.

The Detective went to talk to his forensic team to find out what they knew so far. He would inspect the home himself for further evidence.

CHAPTER 46

The Interrogations

Catherine arrived about 10:00 a.m. the next morning in Detective Farland's office. She gave Detective Farland the list of associates that frequently attended her executive parties. She was seated in Detective Farland's private office, only two-feet away from his desk. She dressed elegantly and appeared a little nervous.

"Mrs. Fitzpatrick can we start from the beginning and you tell me exactly what you know."

"I arrived home around midnight. I called for him first when I entered the house. When he didn't answer, I went upstairs to check the bedroom. He wasn't there. I thought he wasn't home. Sometimes he doesn't get home until two or three in the morning. So I was about to take a bath, but instead I decided on a nightcap before doing so. I came back down to the kitchen to fix myself a drink. I was going to enjoy it by the pool and that's when I saw him lying face up."

Suddenly a policemen came into the room. "Here is the weapon you requested." He showed a .45 Caliber pistol in a plastic bag.

Detective Farland took the gun from the police officer. The officer stood behind Catherine. Detective Farland held the weapon in the bag about six-feet away from Catherine's face. "Have you seen this gun before Mrs. Fitzpatrick?"

"Yes!" Enraged, Catherine stood up. "That's my gun! Why do you have it?"

"Mrs. Fitzpatrick sit back down please." Catherine did as instructed. "So this is your gun? You admit that?"

"It's mine. Why do you have it?"

"When I examined the area where the gun was kept, the glass case was smashed." Detective Farland paused to observe Catherine's reaction. "You didn't notice the broken glass when you came downstairs for your nightcap?"

Catherine was surprise. "No. I only turned on the kitchen light. The gun case and trophies are around the corner in the living room. I went straight to the kitchen, fixed my drink and then to the pool."

"So it appeared you had two weapons in one gun case?"

"Yes. I have two more in another cabinet."

"One of your guns, a .45 is missing from the gun case."

Catherine was in total shock. "What?"

"This one is the other one we found left in the case." Detective Farland paused. He placed the gun on his desk in front of her. "You have quite a few marksmanship trophies in your home Mrs. Fitzpatrick."

"Yes… my friend, September and I enter competitions locally sponsored by the gun club that we are members of. We also go around the states for competition."

"So you are an excellent marksman?"

"If you think that I would do this to my husband Detective, you are seriously mistaken. And with my own gun. Really? "

"You didn't seem to be too emotionally upset until the officer brought in the weapon. Is that because you may have had something to do with your husband's death?"

"That's absurd! Are you implying that I…" Catherine burst into tears. She bowed her head and wiped her watery eyes with her fingers. "I loved him."

Detective Farland watched her outburst of crying and sniffles. None of which he believed were real last night or even now. He reached into his jacket pocket and handed her his handkerchief. Catherine accepted it. "I'm not implying anything." Catherine bellowed louder. "Do you feel like continuing? I want to get everything down while it is still fresh in your mind. If you would like to rest, you may go home and we can try again tomorrow. We may be awhile."

"No, I don't want to come back." Catherine wiped her eyes and gave the Detective her attention once again.

"Detective Barley, my partner found a wine glass and bottle close to your husband's body by the pool."

"Yes. He liked to drink wine and have a cigar while he relaxed in the pool."

"They also found another wine glass by a pool chair in the corner. Was that the drink you fixed for yourself?"

"No."

"Did your husband invite someone over that night?"

"No!... I don't know." aggressively spoke Catherine.

"Why did you fix yourself a drink after you had just come home from drinking with your friend?"

"I wasn't drunk. I didn't know what my alcohol level was and didn't want to risk driving."

"If you fixed yourself a drink, why wasn't there three glasses by the pool?"

Catherine stuttered. "I... I..." She thought. "After I saw him lying there, I put my glass back in the kitchen."

Detective Farland didn't believe that. He leaned forward on his desk. "Are you telling me after seeing you husband died in the pool, which should have shocked you, you didn't drop and break the glass at the pool, but you took it back in the kitchen?"

Catherine was silent. She bowed her head, wiped her eyes and spoke without looking at Detective Farland. "My husband was such a fanatic about items being in place, it was a natural instinct to put the glass back in the kitchen."

"Detective Farland leaned back in his chair. "Um-huh. I just want you to know we are checking the wine glasses for finger prints. We didn't fine another wine glass in the kitchen or anywhere else in the house. We are running ballistic on this gun to see if the bullets match the ones in your husband."

Catherine cried. She looked at him. She mumbled. "You suspect me?"

"Not yet. You aren't being charged right now."

Catherine leaped from her seat. "Right now!"

"I just need a few more questions answered so we can exclude you, Mrs. Fitzpatrick."

"I would like that time now, to recoup, Detective. I don't feel well."

"Yes of course. Officer, please escort Mrs. Fitzpatrick back to her car and take the weapon to ballistics. I'm going to head to the office of Mr. Fitzpatrick to speak with his employees."

Catherine left the handkerchief on his desk and walked out with the officer. Detective Farland stared her down with doubt, as she departed his office.

At the office building of ATSI, Detective Joseph Farland asked Mark to see Johnathon's office. While talking to Mark, the detective sat in Johnathon's chair and rummaged through papers on his desk.

Detective Farland was unimpressed by the elegance of office. "Cybersecurity Systems Incorporated sounds impressive. I'm guessing you are the Vice President, since you are showing me around?"

"Yes sir, you would be correct." Responded Mark.

"How much would you say your company is worth right now?" asked Detective Farland.

"To be exact, I couldn't say without the data sheets, but somewhere close to six-hundred million."

"I see. Mr. Townsend. Can you think of any dissatisfied clients or disgruntled employees that might want to see Mr. Fitzpatrick dead?"

"Well, I don't like to call out anyone, but if you are asking around, you are bound to find out that an employee got fired about a year ago."

"His or her name please?"

"Javier Hernandez."

Mark observed Detective Farland reading papers on Johnathon's desk. "Do you still have an address on file for him?"

"See our secretary Angela at the front desk. She will give it to you."

When the detective pulled out one of Johnathon's desk drawers, he discovered the black book. As he thumbed through the book, he was astonished at what he saw.

"Well... it appears that Mr. Fitzpatrick was a player. Twenty pages of names and numbers in alphabetical order. Did you know about this black book Mr. Townsend?"

"Yes sir."

As the detective turned pages through the book, "Let's see. He has 'E', 'G' and 'F' by these names of women. Do you know what these letters are for?"

"He categorized his women as excellent, good, or fair."

"I don't see a 'P' in here."

"And you wouldn't see a 'P'. As J wouldn't see someone but once if they gave him a 'poor' performance."

"Performance?" questioned the Detective.

"Sometimes he liked to role play with his lady friends. Plus they had to be good in bed as well as intellectually smart."

"I see."

"Do you know the ladies in the book?" Detective Farland handed the book to Mark.

Mark glanced through the list. The book only went by first names. All the names had phone numbers except for... when he reached the letter "B" it didn't have a full name. It couldn't have been their Brianna, he thought... and then he uttered... "No Detective. None of the names I know. It could be anyone. Besides he never told me the names of any of the women he interacted with."

"Very well. We'll find out who they are, except 'B' could be anyone. What about these numbers listed in the back of the book?"

"J never let me see the book. I don't know the names or about any numbers. I'm seeing it for the first time like you are detective."

"Very well Mr. Townsend."

"Do you think you can find out who they are?" quizzed Mark.

"They don't call me 'detective' for nothing." He stood and walked around the office looking for anything out of the ordinary. "Mr. Townsend. Where were you the night of the murder?"

Mark calmly responded. "There was a company celebration that night."

"Is the company always in the habit of celebrating in the middle of the week?"

"It was Thursday Sir. We were giving all of the employees the next day off."

"And why was that?"

"J and I always thought that when our staff does something outstanding, they should get rewarded for it."

"And what was it that they did?" quizzed Detective Farland.

"Our goal at the end of each quarter for this year is to make one-hundred million dollars. This quarter ended in a one-hundred-sixty million dollar yield. We wanted to celebrate all the staff and those that exceeded our expectations."

"So you and Mr. Fitzpatrick held an office party that night?"

"Yes, at the Yacht Club." Explained Mark.

"Why didn't Mr. Fitzpatrick come?"

"He showed up briefly and then excused himself. He said he wasn't feeling well and was going home to rest. He said he would see me at the office that following Monday."

"I see."

"Yes. Well I thought one of us needed to represent the senior staff. So I was at the office celebration until two in the morning."

"You were there all night until early morning?" probed Detective Farland.

"Yes Sir."

"I can ask any of your staff and they will corroborate your story?"

"Any of the staff that was there, yes sir." Calmly stated Mark.

"Alright. Give me the names of all the staff that was there. We will be in touch Mr. Townsend."

"I can have that information to you by tomorrow afternoon. If there is anything else I can do to help, please let me know. Johnathon was like a brother to me."

Detective Farland continued his inspection around the office and headed toward the door. "Thank you for your time Mr. Townsend. If you think of anything or anyone we may need to speak with… here is my card."

Mark took the detective's card. "Yes sir, I will do that."

Mark watched Detective Farland leave the room. After he got Javier's number from Angela he left. Mark stepped out of Johnathon's office and glanced at Brianna's door. It was open and she was sitting at her desk. He went back in the office and sat at J's desk. He punched the intercom button.

"Angela, have Brianna Delray come into Mr. Fitzpatrick's office please."

"Right away Mr. Townsend." Angela's soft voice responded.

A few minutes later, Mark heard a knock. "Come in."

"You wanted to see me Mr. Townsend?" Brianna was a light-brown skinned brunette, very well dressed in black Patten leather shoes, a tight black skirt, and a blue blouse with a wide collar. Her hair was curly and long to her shoulders.

Mark sat behind Johnathon's desk. "Yes, close the door please." She did as instructed and stood by the door. "Do you have any plans for the evening?"

"No, not tonight sir." Brianna spoke calmly.

"Then meet me at the Yacht Club tonight at seven."

Brianna spoke softly. "I am not a member sir."

"Tell them you are there to see me when you arrive."

Brianna quickly agreed. "Very well sir."

"You may go." She left with a baffled expression upon her face. Mark followed her departure with his eyes.

Hours later at the Yacht Club, Brianna arrived a little apprehensive. A waiter greeted her at the door. Mark had been there a few minutes before Brianna. He already had a drink on the table when he saw her walk in. He had Rodney to bring her to the table.

"Have a seat Brianna. What would you care to drink?"

"A coke would be fine Mr. Townsend."

"Nothing stronger. For a young business women, I might have thought with the clients you have been bringing into the business, your social style of drink would be fruity or harsh."

"I do socially drink a small glass of wine with my clients, but I have to drive a good distance to get home from here. Plus I have a low tolerance level for any kind of fruity or harsh alcoholic beverages. More than two glasses of wine is too much. I become either very quiet and mellow or very verbal and gay when I down more than a small glass of any alcoholic beverage."

The waiter awaited their order… "Sir."

"Very well. Rodney, I will have another one of my usual and a coke for lady."

"Very good sir." Rodney left.

"You should check out the menu here. The food is excellent."

Brianna glanced down at the menu and back at Mark. "Right now Mr. Townsend, I really don't have an appetite. Perhaps I could relax a little better if I knew what this meeting is for. I am concerned about why you asked me to come here and why our conversation couldn't have been discussed at the office. Do I have a reason to be nervous?"

"Brianna I will get straight to the point. Were you having an affair with Mr. Fitzpatrick?"

She momentarily went silent. Her head bowed quickly toward the table. Then suddenly, she broke down in a sobering mood. She took a deep breath and sighed. "I didn't mean too. It just happened."

Mark was really astounded, but surprised he didn't pick up on it over time. "Brianna look at me. It's ok." She doesn't look at him. Mark spoke softly. "Brianna its ok." She slowly glanced at Mark. "You two kept that secret very well. How did it happen?"

Rodney returned with their drinks. She paused and stared down at the table, not to allow the waiter to see her eyes swelling up with tears. "Would you care for something from the menu sir?"

"No thank you. Ms. Delray?" Mark stared at her the whole time. Brianna never looked up, but shook her head. "The drinks are fine Rodney. Thank you." The waiter left. "You were about to say…"

She regained her composure and began once more… She started to speak with clarity. "After my first month here, I bumped into Mr. Fitzpatrick in the café' on the first floor. He actually remembered me from my interview."

"Trust me. He knows all the names of his employees. Especially the very attractive ones. Go on."

"He offered his assistance to teach me how to negotiate deals outside of the training classes. So when his wife would take trips out of town and he knew she would be gone overnight, he gave me the combination to the house."

Mark was stunned. He thought he was the only other person that J would allow to have his combinations. "Trips?"

"Yes, like shopping in Paris or weekends at her parents. The trips were few but enough for us to see each other quite a few times. The first time he called me, he said she was gone for the evening. I came over and he was a perfect gentlemen."

"How did you come and go without being seen?" Mark was inquisitive. "There is a woman across the street that makes it her job to keep track of who comes and goes at his home. How were you not seen?"

"There is a back street and bushes leading up to the house around the pool area where the caterers come and go."

"I see… continue, please."

"That night he showed me how to contact potential clients, find their weakness, and exploit their vulnerabilities. Nothing happened that night. He talked about the art of negotiations and what type of technology I was interested in. Two hours later I went home."

"How many times did you see him?"

Brianna spoke with watery eyes and a calm voice. "I didn't count."

"That many…"

"The second time I came and left. Only business was discussed. The third time his wife was gone for the weekend. The advancement came. He had his cook to fix dinner. Catherine had left early that afternoon to visit her parents and the maid was gone for the evening. When I arrived, darkness had fallen. We had a nice quiet dinner for two. We spoke only of work over dinner. As the evening continued, we finished dinner and then he offered me a swim in the pool before going home. I said I would love to, but I didn't bring anything."

"Why didn't you go home?'

"I was infatuated Mr. Townsend."

"Then what?"

"He took me by the hand and we walked out by the pool. The pool lights were dim. He offered me a glass of wine from the pool bar. I accepted. I didn't intend to drink much, but that evening was perfect. The moon was full and the light shined bright upon the water. He explained all was secure around his home and we should take advantage of the moonlight and skinny dip. He had Alexa play love music from Barry White, Marvin Gaye and others. I took sips of wine as the music played. Laughter came suddenly as the wine took its affect over me while I stood in awe of him undressing. Moments later, he dove in the pool."

"You knew he was married Brianna. Why would you stay?"

"The whole ambiance of the evening seemed like a dream. I couldn't help myself. As I watched him undress, his blue eyes and masculine body called every inch of me into the pool. At that very moment it seemed as if it was just the two of us and we were getting to know one another as man and woman for the very first time. The concept intrigued me, that someone of his status would be interested in me. I didn't jump in right away. I sat on a lounge chair and I continued to sip the wine I was poured. When I finished that glass, I poured myself another knowing that was a bad idea. I told him

I was coy and uncomfortable jumping in unclothed as I had nothing to wear. He told me to jump in with my clothes on, if that made me feel more comfortable. He promised to buy me more clothing. Whatever I wanted, when I wanted it."

"That evening?"

"No… the next day or whenever we met again. Mr. Fitzpatrick told me from that day forward I would never want for anything again. That's when I knew his wife wasn't coming home. As I drank my wine faster, I began to feel more relaxed. I just watched as he swam from one end of the pool to the other. He called my name. The way he spoke it, it sounded so beautiful. 'Brianna come join me', over and over again. That's when I couldn't resist his pleading. I finished the wine, undressed and dove in. He didn't try to touch me, even though, at that instant I wanted him to. He asked if I wanted to race. I was in awe that this man was so attentive of me."

"Why not. You're a beautiful black woman. Then what happened?"

Brianna gave a slight smile as if reliving that moment in time. "We went to one side of the pool. We were at least three feet apart and then he said 'ready, set, go'. We both took off. He raced past me, but I caught a cramp about half way and started to go under. He turned and noticed my distress. He caught me around my arms, pulled me out of the water and placed me on a cushy patio couch. He grabbed a towel to cover me. He comforted me by wrapping his arms tightly around me and rubbing my shoulders until he knew I was ok. After a few minutes of just holding me in his arms, he stood from the chair and offered to take me home. He said I could pick my car up later. At that moment, I gradually started to get up. I was just a little unstable in standing. He reached out to catch me around my waist before I fell. I placed my hands on his shoulders. I gazed into his eyes, lovingly. He drew me closer to his warm, naked masculine body. His smile was so intoxicating, I let the towel fall from around me. I positioned my body closer to his. His facial expression screamed of a desire to make love to me. So hypnotized by the entire ambiance of the evening, my heart and soul was his. He asked me once again if this is what I wanted. I ignored his words and without delay, I pulled his lips close to mine. He took my body slowly to the ground, kissing me the entire time. Then he paused, gazed into my eyes as if waiting for me to say 'stop'. It was as if he was asking my permission to proceed. I gave him a look of 'take me, I'm yours' and without hesitation, he thrust himself inside of me still gazing into my eyes. With much delight of physical pleasure that radiated upon my face, he ravished my lips and breast, while maintaining delicate thrusts upon my lower body. I expelled moans of pleasure from my lips and he knew I pleased."

"And that was the beginning?" questioned Mark.

"Yes. That was the beginning of every time his wife was gone overnight or a weekend, I would spend the evening or the weekend with him."

"If he never forced you, why did you continue to see him?"

"At first it was infatuation, fascination, lust or so I believed. When we became physical, I couldn't get enough. It was never the same with him. It was always in one of seven bedrooms, but never their master bedroom. Each room had a different sav-wa-fair."

"He had different rooms for different moods?" Mark was astounded.

"Yes. One was all red for a hot and steamy night of role play and toys. The blue room was just a large master bedroom and a Jacuzzi bath. This was the one I enjoyed the most. This one night… we would lay for hours massaging and kissing one another in all the right places. We poured liquid chocolate, or whip cream, or honey on our bodies. Then after having sex, we would bathe with warm water in the Jacuzzi filled with bubbles, red rose pedals and sweet smelling perfumes. We would lather and cover each other with the soapsuds, laughing, and pushing water into each other's faces. When I would rub the bubbles from my eyes, he would just stare at me as if he saw me for the very first time. Then he took both his hands and smoothly wiped the bubbles away from my eyes and gently touch his lips to mine."

Mark noticed the passion from which she spoke. He noticed her eyes were not upon him, but visualizing that pleasurable occasion that meant so much to her. He continued to listen intently.

"After that moment, he stood over me, held out his hands and pulled me up. Our bodies soon touched once again. His hands worked feverishly over me and I, him. His lips passionately kissing mine over and over again. He moved methodically with his mouth in different places all over my body. He provided me with overwhelming fleshly sensations. I screamed with elation. We soon stepped out of the Jacuzzi. I was like putty in his hands. He swept me off my feet, still kissing me as he carried me to the bedroom. He laid me gently upon the covers. When he climbed on top of me, our bodies were totally wet and we glided over one another like hot butter spreads on a hot dinner. Totally heated with physical and emotional passion, that juices flowed from my inner body, while he thrusted his external rod in to me over and over and over again. I was so drunk into Mr. Fitzpatrick that if someone had called my name with a bullhorn, I wouldn't have heard it. In the purple room…"

"Stop." Mark spoke calmly. "I get the picture."

"No Mark, Mr. Townsend. You don't understand. If we weren't making love at his house, we would take his private jet and fly different places… Miami, Paris, New York, or Hawaii. Any place that I desired was within my asking. Anything I wanted, I could have. And ohhh… in Hawaii we would lay on the beach and watch the sunset and then dine for breakfast the next morning. He'd take me shopping for clothes, shoes, anything my heart desired was at my fingertips."

"How long did it last?"

"Since I have been working with the company, until…."

Mark interrupted…"Did you love him?"

"Not at first. But yes, as time passed, how could I not. What woman wouldn't want to be treated like a queen by her man every time they were together?"

"Did you let him know that?" quizzed Mark.

"Yes. And that's when the affair ended. He never called me again after I told him I loved him."

"Did you kill him?"

"Ohhh… nooo… Mr. Townsend, I loved him too much. The fact that he didn't love me only made me want him more." Brianna paused and sighed. "How strange does that sound. I was happy just to be with him. Seeing him every day at work was hard. I wanted to kiss and hold him. I tried to ignore the fact that I knew every strand of his hair and every inch of his body. But I also knew if I tried to enter his life without his permission, I would have hell to pay. So I was content just being around him and doing my job."

"What about his wife? Didn't it bother you to know that you couldn't be the woman in his bed every night?"

"No. As far as I was concerned… she… was the other woman."

Mark raised an eyebrow in amazement. "Now that he's gone…"

Brianna interrupted. "Now that he's gone, just thinking about the time we shared and the way we made love, still brings me happy memories. I do miss him so. Even though we were lovers no longer, I took great pleasure in just seeing him every day."

Mark just sighed. "Well your secret is safe with me."

Brianna spoke with sadness in her voice. "How did you know Mr. Townsend?"

"I didn't." Mark confessed. "I didn't Brianna. He had a little black book of the women he had relationships with."

"Other women?"

"You mean you didn't know?" asked Mark, surprised at her question.

"No. How would I?"

"When the detective showed me the black book, there were phone numbers beside all of the first names in the book, except for the letter 'B'. Either he knew your number by memory or he had access to it another way. The letter 'B' made me think of you. If you had said 'I don't know what you're talking about' when you sat down just then, I would have said 'my apologies' and left it alone."

"Do you think the detective will figure it out?"

"Maybe... maybe not? Since you didn't kill him, I wouldn't worry about it." Mark took another sip of his drink. "I have another appointment this evening. I must leave. If you would like to dine here, it's already covered." Mark rose from the table.

Tears formed in Brianna's eyes once again as she held her head down. "I think I will sit here and finish my drink."

Mark started to leave, but he paused in his footsteps. "One last question." Brianna turned and stared up into his eyes as tears trickled down her cheeks. "If you had known he was seeing other women, would you have continued to see him?"

"Yes, without question. I had candle light dinners, his pool was filled with an entire bed of red roses, and so many you couldn't see the water. That was all just... for... me. His kindness and mannerism were infectious. Like a drug, I was addicted. I couldn't stop seeing him on my own. I knew he would have to end it."

Mark nodded and walked away.

CHAPTER 47

District Attorney Conversation

etective Farland and Agent Barley, detective Farland's assistant, an aggressive middle-aged man that always wants to get the suspect no matter what the cost. They both sat in the District Attorney's office trying to get an arrest warrant for Mrs. Fitzpatrick.

"Detective Farland what do you have on Mrs. Fitzpatrick? Anything where she searched the internet on how to commit the perfect murder? Any camera footage of her buying poison in a store? Anything to connect her to the murder?" Stated District Attorney Lucas.

"No. Nothing like that. Not yet." Responded Detective Farland.

"So what's your play on prosecuting her?" asked District Attorney Lucas.

"There was no sign of forced entry. However, the alarm was disabled for almost thirty minutes during the time frame the murder could have occurred. There were two glasses of wine by the pool." Stated Agent Barley.

"And she was the only one that had the combination to the house." Stated Detective Farland.

"You don't know that. You yourself said he had many lady friends. He could have given one of them the combination or invited one of them in?" questioned the DA Lucas.

"Yes. That's true, but the house was sacred ground. He may not have loved his wife, but he respected her enough not to bring his lady friends there." Stated Detective Farland.

"How do you know that for sure?" questioned DA Lucas.

"We found out he owed a condominium that housed many of his female guests. So when he made plans to wine and dine them, he housed them or he brought them there." Spoke Agent Barley.

"Did he have clients or others that may have wanted to see him dead?" spoke DA Lucas.

"Yes. Some jilted women and an angry employee." Stated Detective Farland.

"Why don't you suspect one of them?" asked DA Lucas.

"Because all their alibi's checked out." Stated Agent Barley.

"So why don't you believe Mrs. Fitzpatrick with her alibi?"

"She is the only one that benefits greatly from his death. The motive is clear, a scorned wife and his company is worth millions. You know with a company worth a half-billion dollars and his life is insured with the company. The life insurance on him has to be at least that much." Stated Detective Farland.

"Ok let's say you are right. How does that make his wife a murderer? What's your theory?" questioned DA Lucas.

"My theory is she wanted him dead, so she poisoned the wine. It's a slow death, but an effective one. When she confronted him about his affairs while they were drinking near the pool, her anger escalated. She wanted him dead now. She got her .45 caliber and shot him." Stated Detective Farland.

"Her gun case was broken into. We don't have a murder weapon and a neighbor saw a suspicious character leaving her home." Said the DA Lucas.

"The smashed gun case is a mere diversion to throw us off. The person leaving the grounds could have been Mrs. Fitzpatick." Stated Detective Farland.

"Or her friend September." Stated Agent Barley.

"We don't have *the* murder weapon, but I am sure her other gun will match ballistics." Stated Detective Farland.

"And why would either be outside the house where they could be seen?" questioned DA Lucas.

"She wasn't planning on being seen. Mrs. Jenson brought a stool to the grounds with her binoculars to get a better look after she heard the gun shots." Stated Detective Farland.

"Well if you suspect Mrs. Fitzpatrick was already in the home, why was the alarm disabled?" quizzed DA Lucas.

"We are trying to figure that one out?" stated Barley.

"Do you have concrete proof that Mrs. Fitzpatrick has to be the murderer detective for me to issue an arrest warrant?" asked DA Lucas.

"Look! She had every reason to want her husband dead." Stated Detective Farland.

"Agreed, but that doesn't mean she pulled the trigger or poisoned the wine. So how do you plan to make anything stick without proof? All you got is theory and possibilities. None of which will hold up in the court of law. If she doesn't walk now, she will surely walk if a jury hears the circumstantial evidence you have against her."

Detective Farland sighed. He stood and paced the floor. "We haven't gotten all the test results back yet from forensics, but I am sure that it will point to Mrs. Fitzpatrick."

"What about the toxicology report?" questioned DA Lucas.

"That one we do know. He had poison in his body." Specified Agent Barley.

"Any finger prints or DNA on the glasses?"

"Waiting on that test still." Indicated Detective Farland.

"So he was poisoned by the person he was drinking with, but there is no proof to say that was his wife." Stated DA Lucas.

"With an iron clad alarm system, who else could have gotten in to the house? Who else could have poisoned him? Who else could have shot him three times in the head without any sign of a skirmish anywhere in the house or by the pool?" Detective Farland.

"You tell me. She has an alibi." Stated DA Lucas.

"I think September may have been her accomplice. They both could have been in the house." Stated Agent Barley.

DA Lucas was firm in tone. "You're grasping at straws Detectives. So unless you can prove the two of them conspired to murder her husband, I am not letting this go to court. And when I say proof, I mean strong evidence that can put them both away. If not... well let's just say... you tried. Now go find out who murdered Mr. Fitzpatrick."

As they walked out of the DA's office, Detective Farland left the room irritated. "He needs to get the paperwork started for a warrant for her arrest. I am sure all the test will come back against Mrs. Fitzpatrick and her friend."

Agent Barley wanted Mrs. Fitzpatrick as bad as Detective Farland did. "I'll get on it right now and see where we are with test results."

"I will be in my office going over the evidence we've accumulated in this case thus far. Call me when you hear something." Stated Detective Farland.

Agent Barley went to his car, headed toward the laboratory. Hours later, Agent Barley called. "They fired the other .45 that was in the case. They matched that gun with the bullets that were found lodged in Mr. Fitzpatrick's head. The bullet patterns were an exact match."

"Great! Agent Barley. So now we know it was her other gun that was used to kill him."

"How do we know it was her gun and not Mr. Fitzpatrick?"

"Several of their guests from the executive parties I interviewed said how Catherine bragged about being in gun competitions with September and Catherine admitted to purchasing them. Good work on the ballistics."

"Smoking gun." Spoke Agent Barley.

"Literally. Hopefully that will be enough for the warrant for her arrest and we can work on making the rest stick." Smiled Detective Farland.

CHAPTER 48

Arrested

Catherine was soon arrested for the murder of her husband. Days later, she asked to see Mark while she was behind bars. Mark sat in the chair across from a solid glass shield. Catherine did the same. Mark picked up the phone, Catherine mimicked him.

"How did they come to arrest you Catherine? You have September as an alibi."

"My guns in the showcase in the living room. The murderer who killed Johnathon took one and shot him with it. The other one was matched by forensic as being fired from the same type gun." Catherine's eyes began water. Her throat swelled. Words came slower. "Mark I want you to know I would never do anything to hurt my husband. I loved him too much."

"I know you wouldn't Catherine. I saw the love you had for him when I was around you two and especially when you came to see me about taking over the late hours from him."

"I didn't do it Mark. I didn't do it."

"I know you didn't Catherine. They can't convict you. You have an alibi, don't you? What are they saying happened?"

"My lawyers are telling me they think I shot him with my own gun."

"How stupid would that be? See… from that alone, any jury wouldn't convict you because they know you would have been smarter than that. So without the gun there is no way they can prove it was you or anyone else, right?"

"I guess. I don't know." Solemnly spoke Catherine.

"Even if they found the gun, it would have your finger prints on it, it's your gun."

Catherine perked up. "Yes! If someone bashed the case to get the gun, it might still have their fingerprints on it, proving it was an impulsive action by someone else and not me?"

"Exactly. Do you know where the gun is?"

"Of course not Mark. If I did, I would gladly tell them." Catherine's enthusiasm soon demished.

"Don't worry Catherine. There is no way they can pin this on you without evidence."

"There is something else Mark. They found poison in his system."

"What!"

"They are going to try and say I poisoned him while we were drinking wine because two glasses were found by the pool. Supposedly as our conversation heated up over the affairs, I took my gun and shot him in anger."

"Two glasses?"

"Yes. They think whoever killed him, he must have known them. It could have been one of his mistresses."

"You knew about the other women in J's life?" exclaimed Mark.

"Yes."

Mark was shocked that she knew. He tried to pretend he didn't know. "Johnathon was having affairs?"

"Yes."

"Oh my goodness. I'm so sorry Catherine. Well, the other glass could have been the other woman. Right?"

"Possibly. I don't know." Catherine mumbled still in tears.

Mark was inquisitive. "Well how did you find out about the affairs?"

"Totally by accident. I saw him at a club on our anniversary night dancing with Mrs. Russo and we followed them after they left the club."

"You? You were at a club and you knew the woman he was with?"

"I know, I know… clubs aren't my thing. After Johnathon didn't plan anything for our anniversary, we had an argument and September was trying to cheer me up."

"So September invited you out? So how did you know the woman?"

"Yes, well. I met her when Johnathon took me to Italy."

"Well they still don't have any concrete evidence on you Catherine. You're going to be fine. You know I am in your corner every step of the way. So if you need a character witness, just have your attorney call me. You know that you are like a sister to me and I would be happy to testify on your behalf."

"Mark the reason I called you here is for the company."

"The company?" Mark was confused as to her concern for the business while her life was in peril.

"Yes. Please don't let the company fail. Continue managing it as if it were your own. If by some chance I am found guilty, I don't want all his hard work to plummet to nothing. I know you can run it. Promise me you will. I know it's what Johnathon would have wanted."

"Of course, I promise. However, I am very sure you have nothing to worry about Catherine. With all the love you had for J, they will soon see there is no way you could have done this to your husband?"

"Thanks Mark, you know I love you."

"I love you too Catherine and I will be with you through all of this." Mark touched his hand to the glass.

"Times up." Stated the guard.

Catherine displayed a half smile and touched the glass as well. Their hands mirrored each other. She rose and the guard took her away. Mark watched as Catherine soon disappeared behind locked doors.

The very next day Catherine had a surprise visit in prison. To her disbelief, Johnathon's father was on the other side of the glass this time. She had not seen or spoken to him since her marriage day. Catherine sat down behind the glass and awaited the words of this man she barely knew. Catherine picked up the phone.

An expression of resentment claimed the face of this man. "You murdered our son. We hope you rot in hell for what you have done. We tried to warn him from marrying beneath his wealth. Now he has paid the ultimate price so you can inherit his riches."

"Mr. Fitzpatrick I loved Johnathon with all my heart."

"Save your lies for the courtroom." Mr. Fitzpatrick stood with a raged expression and walked away.

The guard removed Catherine back to her cell as she watched Mr. Fitzpatrick disappear behind the doors of the prison room.

CHAPTER 49

The Trial

The courtroom was packed. Twelve jurors in the box. A stern judge sat at the desk. Catherine was solemn. She was dressed in a casual gray dress, covered full body length from her neck to her ankles. The Fitzpatrick's parents had a front row seat behind Catherine. September and Mark sat next to each in the very back of the courtroom. Nicolette sat in the right far corner of the courtroom with her husband. Both the defense attorney and the prosecution attorney stood five-feet eight inches tall, average build, defense attorney with dark hair, and the prosecution attorney brown hair, both in three piece suits ready for battle.

The Judge sat stern and straight faced with a disciplined courtroom. He struck his gavel hard and loud. "The court is now in session, the prosecution may call its first witness."

"Prosecution calls Javier Hernandez." Spoke Mr. Jacobs.

"Raise your right hand. Do you promise to tell the truth and nothing but the truth?" asked the court clerk.

"I do." A calm Javier spoke. He took his seat in the witness box.

"You may be seated." Stated the court clerk.

"How do you know Mr. Fitzpatrick Mr. Hernandez?" asked Mr. Jacobs. Javier spoke. "I was one of his employees."

"What was your issue with Mr. Fitzpatrick?"

"I didn't have an issue with him until he fired me over punching a client." Javier had some anger in his voice.

"Is this your only violent act within the organization?" questioned Mr. Jacobs.

"Of course. Mr. Fitzpatrick was an excellent employer. He treated all of us with respect and the pay was pretty good too."

"So after Mr. Fitzpatrick fired you. Did you want him dead?" grilled Mr. Jacobs.

"I did, after all the hard work I had put into his organization. I felt I desired a second chance."

"So when you didn't get your second chance, what did you do next?"

"I went to his house the following week with the key codes I saw on his desk the day he fired me. When I tried one night, they didn't work. I knew that he had changed the codes. In that instance, I thought of what my girlfriend had told me about having a life together. I changed my mind."

"So... you're only telling us this because Mrs. Jensen saw you that night around ten or so, two weeks after you were fired, correct?"

"Yes." Stated Javier.

"So what did you do then?"

"I left his home and did nothing."

"So you never went back?" asked Mr. Jacobs.

"No. I moved on. My girlfriend talked me into starting my own company. I am in the process of getting a loan for my own business. She said if I can make millions for Mr. Fitzpatrick, I can make millions for myself."

"So your alibi for the night he was killed is...?"

"My girlfriend and I went over to some friend's house to celebrate my idea. We were just enjoying each other's company. We were there until one the next morning, drinking and talking."

"The police corroborated this alibi?"

"Yes you can ask Detective Farland." Spoke Javier.

"Very well. No more questions for this witness your Honor."

"You may cross examine Mr. Barnes." Stated the Judge.

"No questions, your Honor."

"You may step down Mr. Hernandez." Spoke Judge.

"Your Honor the prosecution calls Ms. Cynthia Diamond."

Cynthia dressed in high heels, a female suit coat and skirt with full make-up on, took the stand.

"Do you promise to tell the truth and nothing but the truth?" asked the court clerk.

"I do." Cynthia spoke calmly.

"How do you know Mr. Fitzpatrick Ms. Diamond?" asked Mr. Jacobs.

"I met him at a security conference in New York. He asked me out for drinks after the conference. I accepted. We were intimate with each other later that evening in his hotel suite. The next day he gave me his number and I left."

Catherine stared at her with no emotion. September watched Catherine as she continued to listen.

"When was the next time you saw Mr. Fitzpatrick?" quipped Mr. Jacobs.

"It was a week later he called and asked me when was I going to be in L.A. and for how long? I told him I was coming that Tuesday and if he wanted to get together I would be available."

"And did you get together?" probed Mr. Jacobs.

"Yes."

"Intimately?"

"Yes."

"How many times and months did this *get together* take place?" asked Mr. Jacobs.

"For about three months on Tuesday's and Thursday's. I started to fall in love with him. I told him I wanted to spend more time with him and then that's when he told me he was married."

September looked at Catherine and she cringed when those words were spoken by Cynthia.

"How did that make you feel?" interrogated Mr. Jacobs.

"Angry and betrayed."

"Did you want to kill him?" asked Mr. Jacobs.

"The thought had crossed my mind, but as he so elegantly told me, 'He could ruin my career.'

"Where were you the evening Mr. Fitzpatrick was murdered?"

"I was in New York celebrating my best friend's wedding. I was at the reception until midnight."

"Did Detective Farland corroborate your alibi?"

"He did." Stated Cynthia.

"No further questions for this witness your Honor." Spoke Mr. Jacobs.

"Mr. Barnes do you wish to cross examine?" asked the Judge.

"No questions, your Honor." Stated Mr. Barnes.

"The prosecution calls Ms. Olivia Long." Stated Mr. Jacobs.

Olivia strolled to the stand very well dressed and confident about speaking the truth to the questions she was about to answer.

"Ms. Long how do you know Mr. Fitzpatrick?" questioned Mr. Jacobs.

"I was drinking alone at the Yacht Club one evening going over some notes on my laptop for work."

"Go on."

"He came in that evening alone. He asked me if he could sit down. How can you resist such a handsome man?" answered Olivia.

Catherine held firm showing no emotion.

"Go on." Stated Mr. Jacobs.

"That night I gave him my number. He called a week later with a time to meet him at his condo."

"How many times did this happen?"

"Too many to count." Stated Olivia.

"Did you ever get angry at him?" asked Mr. Jacobs.

"Only once, when he told me he didn't want to see me anymore."

"Go on." Quipped Mr. Jacobs

"Yes, well…" Olivia paused. "We had been seeing each other off and on over three years, until I started to fall in love with him. When I told him I loved him, he dropped me like a heavy weight he couldn't hold onto anymore. He told me he had other women and he was married."

"Did you want to kill him when you found out he was married and had other women in his life?" quizzed Mr. Jacobs.

Olivia yelled. "Not just in his life, in the building! And he was married. I was furious. Yes, the thought had crossed my mind." Olivia calmed down. "However being the professional that I am, I chalked it up to a bad experience and decided to move on with my life."

"Where were you the night Mr. Fitzpatrick was murdered?" questioned Mr. Jacobs.

Olivia answered assertively. "I was working late that evening. I had a presentation to give the next morning. Since each of us have to check in and check out of the building with security. Security can confirm that I didn't leave the building until twelve-thirty that night he was killed."

"Did Detective Farland confirm your alibi?"

"Yes."

"No further questions your Honor." Mr. Jacobs stated.

"Mr. Barnes?" asked the Judge.

"No questions your Honor."

"You are excused Ms. Olivia Long." Stated the Judge.

"The prosecution calls Mr. Giovanni Russo." Proclaimed Mr. Jacobs.

Dressed in casual slacks and designer shirt and a blazer style jacket, Giovanni Russo took the stand.

"Mr. Russo did you know your wife was sleeping with Mr. Fitzpatrick?" asked Mr. Jacobs.

Giovanna looked over at his wife, who bowed her head in shame. Then he looked back at Mr. Jacobs. "To be perfectly honest. I allow my wife her privileges. I realize I have over thirty years in age on her and as long as she is happy, I am happy."

"That doesn't answer the question. Did you know your wife was sleeping with Mr. Fitzpatrick?" grilled Mr. Jacobs.

"I knew she was sleeping with someone, but I didn't know who she was sleeping with."

"Are you telling me you were ok with your wife's indiscretions?"

"I tolerated them as long as she came home to me each time. My wife never gave me any reason to be angry or upset with her. She always pleased me the way a beautiful wife should."

Nicolette stared at Giovanni infuriated, knowing she didn't sleep around.

"Where were you the evening Mr. Fitzpatrick was murdered?" quizzed Mr. Jacobs.

"I was half-way around the world resting with my lovely wife on my yacht in South Africa. My staff and my wife corroborated my location with Detective Farland."

"No further questions your Honor."

"Mr. Barnes?" asked the Judge.

"Yes your Honor." Barnes stood and walked to the witness bench. He stared into Mr. Russo's eyes.

"Mr. Russo." Russo was unemotional to Mr. Barnes wanting to cross examine. "You knew your wife was having an affair and this didn't bother you?" questioned Mr. Barnes.

Mr. Russo spoke calmly with his Italian accent. "I have been married to my wife for eight years. Do you think Mr. Fitzpatrick was the first one?" Nicolette's emotional expression was that of intense fury as he continued the farce of her having affairs. "I knew that one day she may find my passion for physical contact a little less desirable, than that of a younger man. I have thirty plus years on my wife, I expected adultery when I married her. I was at peace with it before I said, 'I do'."

"I see. You are also one of the richest men in Italy. How do we know you didn't just pay someone to kill Mr. Fitzpatrick?" questioned Mr. Barnes

"Objection your Honor." Stated Mr. Jacobs.

"Objection over ruled. Answer the question." Spoke the judge.

"If you didn't hear me the first time, I said I was already at peace if my wife decided to have an affair. I love her very much and as long as she comes home to me, no man is a threat to our relationship."

Mr. Barnes tone raised slightly. "How do you know your wife wasn't in love and planning to leave you? You heard the testimony of the other women. They were in love with this man, what makes your wife any different?"

Russo was slightly angered, but kept his composure. He glanced at Nicolette and spoke. "I trust my wife to keep her word. Not only did she say her vow to me at our wedding, but she made a promise to me on our honeymoon that she would never leave me for anything or anyone."

"You believe her?" questioned Mr. Barnes.

Giovanni was still staring at Nicolette. "With all my heart." Nicolette's expression softened.

"No further questions Your Honor."

"Do you wish to re-cross examine Mr. Jacobs?" Stated the Judge.

"No Your Honor."

"You are excused Mr. Russo. Call your next witness Mr. Jacobs." Stated the Judge.

The prosecution calls Mrs. Giovanni Russo." Spoke Mr. Jacobs.

Nicolette gracefully walked to the stand with elegance and poise, dressed in a tight one piece white and blue dress with buttons centered in the back.

"Mrs. Russo how did you know Mr. Fitzpatrick?"

"He put up the security system in our home in Italy."

"How did you and Mr. Fitzpatrick become intimate?" questioned Mr. Jacobs.

Nicolette glanced at her husband. She couldn't mention Giovanni and the scheme to get Johnathon's business or that Johnathon helped her create her own business. Giovanni shook his head with the slightest of motion. She looked back at Mr. Jacobs.

"He visited us on our yacht one weekend. I thought he was handsome and so we found ways to meet."

"How often was this?"

"Every other week when I came to L.A."

"Did you love Mr. Fitzpatrick?' asked Mr. Jacobs.

Catherine squirmed in her seat. September had an extremely indignant expression upon her face.

Nicolette glanced over at her husband. She was silent for a moment and then she stuttered. "I ahhh…"

"Mrs. Russo. Did you love Mr. Fitzpatrick?" repeated Mr. Jacobs.

"Yes." Nicolette looked over at her husband. He had a non-emotional expression.

"Did you want to see Mr. Fitzpatrick dead?" asked Mr. Jacobs.

"Why would you say that to me?" asked Nicolette.

"It's obvious Mr. Fitzpatrick was causing a strain on your relationship with your husband. The pressure of loving one and being obligated to another could have gotten to you." Stated Mr. Jacobs.

Incensed by his words, Nicolette screamed. "Never!"

"No further questions your Honor."

"Mr. Barnes do you wish to cross-examine?" asked the Judge.

"Just one question your Honor." Stated Mr. Barnes.

"Proceed." Said the Judge.

"Mrs. Russo would you have ever hurt Mr. Fitzpatrick or your husband for any reason?"

"No. I cared for both of them." Nicolette almost teary eyed thinking of Johnathon.

"No further questions your Honor." Stated Mr. Barnes

"You're excused Mrs. Russo." Assured the Judge. "The prosecution may call its next witness."

"The prosecution calls Mrs. Jensen to the stand." Stated Mr. Jacobs.

"Mrs. Jensen, you were watching the house that evening… were you not?" asked Mr. Jacobs.

"Yes I was. I heard a loud noise, but I couldn't see anything."

"What kind of loud noise?"

"Like firecrackers." Stated Mrs. Jensen.

"About what time was that?"

"Around nine-forty-five or ten."

"What did you see that night Mrs. Jensen?" questioned Mr. Jacobs.

"After I heard what sounded like a fire cracker, I heard that same sound a few seconds later."

"Go on Mrs. Jensen." Stated Mr. Jacobs.

"It took a little longer, but I heard that same sound a third time. I tried to wake my husband Harold, but he didn't get up. So I got dressed, took my little stool, walked over to see what I could see over the bushes in their lawn."

"Mrs. Fitzpatrick's lawn?"

"Yes."

"And what did you see?"

"I saw a human figure dressed in military attire tinkering with what I believe to be the alarm system."

"Did you yell at them?" questioned Mr. Jacobs.

Mrs. Jensen was stunned by the question. "Of course not! I didn't want them to see me."

"Did they see you?" asked Mr. Jacobs.

"Yes. They raced toward me. That's when I almost fell off my stool trying to run back home."

"In your observance of this person, where you able to make out if they were a male or female?"

"Well not really. You never know these days, even on forms they have 'other'."

The court room laughed.

"So did their body build look masculine? Or a shapely figure like Mrs. Fitzpatrick?"

Mrs. Jensen looked at Catherine. "They looked average."

"Would you say it could have been Mrs. Fitzpatrick?"

"Objection! Your Honor. Prosecution is trying to lead the witness." Stated Mr. Barnes.

"Objection sustained. Rephrase the question counselor." declared the Judge.

"Mrs. Jensen when did you see Mrs. Fitzpatrick arrive home?" asked Mr. Jacobs.

"Yes. It was almost midnight."

"Was she in her car?" quizzed Mr. Jacobs.

"No, someone dropped her off."

"Was it Miss September?"

"No. I'm pretty sure it wasn't."

"And what did you do then?" asked Mr. Jacobs.

"I raced over to her house and alerted her that I saw an intruder on her lawn." Stated Mrs. Jensen.

"Did she seemed shocked?"

"No."

"So what did Mrs. Fitzpatrick say?"

"She said her house was secure and I should go home. If she needed me she would call me."

"Did you find her reaction strange?"

"How do you mean?" asked Mrs. Jensen.

"Was she pretty calm about it or was she, "Oh my gosh!" type of concern?"

"She seemed pretty calm."

"No further question your Honor." Stated Mr. Jacobs.

"Your witness Mr. Barnes." Announced the Judge.

Mr. Barnes walked to the bench. "Mrs. Jensen how was the suspect dressed that you saw on the lawn that night?"

"With military green uniform, black vest and ski mask."

"Could you tell who was underneath all that military camouflage and gear?" asked Mr. Barnes.

"Not clearly. No I could not."

"Does anyone or everyone in this room appear to have the same shape or build as the person you saw that night?" queried Mr. Barnes.

"I guess. I don't know." Mrs. Jensen seemed confused.

"Did you see anything that could possibly identify the assailant as a male or female or even the color of their skin?"

"No. It was too dark." Thought Mrs. Jensen.

"You mentioned Mrs. Fitzpatrick was calm after you told her there was an intruder on her lawn."

"Yes."

"Did her demeanor surprise you?"

"Somewhat. If it was me, I probably would have been a little more frighten of that fact. But she is young and they do have a security system that would appear to take that worry away of an in-house intrusion."

"How was Mrs. Fitzpatrick dressed when you saw her?" quizzed Mr. Barnes.

"Jeans and blouse."

"Is that typical Mrs. Fitzpatrick, a single rich woman?"

"When she rides with Ms. Jones, yes." Answered Mrs. Jensen.

"No further questions your Honor." Stated Mr. Barnes.

"Do you wish to re-cross examine Mr. Jacobs?" questioned the Judge.

"No your honor."

"You may step down Mrs. Jensen." Affirmed the Judge.

"The Prosecution calls Detective Farland your Honor." Stated Mr. Jacobs.

Mr. Jacobs grabbed the weapon off his table. "I want to present this to the court as Exhibit A."

"So noted." Stated the Judge.

"Detective Farland. Is this the weapon you found at the Defendant's home?"

"Yes."

"Is this the same weapon used to kill Mr. Fitzpatrick?"

"No. But it is the same type weapon, but not *the* weapon. It hasn't been found."

"How do you know this?" interrogated Mr. Jacobs.

"Ballistics matched the missing gun and this gun that was found at the scene. Mrs. Fitzpatrick corroborated the gun that's in your hand was her gun."

"Was it Mrs. Fitzpatrick's gun that killed her husband?"

"Not the one in your hand, but the matching weapon, yes." Answered Detective Farland.

"And the matching one belongs to Mrs. Fitzpatrick?"

"Yes."

Mr. Jacobs placed the weapon back on his table. "How was Mrs. Fitzpatrick when you met her that night?"

"She appeared to me pretty calm, less distraught as other individuals I have encountered about the death of a loved one they just found murdered."

"Did Mrs. Fitzpatrick know her husband was having an affair?"

"Yes."

"Did she admit she was angry about the affair?"

"Yes."

"Mrs. Fitzpatrick also has a friend that used to be in the military is that correct?"

"Yes."

"Why did you suspect Mrs. Fitzpatrick may have murdered her husband?" quizzed Mr. Jacobs.

"Objection Your Honor. Counselor is asking for an opinion." Stated Mr. Barnes.

"Objection over ruled. Answer the question Detective." Stated the Judge.

"There were two glasses found at the pool. Correct?" asked Mr. Jacobs.

"Yes. It would appear Mr. Fitzpatrick was drinking with someone that possibly poisoned his wine."

"Yes and there were no signs of foul play or struggle?" questioned Mr. Jacobs.

"No."

"Which would leave one to believe that Mr. Fitzpatrick knew his assailant?"

"Objection. Counselor is leading the detective to speculate." Stated Mr. Barnes.

"Over ruled. You may answer Detective." Stated the Judge.

"Mr. Fitzpatrick let someone in or someone knew the combination. Would you say Detective?" asked Mr. Jacobs.

"Yes."

"Mrs. Fitzpatrick stated she was at a friend's house. Is that correct?"

"Yes. This friend is also ex-military that taught Mrs. Fitzpatrick how to shoot?"

"Ex-military, yes." Stated Detective Farland. "She taught Mrs. Fitzpatrick how to shoot. That is correct."

"No further questions your Honors."

"Mr. Barnes you may cross examine." Stated the Judge.

Mr. Barnes moved close to the bench to stare at Detective Farland directly in his eyes. Detective Farland was not intimidated by intense stare.

"Yes, there are just a couple of items I need to make clear again for the jury. You've been a detective for the law for how many years?"

"Ten years."

"Are you trained to seek the truth or cut corners when convenient?" questioned Mr. Barnes.

"Objection! Your Honor. No need to insult the witness." Shouted Mr. Jacobs.

"Objection sustained. No need to insult the Detective. Proceed Mr. Barnes with your questioning." Stated the Judge.

"Detective Farland did Mrs. Fitzpatrick have an alibi?" questioned Mr. Barnes.

"Yes."

"She was at a friend's house playing with paintball guns. Why didn't you believe her alibi?"

Detective Farland showed no emotion. "One of her guns was used for the murder weapon and two glasses were found by the pool with no signs of a struggle."

"So that makes her guilty. There is no one else you could have possibly overlooked that could have committed this act of murder?"

"She had the motive and the means." Stated Detective Farland.

"Ms. September said they were at her home until Mrs. Fitzpatrick left around eleven-thirty or so. Correct?"

"That's what Ms. Jones said." Answered Detective Farland.

"Other suspects had a desire to want to see him dead. You checked their alibi's and corroborated them, but Mrs. Fitzpatrick you don't believe. Is that a pretty accurate assumption on my part detective?"

Detective Farland grew slightly annoyed behind his suggestive remark. "Mrs. Fitzpatrick had the motive and the means to execute her husband."

"So this is just a witch hunt for Mrs. Fitzpatrick?" questioned Mr. Barnes.

"Objection!" yelled Mr. Jacobs.

"No further questions your Honor." Mr. Barnes went back to his seat and shuffled some papers.

"You are excused Detective Farland." Stated the Judge.

"Mr. Jacobs. You may call your next witness." Stated the Judge.

"Your Honor the prosecution rest."

"Very well the court will reconvene after the weekend. Court is dismissed."

Week Two of the Trial

"The Defense may call its first witness." Proclaimed the Judge.

"Your Honor the defense calls Ms. September Jones." Stated Mr. Barnes.

As September took the stand, Mr. Barnes got up from his seat. He took the gun off of the prosecutions table.

Mr. Barnes showed September the weapon. "Ms. Jones do you recognize this gun?"

"Yes. That looks like the .45 Caliber Catherine uses at our competitions." Responded September.

"Have you ever fired Mrs. Fitzpatrick's weapons?" quizzed Mr. Barnes.

"No, never."

Mr. Barnes placed the weapon back on the prosecution's table. "Did you have a competition the day Mr. Fitzpatrick was murdered?"

"No. That day Catherine and I did our normal routine of hitting the gun range and a few other sporting activities."

"Like what?" queried Mr. Barnes.

"I believe that day after the gun range we played tennis at her private club. We went horseback riding and then we came back to my house and shot paint guns. We finished up around ten because I do have night lights in my backyard."

"What time did Mrs. Fitzpatrick leave your home?" asked Mr. Barnes.

"After the paint ball game ended, that was around ten. We sat drinking until about eleven, eleven-thirty or so when she decided to leave."

"Ms. Jones do you own military clothing?"

"Yes I do." Confidently spoke September.

"So were you wearing military clothing that night you and Mrs. Fitzpatrick were playing with paint guns?" asked Mr. Barnes.

"No. We had on jeans and blouse with a paint ball vest."

"Why a vest?" questioned Mr. Barnes.

"Because the paint gun shots are fired at the speed of real bullets. They hurt if the body is directly struck with a pellet."

"Did Mrs. Fitzpatrick drive her car home that night Ms. Jones?"

"No. I didn't want her to drive and I had been drinking so I didn't want to drive either. So I called an Uber for her."

"Did you know Mr. Fitzpatrick was poisoned with the wine he was drinking that night?"

September expressed an emotional appearance of shock. "Poisoned?"

"Yes poisoned. Apparently the person he was drinking with tainted his wine while he sipped on it in the pool."

"I had no idea." September maintained a surprise and puzzled expression on her face. She briefly glanced at Catherine with a blank stare on her face and then gave her full attention to Mr. Barnes.

"You and Mrs. Fitzpatrick never drink with Mr. Fitzpatrick that day?"

"No. We never did."

"And you're sticking to the fact that you and Mrs. Fitzpatrick were together at your house that night until around eleven-thirty or so?"

September spoke aggressively. "Yes, because that's what we were doing."

"Did Detective Farland confirm that with you?"

"Yes he did."

"And yet Mrs. Fitzpatrick has an alibi and she is on trial."

"Objection!" Yelled Mr. Jacobs.

"Sustained. Please hold opinions to yourself Mr. Barnes." Stated the Judge.

"No further questions your Honor." Stated Mr. Barnes.

"Mr. Jacobs… your witness." spoke the judge.

Jacobs approached the bench. "Ms. September you were in the military correct?"

"Yes."

"Do you still have your uniforms?"

"Yes."

"You've been out how long?" asked Mr. Jacobs.

"Going on six years."

"Why do you still have your military clothes?"

"They're in a box in a closet. I always think I might get called back to active duty."

"You don't pull these uniforms out to wear them for any occasion?" questioned Mr. Jacobs.

"No. I don't."

"The night Mr. Fitzpatrick was murdered, where were you?"

"As I explained a few moments ago, I was shooting paint balls and drinking with Mrs. Fitzpatrick at my home until she left around eleven-thirty or so."

Mr. Jacobs went to his desk and pick up the gun. "Exhibit A Miss Jones. Do you recognize the gun?" Jacobs gave her the weapon.

September examined it and gave it back. "Yes."

Jacobs put the weapon back on his table. "Mrs. Fitzpatrick is an expert with this gun, is she not?"

"I would say yes."

"Why would Mrs. Fitzpatrick shoot her husband at close range if she is an expert?"

"Objection!" yelled Mr. Barnes. "That's Mr. Jacobs opinion."

"Sustained. Please ask a question Mr. Jacobs." Reminded the Judge.

"I will rephrase the question. Did you and Mrs. Fitzpatrick know Mr. Fitzpatrick was having an affair?" queried Mr. Jacobs.

"We thought it possible."

"Did you and Mrs. Fitzpatrick's plot Mr. Fitzpatrick's murder?" questioned Mr. Jacobs.

"No. The thought never crossed Catherine's mind. She loved him too much."

"What about you Miss Jones?"

"I didn't love him." Firmly spoke September.

The courtroom laughed.

"You didn't answer the question. Did you plot to kill Mr. Fitzpatrick?"

"If I had, it wouldn't have been to poison him or shoot him with my best friend's gun." Aggressively stated September.

"Detective Farland questioned you and didn't believe you Ms. Jones?" spoke Mr. Jacobs.

"That's his problem. We told the truth. We were drinking until eleven or so."

Mr. Jacobs voice grew intense. "Then tell us how Mr. Fitzpatrick was poisoned and shot three times in the head when only Mrs. Fitzpatrick has the code to her home?"

"That would be for Detective Farland to answer that question. He's the murder chaser. We, Mrs. Fitzpatrick and I never saw her husband that evening."

"No further questions your Honor." Stated Mr. Jacobs.

"Do you wish to re-cross Mr. Barnes?" asked the Judge.

"No your Honor."

"You may step down Ms. Jones." Quipped the Judge. "Call your next witness Mr. Barnes."

"Your Honor. Who better to clear this up than… The defense calls Mrs. Catherine Fitzpatrick to the stand."

Catherine took the stand. She had a solemn, confident appearance to her face. She was seated.

Mr. Barnes was confident he had instructed Catherine not to get rattled by any of the questions from the prosecution, because he would ask them first.

"Did you kill your husband Mrs. Fitzpatrick?" asked Mr. Barnes.

"No." Catherine was self-assured in her response.

"Was there friction in your marriage?"

"No, I was always supportive of my husband's work and him. I never complained about anything. I always tried to be the good wife."

Barnes grabbed the .45 Caliber from the prosecution's table and handed it to Mrs. Fitzpatrick. "Exhibit A, is this your weapon?"

Catherine examined it. "Yes. It has my initials on the handle."

Mr. Barnes took the gun from Catherine and placed it back on the prosecution's table.

"You're an expert at firing that .45 Caliber aren't you?"

"Yes." Catherine remained poised.

"How far can you fire your .45 Caliber and be accurate?" quizzed Mr. Barnes.

"One-hundred-twenty meters or a little over a hundred yards." Catherine spoke confidently.

"That's pretty accurate. Is that dead center the target?" questioned Mr. Barnes.

"Yes. It's the reason I have several trophies."

"Do you know how the matching .45 Caliber ended up killing your husband?"

"Only from what Detective Farland told me. He said that my gun case was smashed. This led me to believe that maybe there was an argument perhaps and the other person that was in the house with my husband shattered the case and shot him with my weapon."

"Why do you say the other person?"

"Because Detective Farland also told me there was another wine glass found by the pool and whomever it was, Johnathon must have known that person."

"Did Detective Farland tell you your finger prints were found on the other wine glass?"

"No."

"Did he also tell you your husband was poisoned?"

"He did."

"Did this surprise you?" asked Mr. Barnes.

"Yes. Of course. I don't know why someone would poison him and then turn around and shoot him."

"So on the night of your husband's death you were at Ms. September Jones's house shooting paint guns and drinking."

"Yes."

"No further questions your Honor." Spoke Mr. Barnes.

"Mr. Jacobs." Directed the Judge.

Mr. Jacobs approach Catherine with a stern stare into her eyes. "Mrs. Fitzpatrick. Did you know your husband was seeing other women on different occasions?"

Catherine glanced at September across the room, then back at Mr. Jacobs. "I… thought some of the late nights could have been suspicious. But I never questioned him about it."

"Isn't it true you saw your husband dancing with another woman at the club 'All the Way' and followed him in an Uber to a condo where he entertained other women?" Catherine was a little shocked. She paused. She took a peek at September wondering how the prosecution knew. "An Uber driver reported two crazy women to his headquarters' which alerted the police, but the police said following someone is not a crime."

"Yes, I followed him that night." Responded Catherine.

"So now you knew that your husband was having an affair. Now you have a motive to want to see him dead. Especially since you loved him *so* much. Rage was running through your veins and you plotted to kill him."

"Objection!" yelled Mr. Barnes.

"Sustained." Affirmed the Judge. "Ask a question counselor."

Catherine maintained her composure. "I'll respond Judge. No! That's not what happened! I loved him despite his indiscretions. Someone else shot and poisoned my husband. Why would I bust the glass to get in my own gun case when I knew it was already open? I only locked it when we had guest over."

"How, did someone get past the security system of your home, if no else knew the combination Mrs. Fitzpatrick? When the security system encryption is on, the house is like a fortress. In fact, the security office said someone punched in the code to disable the alarm. The only one that could have known about the combination was you."

"I don't know. Sometimes Johnathon would reboot the system for a system check. He would do it once a month, every month at random. He could have performed it that night."

"Does your husband give out the code to others?" questioned Mr. Jacobs.

"Sometimes he gave out the code to others, but when he did, he would let me know. That day he didn't tell me he gave the code to someone."

"Your neighbor testified that you came home in a cab that night. Why was that?"

"As was explained before, I had been drinking with September that night. We felt it best that neither of us got behind the wheel. So she called an Uber for me."

"You told Detective Farland that September dropped you off that night." Stated Mr. Jacobs.

"If I did, it's because September always drops me off when we are together and it was my first response to him. My thoughts that night after seeing my husband died, wasn't on how I got home."

"Is it not true that you bought September a Mercedes Benz?"

"Yes… what's that got to do with anything?" Catherine, puzzled by the question.

"Why did you do that?" asked Mr. Jacobs.

"She had become a good friend. She is a good friend and that's what good friends do when her ride was a piece of junk."

"You replaced a piece of junk with an eighty-thousand dollar car, why?"

"Because I can!" Catherine spoke aggressively.

Barnes motioned with his hand to lower her tone. "Did you or Ms. Jones shoot your husband with your gun?"

"Of course not!" screamed Catherine. "Why would I shoot my husband with my own gun? That would be kind of stupid, don't you think?"

"I'm asking the questions? Now. Did you shoot your husband Mrs. Fitzpatrick?"

Catherine stated calmly. "No I didn't do it."

"You would stand to gain his empire." Stated Mr. Jacobs.

"It would be hard to enjoy from a prison cell."

"Why did you leave the guns unsecure in the house?"

"Why wouldn't I?" questioned Catherine.

"Your Honor…" spoke Mr. Jacobs.

"Answer the question Mrs. Fitzpatrick." Spoke the Judge.

"I don't have any children. The house is securely locked on a daily basis. There is no reason to lock the gun case. I told you I lock it only when guest are coming over. But the gun case was broken into. I guess the person who killed him didn't know the gun case was unlocked. All anyone would have needed to do was raise the glass and grab a gun. I knew that. So why would I break the case?"

Mr. Jacobs tried to push Catherine into a confusion. He antagonistically spoke. "You plotted. You poisoned the wine bottled thinking he would die a slow death. But as you and your husband argued over the affairs, you grew angry. You shot him point blank, maybe not intentionally that close, but out of anger."

"No!" Yelled Catherine.

Jacob's still spoke quickly and aggressively. "You wiped your finger prints clean of the other wine glass. You broke the glass on the gun case to throw the police off of you and make it seem like someone else was there. Did you not?"

"Objection! Your Honor. The prosecution is speculating." Yelled Mr. Barnes.

"Objection sustained. Ask a question Mr. Jacobs and stop trying to lead the witness." Insisted the Judge.

"Yes your honor, I will rephrase the question. Did you use one of your guns to kill your husband?" questioned Mr. Jacobs.

"I already told you, I didn't. What for? I have access to all our financial accounts. I am, was, the wife of a multi-millionaire. Why would I want to lose that? I have everything I need or want at my fingertips."

"That's true. But you didn't kill your husband for money. You killed him because you found out about his affairs? Isn't that true, Mrs. Fitzpatrick? You found out and you couldn't bear the thought of your husband's arms wrapped around another women and so you shoot him for it? Three times!"

Catherine bowed her head.

"Objection!" Screamed Mr. Barnes.

"Sustained! Questions... Only questions, Mr. Jacobs." Insisted the Judge

Tears began to form in her eyes. September leaned forward and gripped the chair in front of her. She wanted to help Catherine through this emotional moment. Mark grabbed her wrist tightly. September looked at him and leaned back in her seat.

Softly Catherine spoke. "I didn't do it."

"Weren't you hurt emotionally? Didn't you feel the pain in your heart? You're the good wife and here he is stabbing you in the back with all these other women. Remember you're under oath."

Catherine spoke softly. "Yes. It hurt. It hurt badly. But I loved my husband. I wouldn't have killed him over another woman. I would have tried to work it out."

"Well if you didn't kill him, who did?" Catherine bowed her head again with tears flowing. "Mrs. Fitzpatrick, you were devastated by your husband's adultery, wouldn't you have felt compelled to hire someone to commit this crime of passion for you if you couldn't do it yourself?" quizzed Mr. Jacobs.

"Objection! Your honor. Prosecution is leading the witness again." Stated Mr. Barnes.

"Overruled. I will allow the question." Specified the Judge.

Catherine raised her head in disgust. "Someone else? Like who?"

"You couldn't stomach the thought of your husband with another woman, so you had your friend September to do it." September eyes bucked, she almost rose from her seat, but Mark held her down. "That's why you bought her the car." Catherine glanced at September. Her jaw had dropped. "Just admit it! You poisoned him and September shot your husband to make it quick. Just to make sure he was died. How else do you explain poison in his blood stream and bullets in the head?"

"Objection! Objection! Your Honor! Prosecution is still leading the witness. Is he trying to pen the murder on her friend or the defendant?" shouted Mr. Barnes.

"Sustained. Last warning, Mr. Jacobs. Ask your questions or be held in contempt." Stated the judge.

"No! I wouldn't have killed my husband or hired anyone to do it for me. I loved him too much and No! My friend wouldn't have done it either."

"You were wearing a camouflage outfit when you called the police. Ms. Jones gave it to you. That's how Mrs. Jensen spotted you. Isn't that right?"

"No. I was in plain clothing when I spoke with Mrs. Jensen and Detective Farland."

"So if it wasn't you in the camouflage outfit when Mrs. Jensen saw someone leaving your home, then it had to be Ms. Jones?"

Catherine noticed September getting emotionally angry and spoke assertively. "No! My neighbor said she saw someone, I didn't. You need to ask her."

Mr. Jacobs screamed. "Bull! While you were in the house in plain clothes poisoning your husband. You had a few drinks with your husband, got into an argument, grabbed your gun and pulled the trigger! Your friend September was the one waiting outside in a camouflaged uniform to help you get rid of the body. But you didn't count on Mrs. Jensen peeking in the yard."

"Objection! Objection your Honor! That is pure speculation and badgering of the witness." Shouted Mr. Barnes. "The prosecution is grasping at thin air, hoping he can get my client to admit to something she didn't do."

"No further questions." Spoke Mr. Jacobs.

The judge slammed the gavel down. "The court will take a fifteen minute recess." The judge spoke softly to Mr. Barnes and Mr. Jacobs. "I will see you both in my chamber now."

In the judge's chambers, Mr. Barnes attacked Jacobs. "Mr. Jacobs I have asked you to ask a flat out question! If you want someone to confess, go find the real murderer."

Jacobs was clearly angry. "She or her friend or both, is as guilty as ice cream that melts on a hot summer day. Without a doubt. I just can't wrap my head around how it went down."

"How can you be so sure Jacobs? Were you there?" attacked Mr. Barnes.

"Enough counsels." Spoke the Judge assertively. "Mr. Jacobs I have allowed you plenty of latitude with your antics. If you don't refrain from leading the witness, your next thirty days will be in jail. Do you understand me?"

"Yes Your Honor." Softly spoke Mr. Jacobs.

"Your job is to present the facts, not to try and lead the witness on your speculations. Now, I am going to call a recess for the rest of the day unless you are both done calling witnesses."

Both attorney's nodded.

"Good. Then you both take this time to reflect on today, these past two weeks and prepare for tomorrow with your closing arguments. Dismissed."

When the next day came upon them, both sides were ready with stimulating differences. The Judge was seated with a stern glance to the jury for listening to the prosecution and defense.

"Ladies and Gentlemen of the jury both the prosecution and defense rest. We are now going to hear their closing arguments." The Jury sat comfortably awaiting the first attorney to present his argument. The audience in the courtroom was very attentive. The courtroom was so quiet a feather could have drop to the floor and the sound would have echoed though out the courtroom. Then the Judge spoke again. "The prosecution will present its summary first, Mr. Jacobs." Stated the Judge.

Mr. Jacobs stood in a three-piece dark gray suit and black shoes with a pen in his hand. "Ladies and gentlemen of the jury. I have presented that the gun used to kill Mr. Fitzpatrick was the defendant's own weapon that she purchased. Poison was also in his system. It may not be *the* gun, but ballistic proves it is the matching gun from Mrs. Fitzpatrick weapon's case. She knew her husband was cheating on her. Feeling all that hurt, all that emotional pain, she couldn't tolerate it anymore. She poisoned him, when he didn't die quickly enough, she shot him. She plotted, she staged a glass as if someone else was there, and she broke her own gun case to throw the police off her trail. She stage an alibi with Ms. September Jones, a woman she bought an eighty-thousand dollar for. The evidence is clear." Mr. Jacobs smacked the pen on the jury box. "She became incensed, she strategized, and she shot him three times because she was angry. Not only does she get rid of her husband, but she stands to gain his multi-million dollar empire. What kind of new life can a beautiful single woman have without a cheating husband?" Mr. Jacobs glanced across the jury's faces. "The only verdict you can render is guilty. The prosecution rest."

"Mr. Barnes." Stated the Judge.

Barnes stood with a dark blue suit, gray shirt, black shoes, shoulder back and confidence reaped across his face into the jurors' eyes. "Ladies and gentlemen of the jury. The prosecution has proved nothing. Yes... the gun used by the perpetrator was Mrs. Fitzpatrick's. But the actual gun that murdered Mr. Fitzpatrick hasn't been found. Her finger prints were on the gun that the prosecution took from the gun case. But of course, it belongs to Mrs. Fitzpatrick because it's the weapon she used for her competitions. The prosecution didn't prove that she pulled the trigger. And if she wanted to put bullet holes in her husband, she could have shot him from a hundred yards away. Yet the prosecution found powder burns on his forehead, proving that he was shot at close range. The perpetrator wanted to be sure they didn't miss. Yes, someone saw a figure running from the house that night, but who's to say that was Mrs. Fitzpatrick. Yes, Mr. Fitzpatrick was poisoned. Yes, another wine glass was found at the scene, but Mrs. Fitzpatrick's finger prints were not on either the glass or the wine bottle. Where is the proof ladies and gentlemen? And yes there wasn't a struggle in the home which means Mr. Fitzpatrick could have known his guest. This means they were invited into his home. This is all speculation. The prosecution can't even put Mrs. Fitzpatrick at her house at the time of the murder. She was with a friend. So they tried to throw the friend in their assumptions just to try and put the blame on this grieving widow." Barnes pointed at Catherine with a woeful expression on her face. "They showed you no proof ladies and gentlemen, only speculations. With so much doubt swirling around their evidence and witnesses, the only verdict you can render is 'not guilty'. The Defense rest your Honor."

"The jury will deliberate for as long as necessary and reach a verdict. It must be a unanimous decision by all twelve jurors. You may be excused." Spoke the Judge.

Hours passed. September and Mark are in the hallway of the court building. September paced the floor and Mark was trying to console her. Five hours later the jury returned. Everyone was asked to take their seats. The judge sat behind his desk ready for the verdict. Tension gripped the room. September was squeezing Mark's hand. He puts his other hand on top of hers. They held their breath in anticipation of the jury's conclusion. The court room was totally silent.

"Has the jury reached a verdict?" asked the Judge.

A juror stood. "We have your Honor."

The bailiff passed the decision to the judge. The Judge read it. He passed it back to the bailiff to have the verdict read.

"How does the jury find the defendant?" asked the Judge.

"We the jury, finds the defendant… not guilty." Spoke the juror.

September leaped with joy from her seat. Mark smiled and exhaled a sigh of relief. Mark and September embraced each other with smiles of jubilation. Catherine broke down in tears of happiness in her seat. The Fitzpatrick's parents immediately walked out of the courtroom, with Mrs. Fitzpatrick in tears as her husband tried to console her sadness. Nicolette and Giovanni never returned to the courtroom after they gave their testimony. Catherine walked out of the courtroom a free woman.

CHAPTER 50

The Confession

After the trial, Mark went to visit his sister's grave site with a red rose in his hand. Five minutes later his parents arrived with a red rose. The parents, both Caucasian, placed a red rose upon her grave and said a small prayer. Mark bowed his head and listened. Once the prayer was over the parents questioned their son.

"Coming son?" asked his mother.

"No… not right now Mom and Dad. I just need a moment in silence. I will see you at dinner tonight." Solemnly spoke Mark.

"Alright son, bring your brother with you." Stated his father.

"I will ask him Dad."

"Love you son, see you later." Stated his mother.

His parents walked away.

"Love you too, Dad, Mom."

When Mark's parents drove away, he knelt down to the tombstone. He placed his red rose upon her grave. "I wrote this poem for you Penelope, my sister and my best friend. I know you can hear me. I hope you like it. He pulled a piece of paper from his jacket pocket and began reading. 'Our hearts of affection shaped our beginning. Our love stood tall amongst the worst of it all. Nothing could come between us, no wall of hatred, no wall of insensitivity, no wall of unhappiness, no wall of bitterness, and no wall of negativity could break the barrier of warmth and friendship that shaped our lives from the first day we met, until the day that you breathed no more. We…"

At that moment someone walked up behind Mark. Mark felt a presence. He stood, turned and stared at this man. A few seconds later he smiled and embraced him with an affectionate hug.

"I knew you would be here soon little brother. Every year, same time, never fail." Said Mark. "You just missed Mom and Dad, Kofi. They were going to invite you to dinner."

"I accept." Kofi leaned over and placed a red rose on her tombstone. "We did it big Brother."

Mark had a slight smile upon his face. "I know. I wanted him dead as bad as you did. I appreciate you being a patient man little brother and our plan worked without any one suspecting me."

Kofi grinned. "Good. So I can return to New York without hearing you've been locked up for murder?"

"Yes you can and please do it after dinner tonight with Mom and Dad." Mark turned and looked at the grave once again. Tears began to form in his eyes. "I had to do something or I couldn't live with myself Kofi. You didn't hear him talk about Penelope the way I did. Johnathon said after he was done with her, he discarded her… like a piece trash. That was our sister." Mark broke down in tears and knelt once more by her grave. "We got him Sister. He will never hurt another woman again."

"I know Mark. I know." Kofi, placed his hand on Mark's shoulder as he kneeled. "I loved Penelope too."

Mark stood up still staring at her tombstone. His throat began to swell. Tears flowed slowly down his cheek. "Just as if she was my biological sister. She never treated us like we were her step-brothers. In her eyes, we were her brothers." He remembered about the basketball games, the soccer games, and the tennis matches she came to watch him play. He remembered going to her poetry gatherings that he never missed.

As Kofi remembered those moments for himself, tears began to form in his eyes too. "Big brother, I remember the birthday parties we shared, the driving lessons we took. The movies, the study halls, and the support we gave each other in times of doubting our abilities to perform. We talked about everything. Why didn't she come to me or call you Mark so we could talk it out… talk it over?" Tears fell to the ground. "We may have been able to help her through the hurt she was feeling."

Mark sniffled and wiped his tears away. "Maybe it was just too much for her to bare little brother. Or the shame she may have felt for being so venerable to fall in love, only to be rejected by the one you gave your heart to."

"But the communication is what made our relationship so great." Kofi remembered. "There wasn't anything I couldn't tell her or talk to her about. She would always show me the bright side of my adversity, rather than the ugliness I endured being bullied at school."

"I know Kofi. She was strong for the both of us. Maybe to prideful to let us know she needed help." Mark smiled. "I always wondered how she could tell us apart when I pretended to be you. I guess I was too much of a brainy-act when you two love sports and poetry so much more than I did. You and she seemed to have a bond that couldn't be broken. We were lucky to had fallen into the hands of a family that just loved children, no matter what the color of their skin."

"True." Kofi agreed.

Mark was silent for a moment as he still glanced at the tombstone. "Do you think God will forgive us for killing Johnathon Fitzpatrick?"

"I pray that God will have mercy on his soul and ours Mark. I'm just glad Mom and Dad doesn't know anything about what we did. Their hearts would be broken. They taught us to love those that despise you."

Mark gave a sign of the cross across his chest. He looked at Kofi and walked toward the car. "Let's go brother. Mom and Dad will be expecting us soon. I have some things to clear up at the office first."

Kofi followed Mark. "Wait big brother." Kofi was curious. "Our plan was perfect. While I covered for you at the office party, which was a piece of cake by the way with all the info you had given me on your co-workers."

"Good, anyone suspicious of you being my twin?" asked Mark.

"No. I just kept drinking and nodding. That Larry is a piece of work though."

"Yeah. Always telling stupid jokes." Stated Mark.

"Getting back to the accident that was supposed to look like Fitzpatrick had too much to drink and drowned in the pool, what happened that night? Why did you use her gun? The plan was to poison the wine that day."

"It didn't quite go as planned." Mark stated solemnly.

"Obviously, so what happened? You said Catherine should have been with September and J would have been in the pool having a cigar and drinking poison wine. After we switched places at the office party, you were just going to ensure he had drank the wine and lay his lifeless body face down in the pool that evening so it would look like an accidental drowning."

"I didn't get a chance to poison the bottles earlier in the day. A client interrupted that time. So I had to wait for that evening. But it was that simple Kofi. Everything was going according to the plan except for that hick-up. I got there around nine-thirty. The lights flickered, Johnathon called out to me or Catherine to come to the pool area. He was relaxing with his cigar. He was low on wine in his glass, he asked me to pour him another glass and to pour myself one too. I poured myself a glass. I put the poison in his glass. Then I tainted the bottle as well and set it beside him. He didn't notice my actions. I took my handkerchief and wiped the wine bottle down so it would only show his prints. It was perfect. I could tell the poison was taking affect after a half-hour of talking business."

"Go on."

"After he started drinking more wine with the poison, he started talking about how he loved Nicolette and what a beautiful woman she was. He went on and on and on. Then he talked about how he was going to divorce Catherine. I just sat there in my chair in front of him and sipped on my wine while he laid in the pool. After an hour, he asked me to get in the pool. I said okay. I got up. When he wasn't looking, I wiped my wine glass clean and left it beside my chair. As I walked past him pretending I was going to get a pair of swim trunks from his bedroom, I knew the wine was getting to him as I saw his eyes flutter, but he wasn't dead."

"So why use her gun to kill him?" asked Kofi.

"He wasn't dying fast enough!" Mark stated with anger. "I couldn't take listening to him talk about how he toyed with one woman after another. How he loved Nicolette and was divorcing Catherine."

"You could have gotten Catherine put away for life. All you had to do was wait for the poison to work."

"I know Kofi… I know."

"Then what happened?"

"It was almost ten-thirty. He hadn't drank enough to kill himself. When I stepped into the living room I saw Catherine's gun case. I didn't know how long Catherine would be at September's house by this hour of the evening. Then I thought, he should know why he was dying by my hands. While Johnathon was barely conscious, I went to the kitchen, got a pair of plastic gloves and smashed Catherine's gun case. I walked up to him and looked into his eyes. I pointed Catherine's gun in his face and I said, *'You bastard'*. He screamed at me. *'What are you doing Mark?'* I told him, you treated your marriage like a business deal. You treated the women you met like play toys, without any regard for their feelings. They loved you. One in particular loved you so much that when she couldn't have you, she took her own life. Remember Penelope? Johnathon bucked his eyes at that moment. 'That's right! I was her adopted brother. I loved her.' I shouted her name over and over to him. You know he just stared into my eyes and gave me that shocked, bewildered look, like…'I didn't know'. Then I told him that's why he was dying." Mark paused as he relived that moment. Then Mark gazed at Penelope's grave. *'Mark!…'* "Johnathon faintly yelled my name. He started flailing in the water like a stuck fish on a hook. He was so weak, he could barely lift himself out of the pool. He slipped back in. That's when I told him to look at me. He could barely raise his head as his hands gripped the pool siding. I pointed the gun at his forehead… I screamed, 'This is for Penelope!' and fired. He fell backwards into the pool."

"So why three bullets to the head? You had already poisoned him and one shot would have certainly did the job."

"The look he gave me before the first bullet, was such that 'I'm sorry.' He looked so pitiful. I started to leave and then I remembered the words he spoke about Penelope, *discarded her.*"

Inpatient for the answer, Kofi asked again. "Why three times Mark?"

"One for Penelope, one for you and one for me. I shot him at close range so I would be sure not to miss."

"Then what?" questioned Kofi.

"Well, I heard movement on the second shot. It sounded like a bullet being chambered into a weapon. So I hurried and shot him again. Someone else was in the house on the last shot. The patio lights were dim so they couldn't recognize me, the living room lights were off, and so I couldn't recognize them either. All I saw was this figure racing toward the patio door. I scurried out of the caterer's entrance."

"They didn't chase you?" questioned Kofi.

"Why would they? If it wasn't Catherine, they were probably there to do the same thing I had done. Which reminds me…" Mark reached into his blazer pocket and pulled out the .45 caliber. "'Take the gun and drop it into the Manhattan River."

Kofi was shocked. He took the weapon and admired its design. "You still have the gun?"

"I knew Catherine would be blamed. Her finger prints would have been the only ones on the gun. I had to make it look like someone broke in and shot him by keeping the gun."

"You knew Catherine would be blamed?" quizzed Kofi.

"Of course." Mark explained. "She would be the first suspect. Rich beautiful woman kills cheating husband. But, Catherine was supposed to be at September's house until midnight. She told me she would be. Her alibi would be rock solid."

Kofi was perplexed and sighed. "That's really odd. Someone was in the house that knew the combination."

"That's right. Someone got there around ten… eleven-ish." Mark thought. "It had to be Catherine. The lights didn't flicker."

"Maybe? No matter now Mark. No one is the wiser. Catherine is exonerated."

Mark felt no regret, only relief that it was finally over. "Oh well, she's safe now with the trial over. You can't be tried twice for the same murder, if you're found innocent. So after dinner tonight with Mom and Dad, you go back to New York. We will never speak of this again and get rid of that gun. Everything is closed, new evidence could bring the trial to life. Don't let that gun be found."

"Consider it done big brother. Don't worry about it." Kofi smiled. "I believe I will be able to sleep peacefully after six years, knowing our sister's murderer is dead. What about you Mark? Are you going to continue to run the company?"

Mark sighed. "No. I don't want any part of his company? I will resign tomorrow to the board and let Catherine know that it hurts me too much to continue being the acting CEO."

"Then what are you going to do?"

"I'm going to take a year and get myself together. Maybe start my own Tech Company. Who knows? Right now I'm just glad it's all over."

Kofi placed the gun in his jacket pocket, wrapped his arm around Mark's shoulder as they walked to their cars. "One last question. How were you so sure it was Johnathon, Penelope was in love with?"

"Her roommate."

Kofi smiled. "Let's go get some good home cooking."

They both beamed with joy as they drove away.

The next morning Mark was at Johnathon's desk lining things up for Catherine to review. He had called a board meeting for 9:30 a.m. that day. He was going to go over the week's appointments to turn over to the board at the meeting, along with files and financial statements. Suddenly, Catherine walked in unannounced. She stood in front of the desk.

"Mark you know I don't know how to do any of this. Please stay on and turn this company into the multi-billion dollar empire you and Johnathon were aiming for. I know you are supposed to leave today, alerting the board, but please reconsider for a few months. At least to bring me onboard to the functionality of the company. There's a lot to learn. Each floor is designed to do something special."

"I know Catherine. We have a research, parts, fabrication department and many more, but I am going to explain all of this to you this week. I'm just letting the board know where we stand. I'm handing over the specifics to you."

Catherine reached for his hand and held it tight. Mark looked at her grip, then stared back at her and saw the sincerity in her eyes. Mark slowly removed his hand from hers. "I can't learn it all in a week Mark. Just for a year. One more year, until you get me to where I feel comfortable running things."

Mark did his best to sound remorseful over Johnathon's death. "I'm sorry Catherine. Too many memories in this office, this building, I can't, I just can't. I'll give you the names of the best people we have that can keep up the pace of the company, improve the profits and bring you up to speed. I will come by tonight and discuss the financials in more detail with you around eight-thirty. Please attend the meeting at 9:30 in the conference room today, the more you know the better off you will be."

"Is there nothing that I can say that will change your mind? Please." Mark didn't say a word and just shook his head. Catherine had a saddened expression on her face. "I will see you in the meeting and I want you to come by tonight." She walked out the door.

At that moment Angela rang Mark on the intercom. He pushed the button angrily, not really wanting to abandon Catherine in her time of need. But he felt the further away from the crime scene, the better. "Yes Angela." He stated calmly.

"There is someone to see you, Mr. Townsend."

Mark checked his watch. "Send them in Angela."

Angela held the door open for the client and then closed it behind her. Mark stood behind the desk fiddling with papers. The man walked closer to Johnathon's desk.

"How can I help…?" He finally looked over to see the person who entered his office and to his surprise…

"My name is Tate."

THE END OF SERIES I